# Brotherland

A NOVEL

# Brotherland

A NOVEL

GEORGES MELHEM

*Brotherland*
Copyright © 2009 by Georges Melhem
Second Edition, Copyright © 2024

ISBN 979-8-218-35472-5

Library of Congress Control Number: 2024901585

*Brotherland* is entirely a work of fiction. Although it is based on the Middle-East conflict and the general events that occurred there, names, characters, places and incidents are either the product of the author's imagination or are used fictitiously, and any resemblance to actual persons, living or dead, business establishments, events or locales is entirely coincidental.

# Acknowledgments

*Dare and the world always yields. Or if it beats you sometimes, dare it again and it will succumb.* These words by English novelist William M. Thackeray were scribbled under my father's photo in his company's monthly magazine's homage to his career there and in life, against sizable personal odds. I only saw the tribute and accompanying words about forty years later, but I could vividly sense that form of unwavering strength he'd relentlessly infuse in everyone around him, me in particular. From day one. For your unconditional support and unflinching trust in everything I did, or did not, thank you *pa* . . .

To my sister Hiba, for making this "dare again" happen: infinite thanks and love.

For being an often unassuming yet infinite source of inspiration, love and life, I thank my daughter Melany, and my son Mel. May your generation live through better, peaceful times. Your happiness is my fountain of life.

A last thought goes to the innocent victims of this and every conflict, the main prompt behind me writing. May humankind elevate itself beyond Jurassic means of conflict-resolution. May your sacrifices not go unpunished, and may they serve to pave the way for peace.

# Table of Contents

"Out beyond right-doing and wrongdoing
there is a field. I'll meet you there."
*Jelaluddin Rumi, 13th century Middle Eastern teacher*

"If you want to make peace, you don't talk to
your friends. You talk to your enemies."
*Moshe Dayan (1915 - 1981)*

# Palestine, 1948
# Impossible Dreams

# CHAPTER 1

Certain that they are safe under the watchful eyes of their sentries, the people of Dar Moussa, Har Moses, a cozy village nestled in the high grounds west of Jerusalem, sleep with no fear. Dawn is the most peaceful time of the day, with the chirping of sparrows only interrupted by the odd dog bark and rooster call. Narrow streets slope downhill, snaking through a mosaic of red-roofed houses that cluster into a circular red blossom around the village square.

The villagers, Arabs and Jews alike, are confident that the plan devised by their sheikh and their rabbi will keep Dar Moussa magically quarantined from the spreading horror around them. It is the end of May, 1948. A few days earlier, *Huna al-Quds* — Jerusalem Here — broadcast the news: "The United Nations has approved the creation of the state of Israel," and Ben Gurion promptly replied by declaring the State of Israel.

Rejecting the bloody wave of horror and fury that swept over the newly divided country, the villagers unanimously decided they would set an example for the entire world, and show how Jews and Arabs can live together in harmony, as they have for hundreds of years.

Dar Moussa has a plan. Sentry teams, consisting of one Jewish and one Arab male each, are posted on surrounding hilltops, from where they can see the main access roads to the village. Riding horses, they will cut through the hills and olive fields and head directly to the village to warn of any incoming danger. Should an armed party approach, both the sheikh and the rabbi would ride out to meet it, as far out as possible. Dar Moussa stands united, unlike the rest of Palestine, which is now divided into angry and rioting Arabs on one side, and Israelis, dancing the Hora in the streets and fighting the Arabs, on the other. It will remain safe, impervious to the news of massacres and killings. It is protected by its united populace, the wisdom of rabbi Shmuel and sheikh Mahmoud, the swift actions of Mayor Hamid's committee, and the alertness of its sentries.

---

Tarek feels a kick in his thigh, then another. He rises and opens his eyes, squinting under the first beam of morning light. He looks at the bushes around him and the fig tree above as he yawns. "Morning already? Aah, I forgot we were out here. I miss my mattress!" A third, more pressing kick shakes him out of his torpor. "Samuel, don't kick so hard, I am awake!"

Samuel kneels, gazing westward at the main road to their village, in the distance. Sentry duty or not, Samuel often gazes at the road, hoping to catch sight of his parents, who he hadn't seen since they were separated from one another, in Europe. This time though, Samuel's face is pale with horror.

Tarek scrubs his eyes and sits up to look. "What is it, Samuel? What can you see?"

"There! Look! All the way out there. Can't you hear the rumble?"

The sound of engines, muffled by the distance, makes Tarek focus with more intent. His eyes follow Samuel's pointed finger, beyond the olive fields and the flat lands below them, to the narrow asphalt road that leads to their village, and he mutters, "My God . . . trucks . . . many trucks. A whole convoy..."

"There must be a hundred men. Maybe more!" Samuel speaks in a whisper, as if the men in the roaring convoy far away could hear him.

Tarek's eyes narrow as he stares. He rubs them and springs to his feet. "*Yallah*, let's go warn the committee!"

"Patience! We're only minutes away if we cut through the fields. By road, they'll need much more time. Let's take a good look first. I think they're..."

"*Yahoud*! Jews! I can see now," Tarek goes. "Those half-tracks are Jewish; I've seen them in the *Palestine Journal*. M-something, I think. M-Nine."

"They sound so close!"

Tarek frowns. "Look, they're stopping, at the junction. Why?"

Samuel grins. "I pulled the sign down to deceive any strangers. A trick I learned in Europe."

"You went all the way out there during the night? Without telling me?"

"You were snoring like a pig, Tarek! God help Rima when she marries you."

"And I am not letting anyone spoil our wedding! Or bring the war to our village!"

Samuel jumps to his feet. "Let's go!"

At eighteen, Tarek is only two years older than his friend, but he admires Samuel's self-assurance. Samuel had seen terrible things. With his two sisters, he spent the better part of World War Two hiding from the Nazis in the cellar of a kind and courageous Dutch family, but got separated from his parents in the process. Two years ago, he came back to Har Moses, where his father was born, hoping that his parents, if they were still alive, would do the same.

He and Tarek quickly became best friends, and Tarek helped him build his house. Now, as they race down a mule path, just behind the ridge that leads to their village, the two friends push their horses to the limit, riding low, lowering their faces behind their horses' strong necks, shouting and cursing as the horses jump and swerve to avoid thorny thickets. Finally, they cross to the olive fields and the ride gets smoother.

The horses, breathing and snorting heavily, seem as excited as their riders. They rarely have the opportunity to gallop, let alone race. Samuel's horse is in front, its hooves throwing dried soil onto Tarek's face.

Tarek lashes his horse, pushing him to Samuel's side. "Where do we go? Everybody's asleep!"

"To the square. They'll hear us coming in!"

"You think the soldiers will listen to rabbi Shmuel?"

Samuel shouts, "They'll have to. No war in Har Moses!" He laughs, pointing at *Sakhrat al-O'shaq* — Lover's Rock — by the spring at the bottom of the valley, where Tarek would take Rima on romantic walks. "Only love . . . lover boy!"

Lover's Rock . . . . Tarek loses focus for a second.

The two riders clear the last hilltop before the village. They are close, and the fields they still have to cut through are empty or sparsely planted with olive trees. Samuel looks at Tarek and nods his approval for the last "race."

Tarek, about to kick his horse, freezes for a moment before shouting, "Stop!" as he pulls his horse to a stop. He raises his hand toward the bottom of the hill, only a small distance to the east of the village. A group of armed horsemen was heading for Dar Moussa. "Arabs!" Tarek cries. "That's all we need! They're going into the village!"

Samuel reins in and wheels his horse to Tarek's side. "*Elohim*!" — My God! — "Those uniforms . . . they're Arab Legion! They won't go away without a fight. What do we do? Tarek, think!"

"They're looking at us. They saw us. *Ya Allah*!"

Samuel points, his finger moving from soldier to soldier.

"What're you doing, Samuel?"

"Counting. About thirty."

"Great, you can count to thirty. Now what?" Tarek pulls on the reins of his eager horse.

"Calm down," Samuel mutters. "I'll go to the village and tell them what's going on. You go and meet the Arabs. They look disciplined... they'll talk. Try and buy me some time."

"Talk? Buy time? *Wallah*?" — Really!? — "I'll talk about harvesting the olives, the good season we'll have this summer!"

Samuel kicks his horse into a run. "Just don't get killed. Hurry!" Shouting back, he adds, "Tell them about Rima, the new home you're building, the fox that's eating all the chickens! Maybe they can catch it for you!"

The village had to be alerted before the two enemy forces reached it. A clash between the two parties would be disastrous. No one in the village had imagined such a terrible scenario.

# CHAPTER 2

In his Jeep, Ely taps his driver's shoulder, ordering him to stop, then stands and turns back to his convoy, signaling a halt. The men, who had been singing *"Hava Nagila"* at the top of their lungs, go silent, and try to peek ahead from the back of their trucks. Ely looks at the fork ahead and checks his map. There is no fork on the map. He looks towards the end of the left branch, which vanishes at the bottom of the hill, and concentrates on the right side. Ely has memorized every landmark, and every terrain feature . . . Lifting his binoculars up to eye level, he glasses the area where the two roads split, and spots a downed sign. He observes the area ahead, looking for the enemy's Bren machine guns, waiting for his men to close in. Would they have armored cars too? Arab Legion reconnaissance units are known to be operating in the area, and he particularly dreads the Marmon cars with their two-pounder guns. Although the terrain consists of open fields on both sides of the road, a short distance behind that are dense olive groves. Heavy bushes and rocks are scattered over the fields. An enemy can easily ambush them. Ely swiftly turns back to his men and signals his *pluga*, — company — out of the trucks and into covered positions alongside the road. He scans the surroundings for further signs, and glances at his men taking positions. They are his priority.

Noting the relative openness of the surrounding fields and the complete quiet, Ely assesses the danger. He does not totally dismiss the possibility of isolated snipers or camouflaged machine gun nests, but there clearly is no large enemy force in the immediate vicinity. Ely decides to move ahead and gives another tap on his driver's shoulder, sergeant Aaron, who speeds toward the fork. Ely trusts his longtime friend, and relies on him to watch out for roadside dangers, such as mines and booby traps. As they push forward, Ely keeps an eye on the area for imminent danger, and smiles at the sound of the Jeep behind him also taking off. He shouts over his shoulder, "Moshe, you just can't help it, can you?"

Moshe grins back, nodding towards the left side of the road. "I'll handle the left."

As they reach the road sign, Ely hops down, quickly followed by Moshe. Their two drivers scan the area, while the two other men in the back jump out and take covering positions. Ely kicks the road sign with his foot. "No impact. Someone deliberately took it down."

Moshe is silent for a moment. He can hear chirping birds in the fields. "*Someone* is not around anymore. I say we roll." The area is indeed quiet, with no sign of activity save for a single set of horse tracks. Ely waves his company forward, towards the right hand road, and the convoy starts to move. Moshe overtakes him, scouting for ambushes or mines.

Moshe and Ely's friendship is a communion of brothers at war. It was forged during their underground operations against the Nazi regime in Europe, and it's what keeps them operating together. The Hagganah, the Israeli Defense Army in which Ely now serves, is still learning to become a true, disciplined army. As its name suggests, it is supposed to be a defensive organization – its mission is to defend the Jewish people and their newly founded Homeland — although its mission orders oftentimes mean that they end-up in someone else's backyard. Villages are being cleared. Entire populations are being moved away.

Moshe, on the other hand, is a member of the IZL, or *Irgun Zwei Leumi*, which is little more than a structured terror outfit. For them, moving people is often just a postponement of the inevitable: those who refuse to move are savagely brutalized, often murdered.

An uneasy alliance has brought the two men together, in spite of their outfit's conflicting goals and methods. Ely had found himself short of skilled men, and asked Moshe and three of his friends to accompany him. The four men are valorous, experienced soldiers, and well equipped, with a Davidka cannon and a scoped German Mauser rifle that can take enemies out from half a kilometer away. Ely believes that the best thing to do with such IZL men is to integrate them into the "regular" army, where they can be controlled and their expertise put to "good" use.

———

At the sight of the two horsemen, off in the distance, Ahmed raises his right hand, signaling his troops to halt. He frowns as the horsemen separate, one heading toward the village, the other galloping toward his troops. On his signal, two riders bolt to meet the inbound horseman. Another signal, and two more riders dash for the far-off ridge, from where they will have a clear view to the other side. The rest of his men dismount and deploy with the clockwork professionalism he has instilled into them. All their training and fighting with the British is paying off, and the Arab Legion is one of the few Arab forces that has been winning clashes against the enemy. Too infrequently though, in Ahmed's opinion, and only small clashes, not major battles.

Brimming with confidence and pride, Ahmed sits up in his saddle while he watches the approaching horseman with his binoculars, intermittently switching to the ridge, and what may come from there. As the horseman comes nearer, Ahmed relaxes and orders his men to stand down. That innocent-looking teenager is not a threat. He's not even carrying a firearm, and both hands are in clear sight, holding the reins. When Ahmed's two riders reach the stranger, they all slow down, and the legionnaires signal him to continue on, as they escort him back to the unit. Ahmed searches the teenager's face for clues. Why does he seem so anxious, scared?

———

Guided by his escort, Tarek gallops towards the Legion's leader, the only one still on his horse. The others have deployed around him with clockwork precision. *No way will those men back down*, Tarek thinks to himself. *The village will burn.*

Thoughts of mayhem and bloodshed in his own village cloud his mind. Bodies fallen in the streets, houses burning . . . his house burning . . . His family killed . . . Rima . . . He could imagine his father, kneeling in front of their destroyed house, his family gone, his people decimated. The grim scenery swirls around his head until Tarek reaches the leader's thoroughbred. Both the man and his horse seem the same, an immaculate and fiery mass of strength. The man's rifle sits low on his back, as he flicks a whippet onto his eager horse's neck.

Tarek looks the Arab leader straight in the eye as he struggles to calm his own horse. He realizes he has not thought of what he should tell him. The soldier's piercing eyes are disarming, and Tarek loses all speech. Lying is impossible. How about the truth, then? Tarek realizes he doesn't even know the truth.

He stammers, "You must not go to the village!"

"*A'leykoum assalam,*" — Peace be upon you, too — the officer snaps back. He walks his horse around Tarek's, inspecting him from top to bottom. "And why not? Are there any *Yahoud* in town?"

"Well . . . uh . . . the village is mixed, and we, the villagers, have decided not to let any gunmen inside. We want to keep the village neutral. Like... like Switzerland during the War."

———

Ahmed lifts an eyebrow. This *fallah* — peasant — seems honest, but what kind of emissary is this? Why send a teenager instead of the village sheikh or the mayor? Still, Ahmed is moved, and is about to tell the peasant that his fellow villagers, Jews included, have nothing to fear from him or his men, when he hears a galloping sound. His scouts are returning from their reconnaissance to the top of the ridge. "*Yahoud! Yahoud!*" one of them shouts excitedly, standing up in his saddle and hand-signaling toward Ahmed. Firas, his sergeant, interprets the signs: "Company strength, six trucks, two jeeps. Towed mortars."

Ahmed wastes no time. He reaches for his rifle and gives a powerful blow to the *fallah's* terrified face with the butt of his gun. Tarek sags off the saddle, and Ahmed slows his fall, easing him to the ground. He is furious; this boy must have known about the convoy, and must have been trying to buy them time. How could a fellow Arab do this to them? "Traitor!" Ahmed spits on his bloodied face, looks up to his men. They must hurry. "The first one to the village will have the edge. Saddle up."

Ahmed's men mount up and silently follow their leader's pace towards the village.

Firas rides up next to him, and gives him an inquisitive look.

Ahmed is stone-faced. "What? There's an enemy force and we will fight it."

Firas looks worried. "Sir, there's a hundred of them, with mortars and machine guns."

Ahmed acquiesces. "They don't know we're here. We will take covering positions and ambush them."

The sergeant nods confidently. "We all trust you, sir." He turns back to the men behind them, bringing his rifle to his chest, in a sign of devotion, a gesture quickly imitated by all, in total silence. Ahmed looks at him. "How's Jamil, our scout?"

"Still happy about his newborn son. Nothing can scare him. Why?"

"I know. Good soldier. Send him back for reinforcements. If the first contact doesn't go as planned, we'll have to dig in and wait." The corporal slows his horse and gives the young man his orders. Jamil turns his horse around and dashes away.

Ahmed looks back at the speeding messenger. He knows not to expect much — the Arab leadership is lost in internal feuds — but he still hopes they'll answer his call, and send him something to even the odds.

His sergeant interrupts his thoughts. "What do you expect, sir?"

"Well, I *hope* for another platoon, a couple of mortars, and a Piat grenade launcher."

Ahmed circles his hand above his head, and the men line up with him. He looks at one of them, bearing a scoped rifle strapped across his chest. "Rafiq, you're on top of that minaret. Hand signals, you know your job."

Rafiq points to his gun. "Yes sir. Drivers, officers, radio, weapon crews . . . but —"

"But?"

"The minaret, sir? *Istaghfar Allah!*" — God forgive us! —

Ahmed has a shrewd smile. "HE will guide your bullets. They'll have the sun in their eyes and you'll spot for us."

"Yesss sir!"

Ahmed continues, "Take the two fresh guys. Tell them to shoot more and pray less, once we start." Rafiq nods and swerves towards the pious pair, while Ahmed turns to Firas and says, "I want you to cover the west entrance of the village, where they'll come from, with the machine guns. Try to immobilize the trucks in the open, and take as many as you can when they exit."

The sergeant's confidence seems boosted. "We can handle them sir, as long as we have surprise on our side. Salah, up with Rafiq, will spot for me."

Ahmed nods. "Rain hell on them. I'll set up some surprises for them inside the village." The two fresh recruits speed up to Ahmed. "Yes, soldiers?" he asks impatiently.

The soldiers look embarrassed. "We're going with Rafiq, inside the minaret, sir," one says.

Ahmed stares at him and teases. "So I heard . . . Any objections?"

"No, Sir! We'll draw all their blood! Uh . . . It's just, the boots . . ."

"What about the boots?"

"Uh . . . do we take them off? In the mosque, I mean?"

Ahmed sighs deeply and shouts, "*Yallah! Yallah!* Is your gun cleaner than your boots, son?"

"No, Sir!"

"Well you're not going to leave it outside, are you? Move on! Don't worry about your boots."

The sergeant looks at the proud men trotting along. "Lions, Sir. All of them. No one will hesitate."

Salah, the spotter, calls back, "*Insh Allah*, we'll kill them all, sir."

Ahmed clamors, "We're in our right. If Allah wills it, we'll kill them all!"

Back in the fields, Tarek, the young village scout, lies unconscious on the ground, a purple bulge on his forehead oozing blood, his horse standing nearby.

———————

A high-pitched cry of alarm and pounding hooves cut through the rooster calls and dog barks outside Hamid's house. He springs up from his bed, and pats his startled wife on the shoulder, as she sits up. "Don't be afraid, it's probably nothing," he says. "I'll check it out. Go back to sleep." As she mutters incomprehensibly back into her pillow, Hamid's mind is racing. That was a single horse, charging down, and the voice was Samuel's, Tarek's partner. Hamid knows something is happening, and he fears for his son. Why isn't he with Samuel?

Hamid yanks off his sleeping clothes and hastily pulls on his *qumbaz* — his coat. He pulls on his field boots and rushes out to the street, still buttoning up. Other men, some of them still in their sleeping clothes, others barely dressed, emerge from their doorways and hurry towards the square in the dawn light. Everybody is eyeing Hamid for answers, as he dashes towards the village square. But Hamid has no answers; he only has a question: "Where is Tarek?" he shouts, as he makes his way through to Samuel.

Samuel says, "Tarek is fine; you don't have to worry about him."

Hamid sighs in relief. "*Neshkor Allah.*" — Thank God. —

Samuel shakes his head. "But the village is in trouble."

"Why? What's going on?" Hamid raises his hand to quiet the clamor around them.

"A Jewish convoy is coming from the south, about a hundred men. They look disciplined and well-armed."

"Let's go out and meet them!" He searches for the village leaders and spots Sheikh Mahmoud and Rabbi Shmuel rushing his way. He waves them over. "Brothers!" Samuel repeats his news, and Hamid says, "Let's move out. The further up the road we meet them, the better!"

Samuel leaps from his horse, landing in front of Hamid. "Wait, that's not all."

"What else?"

"Tarek and I split up so he could meet a group of about thirty Arab fighters from the Arab Legion, coming through the fields. Tarek is going to try to buy some time for someone to go and meet them. They could be here any minute, and —"

"Where *exactly* is the Jewish convoy?" Hamid asks, trying to ease the mounting tension, and maintain a semblance of control.

"Minutes away, at most. Both groups are heading straight for the village."

Hamid does not hesitate. "We have to act quickly. We have to stop them both!"

He takes the horse's reins, and hops on its back. He looks at the Rabbi and the Sheikh. "You handle the convoy. I'll meet the Legion soldiers." Hamid looks at the worried faces around him. "Remain calm. Stay here in case we need support." Swiveling his horse around, he tells Samuel, "Send someone to alert my wife and daughter." Hamid lashes at the horse, taking off towards the other end of the village.

As he reaches the far end of the village, Hamid spots a column of horsemen silently advancing through the narrow streets. *"I'm too late!"* he thinks to himself. He steers his horse toward the officer leading the troops, searching for Tarek amongst them. All the horsemen wear impeccable uniforms, with rifles at the ready, but there is no horse with his son — there is no sign of Tarek. He is not here. Hamid's heart leaps in his chest . . .

A villager on a horse appears at the end of the street, racing toward them. As he comes near, Ahmed raises his hand and salutes. *"A-Salam A'leykoum."*

The man pulls his horse to a stop, oblivious to the welcoming salute. "Thank God! I'm looking for my son, Tarek. He went to meet you. I am Hamid Abdallah." Hamid pulls on the reins of his nervous horse.

Ahmed mutters to Firas, "Like father, like son: impolite and naïve."

Firas grits his teeth with disdain. "Disloyal too, I am sure."

Ahmed looks up to Hamid, who is trying to make out what the two men are saying. *"Wa a'leykoum a-Salam!"* he snaps back, "Yes, we met him in the field. He tried to keep us from coming into the village."

"Where is he? Did you hurt him?"

Ahmed does not want to tell the man he has knocked the boy unconscious, or maybe even killed him. He grumbles, "He's fine."

Hamid looks relieved but then notices Ahmed about to wave his men on. He raises his hands. "Wait, you can't go into the village. My son is right."

Ahmed stares back at him. "We're already in, and we're not leaving. Why are you trying to deny us sanctuary?"

"Look, there's no room for arguing. There's a column of Jewish soldiers coming in from the west. They haven't spotted you yet, there is no way they could have."

"And what do you propose? How many men do you have?"

"We don't want to fight! We have been living in peace for centuries here, Jews and Arabs together. As I tell my son, as I tell my fellow villagers, and as Islam teaches us, we are all *Ahl al ketab*, people of the Book, just like the Jews, so why fight? Our entire village does not want war. It is neutral, like Switzerland, during the War. We will not allow in anybody who wants to fight. It's the only way to avoid bloodshed!"

Ahmed can't believe what he's hearing. *Where have these people come from*, he thinks to himself. *And where have they been?* His voice heavy with sarcasm, he says, "That's a very compassionate attitude. You should be leading the country, not the village."

"And so . . . you're leaving? You will leave the village in peace?"

Enough with this *fallah*. He yells, "You think *they* will leave!? My orders are to take and hold the village. The Jews will be bringing in supplies and troops on this road. They already hold the area south of the village, and a good portion north of it. That is why we came through the fields. And that is why we will stop them. We have reinforcements coming in. We will keep this part of the country free for our Palestinians brothers. For *you*! Now step aside and let us through!"

"They outnumber you. You'll all be killed. *We* will all be killed!"

Ahmed commands, "In the name of Allah! Get out of the way! If you want to be brave, ask your men to help us. Do you want another massacre here? Another *Deir Yassin*? Your men, women and children cut to pieces, raped, thrown to the dogs?"

"The sheikh and the rabbi, God bless them, are riding to meet the Jews outside the village."

"Good! We'll have time to set up our defenses."

Hamid places his horse in Ahmed's path. "We forbid it!" He panics as the soldiers start to move. "And my son? Where is my Tarek? What have you done with him?" Hamid grabs Ahmed's arms, who tries to withdraw his rifle away.

Firas rushes in and stabs his bayonet between the villager's ribs, working it swiftly into his lungs. Hamid's face warps with pain and disbelief. He tries to speak but only coughs out blood. His limp body falls to the dirt, his soul having left it.

"Damn it!" Ahmed yells, sharply rebuking his sergeant. "He was one of ours. You could have just smacked him."

"Sir, his finger was practically on the trigger. A stray shot now would be disastrous."

Ahmed acquiesces. "Pull his body to the side of the road and tie up his horse." He goes on ordering, "now let's go on, we've wasted enough time." He turns to his men. "Everyone knows his job?" Ahmed gets a sharp nod from everyone. "All right, let's move out to our positions; the enemy is minutes away."

The men bellow in near unison, *"Allah Akbar!"*

An old woman in the village, watching this scene unfold from her window, runs from her house to alert her neighbors. News of the murder is shouted from door to door, window to window. Screams of *"Katalo Hamid"* — they killed Hamid! — and *"Hamid mat"* — Hamid is dead! — race through the village ahead of the Arab Legionnaires, and it's not long before women start bewailing Hamid's death with the ritualistic shrieking. The wailing angers Ahmed. He wanted to befriend the population, but instead of the smiles and gratitude, all he gets as he trots towards the center of the village is screams and closed windows.

Ahmed looks at Firas. "There's no point in seeking out volunteers, now, is there?"

Firas is unperturbed. "He was about to fire, sir. And I don't think getting volunteers from the village was possible in the first place."

"I guess you're right. They have their . . . Swiss minds made up. And, anyway, they're mixed. Half the village would have joined the Jews." As Ahmed and his men move into the village, Firas points to the locals, rushing into their homes, locking their doors behind them. Some of them peek out from behind closed curtains. "You are right, sir. They have their minds made up."

Ahmed thinks of his own family. "All I know is, I want my wife and son to live decently. My wife is from around here."

"I know, sir. I know you can't wait to get back to your son."

"My pride and joy. He must be able to live in peace and honor. The Zionist demons must be stopped."

Firas can't agree more. "What I don't understand is, how can the entire world approve of this? Our British friends! Giving them *our* land . . . Just because they claim they were here a few thousand years ago?"

"It's our God-given duty to defend our land. They will not stay."

Firas turns towards the men, and with his loud voice, says, *"Allah Akbar.* We'll chase them back to hell!" The men reply in unison, *"Allah Akbar!"*

As they reach the village square, Ahmed starts giving orders. Peeking up towards the minaret, across the square, he orders his sniper. "Go. With Salah and the two recruits."

He brings his horse up next to Firas, who is looking down the main road leading to the square. "That's your zone. Take the Brens, hide them inside the houses on either side of the road. Sweeping fire, to cover the entire field."

Firas hesitates. "How far out? The first houses are too isolated."

"Right. Stay close. Have the road in enfilade. I'll position the rest of the men myself."

Firas lowers his voice. "What are our options?"

"If we don't have surprise on our side, we'll have to draw them in, deny them the use of mortars. I'm placing the men in mutually support- ing positions."

"You'll be preparing some surprises for them . . ."

"I don't have much. Just what we carry. Big hearts and some ammo."

"That will do, sir."

"Go, sergeant, may God be with you. Wait for Rafiq's first shot."

# CHAPTER 3

Rima's house is like a beehive, with everyone frantically running around. Omar, her father, has just returned from the square, and has urgently woken his family up to say they will be leaving their home for a couple of days, off to her mother's village, a few kilometers away.

He holds a small bag, in which he has stuffed his *koushan*, the family land deeds, as well as their identification papers, jewelry, and the gold *Napoleons* he hid in a wall recess behind the stove. Rima is weeping, but Omar focuses on his tasks, unflinching at her show of emotions.

He nods towards the heavy bag his wife is trying to carry to their coach. "Essentials only, woman. *Essentials!* We'll be back in two days."

Rima, despairing, looks at her father. "Do we *have* to go? Why?"

Omar is stoic. "As I said, we'll be back in a couple of days, once this thing is sorted out."

Outside of the house, Nour, Omar's wife, lets go of her bag and clutches onto her husband. "Rima might be right. We don't even know what's happening yet. Maybe everything will be sorted out and —"

Omar grabs his wife's shoulders, brings her nearer. He doesn't want to alarm Rima. "Woman, don't argue. And yes, I *do* know: Hamid has been killed by our own."

"What? When? What do you mean our own, what own? Why?"

"Lower your voice. Just now, yes by our own. Arab Legion. He tried stopping them. They are taking positions in our village as we speak. There's a Jewish army coming and we have to leave before they meet RIGHT HERE."

*"Allah Yerhamou*, God bless his soul. My God, this is crazy. Not here. Not Dar Moussa."

"Pull yourself together, and your daughter too. She is only thinking about Tarek."

Nour steps back into the house, pushing Rima and her younger son, Ziad, to speed up. Their dog, Stella, scampers around like mad, sensing the rush and anxiety, adding to it.

Omar's orders for traveling light get lost in a flurry of suitcases, bags, and baskets, all piling up in the carriage, which groans under the load. They all climb aboard, Rima and Nour on the bench near Omar's seat, Ziad and Stella in the back, amidst the luggage. Omar locks the door to his house and stares at the key for a second. He hands it to Rima. "There, you'll do the honor when we come back." He is about to hop in the coach when he notices his father, still sitting on his chair under the porch. "Abu-Omar, we're ready, what are you waiting for? I have all your things packed!"

His father shakes his head. "You know I can't go, son. I cannot leave your mother here, not even for a day. *Allah Yerhamha!*"

*"La Ilaha illallah,"* — there's no God but God — Omar tries to control himself. "Father, she's been dead for two years now. We'll be back in two days, I swear."

"She's still here, as far as I'm concerned, and I'm not leaving her behind."

"Father, we're running out of time. The eastern road out of the village is still safe, and the Jews aren't here yet. This is our last chance —"

His father waves him on. "This is God's will. Go now, take care of your own, and I will man the house. Who will feed your stock? Who will manage the garden? Look, our neighbor is packing as well. I'll be here when you come back. Who would harm an old man? Old Joshua will show up for our daily backgammon. We'll have both sides covered. Go on, the mule is getting nervous. Take your horse too, that'll be one less mouth for me to feed. *Allah ye kun Ma'akom!*" — God be with you!

Omar looks at his wife. She makes a helpless face. He walks to his father, bends down, and hugs him with all his strength. "You're more stubborn than that mule. But you're right. I know you can't leave. I should have guessed. Take good care of yourself, and stay home."

"You'll be back in two days. No worries."

Tears trickle down both men's cheeks. Rima and Nour's faces are damp with tears as well. Only Ziad's mind seems unfettered as he plays with his Dalmatian in the back. Rima can't hold her silence any longer, and she suddenly crashes into her mother's arms. "I heard you speak of Uncle Hamid," she cries out. "Is it true? Where is Tarek? He was on sentry duty. Is he dead too?"

Omar kisses his father on the forehead and walks to his girl. "You must be brave, Rima. Samuel said Tarek is fine, but we have no news from him. I am sure we would have known if something happened. Have no fear my girl. You'll see him soon enough, and everything will be fine."

"How can you be so sure?"

"I am only sure that staying here is too risky. We all heard the ugly stories in other villages. With the Legion putting up a resistance, it's only going to get worse."

Ely stops his convoy just before the last stretch to the village. He looks at the terrain around him, checking it against the map in his hands. He wants to make a quick stop and reconnoiter the village before committing his troops. Ely orders his men to dismount and establish a security perimeter. He hops down and waves Moshe over, as he lays the map on the hot engine lid.

Moshe rushes over and immediately points his finger at their location on the map.

Ely nods. "I'm going to drive into the village to see what we're up against. We may have been spotted or heard by now, and if these people want to fight, I'll try to talk some sense into them. There are Jews in the village, and I'm concerned about them."

"Careful. It could be crawling with *mechablens!*" — saboteurs!

"Can't be a large force, we would have known. I'll try and talk to them, too."

A sadistic look creeps onto Moshe's face. "You talk too much. Why don't you let me —"

"Moshe! We just want them out. Out and as far away as possible." Ely turns to his second lieutenant, Nathaniel, one step behind them. "*Segum!*"

"Yes, sir!"

"You know the orders. You're in charge until I am back, and in case I am not."

"God forbid, sir. The orders, until then?"

Ely points to several places on the map. "Position the men here for defense and quick deployment. The mission is to push ahead and secure this village. So stand ready."

"Fire support, sir? All we've got?"

"Yes. Position the mortars."

"Yes sir. I'll put spotters here and here. They will overlook the entire village." Nathaniel points to a high ground position on the map, a small distance from them."

Ely looks up at the position and nods.

Moshe asks, "What about me? Do I sit by and watch?"

"You get the most crucial task."

Moshe leans in. "Keep talking."

"Go in. Discreetly. I'll give you a short head start. I need first-hand intel. You know your job."

"Done. Going in." Moshe turns dead-serious.

Ely has an uneasy feeling. He grabs Moshe by the shoulders.

"Moshe. I want intel. Only intel. Got that? In and out, incognito, no shooting."

"And this?" Moshe unsheathes a long blade.

Ely dismisses it, shaking his head. "You have a head start, a few minutes, and remember: no contact. That is an order. Use the radio for emergencies. The enemy may be outside the village, or on his way to us."

Moshe nods in approval. "Take care my friend. *Be Hatslaha le hakamat ha Medinah.*" — May we succeed in the establishment of our State.

"*Be Hatslaha!*" Ely and Nathaniel reply eagerly. The men around them echo the same cry. Ely senses his men's sprits lifting.

Moshe tosses a sloppy salute, taps his driver on the shoulder, and they drive away, their Jeep bouncing into the field.

Ely turns to Nathaniel, waves him over and points to specific locations on the map on his engine hood. "Be ready to react within seconds, in case I have to pull back under fire. Smoke shells for cover, high explosive on any source of fire, airburst rounds on enemies in the open. Have the men ready for immediate action."

Nathaniel agrees. "If there are any hostiles in the village, they would probably set up in these vantage points." He points to landmarks on the map. "We'll be ready and set up for them, rest assured."

Ely looks straight into his young officer's eyes, grabs him by the shoulder. "I know."

Nathaniel nods, and Ely turns back, sits in his Jeep, checks his gun, then his watch. "Aaron, we move in two minutes."

Nathaniel starts directing his men, glancing at Ely's Jeep every few seconds, then a long stare as they drive off, disappearing as they turn and take the last stretch into the village.

In his car, Ely remains alert. Is it horse neighing that he hears? There is one last turn before the last stretch to the village, and Ely signals Aaron to take it quickly. As they round the last bend before that last stretch into the village, Aaron looks with amazement at the road ahead. Ely, equally stunned, gets ready to act. He signals Aaron to slow down.

Two horse-drawn carts are bearing down on them. A rabbi is driving the leading one, and a sheikh the second. Barely controlling his horse, the rabbi holds the reins with one hand and his skullcap in place with the second, as he bounces off his bench. Just behind him, the sheikh closely mimics his actions. The rabbi and the sheikh pull up just a few meters shy of Ely's Jeep, blocking it from further progress.

Ely smiles at the sight of the panting religious men as he scans them for weapons. Their horses are exhausted. A Rabbi and a Sheikh . . . odd. Ely looks around him for any trap or ambush. He sees nothing. He looks at the two men catching their breath. Are they really religious men? He looks each in the eye, and checks again for hidden weapons. The two men, however, look genuine . . . and genuinely tired. Ely relaxes a bit.

He flips his Sten submachine gun to the side out of respect for the two men, and pretends to raise a toast to the winner. *"Mazel Tov!* Congratulations, Rabbi, you won the race. Was my car the finishing line?"

The rabbi salutes with a raised hand. *"Shalom Aleichem."* — Peace be upon you.

The sheikh adds, *"A-Salam A'leykoum."* — Peace be upon you.

"What is this all about, Rabbi?"

The rabbi glances at the Hagganeh patch on Ely's shoulder, and answers, "There is a matter of utmost importance we have to discuss."

The sheikh adds, "We have a proposition for you."

Ely wants swift answers. "I'm all ears, but make it quick."

The rabbi starts his small speech. "Ever since these unfortunate events started—"

"Do you mean the declaration of our state? Our having a home and country? Unfortunate?"

"No! We're not discussing politics. I'm talking about all the killings. Can I go on?"

"Of course."

"Well, we decided, in our village, to stay outside the conflict. We can give the country and the world an example of people from both communities living in peace, *kulam achim* — we are all brothers. We've been here together, Jews and Arabs, for decades, centuries. We have mixed neighborhoods and mixed families. We fast and feast together . . . it's our duty to project this image to the whole country and the whole world, starting with our own people. We've heard many horror stories, and we want ours to be one of love, compassion, and understanding."

The sheikh smiles. "Right! Like *Switzerland* in the war. *Kulna ekhwa.*"

Ely is somewhat surprised. "That's a very nice attitude, Rabbi, and I wish everyone thought and acted the way you do. I have my orders, however, to take and hold your village. Your . . . Switzerland. That I will do; but you have my word that no harm will be done to anyone, from either community. We'll be the sole authority, but you can go about your lives undisturbed and unharmed. Of course, I assume you have no armed soldiers in your village, including outsiders." As the two men stare at him, anxious and lost, Ely goes on, unperturbed, "If it's okay with you, I'll make a quick reconnaissance of the village . . . in your company. We'll decide on a place where my men can stay for the next few days. You must have a school we can use. I'm sure the students would love an early vacation."

The rabbi catches his breath. "I commend you for your judgment, son. However, don't you think your troops are better off staying outside the village? We can make a tour of the village, as you propose, and then you can camp wherever you would like in the fields outside the village. It wouldn't be very, how I shall put this, socially acceptable to have so many strangers . . . men, come into our village."

The sheikh looks concerned. "Yes, it would be unethical for our women in the village."

Ely would never consider staying outside the village — his men would be too exposed in an open field camp. He'll pretend to go along, then show the rabbi and the sheikh that he has no choice but to stay in the village. The boys' school he mentioned was on the map. It is a concrete structure; two floors, with dormitories, as it served the region. A perfect staging place.

Ely waves the okay sign to the spotter he knows is watching from behind and says, "I propose that you, Sheikh, tie your coach to the Rabbi's and ride with me, as a sign of peaceful understanding. The rabbi will ride in front of us."

The rabbi looks pleased with the idea, and the sheikh approves. "May Allah guide every one of your steps, Lieutenant." The Sheikh dismounts from his carriage, tossing his reins over to the rabbi, who ties them to the back of his carriage, and climbs into the Jeep's back seat.

Aaron drives behind the rabbi's coach at a leisurely pace. Suddenly, a movement from his flank catches Ely's eye. Moshe, standing in his Jeep and trying not to fall off as his driver frantically tries to control the bouncing vehicle across the fields, coming across to intercept Ely. Moshe is shouting and waving. Ely looks ahead to the village, the first houses, a couple of hundred meters away, the pointed minaret, in their background, backlit by the rising sun. He puts his left hand on the wheel and yells to his sergeant, "Off the road!"

Aaron swerves right, and a bullet thumps into the sheikh's chest. His lifeless body falls out of the Jeep. The rabbi looks back. He yanks on his reins, leaps from his carriage, and rushes toward the sheikh. A burst from Moshe's machine gun immediately cuts him down. He staggers and falls next to his friend. Ely looks at the still-shaking body, as the rabbi, with his last breath, clasps the limp hand of his dead friend.

Suddenly gunfire seems to come from every house on the outskirt of the village. Bursts of bullets from a machine gun rip the ground around them. Ely, Moshe, and their machine gunners in the Jeeps shoot haphazardly, trying to suppress the incoming fire, as Aaron points his Jeep towards the fields. They're too far, and it's open grounds until there. From the distance, Ely hears the muted thuds of Nathaniel's mortar tubes spitting their deadly cargo. The ripping whistle of the inbound shells tears through the air, dotting the path to the fields. The smoke rounds rapidly envelop the air with a thick grey cloud, masking Ely from the shooters in the village. Ely is ecstatic, "Nathaniel, Nathaniel, God bless you Nathaniel!" Aaron follows Ely's signal and stops the Jeep next to Moshe's, as they watch another mortar salvo hit the houses where machine gun fire is coming from.

Ely crouches at Moshe's side, behind his friend's Jeep. "What happened?"

"There's an Arab force in the village, perhaps forty soldiers, all on horses, no vehicles, and only light weapons. They are scattered all through the village, but I suspect they're mostly concentrated in front, waiting for us."

Ely flashes his admiration. "You did all this and came back in ten minutes?"

Moshe hunches. "I had a good look from a rooftop. Had you let me, I would have finished off half of them." He goes on pointing. "They have a sniper in that minaret, but you had the sun in your eyes. Machine guns in the houses overlooking the main road."

Ely shakes his head. "Ok. We'll regroup and check for enemies outside the village before going in. We need to reach the first streets from the fields, the way you went in. And keep our flanks covered. We will then take the village, one sector at a time."

Moshe points to his walkie-talkie. "Nathaniel has already sent units to cover the flanks. You can lead the main line of effort through the field." Moshe points to his crew, with their sniping rifle and small cannon. "I'll walk you in, handle strong points."

Ely is relieved. "Perfect! Let's secure the first houses as a first staging point. We'll surround them and clear the houses with grenades — no need for chivalry here."

Moshe nods. "And then on to the square, and the minaret behind it."

"Tell Nathaniel to keep that one busy until then."

"Done."

Ely resumes his command. Through his walkie-talkie, he barks commands to his platoon leaders. "Double the load of grenades, to clear all enemy positions. Maintain radio contact with the mortars. Report immediately on progress and enemy positions. Watch for guns on higher floors and rooftops. We move from house to house, not along the streets."

Moshe salutes. "Let's go, my friend, let's move the Arabs out; all of them. We won't be needing your loudspeakers to tell them politely. This time, they asked for it!"

Ely grabs his friend by the shoulder. "By the way, Moshe, that was a rabbi you just mowed down. They wanted to avoid bloodshed."

"A rabbi and a sheikh? Together? Where have *they* been the last few years?"

"Well . . . together."

---

Inside the village, Ahmed is busy with hand signals to his scattered troops. The machine gun squads have already started firing, and Rafiq's sporadic shots are zipping by. Ahmed inquires about damage to the enemy. Salah replies with hand signals. A turban and a kippa. "Great," Ahmed mutters, before looking over to Firas, by his side as always. "Firas, our men in front will soon be cut off. Pull them back. No need to mine the road anymore — we don't have explosives to spare, and they know we're here. They'll avoid the main road."

Firas agrees. "I will divide the men into small groups, and hide inside the houses, sir. We'll cover each other, and —"

"And make sure we can always retreat and regroup until help comes. The final meeting point is the school. Spread the word."

"Procedure?"

"Let them draw near, then fire at will. No surrender, no quarters. Maintain visual contact, we fight as one. Make sure the groups cover each other, and peel in turn."

"Yes sir."

The men around them spread out. Ahmed feels proud and knows they will do their job with death-defying bravery. Still, losing the element of surprise has put them all in a tough situation. Unless their request for help is answered, it is just a matter of time, and the men know it. He admires their courage even more as he watches them take up their positions. His thoughts once again wander to his son. *Will he see him again? Not very likely. Nor his wife. It is a very bitter feeling. But not worse than that of retreat. He will stand his ground, and make them proud. Perhaps reinforcements will come, and maybe even in time . . .* Ahmed takes a deep breath. He goes to check on his men, one by one. Soon, any minute now, they will be fighting for their lives, for the life of Palestine, for their sacred land.

# CHAPTER 4

In a street just behind the village square, using a doorway's recess for cover, Samuel is in panic. He has been all over the village, dodging bursts of fire and exploding shells, looking for anyone in charge, anyone who could do something! On the road into the village, he came across Hamid, lying dead in a pool of blood. He must have tried to stop the Arabs. Tarek was nowhere to be found. Many villagers are leaving, fleeing under a hail of fire. The battle for the village is raging. Peeking around corners, Samuel rushes from one street to the next, watching the disciplined Hagganah troops assault the Legion soldiers, who are putting up a staunch and heroic resistance. Again and again, Samuel sees the Arab fighters come under heavy mortar fire, emerge from the rubble, fight again, withdraw, and regroup in yet another house, every time losing one or two of their soldiers, but not without pulling a staunch resistance. The village was also paying a heavy toll, as the Hagannah artillery indulged in every request it received from its advancing soldiers. Samuel flinches with every burst, his body aching and cracking with the explosions that follow. He watches as the Legion fighters and the Hagannah meet in hand-to-hand combat, finishing off one another with drawn knives and bayonets. With each encounter, the survivors' rage and ferociousness seems to double. Samuel watches as stunned enemies are summarily dispatched and their killers quickly hunger for more. As tears run down his cheeks, he feels his heart clutching and his mind focusing on one thing; he has to find Tarek, and get him and his family out. With the Arabs retreating and the Jews taking up the chase, few streets are left unscathed. There is a startling contrast between these unharmed streets that, for now, have escaped both attackers and defenders, and the rest of the village, littered with bodies, broken red roof tiles and shattered stone blocks. The once picturesque Har Moses is slowly falling to ruin, as a raging fire entraps it, consuming it and overwhelming it with smoke, ash, and clouding dust.

Samuel peers out from his hideout and tries to listen to what is happening nearby. Is it horses? He rushes to the corner and peeks around. A group of Jewish soldiers is assembling captured horses from the Legion. Samuel overhears something about outflanking the Arabs, now assembling in the school. He feels the urge to go to them, speaking in Hebrew. Surely they will not shoot him. But what will he say, anyway? *Please stop!?* Samuel knows it is only a small lull in the fight. Tarek's house is not far away, and Samuel decides to go there, taking care to avoid the soldiers. From the undamaged streets, a few daring and curious villagers are emerging from their homes, trying to put out fires, and tending to the wounded. For every lifeless body found, shrieks of death and wails of despair rip the air, as relatives peer out and despair over their loved ones' remains.

Samuel rushes from one hideout to the next, until he reaches Tarek's house. It is all burned out. Two legion horses stand by the entrance door. Samuel's heart fills with horror as he notices two bodies: Tarek's mother, clasping her daughter's hand. The mother and child are riddled with bullets, shot as they rushed out of the house. Mortar shells have left their impact on the house as well. Samuel feels like he is going to throw up. He takes a deep breath and enters the house. He sees two dead Legion horsemen inside, but no one else. Samuel gets out, grabs the reins of one of the horses, hops in the saddle, and heads for the last place he saw Tarek. Should he check again on his own sisters? He knows they're fine. Their street was "lucky" — the Arabs didn't hide in it, and so it was left untouched. Besides, ever since the unforgettable European experience, Samuel had taken extra precautions. He had built a shelter underneath his home, and his sisters would be safely tucked in it, with enough food and water for a few days.

Samuel rides by Rima's house. Abu-Omar and old Joshua lay dead next to their Backgammon game. The animals are dead. Samuel looks for the carriage and the mule, and sighs in relief when he doesn't find them. The horse is gone too, and tracks in front of the house indicate they must have left in the carriage. He notices a note nailed to the door. It's from Rima to Tarek, and it says they've gone to her grandparents. Samuel sighs in relief and rushes to his last meeting point with Tarek, outside the village.

Samuel goes slowly past burning houses and past the street where Hamid's body lay. He goes past the last house, and gets his horse into a soft trot. He barely clears the last bend before heading east that he notices a horse carriage on the side of the road. It had been struck by shells, and the horses were dead. Samuel heads for it and jumps off his horse as he reaches a dead woman's body. A dead man laid a few paces away. He fights his revulsion and quickly checks the limp bodies for life. They are still warm, but lifeless. The unmistakable muffled cry of a child breaks out. Where is it coming from? A half-burnt crib is in the coach, with one word inscribed on it in English, "Amir." The sheets move and heave, and another cry breaks out. Samuel peels out the sheets and grabs the child, who responds with another burst of crying.

He looks around, as if things could help, as if the dead could awaken. Samuel hears galloping in the distance. He snaps the sheets, wraps the child with them, and hops back on his horse, bolting away towards where he had last seen Tarek. As he clears the hilltop, he sees Tarek's horse, off in the distance. Samuel draws near and can see the horse licking his friend's face as he lays on the ground.

Much to Samuel's relief, Tarek moves as Samuel's horse comes to a halt beside him. Samuel jumps down, carefully hugging the baby against his chest with one hand. He offers out his other hand and helps his friend struggle to his feet. Tarek touches his bulging forehead, and blood oozes between his fingers. He mutters, "They didn't listen to me, did they? How about the Jewish soldiers? Did they listen?"

Trying to keep his balance, Tarek stares in the distance at the smoke rising from the village, just across the hill. He points with a trembling hand and asks, "What? What happened? *No one* listened!" His gaze shifts to the baby wriggling in Samuel's arms. "And what's this? A baby?"

"Yes," Samuel replies. He lifts the tip of the blanket to show the baby's face. "I don't know whose. 'Amir' was written on his crib. Both his parents were killed. He must be a couple of months old. There's no telling who they were . . ."

Tarek, wide-eyed and staring back at the village, asks, "The village! My father, where is he? The sheikh, the rabbi? What's all that shooting? Explosions! Smoke!"

"I'm afraid I have terrible news."

"Those bastards! All of them! They brought their war into our village. It's all in flames. Why aren't we doing anything? Where's my father?"

"They've done all they can, and more. I told you I have terrible news."

Tarek pauses, panic in his voice. "My father . . ."

Samuel lowers his head, as a tear runs down his cheek. "I'm sorry. I'm so so sorry . . . Your father tried to stop the Arabs. They . . . killed him."

Tarek falls to his knees, as his eyes stare at the burning village. He chokes as his breathing falters. "It's my fault . . ."

"Of course it's not your fault — don't be a fool! You have to be steady, Tarek. I have more bad news, and there's no way I can give it to you in small pieces."

Tarek shakes his head in disbelief. "We'll make a dash for my home. My mother must be devastated. My sister must be panicked. And I have to find Rima."

"Will you please listen?" Samuel shouts. "Arab fighters took refuge in your house. It was shelled."

Tarek stutters, "My . . . my mother?"

Samuel tries to steady his voice. He can't. "And your sister."

Tarek grabs his head in his hands, bending over until his bruised face hits the ground. "That can't be true. Why, God, why? Allah is not so cruel. My little sister can't die; she hasn't done anything. Why? That's impossible! Why would anyone kill her?"

Samuel puts his knee to the ground, next to his friend. He runs his arm around his shoulder. "Rima's family has left. I passed by her house. She left a note saying they went to her mother's family's house in the next village. They should be safe."

"I can't believe what you're telling me. It's not possible! How could it be?"

"I'm sorry. There are no words that can heal your wounds. You have to be brave, and keep your faith in God. Only through Him will you find comfort."

"I still have to go back. I need to see them. They need a proper burial." He reaches for his horse's reins.

Samuel steps in front of him. "You can't. The Jewish soldiers will kill you. They'd take you for a Legion Soldier. It's better for you to go find Rima, and then come back in a couple of days. That's what your father would want you to do."

Samuel knows this is the only chance to make his best friend avoid the fighting, to save his life. He adds, "The Jews had the edge. The Legion soldiers pulled back into the village, and the Jews went after them. Methodically, street by street and house by house. They kept pushing forward, shelling them out of their hiding places. They have heavy mortars, and rained hell on the village. I think they retreated towards the school."

Samuel pauses in trying to get Tarek's full focus. "Listen to me! Go to Rima! I'll send for you in couple of days. I'll take care of your family. If there's anything you should do right now, it is to stay alive. Think like your wise father would, do as he would want you to."

Tarek's trembling voice betrays his despair. His voice, like his body, quivers. "My family is dead! *Allah Yerhamhum*, God bless their souls. How can I leave? Maybe it's better to die . . . I'll be with them again."

"Tarek! God forbid! Think of Rima. Think of yourself. Think of me as your father talking—wouldn't he say the exact same thing? And wouldn't you listen? Listen to me. I'm Hamid, talking to you, ordering you to stay alive. *Just stay alive!* Go to Rima. They're finishing off the houses with incendiary grenades, for God's sake!"

"Incendiary? In Dar Moussa . . . so much for our Switzerland. Our village of peace and brotherly living... now a living hell." He turns his reddened eyes to Samuel. "What will *you* do? Where will you go?"

"I'll go back to the village. My street was relatively spared. I'll join my sisters."

"Your sisters . . . Are they okay?"

"They must be in the shelter. I'm sure they're fine. Please go now."

Tarek nods. "The shelter. You were right about that . . . I know I should go, but I can't get myself to do it. What will I do? How can I go on living? What for?"

"Here's one incentive." Samuel hands the baby to Tarek. "Time to do some good."

Tarek looks at the child in his arms. "Are you crazy? What can I do with him?"

"Find someone to take care of him. I can't do that in the village. His name is Amir, maybe he'll respond to that. He looks healthy. He'll need milk soon, though, so you'd better get going. The sooner you go, the sooner you'll catch up with Rima's family."

Tarek looks dazed and lost. Clutching the baby, a sense of resolve comes over him. "Ameer," he says to himself quietly. "He seems so unaware, so innocent." Tarek looks up at Samuel. "He should live, in spite of all."

———————

Ely, Moshe, and a dozen other men are on horseback. They are galloping out and away from the village, in order to outflank and surround the Arab fighters holed up in the school, on the other side of the village. Ely looks at Moshe, riding by his side, "They're not like others we've seen . . ."

"Good fighters. Organized."

"Still, we'll get them. They're cornered now."

"We have to rush, they may have reinforcements coming."

"You're right Moshe. Hey, what happened here?"

Ely points to a burnt carriage a short distance from them. Two corpses, a man and a woman, lay on the ground. The horses were dead too.

"Dead Arabs. Nathaniel must have handled them."

Ely steers his men towards the carriage and hops down from his horse. He points to two of his men, indicating for them to stand watch. He kicks over an English book, "They're not Arabs, I don't think so."

Moshe is looking towards the village, thinking about the battle continuing on inside it. "What they are is dead, this we know for sure. Let's continue on. We have to be in place when our men attack the school."

Ely is startled by the sound of an infant's laughter. He motions to his ears and looks at his sergeant. "Listen! Do you hear that?"

The sergeant dismounts and searches through a bloody bundle of sheets beside the dead woman's body. Peeling back layers of cloth, he looks up at Ely. "You're not going to believe this, sir."

"What is it?"

"A baby. He's alive." He looks into the wagon. "It reads 'Amir' on the crib, sir, in English. The blood on these sheets is not his, it's his mother's!"

Moshe curses, *"Ben zonah!"* — Son of a bitch!

Ely is equally struck. "I'll be dammed!" He gently takes the baby boy into his arms and is rewarded with another giggle. The baby's face, his voice, his clenching hand as Ely touches it with his finger . . . Against the raging battle in the background, it all seems divine. Amir tugs at the sheets wrapped around him, and giggles as they tickle him.

Moshe shouts, "Give him to me!" He draws his handgun.

Ely steps back and turns away to protect the child. "Moshe! Are you MAD?"

"Our men are waiting for us to reach our position, Ely, and they're in a tight spot until we do. We can leave him here for the foxes, or we can put him out of his misery."

"He seems pretty alive to me. Hungry for life too . . ."

"Ely! Our men are waiting. Let's just do him in and go."

"Would you kill him if he were a Jew?"

"He's an Arab!"

"How do you know? We both use Amir." He points to the books scattered on the ground. "And there's the Old Testament . . . well, there's a Koran, too. Looks like an educated family."

The child laughs again.

Moshe says, "Ely, *please*, let me finish him off and forget the whole thing."

"He's the only one laughing in a hundred-mile radius, and *you want to kill him?*"

"Ely, don't you understand? He'll be eaten alive if you leave him here."

"He should live! Sara and I have been trying for two years now. He's a gift from God. She'll be delighted, and so happy to care for him."

Moshe spits with sarcasm. "Yeah. Give him a gun, he can help us out."

"That's enough, Moshe. I'll take him."

The baby's laughter, his call for life, has been heard. Ely will answer it. He looks at his sergeant. "Aaron, go find some clean water for him to drink."

Aaron says, "They should only drink milk at this age, sir. He's no more than a couple of months. I know from my children."

"Well, then, you're his babysitter. Okay? Find some milk. Guard him with your life. Your mission is milk, and you're dismissed from combat for now. Go back the way we came, the sector is secured. Find a nursing mother in a safe area. Tie your horse in front of the house where I can see it. I'll be with you as soon as we're done."

"Yes sir! This is a first!" replies Aaron, holding the baby gently to his chest and galloping away with him as Moshe mutters, "Great, now we're one man short."

Ely is swift to rebut. "Oh no. We're one man extra."

Hiding behind thick bushes just a hundred meters away, Samuel, having convinced Tarek to go find Rima, has seen and listened to all of this. Patting his horse and whispering in his ear to make sure he remains calm, he watches the Hagannah sergeant take off with the other child. They are twin boys, and they are now separated, heading in opposite directions. Samuel resists his instinct to step forward and tell the officer the whole story. He hesitates, but now the men are on horseback and away before Samuel can change his mind. Samuel wonders—what kind of miracle happened here? Dear God, bless both him and the baby. And the other twin too.

Approaching the burned coach, Samuel dismounts and tries to find more information about the twin's identities. He can't help wondering if they were Arabs or Jews. Someone had clearly been here before him, as nothing of value was left. Nothing that could indicate who they were, or where they came from either. Samuel wishes the burned bodies could talk one last time.

He notices a picture frame lying on the ground, half broken: a still intact picture of the twin boys together in their crib. Samuel pulls it out and puts it in his pocket. It is time to get to his sisters, Irene and Clara. Surely they must be worried sick about him. Then . . . he'd need to take care of his friend's family.

Entering the village, Samuel could see the last of the Legion soldiers, entrenched in the school as they make their last stand. The battle is nearly over. Perhaps some of the villagers would know more about the twins' family. His mind is plagued with questions. How will he take care of Tarek's dead parents and sister? Will the village find its way back to normal life after those events? When will all the fleeing Arab villagers come back? After so much violence and death, can there ever be "normal" again? And about the twin boys, what can he possibly do to help? Maybe he can help the one with the Jewish officer. He'll look for the sergeant's horse.

———

Omar is trying his best to untangle Rima from her mother. The two are clasped together with desperate strength. Tarek watches helplessly, a lost look on his face. Rima holds on to her mother, crying in her ear, "Why don't you come with me? There's plenty of room in the coach!" She drags her mother to the porch, pointing to the carriage outside. The village sheikh is busy swapping the harness from the mule to the horse.

Rima's mother wipes her tears and speaks firmly. "You have a new life now, *habibtee*, my love. You have a husband; and a child, a blessed gift, and a mission from God."

Rima shakes her head. "This is too fast for me. And you're staying behind."

"Rima, you know I cannot leave my parents —"

"Neither can I!"

The sheikh walks up to Omar. He nods towards Rima and her mother, hinting for Omar to step in. "It was a quick ceremony, but the wedding was done properly. The child is theirs too. Now they have to go. It is the will of God." Neither Omar nor Tarek respond to the Sheikh. Ziad is on a couch, making faces to Ameer on his lap. He gets up to his sister. "Rima, will you hold him please? I have to fetch Stella." A muffled cry seems to shake Rima loose from her mother.

The Sheikh looks at her. "Be brave my girl," he says. "Lamia and Ramez, our neighbors, are leaving as well. They are ready. Lamia is nursing her child; she will help you with Amir."

Rima turns towards Ziad, grasping Ameer with both hands and holding him to her chest. She looks towards her father, tears running down her cheeks.

"Go on my love," Omar says through his tears. "May God bless you and be with you and your family. Don't come back until it is safe, even if it takes a month!"

Tarek puts his hand on Rima's shoulder and walks over to her father, who hugs him firmly. "I entrust you with her," Omar says. "This is what you both want and now you have our and God's blessing. Take good care of my daughter. Take good care of yourself, my *son*."

"I will, Uncle Omar. I will." Tarek turns tentatively to Rima's mother. She clenches him as tightly as she did her daughter. "I know what you feel. I am so sorry for your loss. Your parents were family to us. You have to turn to God, for hope, and for strength. Nothing less will work for you, my son. Have faith. May God protect you."

Tarek takes a deep breath and steps back. He holds Rima's mother by the arms. "I will take care of us all. God willing, we'll be fine . . . and back soon." Tarek turns towards the Sheikh, who hands him his marriage deeds and winks. "I have changed the dates on purpose. It says here that you were married a year ago. Ameer is now your legal son, as you asked."

Tarek smiles with approval. "God bless you, Sheikh. When this is over, I will need you to come with me to our village, for my parents. You know, Sheikh Mahmoud . . ."

"I know. I will. Do not worry. I know Samuel. I know he'll do things properly."

Tarek nods, looks at Rima, and gently ushers her along.

Rima looks at her mother, shakes her head in despair. "No. Mother!" She pulls Ameer to her left side, and extends her right arm towards her mother, as Tarek walks her to the door. Her mother rushes in, grabs her hand, and pulls it to her lips, kissing it. She tugs more and ends up clutching Rima, Ameer, and Tarek. "*You're* my heart. My heart is being pulled out. My heart, my soul . . ."

As the Sheikh taps him on the back, Omar at last intervenes. He can barely talk. "This is God's will. It is for the best. This is goodbye, not farewell. We will be back together soon."

As Omar separates his wife from his daughter, Ziad draws everyone's attention. Standing in the middle of them all, holding a small pack and accompanied by Stella, wagging her tail, the young boy declares, "I am going too. I will help them."

His voice falls on stunned ears. The Sheikh is the first to recover. "Maybe you are right, my son. Maybe you should go. Maybe it is God's will for all the young to go."

Rima's mother looks pale. She collapses onto the couch, unable to even respond. Ziad rushes over and starts smothering her with kisses. "Don't worry mother. I am sad too. But we will be back. I promise I will be back very soon."

Rima's mother is completely stunned. She mutters incomprehensible words. Ziad goes on, "We will be back . . . very quickly mother. And we'll go back to our home, with Tarek and Ameer."

Omar looks at the Sheikh, then at Tarek. They both nod. Tarek moves towards Ziad, and pulls him to his feet. "Let's go little brother."

Omar firmly escorts Rima out to the coach. She screams over her shoulder, "I will be back for you, mother! I will be back!"

Tarek takes over from Omar and eases Rima up into the coach, as she holds Ameer with one hand, and uses the other to climb. Ziad rushes to his father. He seems to realize what it means to go . . . "I love you father. You are the best father, and I will always love you . . . We won't be long, will we?"

Omar kisses his son on the head. "God will unite us soon, my son.

God willing, we will be together before long." Omar looks at his two children and at Tarek. "We will be thinking of you every second of every day. We will pray with every thought."

As Omar reaches out to kiss Rima's hands, she bends over and hugs him one more time. "I love you father. Take care of mother. We will be back. Soon."

The Sheikh walks into the emotional parting. "Omar, you should go back to your wife. Tarek, Lamia and Ramez must be set, too. They'll join up as you ride past their house."

---

Tarek had been so busy with Rima's family that the fate of his own parents had remained a dark and heavy cloud of denial that had not yet settled. Now, as he steers his horse down the beaten road, he can't help thinking of his parents' final moments. Tears run down his face, and he struggles to breathe normally. Did they suffer? Did they cry out for help? Did they hope Tarek would come back for them? Samuel said it was quick, and no one suffered. But how can you not suffer? Did his mother know her husband was dead? And what about his sister — who would harm a helpless child? Did she watch her own mother die? Or was it the other way around? How did it happen — exactly?

Rima rests her head on his shoulders. She too has tears in her eyes. A small murmur from the bundle on her chest brings a shy smile to both of their faces. Ziad is busy in the back keeping an eye on Stella, who jumps in and out of the carriage as it rolls along. Tarek wipes Rima's tears off with his sleeve, kisses her still wet cheeks. She looks into his eyes. "I am so sorry about your parents. God bless their souls," she says softly. "I feel ashamed worrying about mine."

Tarek nods. "There's no use worrying about mine, they're in God's hands. I just wish I had been there to defend them." Tarek's voice trembles as he adds, "They must pay. ALL of them."

"Who? The Legion killed your father. Samuel told you your house was bombed by the Jews. You want to kill both? Everybody? What would Uncle Hamid say?"

"God bless his soul. His ways obviously don't work. We have to think of something else." Tarek's eyes turn into an expression of death. "We have to defend ourselves. By force. Not relying on others. Look at us. No one should be forced away from their home."

———

It is late in the evening, and the battle for Dar Moussa is over. Ely and his men have fought bravely, and indeed they had to, considering that none of the Arabs surrendered. Ely has been driving for almost two hours, and, at last, the city lights of Jerusalem's suburbs appear in the distance. Sergeant Aaron is riding next to him, while Moshe sits in the back, cozying up to a beautiful young girl holding a baby in her arms. Ely turns towards her. "Liz, how's Amir doing?"

"Fine. He's drowsy from the drive."

Aaron looks back and leans over Amir. "It's good that this boy Samuel found us a nursing mother in the village. He really saved the day—"

Moshe mimics Samuel's voice. "Except them, except the owners . . ."

Ely laughs. Liz frowns. "What?"

Ely explains, "The boy was having at us for burning the village. So Moshe explained that the UN gave us this land, and the whole world had agreed to it."

Liz nods, "Oh, I see . . ."

Moshe has a sadistic look. "Don't trust him. He's a kidnapper."

"Right. And you wanted to kill the baby. *Finish him off*, as you said."

Ely and Aaron laugh, as Liz glares at Moshe. "You did NOT!"

Moshe is about to come up with something, but Ely is faster. "Moshe, that child is a miracle. It is sent by God." Ely winks at Liz. "You've had your own miracle, too."

Moshe's eyes turn mellow, much unlike him. "Yeah. Who would have thought? We lost track since Europe; since the war, back in —"

"When I saw Ely's name on the promotion list," Liz interrupts, "I thought that you shouldn't be too far. So I proposed to my colonel that I'd ride with the resupply convoy that you requested, and come find you."

Moshe looks at Ely. "You're a captain, now. You can kill more. *Use it.* We have more mortars and light tanks —"

"Can we talk about something else, please?" Liz cuts him off. "I have an infant in my lap, and I am sure Ely has a bright future in mind for him. A future with no war."

"Well," Moshe replies, unmoved, "That's why we do what we're doing."

Ely says, "We all fought in Europe to guarantee our survival. Now that we have a state of our own, let's build it to last."

"Our nation is under attack, Ely. We have to—"

Liz jumps in, "Stop the attackers, make peace, start a new life. There can be no nation without people in it. Put that in your stubborn head, Moshe."

Moshe grins. "A new life? Are you proposing?"

"Same old devil, aren't you?"

Moshe moves closer to Liz. Tender gestures are quite unlike him, but it makes Ely happy to see it. Early in the war, the Nazis had killed Moshe's wife and daughter. They forced him to watch while they burnt his house, with his family inside. He met Liz late in 1944, and although they immediately took to each other, Moshe couldn't let their relationship move past friendship. He was not ready for it. Ely wondered, would now be the right time for them? And what about "his" baby? Is this the right thing to do, adopting a child? Without even asking Sara! He remembers that magical moment when Amir giggled in his arms. Surely there was something divine in that moment.

Aaron looks at Ely. "I know what you're thinking, sir. You did the right thing. You really did."

Ely nods. Aaron extends his hand, and Ely grasps it firmly. Aaron may be his sergeant, but he's a friend first, and a brother in fighting. The bonds of battle are as strong as those of birth, for they, too, are forged in blood. Ely is brought back to earth by the sweet voice of Liz, singing softly "*Noumi, noumi, tinoki, aba halach la avoda*" Sleep, sleep my little baby, father has gone to work. Another bond is materializing in the back seat, as Moshe softly kisses her neck. Amir purrs gently, as he sleeps tight in Liz's arms.

They drive through the city's quiet streets, and soon enough, Ely is pulling up in front of his house. He turns the engine off, takes a quick look at his house, his tidy garden, and inhales deeply as he stares at the blossoming roses.

Moshe taps him on the back. "You're on, my friend. Take your son to your wife."

"Moshe, I thought I softened you up!" Liz cries, taken aback. "Ely, never mind him. I'll hold Amir. Just go to Sara. She's in for a surprise. Well, two surprises."

Ely smiles at her. "Three surprises. There's you as well. She hasn't seen you in three years."

Before Ely gets out of his car, the front door opens, and Sara is on the porch. She steps towards them and rushes to hug her husband. "Ely!

Thank God you're ok." She looks around at everyone. "Shalom, Aaron, Moshe . . . oh my God! Liz? . . . Liz!"

"It's me!"

"Here, in Jerusalem? How did this happen?"

Liz hops out of the Jeep, and gently puts Amir in Ely's arms. Liz and Sara instantly clutch in a tight embrace, tears of joy running freely down their cheeks. It takes the men a few minutes to get them into the house. Aaron looks at Ely. "I'll stay in the Jeep sir, in case something comes over the radio."

"Thanks, Aaron. We won't be long. Take a short walk to stretch out. If the radio crackles, you'll hear it. But first come in to freshen up."

Sara turns to hug her husband.

Ely says, "Easy now, we don't want to squash this little fellow!"

Sara lets out a small shriek, waking up the hungry baby, who promptly makes it clear that his problem should be solved immediately.

"Is there anyone with a baby in the neighborhood?" Ely asks.

"Yes, but, what do you mean, what . . . who is this?"

"We found him on the battlefield, his name is Amir, and his parents are dead."

"Why did you bring him here? He needs parents! But never mind; right now he needs milk. I'll go to my friend down the street. She has twins. She's well appointed," Sara adds, extending her arms in front of her chest to mimic her friend's large breasts.

"I'll go with you," says Liz.

"Well, why don't you take Amir with you?" Ely hands the child to his wife. "Don't be long; we may be called back any time."

Liz responds, "Okay, we'll be right back." Liz grabs Sara by the elbow and steers her out the door. She leans towards Ely and whispers, "I'll explain it to her." Ely nods back and sighs in relief. Liz's help is quite timely . . . He had no clue how to put it to Sara.

Liz takes a deep breath and looks around the quiet neighborhood of Rehavia. "Looks like a nice place to live. Clean street, lovely trees, nice homes with small gardens — like a village, only bigger. Do you know all the neighbors?"

Sara smiles. "We're friends with everyone around here. They've all gone to sleep already, as you can see . . . at least those who are home, not out there fighting. We're in the middle of Jerusalem, and yet we enjoy the calm and serenity of a suburb. We love it here. Now that we're not under siege anymore, we have everything we need close by: Angel's bakery; the small well-stocked grocery owned by a nice German Jewish couple, the Roffmans; even a lovely flower shop, owned by Yehya, a Yemenite Jew — look at all those beautiful flowers . . . the neighbors are nice and helpful. If we could only have peace with the Arabs on the other side, it would be ideal. See that house on the corner, at the end of the street? That's where we're going."

Liz thinks she has better tell Sara about the baby before they get to their destination. "Sara, that child is an orphan, and no one knows where he belongs."

"You mean, nobody knows who to take him to?"

"Well, Ely seems to have an idea."

"I'm glad he comes upon such ideas even when he's fighting. Maybe it's not all about death and killing, after all. I have had enough of violence and wars." She smiles down at the baby. "Look at him; he seems so happy in my arms."

"Ely actually has plans for Amir, but it involves both of you. He said that you had trouble, uh, with your pregnancy. And then this child just appeared in his path in the middle of a battle. He sees it as God-sent."

Sara stops walking and stares at her friend. "He wants us to keep him? As our own?"

"Well?" With a smile, she shoves Sara in the back to get her moving again. "Keep walking, or he'll start crying again!"

Sara continues to walk, fumbling. "Well, I don't know . . . I mean, he looks lovely, and he's so cute, but you can't just throw a baby in my arms and call him mine! I have to think about this, I have to get used to the idea. It might not work out, or maybe . . ."

"Are you afraid you won't love him?"

Sara gazes at the baby. "How can a woman not love such a cute baby?" she says musingly, looking tenderly at Amir. "But this is too fast. It's unknown territory for me." She hugs the baby close.

"Well, you don't have to force anything or hurry a decision. Take your time and think about it as keeping him for a while, and taking care of him. Things will come naturally."

"And what about him? Maybe *he* won't love me?"

Liz smiles. "That I can say for sure. He will adore you! He doesn't know anything, anyway. He's only a couple months old. The little that's in his little mind won't stay there for long."

"And I should decide now?"

"No, you don't have to decide anything now. Just take care of him, if you think you can do it. Ely is too busy now anyway, so you have a few days to think it over. Babysit him for a while, and then see if it works for both of you."

Sara is apprehensive. "I'll ask my friend Linda what she thinks. She'll have to help me anyway."

As they turn up the sidewalk and go through an open garden gate, Liz notices the nicely maintained greenery, and flower bushes flanking two neat wooden benches. She's about to voice her admiration when, as they reach the slightly open door, she catches sight of Linda's silhouette.

She whispers to Sara, "If that's your friend, then she shouldn't have any problem feeding an extra child. Her breasts are twice the size of yours and mine put together!"

Sara smiles as she opens the door. "Good thing she's awake."

———

Ely is nervously counting the minutes. When Sara and Liz show up at the front porch, would Sara have a stern look of disapproval? Would Liz's face bear failure? But as they appear far down the road, Ely can see they don't even have the baby with them.

"Where's Amir?" he says, when they arrive.

Sara smiles. "Relax. It takes a good fifteen to twenty minutes to feed him, so we left him with her, and we came here to talk. Her children are asleep, and her husband is home, so she'll be fine."

Ely is silent, an anxious look on his face. Moshe steps in for his friend. "Did you two . . . talk?"

"We decided, well, Sara decided . . . tell them what you decided!" Liz says, pushing her friend forward.

"I obviously can't turn myself into a mother and love someone else's child just like that, on the spur of the moment, even when he's so cute . . ."

Ely grins, his breath still in . . . Sara goes on, a smile gradually easing across her face. "However, I'll give it a go. I'll keep the child and take care of him for a while. If we take to one another, then I'll agree with you that it's a God-sent miracle. We'll keep him. Can you be sure no one will claim him?"

"Yes! Absolutely! I asked around a lot, the entire village." Ely assures her. "No one knew him or his family. A Jewish boy from the village helped us. We don't even know if he's Jewish or Arab."

Sara seems to have a motherly meltdown. She goes, with a resolute tone, "That doesn't bother me. We'll raise him as a good, God-loving Jewish boy."

"That's it then, we keep him! You'll be a great mother, Sara!"

Their heads turn to the sound of a loud "pop!" Moshe emerges from the kitchen with a bottle of wine. "Let's celebrate!" he says. "I stole this from your victory case." Moshe glances at the bottle. "*Rishon le Zion.* Our own wine!" He hands the bottle to Ely.

"*L'chayim!*" — To life! Ely shouts, "And to Amir, and his mother." He grabs Sara by the shoulders and pulls her to him.

"*L'chayim!* To Amir and to all of us," answers Sara, gazing into her husband's twinkling eyes.

Aaron comes through the open door. "Congratulations, sir —"

Sara grabs his hand and pulls him in. "Come on Aaron, celebrate with us!"

"Just a small sip," he says. "I'm sorry to say I'll be driving your husband away, now. Orders just came in . . ."

Sara returns to Ely's embrace, as Moshe asks, "Any specifics?"

"Reinforcements to the unit we crushed. They came in late and gathered in the next village."

Ely kisses Sara and lets go of her extended hand, a regretful look on his face. "I have to be with my men. We have to attack before they do."

Moshe concurs. "My thoughts exactly. Let's move."

Liz gets up to go with the men. Sara is shocked. "Liz! You're not staying here?"

"I am with the reconnaissance squad. I have to be there."

"Her Arabic skills are invaluable," Moshe explains. "She translates all their communications for us."

Sara has a disappointed look. "I should have known. So you just drop in for a few minutes, hand me a child, and go back to your war?"

Ely reassures her. "We're building our nation. We have to do our part. And you have to do yours: take good care of Amir. I won't be more than a few days." Ely puts a quick kiss on Sara's lips and whispers to her ear, "I love you."

Ely and his team head out towards the Jeep. Aaron is already at the wheel, engine humming.

Sara rushes out behind them, a shiny box of 'Elite' branded chocolates in her hands. "Take these. They're *ours* like the wine, so you can have the good taste of home."

———

After another long drive, made easy by the clear night weather, Ely rejoins his unit. Over the last few hours, his men have been resting, tending to their wounded, caring for their dead, and looking after their equipment and machinery. Reinforcements have been integrated into their unit, boosting their capacity and adding to their firepower. Ely gathers his officers to plan their next battle. The meeting will take a couple of hours, at least. Moshe and his team have already set out. Ely puts away any thoughts of the miracle child and dismisses the fears about their future that had plagued him during the drive — What if someone popped up to claim him in ten years? And was Sara getting along with him? Instead, Ely focuses on the map before him. He has a duty to do — for Amir, for Sara, for his entire nation. Tomorrow will be another harrowing day.

# 1956
# War and Death

# CHAPTER 5

Eight grim autumns, eight cold winters, and eight scorching sum-
mers . . . There were no springs. Not in the derelict West Bank refugee
camp they ended up in.

Rima looks around her, at the maze of randomly erected tents, some
of them as large as a small house. Whole families live in one-room
shacks built by the United Nations. Nearby, children run barefoot,
women wash clothes, others prepare cooking fires. Old men queue up
with their refugee registration cards to receive food supplies. This is the
"paradise" that the ordeal of eight years on the road has led Rima to.
Time is fleeting—the days, the months, the years. They are nowhere
nearer to the villages they fled from. Everything is getting worse, and it
troubles her that people seem to be getting used to it. Everyone is aging.
Even children seem to be aging, rather than growing up. Every day,
children battle disease, women battle the hardships of life, and men
battle the enemy. Occasionally, some would lose. Their homes are a distant, cold memory. Cold like the brass key to her former home. She still
likes to feel that key against her skin, having held on to it for so many
years. She pulls out of her grim thoughts. The camp has also proven to
be an ideal place for a child to hide from his mother, if he so wishes, and

at the moment, Ameer is nowhere to be seen. Rima scans the makeshift playground — a small clearing in the adjoining olive fields where the children play their war games — but he isn't there. He isn't in the "classroom" — a patched awning the teacher had stretched under the large oak tree in the middle of the camp — either.

Holding the cotton shirt she's been trying to get Ameer into for the last fifteen minutes, Rima is about to start yelling for her son. It is one of those late October sunny days, and a fresh moist breeze blows in the air, unlike the heated atmosphere that blasts with every frenzied radio wave, every fiery TV broadcast, all calling for war. All calling for obliterating *essahayeneh*, the Zionists. Still, it is not warm enough for an eight-year-old boy to be running around half-naked. To make matters worse, his brother Rabih, younger by two years, follows his every move.

Rima decides to abandon her search, for the moment. She will punish Ameer later, instead of herself now. She and Tarek had been doing their best to give their two sons as much decision-making responsibility as they could, knowing that if something bad were to happen to them, Ameer and Rabih would be facing life alone, and the more prepared they were, the better. Of course, the extra confidence and independence that Ameer and Rabih have acquired often backfires on Rima, whenever she tries to rein them in.

Rima plops down on her "coffee bench," a fallen tree trunk. Her friend and companion for several years, Samar, is serving their preferred drink. Black, no sugar. "Just like our everyday life," Rima jokes. She admires Samar's serenity and wonders how she achieves it. Samar looks, as always, quite relaxed despite her inner anxiety. Like Rima, Samar is from a relatively well-off family and wasn't used to the rigors of camp life. Others who could afford to have settled in a safe country; less fortunate ones fled to Lebanon or Jordan. Both Rima and Samar's families have decided to stay in Palestine, with their people, in their land, and reclaim their homes.

Rima turns to the sound of trucks nearing the camp. The UNRWA vehicles maneuver into the camp, and their crews set foot on the ground. They already look tired.

Samar points to them. "Those brave people, helping us whichever way they can."

Rima hunches. "Look at *our* people, rushing towards them. And for what? Canned food, used books, overused clothes?"

"At least we get some medication. Not all we need, but it's good to know that someone cares. Those doctors are all volunteers."

Rima persists. "What we need are volunteer soldiers. Doctors won't bring us back our homes, our villages."

Samar nods. "That promise about going back? That was a lie."

Rima pretends not to hear. "Oh God! If only our men were here. Then the children would at least listen to us. Maybe they would quietly sit and listen to their stories!"

Samar slowly shakes her head. "I'm not sure those stories they tell each other are such good examples for children. Military operations, killing people? A dozen of them go out, one or two don't come back. This isn't good for the children. Haven't you noticed how Faris has been behaving ever since they brought his father back, all torn up?"

Rima nods. "He's mad! If he doesn't find a person to beat up, he taunts cats. Poor Faris! It was a crime to let him see his father's mutilated body. He's barely eight!"

Samar raises both her arms. "What could we do? Everything happened so fast. It was hysteria."

Rima turns to look at two small boys, both about Ameer's age, standing by themselves, near the infirmary. Weary faces more appropriate to tired old men, she thought. They are both new to the camp and orphans — their father died in battle; their mother committed suicide — and since arriving, they rarely talk or play with other children. "I'm just as worried about Khalil and Khaled," Rima says.

"Who's taking care of them now?" Samar asks.

Rima points at a threadbare tent halfway down the lane. "Their grandparents, but they're barely able to manage as it is. Those boys keep climbing up the hill, hand in hand, gazing at the sky. Someone told them that's where their parents are now. They barely eat, rarely play. At least they talk with Ameer. He seems to be able to communicate with them."

"They should attend classes. Maybe the other children's company would help them." Samar has barely said this when the teacher, Mr. Halim, walks into his 'classroom' and starts ringing a cowbell hung on a branch of the oak. "He must have read my mind! It must be story time. Still, I bet they'd rather play war."

Rima finally sees Ameer, his dark curly hair falling across his handsome face. He walks over and takes Khalil's hand, and Ameer's friend Faris, emulating his moves, comes from behind a nearby tent and takes a reluctant Khaled by the hand. They all head for the 'classroom.' Ameer definitely has a sense of responsibility. At such a young age, Rima is pleased to see him so often acting like an adult, especially with Tarek away so often. To deal with the turmoil of his young life, he has taken on the world as a protector — of his mother, his younger brother, his neighbor's friends — and waiting for his turn to go fight the enemy like his father before him.

Samar stands and looks around. "I am still looking out for my children. And your Rabih."

Rima hears familiar shouts and sees two young boys and a girl racing from the back of the camp. "Thank God for Mr. Halim! Here they come, running not to miss the story. He really knows how to reach their little hearts. Ameer told me they're all eager to listen to the second part of *Sinbad the Sailor*. So much better than violent stories."

"Sami loves the classes. So does Layal. She loves to be around Ameer. They all like being around him. Rabih follows his every step!"

Rima turns to Samar, suddenly looking stern. "I think you and I should make a deal, a promise."

"About what?"

"Both of our husbands are the top soldiers in their outfit. They're the officers in charge . . ."

Samar raises her hands up. "What can we do? What can *they* do? It's not like we have any choice. I look at Wassef and I miss the peaceful, pleasant person he used to be. That caring young man I married is gone. He seems like an entirely different person now. It all seems like a different life, *another* life."

"Well, it *is* another life," Rima says. She points to the makeshift classroom and goes on, "Refugee junior high — grab your books and be sure you run to class." She gestures toward the canvas-topped infirmary. "Refugee hospital — don't get sick, don't get hurt, but if you do, we'll finish you off." Then she points to a ragged cluster of tents. "Refugee hotel — sorry, no running water and no heating. Insects on the house!"

Samar has a bitter look. "Mosquitoes are the only creatures to get their full complement of hot meals. But . . . what was your point, about our husbands?"

"They keep going on dangerous missions. They'll keep going until—" Rima turns her misty eyes away; the thought always left her sad and breathless. "Until one day they won't come back."

"God help us! I'd rather not think about it." Samar gazes at her children.

Rima pulls Samar's arm. "You'd *better* think about it. Learn from the others, the many widows. Some day we may be on our own, with our kids. I have Ameer and Rabih. You have Sami and Layal."

"So what should we do? I can't think about it. I'd be completely lost without Wassef!"

Rima's voice rises in vehement denial. "No, you would not! I used to think the same way, but look at us now. We've been like close sisters, living without their help for years."

"Don't you love Tarek anymore?"

Rima puts her hand on her chest. "I worship the soil he walks on. He has been my only reason to breathe since I was a little girl."

"So what has changed?"

"Everything has changed! Do I need to show you again?" Rima gestures around the camp.

Samar says, "I mean, what has changed between you two?"

Rima takes a deep breath and pauses to gather her thoughts. In a calm voice, she says, "Now I have children. I don't know when and where our plight will end." She pulls the blackened brass key from her pocket. "This key to my house in the village is useless. But I intend to make it through, whatever odds we face, with my children. Hopefully with my husband, too. Maybe our dream of return will come true, but I'm realistic — we are refugees now."

"Rima, this key only opens the door to our dreams. What should we promise each other?"

Rima reaches for Samar's hands, gripping them firmly. "We should vow to take care of each other, and each other's family, whatever may happen to us. If, God forbid, my husband goes one day and doesn't come back, I don't want to follow him. Not physically, and not mentally."

Samar squeezes Rima's hands in return. "Me neither." She adds, "You will always be my dear sister, and we will always take care of each other and our children." The two women grasp each other's hands and hug to seal their vow.

Rima sighs. "We've lost our youth, our lives, our homes, our families, and our every reason to live . . . we lost our parents . . . but not our kids. We owe it to them to get them somewhere in life — anywhere but here."

Samar adds, "This insanity can't go on forever; we've been going from camp to camp for years!"

Rima looks toward the sky, as if hoping Allah would send an answer. "Will we ever go home again?"

"You don't have a home anymore! Either it's been pulled down, or someone else is living in it. Jordan has taken the West Bank. Egypt has taken Gaza. They all betrayed us. We Palestinians can't rely on anybody else to remake our lives for us, not UNRWA, not the other Arab Countries. We can rely only on ourselves."

Rima is less pessimistic. "I don't know. It's better to be under the control of Arabs than to be under a foreign leadership. Imagine living under the Zionists! We ought to be happy that the Arabs are refusing that UN resolution on partition — at least they're supporting us!"

Samar is unmoved. "I'm not at all sure about that. I hear that in Haifa, the Palestinians who have not fled are living quite well. They have houses, they have jobs. What's left for us? Where will we build our homes?"

Rima is perplexed. "You talk about home all the time, but you will give away half of it to the enemy. We should not accept this *nakba* – catastrophe, as a permanent situation." Rima looks southwest, in the direction of her village, as if she could fly back to her dreams.

Samar guesses at her thoughts. "Stop dreaming, my dear Rima. Be wise."

Rima turns nostalgic. "I dream about it all the time. Maybe not the home I came from. Maybe that's gone. But I dream about my mother, my father, and what must have happened to them. I wonder where they are, and if they're still alive. My mother's village . . . they told me every house was burned and razed to the ground, and no one made it out. As for us . . ." Rima's voice softens. "I can still see my poor little brother, when those Zionist bastards bombarded our first camp. He ran after his dog to bring her to safety while the bombs were falling. He got to his Stella, turned back to me with a happy smile, and disappeared in the blast . . ." Rima cannot stop her tears. "I had promised my parents I'd take care of him! I miss him so much. Ziad, *habibi*," — my love. She cries, her voice breaking as she looks to the heavens. "Where are you? What are you doing *now*?"

Samar hugs her and wipes her tears with her sleeves. "Ziad is in good hands," she says, sweetly. "In God's hands. He is happy and well."

For Rima, memories of her family are like an infected wound, deep in her heart, that will never heal, always seeping sadness and hatred.

Forcing a smile, Samar continues, "In the meantime, let's just hope our men come back to us safely, and soon."

"I'm sorry if I scared you," Rima says, sniffling. "Don't worry about today, though, they have a reconnaissance mission." Rima stands up and stretches her stiff back.

Samar seems to drift away. She says, "Our so-called Arab friends keep using us for the most dangerous missions. They hide behind our cause in order to show off before their people. But what did they accomplish? So far, we would have been better off without them. And . . . they fight each other more than they fight the Israelis! If the Arabs ever joined ranks, we'd be back in our homes in no time. May God forgive them." Samar pauses for a moment. "I can't think about this. It's driving me mad. Sometimes, I'm not sure how much longer I can last in this camp. Everything about it is a nightmare. I'm constantly afraid the children will get sick. I never know where we're taking them, and—"

"We're still alive." Rima grabs Samar by the arm and pulls her to her feet. She says firmly, "and we have our children to care for, remember? Now we're linked by our solemn vow." She looks towards the 'classroom.' Let's go give the poor teacher a hand. Maybe we can learn a bit about how he handles those children!"

Rima and Samar walk arm-in-arm toward the children, who are gathered around their teacher under the oak tree. The teacher has managed to captivate the children with his storytelling. The story of Sinbad the Sailor, as he smartly overcomes a multitude of odds on his long journey around the earth captivates the attentive minds. Rima stops near the oak tree. "Looks like today's episode is over . . ."

Mr. Halim, seeing the ladies approaching him, turns to them gently and says, "Hello. Come sit with us. I'm teaching the children about merciful Allah and the hidden beauties of the world, the ones we have to find by looking in the right direction . . ."

Samar is inquisitive. "What are you teaching them about Allah, Mr. Halim?"

The children shout in unison, "Allah is peace, Allah is serenity, Allah is love!"

Rima asks, "Are you a Christian, Mr. Halim?"

Mr. Halim scrutinizes Rima. "No, but what's wrong with being Christian?"

Rima smiles. "Dar Moussa was named after a Christian saint. We had many Christian friends . . ." She pauses before grinning. "Don't teach them that thing about the other cheek. It's the only one we have left!"

"What I teach them is that we're all brothers, that we should not harm fellow humans, and that this war, like all wars, is wrong. In war,

even the winner loses. We're all children of Allah, and we must there-
fore live as brothers and not kill each other. All this violence is wrong.
It is against *all* religions."

Other mothers are arriving to pick up their children. Samar says,
tongue in cheek, "That's wonderful Mr. Halim, and we all thank you.
But can you also please teach them how to wash up and be ready for
dinner in five minutes?"

---

Later that same day, Rima is busy with her daily laundry, struggling to
make do with whatever water is available. The men will be back soon,
and she looks forward to gathering around for dinner.

A slight breeze continues to cool the air; hopefully, this will be a
mosquito-free evening. Rima is looking forward to this dinner in particular because they have been promised that the goats they received in
return for the men's valor in combat against the Zionists will be slaugh-
tered that night. Given the paltry pay the men are given, a miserly few
Jordanian dinars per month, those goats were well earned. For now, a
lot of meat was going to be available, and she doesn't want to miss that.
As soon as the men return, the fire will be lit and the meat put into
large pots to boil and on charcoal grids to grill. Young mouths are salivating, and Rima is happy that tonight, the children will be well fed.

# CHAPTER 6

Amir is sitting on Ely's bed, his eyes fixated on the disassembled pistol on the bedside table. Ely is on a chair facing the bedroom window, with a view of the garden, where bright sunlight is pouring in. It is late October, and he notices the cool breeze morphing into cloudy skies. *Just what we need*, Ely thinks. *Rain on top of the rest of our troubles.* The eight years since the war of independence had not been quite the peaceful times that everyone hoped for. Ely's crack unit, now expanding and merging with others for larger operations, is constantly involved in retaliatory raids against enemy infiltrators. With each of their clashes, the prospect of peace is fading further away and people on both sides are becoming more and more adamant about destroying the enemy.

Ely looks back down at his handgun. He meticulously rubs every part of the Browning 9mm and lays them on a cleaning towel on his bedside table. Reassembling it, he works the action, and inserts a full clip.

Amir studies his father, mesmerized by the gleaming metal of the gun. Ely knows that his son looks up to him, and dreams of the day he too will be wearing a uniform and fighting those Amir calls 'the bad ones.' Amir, like most of his friends, is growing up, maturing—all too quickly, perhaps—in a military environment. His games, his thoughts, his worries, they all center on the ever-present idea of war. Finally, Amir breaks the silence. "Can I hold it, please? I want to play with it."

Ely frowns. "You cannot play with it, it's a real gun. It is very dangerous. I will make it safe and let you hold it. Remember, you ONLY play with your toy guns. Not the real ones."

"But you're always playing with it! You carry it all the time."

"I'm not playing with it. I clean it to make sure it works when I need it. And I carry it because I have to. It's for protection." Ely assumes a shooting stance, pointing the gun out of the window, leaning into the sights. "Protection only. You understand?"

"From 'the bad ones,' who come to kill us?"

"You got that right. But you have to remember that not all Arabs are bad guys — we have some good and kind Arab neighbors, like the Shehada family — you play with their son all the time. He is a nice boy." Ely hands the gun to Amir.

Amir grabs the heavy gun by its handle and tries to control it. Ely shows him how to make sure there is no clip in the gun and how to be sure that the barrel is clear. "Stay on the bed Amir. Feel its weight? It can hurt you just by falling on your toes."

Pointing the gun at imaginary foes outside, Amir shouts, "Boom! Boom!" His gaze drifts briefly before he looks back at his father with serious intent. "What do they look like, 'the bad ones?'"

Ely wonders whether he was overdoing it in treating Amir like such a grown-up. That innocent look now seems to have become one of cool determination. "Well, they're people, just like us."

"If they're just like us, then why are they bad?" Amir hands the pistol back to his father.

"The people in the countries around us don't want us to stay here. They want to chase us away. They want to throw us into the sea!"

Amir's eyes widen. His mouth too. "Into the sea?"

"That's what they say . . . So we have to defend ourselves, and some-times fight —"

"Are there many of them? More than us?"

Ely can see the anxiety on his son's face. "Yes, there are. Many more than us."

Amir pouts. "So they'll win! They will throw us in the sea!"

"Oh no, they won't, son! Don't worry, your father and our strong army will defend all of us, and I promise, you will not get hurt!" Ely ruffles his son's dark hair, clearing a curly lock from Amir's forehead, and gives him a reassuring look.

Amir rolls back over and looks at Ely through his dark, earnest eyes. He hesitates for a moment, and then asks, "*Aba*, will you die like Ethan's father? Will Mummy and me be left alone?"

Ely sits on the bed and draws his son onto his lap. "Don't worry, my son, I'm not going to die. You know your father is the best!" Ely holds Amir's head with both hands, then kisses him on his forehead.

Amir tries to smile, but his eyes are pleading. His voice trembles. "*Aba*, please stay home, always! I hate waiting for you. I'm always afraid you won't come back."

Ely hugs his son. He and Sara have always made sure that they explain what's happening in the world to their son in a way a young boy could understand. Amir is turning out to be a confident and smart boy. The downside is that there isn't much Ely and Sara could hide from him. Ely whispers in his ear, "I hope the day will come, my son, when I will indeed be home with a normal job, and not have to pack my gun."

Amir whispers back into his father's ear, "Mother cries when you're gone. Then Liz comes over with Debbie and Dina, and we play until late at night."

"Do you like Debbie and Dina?" Ely asks.

"A lot!" Amir says. "Dina's still a baby. She's only four." Amir counts the years on his fingers. "Debbie is between Dina and me. And we can stay up a lot later."

Ely laughs. "What else happens when I'm gone?"

"Mummy and Liz laugh all night. They don't let me sleep."

"Should I punish them?"

Amir giggles. "Oh, no, I love it. I stay up with Debbie and play with my toys. We listen to Liz tell jokes, but sometimes we don't understand. Mother says it's dirty jokes. How can a joke be dirty, *aba*? We can't even see it!"

"Oh, I see. Now you're going to end up with a twisted mind from all those dirty jokes." Ely shouts to his wife, "Sara! What are you doing to our boy?"

Sara comes to the door, sniffling and wiping tears from her eyes. "I'm sorry, I was listening to you. I can't bear it when he says 'Daddy, please don't go!' Amir is right, Ely, I'm afraid it's going to be your epitaph one day."

"Don't talk like that. You know I'm a careful soldier. Liz should be worried, not you!"

"Hasn't Moshe wised up a little? Regular army work isn't helping?"

"Moshe will never be regular. He does what he does best, and that is all sorts of special jobs. Still, we have a lot of hotheads, just like the Arabs do. Let's just say, when our men get overzealous, Moshe is surely not the one to calm them down."

Sara sits next to Amir and asks, "What does it look like out there, on the front, I mean? You never really tell us. I know it's not like Europe."

"There isn't a front. Not in the true sense of the word. All we have is those *fedayeen* infiltrators that the Egyptians are sending against us.

Don't worry Sara, we're taking care of them. As it says in the Bible: '*Ha mashkim le horgekha hashkem le horgo!*' He who comes to kill you, rise and kill him first! But now, it seems we have a big engagement coming."

Sara lowers her voice. "I hate that."

Ely shrugs. "What's the difference? At least we get the job done once and for all. As Moshe loves to say, 'If they come in big numbers, we'll kill them in big numbers.'"

Sara replies, "*You* don't say that!"

Ely shakes his head. "I would prefer for them to come in numbers to make peace, not kill us. Then they will find us ready partners." He lifts Amir from his lap and sets him on his feet. "Why don't we all go to the sitting room, eat your delicious *souvganiot*, and play a Domino game or something?"

Sara follows them, saying in a near whisper, "When you go on a mission, Ely, I trust you. You're the one in charge, and you're good. But in a big battle, soldiers are always sacrificed just for the sake of the war. I hate it. We've seen enough death in Europe. We came here for peace. And these poor Arabs want to live, too."

"You're wrong to think our commanders sacrifice our soldiers easily. From what I see, our army cherishes its soldiers the most. We're way too valuable, not to mention too precious in number. And if the Arabs want to live and to have a Palestinian state of their own, they should stop infiltrating our land and killing us. One day they'll understand, and we'll live in peace, as we should."

Sara fetches the platter of sweets from the kitchen and returns. "I hope and pray you're right."

Amir looks up at his father and says, "Me too, father. Mummy taught me how to pray, and I pray so that you come back . . ."

"That's good, my son. Faith is a good thing." And then he adds, "You have to learn what's right from what's wrong."

Ely sits on the carpet and motions Amir to him. "Let's enjoy the evening, son."

Amir jumps on his father. "Yeah! Let's wrestle! I'll take you down!"

"Let's see how strong you've become," Ely says playfully.

"I'll poke your eyes!" Amir yells, sending his forefinger straight at his father's eye. Ely barely manages to squint in time.

"Who the hell taught you that one? Certainly not me!"

"Ethan did! He's teaching us how to make war."

Ely turns toward Sara, rubbing his reddening eye. "Ethan?"

Sara lowers her arms. "He's the neighbor's son, from down the street. You know, the father who died in Rehavia's shopping area? Ethan's become quite aggressive since then. I fear Ethan is becoming Moshe, only worse. He seems to have no feelings anymore, and no moral code. He takes it out on everyone."

Ely warns, "Ah yes, the friend you just mentioned. But I don't like this. Amir, you should stay away from this Ethan kid."

Amir protests. "Oh, no, he's nice. He is coming later with his hunting gun to shoot in the garden with me. He's nice, father, you'll see!"

"What?" Ely turns toward Sara with a frown. "Our boy plays with this boy and his gun?"

Amir says, "Dad, he's nice to us. He just hates Arabs, because they killed his father. He loved him so much. We all hate the Arabs. Ethan says we must kill them all."

Ely is horrified by what his young son is saying. "That's wrong! You don't say things like that, and you shouldn't even think that way!"

"But I just want to be like you. Everybody says you're the strongest fighter and you beat the Arabs all the time."

"In war, we kill our enemies because they attack us." Ely says, "We don't go around killing people for no reason. We only do it to defend ourselves. *Only!*"

Amir lowers his eyes. He is quiet for a moment, and then he says, "Ethan is going to kill Suboh."

"Suboh? The man who works in our garden?"

"And his whole family. So they don't grow up to fight us."

Ely stands up, stunned. He glares at Sara. "I leave my son for a couple of days, and this is how I find him? Don't you pay attention to where he goes and who he talks to?"

He looks back at his son. "Amir, this is not OK!"

Sara looks back at Ely. "Well, I'm so sorry. I'm sorry I can't keep Amir from playing war games while you're out fighting a real war. Ethan is really a nice boy, very polite and well mannered. Amir, don't believe him about killing Suboh and his family, I'm sure he was just joking." She turns back to face Ely. "You should see the other kids. Some of them are simply not normal."

A knock at the door breaks the tension. Amir grabs his father's gun and tries to point it at the door as if to defend his home.

Moshe lets himself in. "*Shalom*, everyone!" He looks at Amir. "How's my favorite little soldier doing? Happy your father is home?"

Sara frowns at the word soldier.

Moshe points helplessly at the gun in Amir's hands as if to say, "Not my fault."

Ely takes the gun from Amir and says, "That's *it!* No more guns for you! Not real guns, not toy guns. Nothing!" He angrily points to the magazine in the grip. "Do you see that? It's loaded!"

Sara sighs, looks at Moshe and invites him in. "Welcome, Moshe. Have a seat. Where are Liz and the girls?"

Moshe steps into the sitting room. "How are you, Sara? They're coming right behind me." He hands Ely a white envelope. "Here, our orders. A bit unofficial, but I was there when the commander came in, so he gave me this envelope for you."

Sara moans. "You paratroopers started as Unit One-oh-One. You didn't miss a fight. Now it's the two-oh-two, and it's getting worse. I hope there's no three-oh-three!"

Ely answers with pride, "Well, we're paratroopers. That means things begin with us and they end with us."

Sara looks desperate. "And we will all end with them, too!"

Moshe closes in on Ely and whispers, "Looks like I walked into the middle of something here."

Ely holds up the envelope. "Any idea what the orders are?" Moshe shrugs unconvincingly. "You're the boss. You read them."

"Yeah, right. You always manage to be the first to hear everything."

Moshe smirks. "I have friends. Good friends. High places."

Ely reads quickly, then looks at his wife. "Well, it's both good news and bad."

"Please, the good first." Sara says, clenching her fists.

"We're home for another two days, so we can go to the beach in Tel Aviv like you wanted."

Amir and Sara jump up and cry happily in unison. Ely nods to Sara, who returns a stern look and grabs Amir by the hand. "Let's go pack."

Moshe interrupts, "An extra break . . . and now for the second part?"

Ely crumbles the paper. "After that, we're assembling at brigade strength. You know what that means."

Moshe raises a fist. "Yes. It means we're finally going to knock Nasser out. We have both France and Britain with us. We're fighting the Reds, and Europe is on our side."

Sara interrupts, "Europe?"

Moshe is confident. "The French and the British want the Canal back. They are part of the effort."

Ely raises an eyebrow. "The fighting is mostly on the Jordanian side, and the British have a Treaty with Jordan . . ."

Moshe shakes his head. "The Egyptians will think we're going to hit Jordan, but our real target is the Egyptian army. The organization is perfect. Reservists can reach their rally points quickly, we're extremely mobile, and our military is much stronger than theirs." Once again, Moshe knew more, and knew it first.

Ely says, "I think the Egyptians' conflicting doctrines are going to hurt them. Russian equipment, old-fashioned British training..."

"Yes. I read your report. Its time has come. They loved it at the HQ."

Sara steps in and dismisses their plans with a wave of her hand. "Later, later. Right now, we have forty-eight hours to enjoy."

A loud knock at the door breaks the conversation. Ely looks at Amir. "That must be Liz."

Amir dashes to the door. Liz is there, trying to control a bunch of kids as they all rush in at once. Ely notices them hesitate when they see him. He waves them in. "*Shalom*, Liz, come on in." Ely recognizes Debbie, Dina, and guesses Ethan, but not the two youngsters with them. "You two guys are new to me," he says, gently pulling them in.

The boys are about Amir's age, wearing shorts and rounded hats, one blue, one white, and shiny shoes. They are holding toy guns, and stare at the real gun on Ely's hip. The taller one says, "I'm Ron, and that's my cousin Benjamin."

Liz smiles, "They're Ethan's cousins. Their families just moved in."

Ethan spots the platter of *souvganiot* that Sara has put on the coffee table in the living room and leads a rush to the treats.

Ely is happy to have everybody gathered at his place. Later in the evening, he'll have time alone with his son and wife. Right now, he wants to learn more about his son's friends, and how they are coping with the heated atmosphere infecting the country.

Ely gathers the children for games. He entertains them with a few card tricks, then moves on to one of his favorite games: word association.

He gives them a word, and the children answer with the first thing that comes to mind. Besides improving their language skills, it gives Ely an insight into their thoughts.

Sara watches with a wry smile. "Just like a military interrogation."

Ely gives her a wink. "Ethan, you go first — answer with one word: gun."

Ethan barks, "Kill, kill, kill!"

"Okay, that was expected, but you don't have to say it three times." Ely laughs. He turns to Ron. "Ron, answer with one word: war."

Ron's answer comes quickly. "Always." Ely decides to try some non-war-related words, but he can't seem to get the kids' minds off violence. Amir replies to "toys" with "gun" and when Benjamin hears "game," he shouts, "war!"

After an hour of varied games, Amir's friends get up to leave. Ely, Sara, Moshe, and Liz spend the rest of the day with their children in the small garden behind Ely's home. For a little while, Ely relaxes. He likes the aroma that fills the air from his lemon tree, and the kitchen is only a step away, with a fridge full of food and mint lemonade.

Everyone wants to make the most out of their time together. Evening comes, and the weather turns milder, a refreshing change from the heat of the day.

Gazing at the stars above, Ely reflects with sorrow that, under the infinite splendor of this very sky, men would soon unleash a wave of terror against their fellow humans with one of the cruelest inventions of all, war. It was little more than systemized murder.

# CHAPTER 7

A loud tumult fills the camp. The men are returning from their mission, and Rima can hear the brouhaha coming in like a tidal wave, all the way from the other side of the camp. Many families have someone on that patrol—a father, a son, a brother—and everyone rushes from their tents, anxious to check on their loved ones.

Children, ignoring their mothers, bolt away and outrun everyone. Like Ameer and Rabih, they all have their fears, nightmares, and torments to be quenched. This time, a routine reconnaissance mission ends with everyone happily reunited. Surrounded by children and women, the men start recounting their adventures and missions. Loud laughter fills the air, couples exchange romantic looks, and children, calmer now, silently cling to their fathers.

The men are back.

Most of the refugees in the camp put aside their misery long enough to enjoy the exceptional evening meal and copious *meze*. Those with a more recent personal loss than others wander off, unable to hear even a joke in the background, and stray in the exposed and roofless world of their camp, gazing up into the unforgiving skies. Eventually, they will be joined by a caring person from the larger family, who draws them back into the fold, offers them some dinner, and gives them a reality check. Life goes on, past death.

After making sure everyone has been served, Tarek and Wassef gather their families in Rima's tent, preferring to defer their socializing until the children have fallen asleep. Rima knows Tarek would be heavily scrutinized by everyone in the camp. As the military leader, he is also the de facto community leader, known for both his boldness and wisdom. He would soon have to answer questions about the battles they are losing, the whereabouts of that long-promised Arab military and financial support, their worsening situation, and their ultimate goal, their return. Rima wonders what Tarek could possibly say. Things have never looked so grim. Incessant raids by both sides may soon lead to full-scale war.

The refugees, like most of the Arab people, seem to have a blind faith in the charismatic Egyptian leader, Gamal abd-el Nasser, who gives heated, patriotic radio speeches about how the Suez Canal belongs only to Egypt and not to any colonial power, British or French. He is skilled at stirring up emotions and rallying Arab public opinion. He has already managed to drag Arab populations into the streets, chanting angry slogans and death wishes for Israel and calling for all-out war to erase the Zionists from the map of the Middle East.

Tarek, however, is more pragmatic in his approach. He tells Rima that Nasser is leading them straight to defeat. By turning to Soviet Russia and aiding the communists in Yemen, the Egyptian leader had alienated both the West and the oil-rich Arab kingdoms like Saudi Arabia. His decision to seize the Suez Canal is not acceptable to the West, the British in particular, which will side with Israel in the inevitable conflict. Meanwhile, France is incensed by Nasser's support for the Algerian resistance movement.

For now, however, Rima decides they will enjoy their family reunion while it lasts. She asks their good friend Nabil to make sure they receive their share of the sweet-smelling meat skewers coming off the fire.

Nabil delivers a dozen skewers, which disappear before the plate even touches the table. Nabil laughs. "By God's name! I'll go and get more . . . and some salad. Some bread as well, from the old lady at the oven.

Tarek looks at Nabil and says, "Don't forget to make sure everyone gets a share. I did my first round, it's your turn now . . ."

Rima likes her husband's trusted friend and fellow soldier. "Nabil is a good man," she says, after he leaves the tent. "Decent and caring."

"Good soldier too," Wassef adds. "Will you give him a command, Tarek? "

"Soon enough he'll have his own platoon."

Rabih asks the question everyone dreads. "Father, are you staying for many days this time?" He looks straight into his father's eyes, holding up his fingers for a count.

Ameer jumps at his father's neck, in a burst of emotion and admiration. "Forever! Father's not going away anymore."

Sami and Layal join Ameer. "Our father too!" Layal cries. "Will you stay?"

Sami has something else on his mind. "Will you take us hunting tomorrow Dad?"

Layal cries, "Yes, yes, please dad! Take us hunting!"

Sami says, "Girls don't go hunting. Only boys."

Wassef smiles and reassures her, "We'll all go tomorrow. We'll hunt, pick flowers, and do some shooting as well."

Ameer says, "Yeah, and I'll shoot your rifle!" He tries to avoid his mother's look, knowing she'd strongly disapprove.

Instead, she smiles and grabs his hands for an inspection. "Before you do anything, you have to wash your hands. Then we'll go to bed."

Tarek stands up. "Your mother is right, children. It's time for bed. We have to wake up early if you want to catch some birds. Kiss your mother goodnight and let's go."

Ameer is delighted. "You're going to put us to bed?"

"Can Sami and Layal sleep here?" Rabih asks. "Yes? Please?"

Rima would have preferred to have things reversed, with her children staying over in Wassef's tent. She wants to talk with her husband. And she needs to be close to him, to be comforted by his body, enjoy some romantic time alone, if that is at all possible. She hasn't seen her husband much lately, and she needs him to take care of her, give her his attention. Being the wife of the camp's leader, Rima would often have to address the other women's complaints, as well as manage the camp's daily life. Now she needs her own share of consoling, to try to find a hint of reason in their diminishing way of life. Or was it, as it often felt, a gradual way of death?

---

Tarek hurries the children to their beds, which are little more than a couple of salvaged flat wood doors propped up on concrete blocks with mattresses on top. As Tarek tucks the children in, Rabih asks quietly, "When will we have a real home? With real beds."

Ameer looks his father straight in the eye and says, "And when can we go to a real school? You always tell us to learn things, and I love to read books, just like you!"

The question startles Tarek. "A real home? A real school?" He has succeeded in avoiding Rima's inevitable questions, but now he is stuck with a bunch of inquisitive children.

Rabih says, "I like this tent! It's nice. But a real home is nicer, like in the books."

Layal says, "I wish I lived in a palace! Like princess Shahrazad. In 'One Thousand Nights.'"

Tarek smiles. "One Thousand *and One* Nights. And that's a castle, not a home. Don't even dream about that!"

Layal says, "Daddy says I'm his princess. A princess needs a castle, not a *tent*."

"Listen, children, I'm going to try to explain something. It's complicated, and I can barely understand it myself."

Ameer frowns. "But you know everything!"

"Who told you that?"

"Mother. She always says, 'Your father knows this, and that . . . everything.'"

Tarek laughs, pleased by his son's admiration. His wife's too. "Your mother loves me very much, then."

Rabih confesses, "She cries in her sleep when you're gone."

Ameer adds, "She says not to worry, it's only a bad dream. Then Samar and Layal and Sami come over, and they sleep here. Mother and Samar stay up all night. Sometimes we go to their tent, and I like that. It's a change."

Tarek puts thin blankets over each of the children. To Ameer, he says, "You're the man in charge when I go, aren't you?"

"And if the enemy comes, I know where the guns are."

"Never go near the guns! Not without asking. Understood? Now I'm going to tell you a story." As Tarek wonders what story to tell, he thinks back to when he was the child waiting for a story. His sister cuddled in his lap, and if the story got scary — such as the one with an angry witch, for instance — she would clasp his hands tightly. Nothing hurts more than memories of his little sister. She was their family's little treasure, loved and cherished by them all. She made them laugh, too, especially when she ran after their chickens, clumsily trying to catch one.

Tarek clears his throat and begins a story about Layla el Hamra —
Red Riding Hood. Soon enough, everyone but Ameer is asleep. Before
giving up to the call of the pillow, Ameer nervously says, "*Yaba*, if you
have to die to get us a real home, then I don't want it. I don't want a
home without you."

Tarek feels a wall of emotion come over him. "We'll stay together,
my son, we always will. And we'll have our real home, I swear it. I promise I will build a house and you will have your own bed in your own
room. In the meantime, we have to hold on to what we have and make
the best out of it. Until we get that house, you have to prepare yourself for the decent life that awaits you. That means you have to keep up
your good work with your books. And make sure your brother does
the same. You will not get anywhere in life without the proper tools. A
solid education is your best tool."

"Shooting too! Tomorrow . . . So I can go kill the enemy with you
when I grow up."

Tarek sighs. The first lesson in the art of killing and destruction is
scheduled for the next morning. This is not what he would have liked
to teach his son. From a faraway tent, he listens to a sad tune by Om
Kulthum, "*laylat hob*" — night of love.

---

Even though it is past midnight, Amir isn't feeling at all sleepy as he
sits, still in his pajamas, on a small chair in the corner of the dining
room. Earlier in the day, he heard his mother complaining about turning their house into an army headquarters, what with all his officer
friends coming in for a briefing. He kept awake in anticipation for that
moment, and now it's here.

Ely, Moshe, and some other officers are standing around the table, finalizing plans for an upcoming mission. Ely and Moshe had gone over them the night before, and now they are working out the details with the others. The map they are scrutinizing depicts the Sinai Desert. Ely puts miniature wood blocks to mark their positions and those of the Egyptian army. He scribbles diagrams on the blackboard in the opposite corner, erasing and redrawing as each of the men adds an opinion. Amir listens desperately to every word, trying to decipher the map. He follows his father's hand as it moves a wood block on the map, using it to attack another block. One of the officers moves his block to the flank, and now Amir understands: They are not just playing with blocks. They ARE the blocks. Each block is an officer and his unit, commanding his units toward the dying enemy, racing across the desert, unstoppable. Would he be leading one of those units one day? Or would he be flying one of the airplanes that zips overhead and blow up enemy bunkers? The fascinating words he hears are like a mysterious world, existing for now only in his imagination. *Dakotas* for the paratroopers, *Meteors* for bombing, *Mystères* for fighting . . .

As the officers drill Ely with questions, Ely signals for their attention. "The French and the British want us to mount our own attack, so no, no direct help from their side. They just need us to spark things up so they can move in as peacekeepers and take the canal back. They'll knock out the enemy's air force, bombing the airfields as early as possible."

A young officer asks, "What about the other fronts, sir? Jordan?" The name on his field jacket reads Gideon. Amir doesn't know him, but he seems to look up to his father, and his father seems to like him.

Moshe answers, indicating areas on the map and routes for the troops. "Our buildup has been interpreted as preparation for the Jordan front, as we anticipated, and they don't expect the British to intervene because of their treaty with Jordan. We can take the Egyptians by surprise if we keep them thinking that our intentions are only retalia-tory raids."

Ely puts his finger at a point on the map. "Our objective in the first stage is this pass, deep in enemy territory. We don't need to take it — blocking it will do. Our real aim is to put pressure on the city of Suez, west of the pass."

"How do we get there?" inquires Gideon.

"How do we get back?" another officer named Uri, asks.

Ely is confident. "We'll drop by parachute just outside the pass. We'll have a couple of heavy mortars, as well as the recoilless guns. They'll be under your command, Nathaniel. You're the best when it comes to artillery. We can't pack a lot of ammunition, so every round counts. The whole battalion will air-drop, and our lieutenant colonel is, of course, with us. Aaron, please distribute the orders."

Amir holds a hopeful hand out for an envelope too, but Aaron smiles and gives him a blank paper. "Make a nice drawing for your father," he says.

Ely says, "You all have your orders now. Any questions?"

"Are you sure about the enemy's strength there?" Gideon asks.

Moshe says, "Yes, we are. We wanted to fill you in for the last-min-ute touchups to the plan. We're good now, and it's perfect. We'll wreak havoc upon them."

Ely goes on. "As I noted in the orders, the remainder of our force will drive in by land, under the CO's command. We'll try to make it look like we're arranging an escape route for the airborne force. Instead, our orders are to take as much terrain as possible before the cease-fire. But our mission at the pass is only stalling and containment."

Nathaniel asks, "Do the British and French know about our plans?"

Moshe draws a line between their forces and their allies. "Their pri-ority is the Canal. Ours is to take ground. We need to secure Sharm el-Sheikh, we need to give Eilat breathing room, and we need to stop incursions, especially from Gaza and the inner lands." Moshe pauses, then looks at the men. "If you have any comments or questions, now's the time. Gideon?"

Gideon doesn't need thinking time. "We're going deep into their territory, Ely, how can we guarantee we won't be isolated?"

Ely has a confident look. "We're paratroopers; we're supposed to be isolated. Phase Two will have us fall back to take on Palestinian camps and Egyptian positions in the urbanized areas up north that are too close for comfort. But we can't concentrate on them until the main Egyptian forces are out."

Moshe adds, "Ely has already told you about the enemy's operating procedures. Surprise them and they'll stumble. They flee instead of maneuvering, or just surrender. Their officers have no initiative and take no risks without written orders. We'll keep hitting them with an ever-changing battle plan to keep them on the defensive. Our planes will cut their communications and this will effectively behead them. We will succeed again. We always do."

"When do the ground forces leave, sir?" asks Lieutenant Uri.

Ely answers. "Immediately after we take off. The desert drive is their worst enemy."

Ely sweeps each officer with his gaze. "Last two things: First, speed is critical. We've teamed up with the British and French, but our targets aren't the same. We have to secure our objectives before they hold the Canal and declare a cease-fire." Ely pauses for a sip of coffee, which Sara had unobtrusively brought over, with some fresh *souvganiot*.

"The second thing is that this is a real war. The first since the War of Independence. Remember that. And be smart. We have to make a clear statement to the world that we must secure the land of Israel. The only way to achieve that is to have more of it. We can't survive with their guns at our doors." He raises his palm and rams it straight at the table, causing the miniatures to fall over. "Let's move them back!"

The officers rise and salute. Some start chanting, *"Yam Yisrael Chai!"* — The Nation of Israel is alive!

Amir stands up and joins their singing, his higher pitch mixing with the manly voices. He is among them, he is one of them. He is driving his tank, the French one with the weird name. *Something*-X 13. He is shooting his gun. His enemies are falling. He is the hero.

# CHAPTER 8

Sitting on top of the sandbag barricade his men have erected in the street, under the hot sun of the desert just outside Khan Yunis, in the Gaza Strip, Tarek observes the road ahead through his binoculars. Tired, sweating, and hungry, he is eager for Wassef's reconnaissance unit to come back. The Egyptian armored battalion they are supposedly there to assist has either bogged down with mechanical problems, or . . . or is being used for the evacuation of their infantry. Soldiers in ragged clothes cluster on top of every retreating tank, but Wassef is nowhere in sight.

Nabil, his sergeant, looks at him and says, "Sir, we have to find Wassef. His unit will be surrounded soon. The Egyptians are packing up and running away!"

Tarek frowns. "Yes, we must go back in, I'm afraid."

The scars on Nabil's face widen as he smirks. "Yes, sir, we must. They're not coming back otherwise, and soon, they'll be all by themselves on the firing line. We have to bring them back."

Tarek nods and turns back to the road, saying, "You're right, *Raqeeb*. Gather up the men. We're going to go in and get them. If something happens to Wassef, I'll never forgive our Egyptian 'friends'."

As Nabil barks the orders to the men, Tarek grabs him by the shoulder and points to a cluster of dense streets on the outskirts of the abandoned town in the distance. Smoke covers the area. "They're caught up over there. Still in position."

Nabil hesitates. "God help them. That could be in enemy hands."

Tarek isn't convinced. "I hear small arms fire. They're still fighting." He turns an ear toward the village as a machine gun burst rings in the distance. "Hear that? That's a Degtyarev, Wassef's Degtyarev. Short busts, sounds like he's running low on ammo. It must be Wassef. Let's hope he waits for us. They don't have enough manpower for a clean retreat. They'll be sitting ducks for the Israelis."

A corporal rushes in. "The men are ready, sir." Tarek and Nabil inspect the company, tired and bloodied men aboard the five derelict trucks they managed to salvage.

"Ride with me in the Jeep, Sergeant, I'll need you to signal orders to the trucks. We'll have to step on it to avoid the planes." Tarek orders his small convoy forward.

As their convoy races up the road, the sergeant says, with another scar-twisted smile, "It's going to be a very long ride, sir!"

Suddenly, the sound of a diving propeller airplane cuts through the air. An Israeli Mustang is coming at them. An Egyptian tank with one of its tracks blown away stands askew, just off the road, smoke billowing from its hull. The tank commander opens up on the fighter jet with his heavy machine gun, diverting its attention. It was a fatal act of courage. The mustang diverts slightly and fires his rockets at the tank. The commander is still firing as the fire from the explosion engulfs him and his machine.

Tarek lowers his head to avoid the blast as they drive by the burning carcass and shouts, "Brave man! He saved us. That plane was coming for us! Are the men okay?"

The sergeant looks back. Shells are falling all around. "All made it. So far."

They come to the entrance of the town, and, before going any deeper, Tarek spots a dense grove of trees and tells his sergeant, "I'm going to stop here to dismount. Signal the men. The planes can't see us under the trees."

The sergeant signals the order. As the men jump off their trucks and run to the cover of an abandoned house, he points to the next street over and says, "Sir, all I can see is fleeing Egyptians looking at us like we're devils!"

"They must think we're crazy. You stay here, Nabil, with half the men. I'll go for Wassef with the rest."

The sergeant looks at Tarek. "Since when do you spare me from the action?"

"I'm not sparing you. I need you to guard our trucks so we can get out. Those retreating soldiers will take them if they have the chance."

The sergeant nods. He adds, in a rare worried tone, "How will we get out, sir? We barely made it in."

Tarek points to a platoon of brand new Egyptian SU-100 self-propelled guns, with fresh desert paint. Soldiers are humming around them. "You see those tanks getting ready to leave? They'll divert the planes away from us."

Tarek can see the relief on Nabil's face. He gives a final nod and puts a hand on his shoulder, as if to wish him farewell, and waves over his unit. Thirty proud and battle-hardened men who would follow him anywhere come forward. He divides them into squads, and they all swiftly rush through streets filled with debris, dodging incoming mortar fire and zipping bullets, until they reach what must have been a second line of defense. With hand signals, Tarek quickly directs his men to cover each other. He then moves ahead across the street, his platoon behind him, until he reaches a burning barricade. He orders his squad leader, corporal Yussef, to stay put.

Behind the barricade, he finds two of Wassef's men dead. Tarek guesses there would be more dead men in the makeshift bunker further up the street. He dashes across and leaps inside, landing on two bodies. As he focuses on the last bunker ahead, he hears the familiar sound of a soldier running behind him.

Yussef drops in next to him and shouts, "Look, there's someone moving in that barricade!"

Tarek reprimands him. "I told you to stay behind and wait."

The man smiles and says, "You did. But we need to cover each other as we cross." He points to the bunker as a burst of fire rips the air. "That's Wassef. He's alive!" Another burst from the gun shatters the air. Yussef starts to head out. "They're alive. Let's go get them." Tarek grabs him by the arm to stop him. Yussef objects, "Let's get them before it's too late!"

Tarek forces Yussef down. "Listen! I'm going first, alone. I'll come back for you, or wave you in. Wait here. That's an order. Cover me but only if you have to. No need to draw attention. They don't have much firepower covering this street. They must think we're done here."

Tarek rushes to Wassef's trench. He finds his companion, leaning back against a wall, shaking and bleeding severely from a stomach wound. He holds on to his machine gun. Next to him lie the bodies of his sergeant and two other soldiers.

Tarek points at them, inquiring. Wassef shakes his head. The men are dead.

Wassef looks up at Tarek. "Thank God. I knew you'd come, I told the men you would. I told them we shouldn't get out in the open, where they would hunt us down like rabbits. I told them we should resist until you come. And you did."

Tarek eases his friend to a more comfortable position. "You did well, my friend, you stalled them and forced them to divert. You and your men, alone. They'd be on us otherwise, and we'd be all dead. I'll get a stretcher. We're getting you out."

Wassef reaches out for Tarek's sleeve. "You have trucks for the men? They must be relieved."

Tarek looks away, clamping his lips.

Wassef mutters in disbelief, looking haggard, "What . . . My men? No!" He collapses back onto the wall, coughing blood. "I'm up front! *They* are dead? All of them?"

Tarek shakes his head and points to the sound of whizzing mortars a few streets down from them. "Mortars. The Egyptians fled and opened your flank. They had eyes on you. You're the only one left. They all died fighting." Tarek stands. "The Jews are busy with the Egyptians two streets from here, and have few people covering this street. We have to move. Now!"

Wincing with pain, Wassef rips off his chest pouch and jacket, uncovering another wound, in the middle of his chest. Blood flows with his every movement. "I have bad news, Tarek. You made this trip for nothing."

Tarek looks in horror at the wound, trying to hide his despair. "Don't be a fool. We both know you're impossible to kill. I'll get you out right now!"

As Tarek turns to call for a stretcher, Wassef pulls him back. "Wait. There's something..." Tarek can tell these will be his friend's last words. It's not the first time he's watched one of his men die. But Wassef... he called him *ya akhoui* — my brother. Tarek kneels next to him.

Wassef can hardly breathe. He manages to mutter, "Take care of my family like you would your own. I know you will, I know you and Rima will . . ."

Hoping to keep his friend alive a few more seconds, Tarek says, "*Insh*

*Allah*, you'll take care of them yourself. Hang in there! You can tell them all about how you saved the day by stopping the enemy. Sami and Layal will be so proud. It's going to be the story of their lives. Sami will talk about it forever!" Tears spill from Wassef's eyes as he moans and winces in pain.

Wassef struggles with his last words, coughing up his own blood. He looks down at the blood pouring from his chest. "The story of their lives. I can imagine them, I can see them, I am their hero! Do they . . . do they know they're my heroes, too? Does Sami know he's my hero? My Sami, my Layal . . . *awladee* — my children . . . Samar, my beloved Samar . . . take care of her. I wish I could hold my Layal one last time, just to tell her it's all right . . . my brave Sami . . . my boy . . . who will love him like I do? Aah, my children . . . take care of my children . . ."

Wassef raises his head, points to Tarek as if to say 'you', then exhales loudly and collapses, lifeless, one last gush of blood spurting out of his punctured chest.

Tarek suddenly realizes that Yussef is behind him again. Yussef mutters, "God bless his soul. He's in Allah's care now, sir. It's too late for him."

Tarek stares at his friend's open eyes.

Yussef squeezes his shoulder. "But us, sir, we're still here with the Devil, and it's not too late. Your men are waiting. I can hear the Egyptian tanks moving out. Only you can get us out of here, so let's go!"

"How can I leave Wassef here?" Tarek whispers, "My best friend, my brother — dead . . ."

"If we stay, it will be forever. All of us. The men's lives are in your hands. Come on, let's carry him back."

———

In the desert mountain pass, Ely leads his troops uphill, under both heavy fire and the scorching afternoon heat of that last day in October. They are painstakingly shutting down enemy positions, one by one, but paying a dear price for each. Like him, his fellow commanders lead their men forward, obeying the careless orders of their Commanding Officer. Not happy with merely taking the eastern side of the pass and blocking it as planned, the CO ordered them to take the whole mountain pass. They have already lost a number of good men clearing the caves below.

As Moshe rushes towards him, his footsteps closely tracked by bullet impacts from a machine gun burst, Ely doesn't hide his feelings about the mission readjustment. He keeps his voice down, so the men don't overhear, and his head low, as the machine gunner in a bunker about a hundred meters up has him pinned down behind a rock. Moshe crouches next to him and turns back towards his sniper. He quickly points to the bunker, signaling an estimate of the distance.

Ely can barely contain his anger as he grumbles, "Are you happy now? We're fighting uphill against a dug-in enemy. This is suicide! Our orders were to hold the east side. You should have stopped him, Moshe; you should have at least tried."

Moshe is unmoved, and doesn't even look at Ely as he says, with a stern voice, "What's your problem? We're moving ahead, and they're moving back. We're winning."

Ely points to the corpses of two dead men in the open, on the way up the hill, *his* men. "*That's* my problem. Look at them! My men! Dead! What about their families? If this is winning, what would losing look like?"

Moshe answers with a grin, pointing to the enemy bunker as one of Ely's men, encouraged by the covering fire from his sniper, blows it up with a demolition charge. "*That's* losing!"

Ely has no time to argue. He seizes the opportunity to move his men up to the destroyed bunker, and the dominant grounds around it. He signals them forward, one squad at a time. Each squad covers the other with suppressive fire as they close the last few meters to the top of the hill, dispatching the remaining resistance scattered among a handful of foxholes. The rest of the enemy is now on the run. Other units give chase, finishing them off, paying no attention to raised hands and white flags. The shooting slowly subsides.

Ely's men gather around him. They are exhausted and many are wounded. They glance at each other with inquisitive whispers and looks about the missing men. They're sometimes answered with a negative nod by their team mates. Ely orders his sergeant, "Secure the area and give me a quick report. Tend to the wounded and gather up the men. I have to contact the CO."

A sudden burst of firing, followed by two muffled explosions, sounds ahead. Ely watches as, in the distance, retreating Egyptian soldiers blow up what seems to be a hidden dugout. It was so well camouflaged that no one had noticed it, even them.

Ely looks with his binoculars and dictates the scene. "An Egyptian platoon, or what's left of it, has come across a concealed position in the rocks. Maybe they tried to hide there themselves. It must be our people inside, although I have no idea how they got up there. They blew it up."

Moshe looks at Ely, visibly annoyed by the unexpected loss. "We should check it out, quickly. Maybe there are survivors."

Ely nods and waves over his corporal. "You're coming with me. Get your squad moving!" He turns to Moshe, knowing his friend's insatiable curiosity wouldn't let him stay behind. Lips tight, he says, "Come along, Moshe. Bring your men too. There might be a few surviving Egyptians as well."

Ely and his men, swift but cautious, quickly reach the hideout, a group of rocks standing in a natural half-circle. His corporal says, "This is very well concealed . . . No wonder the Egyptians didn't notice it at first. I'm sure none of our men would—"

"Whoever did the camouflage was a genius," Ely interrupts. Indeed, camouflaged canvas, now shattered and torn, was covered with mud and dry sand, closing all gaps around the small cavern in the rocks. Smoke is rising from it, and dust from the explosion hasn't completely settled.

Ely hears something. "Someone is moaning. There's someone in there." Signaling his men to lie flat, he calls out, "We are the two-oh-two! Who's in there?"

A barely perceptible voice responds. It sounds like Hebrew. Ely signals Moshe to follow and cover the right side of the interior. He nods to his corporal and points to him. *'You're in charge.'*

Trusting his instincts, Ely rushes in. His feet slide and he falls flat on his butt. Moshe lands on his shoulders and starts to curse. The area inside the rocks was dug about one and a half meters deep.

Ely looks around. There are four bodies, all in Israeli military gear. They all seem dead. One was a woman, face down. A mound of radio equipment, power packs, and supplies have been blown all over by the Egyptian grenade. Smoke, dust, and burnt powder still hang in the air.

Moshe rises to his feet. "Anyone alive? Move or speak!" One man, lying on his side, manages to raise a hand. Moshe rushes to him as Ely shouts to his corporal, "All clear! Medic!"

Moshe turns the soldier to face him. He is a young officer from the signaling unit, and he grimaces as he sees Moshe. The light in his eyes is already fading. "We were sent to intercept and disrupt their communications. We all volunteered, at the last minute. We were broadcasting on their frequencies . . . I don't know what happened; there wasn't supposed to be any fighting our way. Your orders were only to block the pass."

Moshe avoids Ely's stare. He says, "Don't worry, son, help is on the way."

The young officer's shaky finger points to the woman's body, "We tried to protect her, we . . . I'm so sorry . . . Sam jumped on the grenade . . . then they threw another . . ." The soldier exhales his last breath as his hand slumps down.

Ely feels a chill. He looks at his friend, who freezes for a moment, then leaps to the woman's body, half-baked by fallen debris. Ely jumps behind him, holding Moshe by the shoulders as he kneels and turns the limp body to face him.

It is Liz. Moshe holds her, eyes wide, face frozen. Neither he nor Ely can speak.

Ely eases down beside him and checks her throat for a pulse with his fingers. He looks at Moshe, not daring to say anything, and shakes his head.

Moshe rises up suddenly, lifting Liz's body in his arms, howling. "No! No! No! Not my Liz! Not my Liz! Noooo . . ."

Ely watches as Moshe turns in circles, holding Liz's body against him, like a baby, screaming his denial. Then he stands in place, clutching her lifeless body, kissing her dusty cheeks, her neck, her forehead, as if to revive them.

The corporal and the rest of the men have gathered around the rocks, peering inside. Ely looks up and gives them an order. "Back off, Corporal, nothing here for you or the medic. Not anymore."

Moshe falls to the ground, his dead wife lying across his lap. He rocks back and forth, mumbling incomprehensible words. "*Imma Shmam!*" he yells. Cursed be those who killed her. "Curse them for generations and generations!" Ely looks back to his corporal. "Go back and send in the sanitary unit. We need to evacuate —" Ely notices the sudden astonishment on his corporal's face, and instinctively looks back at Moshe.

Ely jumps to Moshe's side and snatches his Colt out of his hand before he can insert the muzzle into his mouth. In a rage, Ely slaps him, and slaps him again. He kneels and shakes Moshe violently. "You stupid fool, what are you trying to do? Huh? What are you trying to do? Just when we need you the most, Moshe? Are you mad?"

Moshe just looks at Ely with complete apathy. "Liz is dead. And it's my fault. I just want to be with her . . ."

Ely stares his friend in the face, shaking him. "Liz is dead, but you have two young angels at home! Don't you DARE fail them, don't you dare! I won't let you, you hear me? I won't let you! Liz wouldn't let you! Do you hear?"

Ely looks again into Moshe's blank eyes. "You owe it to them! You have to get back to them! We do what we do for the ones back home. Isn't that what you always say?"

Moshe nods, and whispers into his dead wife's ear, half-choking, he tries to mutter a few words, but cannot. He draws in a long breath and mutters in her ear, "Just for you my darling, my soul. Just for you and the girls. I won't join you now. Not yet."

# CHAPTER 9

Tarek and his men enter the camp silently. They have not sent news of their return. They are on the run, and they are missing an entire platoon, as well as other men from the company. Each of the able men heads for his tent, some of them assisting the wounded. Tarek, soaked from the first rain of the year, smudged with sweat, blood, and mud, is greeted by Ameer and Rabih who jump to his chest. Tarek puts a knee down to better grab them and looks towards Rima. He feels guilty, angry, and sad, very sad. He knows Rima will guess something is amiss from the first eye contact, and she obviously does. She rushes to him, her eyes two wide question marks. Tarek wishes *everything* would go away, and he could hug his boys for eternity. But no, this is still reality, awful and heartless in its overwhelming emptiness. Tarek slowly tilts his head towards Wassef's tent, and shakes mournfully. Rima spots the tears he can't restrain. She freezes in disbelief.

Tarek looks again at Rima and tries to speak, but finds no words. Another issue haunts him. He knows the Israelis will soon overrun their camp in retaliation for their valiant stand. He lets go of the boys and heads for the corner where their suitcases are piled. Rima's voice trembles as she pulls at his sleeve, finally daring to speak. "Tarek! *Thank* God!

What happened, Tarek? Are we leaving the camp? You look hurt. Let me have a look. You have to clean the wounds and stop the bleeding." She begs her husband, "Will you please listen? And ... Where ... where is Wassef?"

Tarek realizes that if he is going to get any help from his family, he will have to explain. He faces them, takes a deep breath, and says, "My wounds are nothing. We're facing a catastrophe. Another catastrophe. We had to sneak back here from Gaza. It took us more than ten hours. Now we have to pack and leave. We should have done it before, but I knew you were tired of moving." Tarek gathers his land deeds, their birth and wedding certificates, and the little cash they have. He also gathers the gold pieces that were the present he gave to Rima in front of the Sheikh who had hastily wedded them eight years ago. It was Rima's father who initially gave him those pieces. They were a family inheritance, the *Napoleons* that Omar had stashed away for emergencies, as his father had, and before him, his grandfather. Tarek quickly draws Rima's attention to all their family essentials: clothes, blankets, mattresses, dishes. Everything that could go had to go.

Rima says, "We're leaving? The whole camp?" She hesitates before throwing, as in a last attempt of forced denial. "Wassef?"

Tarek turns to Rima and holds her by the shoulders, wishing she'll guess what he cannot say.

Rima lowers her eyes. "Isn't Wassef coming?" Her voice breaks, yielding to her fears. "It can't be. I have to go see Samar."

Tarek hands her the suitcases, and says, "Keep packing. We have to leave within an hour." Looking at his boys, he adds, "Same goes for you. You have your own bags."

Ameer doesn't budge. Instead, he faces his father with a challenging look. "Tell us what's happening!"

Tarek knows Ameer will not give up. "The Zionists know we came from here, and they're looking for us. Arab forces are either on the run or defeated. Every soldier's family is in danger. I told my men that they should pack."

Tarek looks in the direction of Wassef's tent. "I have to go see Samar and —"

"Where is Wassef? Why don't you answer me?" Rima is shaking and trembling, as reality seeps in.

Tarek strides toward the tent entrance. "I said, pack whatever you can. No furniture, just clothes, food, our belongings. Throw in the mattresses, if you can. All of it has to fit in the truck."

Ameer jumps in front of his father, resolve turning into distress. "Where is Uncle Wassef, father? Why don't you answer Mom?"

Rabih says it for everyone else. "*Estach'had*? Martyred? Poor Sami and Layal!"

Again, Rima hides her face with her hands, and Tarek kneels to face his children. His voice breaks as he says, "Yes, Wassef is . . . he's gone. God bless his soul. We have to gather our courage and strength now." Tarek says the words for himself as much as for his family. "His family needs us."

How can he face Samar? Besides the deep feeling of sorrow for the loss of his friend, Tarek is full of rage, guilt, and lust for bloody revenge. But now, he has to go to Samar. He swore to Wassef that he'd take care of his family as his own. He steps out of the tent, Rima at his heels. She races past him, hands over her tearful face.

Samar is standing in front of her tent, a dire look on her face, as she and her children watch others frantically load their belongings into cars and trucks. Some other women are also standing in front of their tents, waiting in vain, avoiding each other's eyes. Like Samar, their men have not returned. Samar turns to Rima and Tarek, her eyes shifting from face to face, and she understands. The sweat, blood, and tears on Tarek's face . . . Rima's face . . . Ameer . . . Rabih . . . she doesn't need any explanations. She gasps, "No!" and falls unconscious to the ground.

Sami and Layal kneel beside their mother, begging her to speak to them. Rima is quick to act. Grabbing them both, and pulling them gently, she says, "Your mother's fine, children. She just fainted."

Ameer and Rabih cluster around her. Glancing up at Tarek, Rima says, "Why don't you take the kids to our tent and talk to them? I'll take care of Samar, and we'll pack in a few minutes."

Tarek acquiesces and gathers up the children. How could he explain to his best friend's son and daughter that their father was gone? In Tarek's mind, he could see Wassef still dying, again and again, the bloody and poignant last seconds prolonged to infinity, his last words forever hanging in Tarek's ears. His family . . . take care of them . . . love them . . . as he would his own. Tarek's mind feels like gunpowder, about to blow his head into splinters of flesh and bone. He realizes that the children, in tears now, need comfort as much as explanations.

He leads them into his tent. "Come with me, children. We have to talk."

Sami tries to hide his trembling lips with a manly voice. "My father is dead?"

Ameer says, "Uncle Wassef is a martyr!"

Layal cries, "And what about Mommy? Is she dead too?"

Taking the six-year-old into his arms, Tarek does his best to comfort her. "Your mother is fine, little angel. She is very sad and shocked by the bad news, and she fainted, but she will be fine."

Sami grabs Tarek's shoulder. "Are you sure my father's dead? Maybe he's just wounded?"

Tarek answers, "I was with him when he . . . when it happened."

"How come only my father is dead?"

"Many have died. Many good soldiers have. All the men in the camp are soldiers. It's our job, and that's what we do. The Zionists took our country and put us out of our homes. We have to fight those people to take our homes and our land back."

Ameer, having reached a conclusion of his own, shouts, "And we're losing! We're dying, and we have to move all the time. It's not fair!"

Tarek eases Layal down and holds his arms around Ameer and Sami, bringing them to him. "Yes, it's unfair. All the countries in the world are helping the Israelis, and no one is helping us. Not even our Arab brothers."

Sami looks at Tarek, and then at Ameer, his face showing his confusion. "My father said there are many of us. He said the Arabs can help us win."

"Your father wasn't wrong. There are many Arabs, and they can help us win. But their commanders are no better than their politicians. That's why we suffer so much."

Layal cries, "We lost the war? Again? *And* my father died?"

Tarek feels the question more than he hears it, as it bounces from his heart to his mind, not finding anywhere to rest. "We haven't lost the war yet, and—"

"Then why are we moving?" Ameer says.

"Well, we lost a battle. Soon, the Israelis will be here."

Sami asks, his voice thin with worry, "Will they kill us? Like they killed father?"

Tarek shakes his head firmly. "No one will kill you, but we have to move on. We're not taking any chances. We don't want to live under an occupation, do we? We're free people. Free and proud, just like Wassef says."

Layal says, "Did my father cry when he died?"

"Your father died like a hero. More than twenty enemy soldiers surrounded him. He took half of them and pushed back the rest before we made it to him. He died a proud father, with your names on his lips."

Rabih speaks for the first time, with a calm voice that seems to contain mountains of resolve. "Uncle Wassef is a hero. We all should be like him."

Tarek is glad to hear his voice.

Tarek gently draws Layal back to him. He looks at her and Sami and says, "Your father told me to take care of you and your mother, like my own. I promised him I would. I told him he has a very brave boy and a very courageous girl. He said he needed you to be strong so you can take care of your mother. He said you are his heroes, just like he was yours. And that will always be true."

Sami straightens. "I'll take care of mother. Don't worry, Uncle Tarek."

Layal adds, "And me too. Can I see her now? She must be crying!"

"Of course you can see her."

Layal says, "And father, when can I see him?"

Sami snaps, "Our father is dead. You'll never see him again, Layal. Never!"

Layal breaks into tears. "But I want to see my father, even if he's dead."

Lowering his head, Sami whispers, "We'll never see our father again."

Tears run down Layal's cheeks, as she clings to Tarek. "Is it true, Uncle Tarek? I want to see him. I want to play with him. He promised he'd always comb my hair, and read me stories at night." Pulling her head away from Tarek's shoulder and looking into his eyes, Layal cries, "It was a promise. He has to come back. Father always comes back!"

Tarek knows too well about that promise. He makes the same one to his children, every time. How easy it turned out to break. "It will be a very long time before you see your father again, my lovely girl. For now, when you want to talk to him, you talk to him in your heart. Wassef will always be with us. He's like an angel now, looking at us. He wants you to behave as if he were with you, all the time. We'll love him as if he was here, and when you want to feel his love, all you have to do is look at the sun and feel him in its rays. And I will be here for you, always. This I swear."

Layal softly says, in between hiccups, "And at night? How can I see my father at night? There's no sun in the night."

"Look at the stars and imagine his sparkling eyes, watching your every move. Say a short prayer for him. Tell him you're a good girl, and ask Allah to take care of your father."

Sami says, "What if Allah doesn't?"

"What do you mean?"

"What if Allah doesn't take care of Dad?"

"Allah takes care of everyone, and especially your dad, because he lived an honorable life, and was the best father. We still have to pray, because it's a sign of submission to the will of Allah."

Sami asks, "It is the will of Allah that my father had to die?"

"Allah created the universe. Allah doesn't decide who dies, but we do say that it's His will. Allah will take care of Wassef, this I know for sure."

Sami rebels. "I am angry with Allah if it is his will that my father should die!"

Ameer takes his father's hand and asks, "Is it Allah who makes us evil, or good?"

"We can't use Allah as an excuse for doing bad things."

"*Wa el-yahoud?* — and the Jews? — What does Allah give them?"

"We're all the same in the eyes of Allah. When we die, he will decide who did the right thing in his life, and who was a bad person."

Ameer's words are full of venom. "I hope all the Jewish fathers go to hell. And their children too."

Sami speaks with a soft, confident tone. "We'll kill them all. Send them to hell."

Ameer joins ranks with Sami. "Yes, we will. You have to train us, Father, so we can go fight with you. You always say no one will get us our land back, except us. We *will* fight! We will kill them and get our homes back."

Rabih mimics choking someone. "I'll kill them with my hands, like this!"

"You're still too young, my boy, but trust that I will train you."

"I want to train too," Layal says. "To avenge my father."

Rabih says, "Not you, you're a girl!"

"Everyone will train. At one point or another. But we must not forget our other priorities, like education. That was Wassef's dream, and we shall not fail him. Now, how about comforting your mother? We must all stick together."

Tarek shepherds the children back to Samar's tent. Her face warped from crying, she hugs her children as if they might leave her as well. As if she wants to fill her hollow self with their bodies.

Layal turns her small lips to her mother's ear and whispers softly, "Don't worry, Mama, Uncle Tarek said Daddy is still alive in our hearts. And we can talk to him when we need to. We don't really die, we just go to Allah."

Samar, incapable of speech, pulls her children tighter to her heart, tears flowing freely down her cheeks.

---

Despite the late evening hour, the street outside Sara's home is in full parade. It is November 5th, and the war has ended, with a swift victory for the Israeli army. Happy teenagers zip by, honking in their cars, singing patriotic songs and yelling shouts of victory, while waving blue and white flags with Magen David. It is as if the entire country is shouting and dancing away its relief at the end of combat.

Inside her house, Sara has just called her husband's headquarters and was told that Ely is on the way. She can't wait for him to return, so she can celebrate with him and their close friends.

She looks at Amir, who seems indifferent to the late hour. He looks so excited to have his father, his hero, coming home. Staying up late is just one of his ways of showing 'adult' behavior, and this time he has a good reason to do so. Sara closes the book she is reading to her son, about the first children pioneers who had come to Zichron Yaacov. "Are you sure you want to wait up? Wouldn't you rather go to sleep, if I promise to wake you?"

"No, no, and no! I want to see him. I want to open the door for him when he comes. Let's watch TV, it's full of soldiers, maybe we'll see father! Why isn't he here yet?" A loud knock at the door saves Sara the trouble of answering.

"*Aba!*" Amir screams as he scrambles off the couch and races to the door.

Ely's resounding voice comes back. "It's me."

Sara sings her way to the door. "Coming..." She helps Amir swing it open, expecting a fresh and eager Ely. She hardly recognizes him, still in his battle uniform, uncleaned and coated in mud, sweat, and blood. Ely holds the hands of Dina and Debbie, Moshe and Liz's girls. He doesn't put on his usual homecoming show and makes no move to hug Sara, or even kneel to grab Amir.

Despite her surprise, Sara is overwhelmed with excitement.

Oblivious to his condition, she wraps her arms around his neck and cries, "It is over! You're back home!" She steps back for a moment to look at her husband. "You always take a bath and change before coming home . . . And where are Moshe and Liz?"

Ely remains mute. Sara scrutinizes his eyes. Two windows with their curtains closed. Leaning toward him, she whispers darkly, "What happened?"

Ely mutters mechanically, "I'm going to get Moshe. Stay here and take care of the girls. They were with the sitter, and I had to wake them up. Amir, help Mommy. I'll be right back."

Sara reaches for him, but he refuses to lock eyes with her. "I have to go. Moshe's alone now."

Sara is dumbfounded. *Moshe is alone? How? Where is Liz? Impossible . . . What could have happened to her? An accident?* Sara coaxes Ely inside. "Bring the girls in first, then go get Moshe, OK?"

Ely relents and leads the sleepy girls together to the living room couch.

In a teary voice, Debbie blurts out, "*Ima* is dead. *Aba* said it's all his fault!"

Sara glances at Ely. He shakes his head, and silently turns to leave. Sara has never seen him like this. He looks completely worn down, and the sparkle in his eyes is like a dying candle, drowning in a pool of its own wax. A tear runs down, then another. Sara, still impervious to the news, motions for the girls to sit on the couch. She sits next to Debbie and puts her arm around her. "How could it be your daddy's fault? This is impossible!"

Dina blabbers between tears, "*He* said, 'I didn't know, I should have stopped Adam. I should have stopped him in the beginning.'"

Amir says, "*Aba* says Uncle Moshe's one of the best soldiers. It's not his fault."

"My tummy hurts," complains Debbie. "I feel bad."

Dina says, "Me too. I want to go to the bathroom. Will Mommy be dead tomorrow too?"

"Debbie and Amir, why don't you watch TV? I'll take Dina to the bathroom. Do you want to go, Debbie?"

Debbie takes a deep breath. "I'm okay, but the TV is all about the war. I don't want to hear anything about the war. I hate war. War killed my Mom!"

Dina's eyes sparkle. "Do you think they'll show us Mommy? They're showing soldiers!"

Debbie shouts at her sister, "Mommy is dead. You can never see her any more. Never! Don't you understand?"

Debbie starts to shake, and Sara rushes to hug her. She kisses her forehead and pulls them both in a tight clutch.

"Children, let's be calm. Debbie, you're right about the TV. Let's leave it off. I don't want to hear anything about the war either. I'll be right back with Dina. Amir, will you see if Debbie needs anything?"

Amir takes Debbie by the hand and brings her over to the couch to sit next to him. He wipes her tears with his bare hands and hugs her tight to stop her sobbing.

Ely and Moshe are entering the house. Moshe looks distorted and pale from pain. Sara rushes to embrace him, and he stutters to her ear, "I . . . I killed her, Sara. I killed my Liz. It's all . . . all my fault." Moshe steps back and stares at his girls with sorrowful eyes. "Look at those two angels. What's going to happen to them without the love of their mother?"

Sara struggles to stay calm. "I guess you're going to have to love them twice as much now," she says to Moshe in a soothing voice. "We're here for you, but you have to stand up for them. And you have to stop blaming yourself."

"I'm not sure I know how to love anymore," Moshe says. "Not after the war in Europe. Not after this." Moshe gazes at his daughters and adds, "I wish I was the only one to pay the price, but no, that's not enough. They have to suffer, too. My girls have to pay their father's huge bill." He lowers his head. "What can I say? It's *Hayin Hara*" — the Evil Eye — "and it's following me everywhere. I was born under an evil star."

Sara guides Moshe to a corner and whispers into his ear, "Listen here . . . Stop letting them hear you say it's your fault. Even if it's true, which of course it isn't, you have to stop saying it. Do it for your girls. Do you want them to lose their father as well? Do you want them to hate you, too? To see you as their mother's murderer? Then they'll lose both their mother and their father. You have a difficult task coming your way, Moshe, and the sooner you get started, the better off you are, and so are your children."

Ely takes Sara's arm and says to Moshe, "I'll take Sara to the bedroom and talk to her about what happened." He nods toward the girls. "In the meantime, Moshe, do as Sara says." Ely motions Sara toward the bedroom and gives Amir an 'I'm counting on you' nod.

Moshe sits on the carpet and snuggles his girls beside him, rocking back and forth. They hold each other's hands and weep together. Amir joins the heart-wrenching scene by resting on Moshe's back, his arms spread on Debbie and Dina's shoulders.

In the bedroom, Ely sits next to his wife on their bed. "We didn't know it, but Liz volunteered for a secret signaling mission deep behind enemy lines, and right in our path. Their position was uncovered as we drove the Egyptians back."

Sara says, "But how? How did this happen?"

Ely gazes angrily into the distance. "Well, we shouldn't have been there in the first place. We were supposed to hold our ground, as ordered. Then, Liz's unit could have sneaked out just as they went in. Instead, our push drove the enemy right onto them."

Moshe walks in. "I didn't know Liz was there. How could I know?"

Ely glares at him. "Would you have stopped the CO, if you knew?"

"Of course I would. Well . . ." Moshe hesitates for a second, but Ely has trapped him. "I don't know . . . OK?" He pauses, and then says hesitatingly, "I think I would have."

Ely harshly articulates every word. "That, Moshe, is criminal behavior. You don't mind sending our troops to an irrelevant death, just as long as they're not family?"

Moshe points to his chest. "I was there, just like anyone else. This isn't fair."

Ely lowers his voice. "I'm not talking about you and me. Our CO was up front, as excited as the rest, but that doesn't excuse him for making bad decisions. Dying with your soldiers doesn't make you a better leader. There's no chivalry here. Not one of those men died for a good reason. That's the only point that matters. We all volunteer for high-risk jobs, but we do it because we have confidence that our death, if it happens, is necessary. Those people died in vain. And the same goes for the Egyptians we killed along the way."

"What do I care about the Egyptians?" Moshe cries, "My poor Liz!"

"Moshe, just imagine all those families," Sara says, as her voice trembles. "They lost a father, or a son, or a brother. On both sides, and for what? Nothing! Poor Liz, my best friend, my sister is dead, and I will mourn her all my life. But how can I also not mourn the deaths of all those young men? So many families in mourning."

Moshe's shoulders fall, his face desolate, he moans. "You should have let me shoot myself, Ely. Why did you stop me?"

Ely puts his hand on Moshe's shoulder. "Steady, Moshe. I'm not going to try to make things easy for you. There's no room for argument, and there's a lesson to be learned. Many homes are in mourning today. A few of those could have been happily rejoicing in the safe return of their father, brother, or son. Yes, Egyptians too. It wasn't your fault, but, to be fair and honest, you could have tried to stop it. As for shooting yourself, you'll find your answer in the living room. Two answers. I can't give you any better ones." Ely leaves them to sit with the children on the couch.

Sara looks toward the girls, tries to steady her voice. "Ely is right, Moshe. Let's not talk about what happened any more. Liz is not with us any longer. I still haven't absorbed that, nor will I anytime soon. But we all have to be here, in full, for Debbie and Dina."

His back to the wall, Moshe squats, his head in his hands. "They're going to miss her like mad. Me too . . . Oh, God help me!"

Sara doesn't let Moshe falter. "We have to make it clear to them: Liz is gone, for good. Nothing and no one can replace her. But we have to do our best to fill the void."

Moshe looks up at her, tears in his eyes. "Right now, I still can't believe it's true. I feel like she's going to knock at the door any second, wearing her army outfit, or maybe a sexy dress, and her smile . . ."

Sara kneels beside him. "Listen to me, Moshe, please. Liz isn't coming through that door. And you're sleeping alone, tonight and every night. Keep your head right here on planet Earth, where you're needed. Do you want to die with Liz, or live with Debbie and Dina? You choose."

"Of course I will do my best. For them."

"Just *be* there. In full. They don't need a ghost for a father."

"They have a ghost for a mother."

Sara grasps Moshe's shirt and pulls. "Don't think that way. You can't and you shouldn't. We will pray for her, but we'll do what she would want us to do."

"And that is?"

Sara holds his hand tenderly. "Go on with our lives, dear Moshe."

Sara gently lifts Moshe's chin to meet her gaze. She won't be able to contain her emotions much longer. "We'll get our courage from our children. Don't let her death be pointless. They deserve a better life than the one we've had. Let's make sure they get it. Let's make sure they get what we paid for with our blood. If we can have peace in this land, then her death will not have been in vain."

Moshe says, "I realize now what Ely was saying when he asked to stop the attack."

Sara holds Moshe tight to her chest. "What did Ely say?"

"For every dead soldier, we're one home behind in building our country."

# 1967
# Baptism of Fire

# CHAPTER 10

Morning, June 6. Taking advantage of a staging break, Ely heads for his son's regrouping point in the desert, hoping to see Amir before he takes off on another mission.

Aaron, his faithful and long-serving sergeant, is driving the Jeep; Moshe rides in the back. Ely jams his foot against the floor as if trying to force extra speed out of the car.

Aaron taps the dashboard. "This is all she's got, sir. We're almost there, this is the base camp. You can calm down."

A few seconds later, they reach the entrance gate. Two soldiers on guard stop them, salute, and check their papers carefully. "All in order," says one of them, about Amir's age, lifting the gate and waving them inside.

Ely grumbles, "Amir and those boys ought to be in college. This is no place—"

"You were doing even more dangerous work when you were his age," Moshe says, his mind focused on battle.

"So that he wouldn't have to. So that *he* wouldn't have to! And this is not *work*."

As they drive into the base camp, passing by one hangar after another, Ely points to an empty spot next to one hangar's doors. "Pull over there! See those markings on the tanks? That's his unit."

Moshe grips his arm. "Will you relax? We know Amir's all right, and you'll have a good fifteen minutes with him."

As the Jeep slows to a stop, Ely hops out. "Come on!"

Ely dashes to the hangar door. The air inside reeks of diesel fuel, hot metal, burned oil, and exhaust smoke. From a record player somewhere, an oddly cheerful love tune —"*Ahavtiha*," I Loved Her — sounds out, contrasting with the brash cacophony of singing soldiers. Some of the men carry ammunition boxes, while others are busy changing tracks on tanks, repairing battle damage, and loading weapons. Ely scans the hangar until he spots a tall young man in dusty fatigues striding toward him. Through layers of sweat and dust, Ely recognizes Amir's hearty smile.

Moshe joins Ely and squeezes his shoulder. "See? He's still in one piece."

Ely gazes at his approaching son. He is the embodiment of the perfect warrior. His strong figure, his determined walk, his sleep-deprived yet alert eyes. Ely mutters to Moshe, "He and his friends, all those young men. They are the product of our failure."

Ely rushes forward and hugs his son. He clears his throat to overcome a choking feeling. "I was so worried about you. I heard you've just been through one hell of a battle."

Amir takes a step back. "Not us. The *Egyptians* have been through hell."

Moshe puts his hand on Amir's shoulder. "You'll soon outrank us if you go on like that."

Ely takes Amir's face in his hands and says, "Or you won't make it. You've got to be careful, Amir."

Amir smiles, swivels and, putting his arms across Ely and Moshe's shoulders, guides them outside. "Let's get a breath of fresh air. I've been inhaling exhaust and fuel vapor all day."

Ely withdraws a bit and eyes his son, from the boots up. He mocks, "You're taller than me in those boots." Then he notices the blood on Amir's chest and bandages on his hand, and asks anxiously, "What's this? What happened?"

Amir answers with a shrug. "Don't worry. It's nothing. Our lead tank got a direct hit, and we had to evacuate the men."

Ely squeezes his son just above the waist. He notices a grimace of pain. He knows his son was not one to wince easily, certainly not without a serious cause. "Now what?" He stops and tries to unbutton Amir's shirt. "Let me see."

Amir pushes his father away. "Father, stop! We only have a few minutes, and you want to inspect every inch of me?"

Moshe asks, "Were you hit?"

"It's a small burn," Amir says impatiently. "I was evacuating the crew from the lead tank."

Ely asks, "Casualties?"

Amir looks away. His brown eyes become darker as he answers with a sad tone, "All of them, the whole crew. We got the commander out of the tank before it blew, but it was too late. They had T-fifty-fives. It was a direct hit. We were at close range and their shell went right through. The commander was seriously hurt, and the men inside were burned so badly they didn't survive."

Ely inspects his son. Amir's jaw is tight and he is obviously containing his pain. This had been his baptism by fire, and Ely wants to talk him through it. Ely pats his son's back gently, and, looking into his eyes, says, "More will die, son, maybe many more. You have to be ready for that. You do whatever you can to minimize it, but that's all. Victory doesn't come cheap."

Amir nods. "I know. This is going to be our way of life." He takes a deep breath and adds, "But I'm not scared. Those M-forty-eights are the best tanks, and we'll finish the Arabs once and for all. This time will be the last time!"

Amir's vehemence catches Ely off-guard. He has only been at war for a few hours. Has he turned into a reckless killer, with little value for his own, and his enemy's life? "Son, first of all, you *have* to be scared! Second, you cannot simply 'finish the Arabs once and for all!' There are two hundred and fifty million of them, against four million of us. Our aim is not to kill them all, but to show them, as David Ben-Gurion used to say, that there's a high price to pay for Jewish blood, and that we're here to stay."

Amir grins. "And that we will. Don't worry about me, or the rest of my crew. We remain sharp at all times."

Ely says, "Good. You have to control your environment. When you can't, it's time to relocate, to change your environment. I hope you're right about this war being the last one. I don't like the idea of you stuck in this tank —"

"I've applied to the infantry unit." Amir waves his hand. "So I can later move on to the paratroopers, like you. I am not staying here."

Moshe laughs. "Like father, like son. He's in your every footstep, and probably doing you one better." Moshe's face sobers. "How are your men taking it? Do they know you're leaving them?"

Amir has a cheerful smile. "They want to come along. They're all eager to go."

Ely squeezes at his son's shoulder. Amir's popularity notwithstanding, this was war, not a camping trip, or a Boy Scout expedition, and he is concerned about the apparent nonchalance of his son. "I just hope you're also eager to come back. There's no point in winning if you don't come home. And, son, you have to know there's no home if you're not in it, not for me and not for your mother. Remember that."

Moshe adds with sorrow, "Soldiers will die. The point is not to take unnecessary risks. Don't let any of your men die a stupid or, worse, avoidable death."

Amir answers with one of his father's favorite sayings. "*Elohim* calls the shots, but we can still duck."

Ely approves with a smile, and points in turn to his eyes, ears, and brain, saying, "We duck, and we keep our eyes and ears open. And our minds clear. You have to know where the danger is in order to deal with it. You've already received a lieutenant's commission, well ahead of all others, including myself when I was your age. I am proud of you." Ely pauses for a second, to get Amir's undivided attention. "Amir, it's a huge responsibility. You're deciding on life and death, and battle-critical issues. Always know what you're getting into, and how to get out. Let your radioman keep you informed about dispatches, the latest news about the enemy, and who's nearest to you if you need help."

"*Aba*! We've gone through this a thousand times."

Ely persists. "A couple thousand more and it will be instinct, as these things should be." Looking at his watch, Ely adds, trying to hide his rising angst, "Moshe and I should go." He turns to leave.

Amir steps in front of Ely, his expression serious. "You had a sad look when you saw me, and I heard what you said to Moshe. What did you mean with 'your failure?'"

"It's not you." Ely pauses and then decides to say what he felt. It was a mountain of feeling, accumulated over the years. "I, well, we, my whole generation, devoted our lives—and our deaths—to clear the field for you, the next generation. After the Second World War, my generation felt doomed. The *Shoah* took away a third of our people. We wanted to make sure you wouldn't go through the same ordeal, so we found peace of mind in believing that the War of Independence and then later, the Fifty-Six War, were necessary. We wanted to prepare a peaceful home in a safe country for you. We all hoped to achieve it before you grew up, so you could have a normal life — and, seeing you here, a battle-tested warrior, *this* is our failure, my son . . ."

Amir says, "But, Pa, I have a normal life. I'm nineteen, I have a girl that I love, and now I'm going to war, to fight for my country."

Ely points to the tanks and buzzing activity around them. "Going to war is not a normal life, Amir. A normal life for someone your age is going to college! Movies, parties, sports . . . all those *other* things you love to do. Not war. Not worrying about an ambush on the way back from a family picnic. Not having to carry a gun, ready to fend off saboteurs. And it's not having to obsess over your children's safety every minute of your life!" Ely catches his breath. "My generation built this country from swamps and desert, made it a place for modern technology in every field, but we failed to finish the job — we failed to bring peace with our neighbors. Twenty years from now, you will be like me, and all you will want is for your smartly dressed son to wave goodbye and take off with his girlfriend in your car for a party. Believe me, you will not want to see your son wearing fighting gear, wincing from the pain of a battle injury, jumping into a tank and waving goodbye. That's why we failed."

Sergeant Aaron waves from the Jeep. Moshe says, "We'd better get moving."

Amir shakes his head. "Maybe you're right, dad. Let's see what happens after this one." Amir glances inside the hangar. Some of the men are hopping into their vehicles; others are running to the tanks outside. "Yeah, our unit's moving out, too."

Ely sighs and hugs his son. "I can't get enough of you, son."

Amir stands back and looks at his father. With a serious tone, he asks, "When this is over, can I really use your car to go out?"

Moshe and Ely burst into nervous laughter. Ely says, "You can have my car any time."

Amir looks at Moshe. "With Moshe as my witness. Debbie will be glad to hear this. I told her I'd come and pick her up in my tank as soon as possible, before I'm back to infantry."

Moshe laughs. "I heard you two already had a joyride in a tank."

Ely tries not to laugh. "Yeah, what did you do, *exactly*?"

Amir shrugs and says, "She dropped by to visit when we were on the driving course with the tanks, and my driver asked if she wanted to give it a try, and she said yes."

Ely says, "So it's your driver's fault?"

"Oh, no. *I* gave the okay. As we went to the firing range, we had to go through the driving course gate, and she missed the gate. That's all."

Moshe laughs. "She destroyed a guard kiosk. If the guy hadn't jumped out, she'd have crushed him!"

Ely laughs as Amir goes on saying, "He hung on to the cannon, and Debbie kept speeding up as he screamed and shouted."

Ely hadn't heard that part. He looks at Moshe, who shrugs. Ely asks, "And how did it end?"

"She drove into the mud pit. That's where the guard landed."

Through his laughter, Ely looks to Moshe. "So, how did you clean this up?"

Moshe says, "Let's just say it took a couple of phone calls upstairs." With a jesting glare, he points at Amir. "Not that I appreciate that kind of behavior with my daughter."

Amir replies with a serious tone, "She's my soul. Always has been, always will be." He adds with a wink, "Lousy driver though."

Ely says, "You make a fine pair. It's probably ok if she can't drive a tank."

"So, do we have both your okays?"

Moshe frowns. "Okays for *what*?"

Amir's face falls at Moshe's tone. Ely bursts into laughter, quickly joined by Moshe.

Ely says, "We approve. We've never talked about it with you two, but we've been watching you; Ethan and Dina too . . ."

Amir's excitement builds, "I'll call Debbie right now, and —"

Ely puts his arm on Amir's shoulder, interrupting him. "Listen here! You're going to battle, son. For now, concentrate on that."

Ely gives his son one last hug. To his surprise, cold-blooded Moshe does the same.

Ely climbs into the Jeep and shouts over the noise of a tank roaring out of the hangar, "Take good care of yourself, son! *Tnuah Ve'esh!*"

"*Tnuah Ve'esh,*" — Fire and Movement — Amir shouts back, his voice drowned by the sound of the tank's engines shaking the air, their tracks tearing into the asphalt. *Fire and Movement.*

# CHAPTER 11

Under the hot midday sun, in camp Kalandia's square-shaped yard, worried faces gather around a man with a transistor radio tuning from one station to another. The Voice of Israel, from the Israeli broadcast service, has announced that war had broken out that morning. A surprise Israeli attack on Egyptian airfields. Tarek sits on a thick wood plank, used as a bench, debriefing his men. He has just brought his unit back from patrol, where they had come across an enemy formation.

Tarek hangs a blackboard on a wooden pedestal. It is the blackboard that Mr. Halim once used to teach the children about peace and respect, years earlier; now, Tarek is using it to teach the young men about tactics and ballistics. He sketches terrain features, their positions in white chalk, the enemies positions in red chalk. He then proposes different scenarios and asks the young men to come up with suggestions.

Tarek is particularly proud of Ameer, who has skillfully assumed command of his five-man squad and carried out his orders well. That said, his son's overzealous behavior under fire was of a great concern. Ameer and some of his friends sometimes acted as if they wanted to push the concept of the *fedayeen* — the volunteer martyr fighter — to its ultimate meaning.

Tarek finishes and dismisses his men with comforting words. "That's all for now. You did all right this morning. You'll be fine in the afternoon, too."

Ameer speaks up. "Where are we going? What's our mission?"

Tarek retorts, "*You* are going nowhere. Not until you learn to control your impulses."

Ameer can't believe what he's hearing. "Me? I followed orders." Turning to Faris, he adds, "Of course, I can't say the same about all of us, though."

On that morning patrol, Faris had suddenly jumped from cover to toss a grenade at an enemy machine gunner. With an innocent expression, Faris spreads his arms wide in denial.

One of their friends, Faysal, nods toward Sami, who had yet to fire his machine gun at enemy soldiers, despite having had the opportunity. "Some of us are innocent for real."

Sami stands up and cries, "It jammed! It wouldn't fire!"

Faysal snatches Sami's weapon from him. "This one? Ha!" He fires a burst into the air above Sami's head, causing everyone to cover their ears and curse. Faysal looks around proudly before tossing the still smoking gun back to Sami. Tarek does not react. He watches the young men sort it out without interfering. This encourages Faysal to continue his taunting, using Sami's ambition of one day being a doctor. "Some people need fixing, doctor, and others need killing."

Sami stands up. "Well, I prefer fixing to killing! Any problem with that, *killer*?"

Layal, lingering just outside the circle of men, leaps to her brother's aid. Tall and proud, her long dark hair flowing over her shoulders, she resolutely strides over to the group, heading straight for Tarek's assault pack, on the ground by the blackboard. All eyes are on her as she snatches a hand grenade from it and pulls the pin. "How do you handle this, *killer-boy*?" she bellows as she tosses it at Faysal, who catches it and freezes in panic.

The young men dive to the ground, but Tarek doesn't budge. Like many other seasoned fighters who carry war equipment into their homes, he had wrapped tape around the grenade's lever as a second safety measure. He looks on with amusement at Faysal, holding the grenade in his trembling hands, while a wet stain spreads at his groin.

Layal calmly takes the grenade back and reinserts the pin. She points to Faysal's wet spot and says, "Do you need a doctor for your incontinence problem, *killer-boy*?"

Everyone bursts into relieved laughter, and then applause and whistle at Layal's audacity, as she heads back to Tarek's pack and puts the grenade back in it.

Tarek shakes his head. "Enough! Break it up! That was an extra lesson, for all."

As the men disperse, he catches up to Layal. "A lesson for you as well. Two actually. You should let Sami handle things himself." He points to his sack. "As for that stunt . . . never again! Am I clear?"

Layal sighs. "I know, I know."

"That was *not* the thing to do. Should I even ask you where you learned to handle these things?" He looks at Ameer, the obvious culprit. "Maybe not."

Ameer is now a mature adult, and an affirmed fighter, despite him still being a late teenager. Their quest as a people for independence and land has somehow ascended to his personality, as he often behaves of his own "free" mind. The hardship of their lives is a perpetual test — you either succeed or fail — and in young men it produces either early maturity, or a lifetime of submissiveness. Ameer has clearly made his choice: he is already distinguishing himself as a leader.

Tarek takes Sami, Layal, and Ameer into his tiny steel and concrete block house the likes of which UNRWA built throughout the camp. The small structure feels cramped, with mattresses and freestanding cupboards stacked wherever they'd fit. As they enter, Rima stops her housework and greets them with a grim look. She puts her hands on her hips and nods toward Rabih.

Rabih is busy checking a gun and a battle pack. He has an olive battle outfit on and a black and white Palestinian *keffiyah* around his neck, and before Tarek can say anything, Rabih remarks with a nonchalant tone, "I need a couple of minutes. Do we have orders?"

Tarek tries to contain his anger as he walks to his youngest son. "Whose rifle is that? A brand new Kalash! And the pack? Where exactly do you think you're going?"

Rabih looks up at his father with determination and says, *"Raje'e al beyt!"* — I'm going home. He points his finger to his father's chest. *"Your* home."

"We all want to return," Tarek replies. "But each of us has duties and responsibilities." He is not about to let his sixteen-year-old son go to war.

Rabih stands to attention. "Right. Only soldiers fight. I am a soldier."

Tarek puts his hand on Rabih's shoulder. "You know the rules. In my command, no one fights until they finish their training. And not all men from the same family can fight in the same unit."

Rabih opens his mouth to protest, but Tarek cuts him off with a stern look. "Besides, someone has to guard the camp."

Rabih's face lights up with a hopeful smile. "The camp is in danger? Or are you just trying to make me stay?"

Tarek shakes his head. "You're not a soldier until you can obey my orders." To the worried faces around him, he adds, "No, the camp isn't in danger. We're under UN protection. But I need able hands in my absence." He points at Rabih. "I need you."

Rabih starts to argue, but Tarek isn't finished. "I need you to give that rifle and your gear back to the quartermaster. We need every weapon for our next mission."

Ameer jumps at the chance to ask, "What's the mission? Where are we going?"

Some of Ameer's friends come in, led by Faris. They all serve in Tarek's unit and are coming for information. They must have heard Ameer's question.

One of the men asks, with a worried tone, "Are we joining an army? Like in Fifty-Six? Or are we operating alone?"

Faris says, "Don't worry, Tarek will get us permission to operate alone. That way he'll decide what to do —"

Tarek raises his hand for silence. "We'll get our orders from the joint Arab command, but we'll have freedom of movement on a tactical level." Tarek goes on with a worried tone. "I'm not sure how the Arab forces are doing. They claim they're winning, but apparently the Israelis made the first strike. The one we begged our leaders to do." He lowers his head. "If that is true, then they probably crippled the Arab air forces."

One of Tarek's men laments, "Damn luck! We should have attacked first. It was our big chance, and now it's gone before it even started."

Another adds, just as desperately, "We lose territory every time they start a new battle. Not to mention men . . ."

Rabih is a ball of nerves. "Are we going to have to leave again this time?" His hatred for their camp life was obvious, and every major battle seems to only make things worse. "I refuse! I'm not moving, except to return home." Looking at his father, he continues, "Your home, Father, the one mother has a picture of. I'll go there, or die here, standing my ground."

Tarek sits on a wooden chair and asks everyone to squat around him.

"I won't tell you fairy tales. I've seen the Arab forces, I've trained with them, and I don't like what I saw. They haven't learned their lessons from the previous battles. They're still relying on major confrontation lines, huge concentrations of troops, archaic chains of command, and a conflicting mix of Russian and British doctrines."

One of the young men objects. "Nasser knows what he's doing, and he'll win. Didn't you listen to him on the radio? *La Istislam.*" No surrender.

Tarek shakes his head. "Don't believe that nonsense, son. Propaganda on the radio won't melt tanks, and it won't shoot down an air force. Nasser's foreign policy makes enemies out of everyone. The rich Arab countries, the French, the British, the US, and anyone else who could *actually* help."

Ameer raises his hand. "The Russians are with us. They won't let the Israelis win."

Tarek shakes his head again. "Ha! They haven't given the Arab forces the heavy bombers they need, they haven't trained them properly . . . and I haven't even mentioned the much-needed coordination between Arab armies."

Sami stands, a frustrated look on his face. "Then what's the point in fighting if our fate is already sealed?"

Tarek motions him to sit back down. "I have one more thing to say. We may win this one, or we may lose; only Allah knows, and only Allah decides." Looking at Sami, he continues, "I vowed a long time ago, when Wassef died, that I would never again let someone else's bad strategies take one of my men. If we're going to die, then it will be our fault and Allah's will."

Ameer asks, "What are you saying?"

Tarek speaks slowly. "You know about the new Palestine Liberation Organization. From what I'm hearing, they've been impressed by our fighting and the way volunteers are constantly flocking to our unit. And they've asked us to join them."

Ameer raises his fist. "The PLO will fight and win the war by itself!"

Tarek nods. "In the end, victory will be ours. We will win. We're right before Allah, we're right before our land, and we're right before our children. And we have nothing to lose. It can only be victory for us."

Tarek stands and walks over to Rima. Standing beside her, and looking at the eager young soldiers assembled around him, he says, "I wanted to say this just to my children, but we're all one big family here. It's my wish for everyone here to join *el-Munazameh*." — The organization. — "We Palestinians will fight the war for ourselves, with our own command, our own decisions. We already know that an Arab defeat every ten years won't bring our Palestine back to us. We need a new way."

The men all stand and shout, "*Fatah! Felasteen tabka hurra!*" — Palestine remains free!

Rima pinches Tarek in the back and whispers in his ear.

He raises a hand. "Calm down, I'm not finished." He looks back at Rima. "Rima insists that I tell you that I don't approve of their attacks on civilians and innocent people. We will not take part in that."

"And the Jews? Will they do that too?" Faris asks with a bitter tone. "Stay away from our women and children? And our homes?"

Tarek scowls and points at Faris. "As long as you're under my command, you will obey my orders! We do what we think is right, no matter what." He waves his hands to dismiss his guests. "Go. Get ready. We're moving out."

Ameer, still excited about the decision to join the PLO, shouts, "*Felasteen tabka hurra!*" His cheer is echoed again and again as the men leave. This decision is the much needed answer to their enduring frustration from the lack of a Palestinian leadership to their struggle.

It is a new horizon, a new dimension, and a source of hope in their plight. Now, *everything* seems possible.

———————

Rima has her arms around her husband and Rabih as she leads them out of their house. "Let's go to Samar's." She smiles at Layal. "Your mother has fixed lunch for us. Here, take some olives and tomatoes." She gives Ameer a small package. "You take the bread."

Tarek says, "Right. Let's go."

Up ahead, Ameer walks with Layal. Rabih points at the two and says mockingly, "They're in love, they're in love!"

Layal hides her red face behind her free hand as Ameer wheels around. "Shut up, you silly fool!"

Rabih cowers behind his father as Ameer steps toward him. Tarek grabs Ameer and pulls Layal in as well. He hugs them. "What is it? Am I missing something here?"

Ameer's expression changes to confusion, and Layal's face reddens some more. Tarek has a wide smile, and bumps his forehead against his son's, and then looks into Layal's eyes. "Do you think I'm blind? We all know you two are . . . together. You remind me of myself, except that in my day seeing a girl was forbidden."

Rabih seems delighted. "And you disobeyed? Mother as well? Aha! Now I have something on mother." He takes Rima's arm and pretends to slap it.

Ameer beseeches Tarek. "We're serious, Father."

Tarek laughs. "I know. Your mother and I talk about you two, and we've talked with Samar. We're all waiting for you to make an official announcement. I can't think of either of you without the other. You've been together since you were born."

Layal blushes. "We're very . . . comfortable together."

Samar comes out when they reach her house and Tarek winks at her. "So, when's the big day?"

Ameer pretends to be surprised. "What?"

"The big day." He slaps his son on the back. "*When* is it?"

Ameer looks at Layal, and then at Samar. "It's too soon. We don't know where we'll be tomorrow. Maybe when this whole thing is over, and we have a decent place."

Samar, overhearing the conversation, shines a bright smile Tarek hasn't seen in years, and invites everyone inside. She hugs Layal, and Tarek sees joyful tears return a long-forgotten luster to the happy mother's eyes.

Samar's lunch is served on a blanket set on the floor. They gather around the different plates — goat cheese, radishes, green onions, olives, green salad, and various *meze* — enjoying the few moments of calm. In a couple of hours, he and Ameer would be going to war. Will they make it back safely? What would the future throw at them? More death and sorrow? Peace and happiness? How long would it take? How much sacrifice? It is all in God's hands . . .

# CHAPTER 12

Under the desert sun, Amir's armored platoon is sizzling in its M-48 tanks. As he inspects the area ahead with his binoculars, a gust of wind blows sand into his face. His orders are to close a pass in the desert with his armored platoon. Early on in the war he lost his Captain, to an enemy tank's fire, and his Lieutenant was dispatched to support an infantry unit. Four of Amir's remaining nine tanks had run out of fuel. And nine was already a very small number, considering what they are up against.

Amir adjusts his microphone and barks to Ethan and his sergeant, Caleb. "Everyone dismount! We'll hook up the disabled tanks to tow. The sooner we get there, the sooner we can get into position."

Ethan hops down from his tank and strides over to Amir's, raising a cloud of fine dust. "We'll use twice as much fuel. Why don't we siphon some off?"

"No. No time. Every second counts. We were supposed to be at the pass by now. We have to block it."

The fallen faces of his men tell him they need encouragement. They have just won another harrowing engagement, but they are exhausted. The prospect of going through it all again has them shaken. It is the law of attrition: their losses may have been few, but given enough confrontations, the unit would eventually succumb to the odds. It was only a matter of time.

As the men dismount their tanks, Amir climbs up on top of his. He looks at their weary faces and tries to sound as upbeat as he can. "Soldiers, we have won a battle. But the war is still on, and the enemy is still looking for a gap in our lines."

Ethan, who was working on his tank's tracks, bangs his tank's armor with a hammer and shouts, "The rest of the unit's facing an Egyptian formation while we're out here getting a tan. Come on, let's move!"

Amir nods in sympathy to his outburst. Slowly raising his hand, he says, "We have to stop the enemy units from getting through the pass. If we can beat them to it, we can take advantageous firing positions and ambush them. If we get there late, we lose the advantage of terrain and surprise. Remember: tanks that get through us go straight to our homes. Our parents, our families, our nation. Let's go to work. We have a job to do!"

Caleb climbs onto a tread and shouts, "You heard our *segen!* If we want to keep our loved ones safe, we have to do our job first. Amir got us through our first battles, and he will get us through the next."

The men cheer, "*Yam Yisrael Chai!*" — The nation of Israel is alive.

As the men climb back into their beasts of steel, Amir looks at Caleb. "Thank you, Caleb. The men trust you."

Caleb stares at him. "After what they saw today, they trust you. You keep this up, and those guys will follow you to Hell and back."

"I hope we won't have to go that far."

The tanks are set up within minutes, and Amir gives instructions to Ethan and Caleb. "I'll drive ahead to scout the terrain. Ethan, you take command if something happens to me. Drive the last tank and watch our backs."

Ethan nods. "Yes. I've told the men to ditch the disabled tanks if we get caught in transit, but only after firing as many rounds as possible, and not before the enemy has a range on us."

"Great. Caleb, you're in the first tank behind mine. Maintain a safe distance. All commanders up, scouting in sectors, as usual. That desert dust is a pain, so wear your goggles. Cover the main gun barrel and the machine guns."

The convoy moves forward, Amir in front by a couple hundred meters. They soon reach the pass. There is no enemy in sight. Amir drives in to look around and then returns to his group. As the dust swirls around them, he lays a map across the top of his turret, and signals Ethan and Caleb to climb up to him. Amir indicates a place on the map. "Caleb, have two men climb up this ridge. They can see deep into the pass from there. No firing, hand signals only. I want total radio silence, understand? Spread the word."

Caleb turns around to his crew, standing in the shade of his tank. He gives hand signals, and two of them dash away towards the ridge. Caleb turns towards Amir. "You can count on them."

Amir agrees with a nod and turns back to the map. "We can position the disabled tanks behind the cover of these rocks and depressions." The three men look at the map, then at the location of the rocks near them.

Ethan approves. "Only their turrets will show, and the guns can traverse freely across the field of fire."

Caleb adds, "When the enemy stumbles onto them, it will be the last thing they see."

Ethan goes back to the map. "Good. Where do we put the other tanks?"

Amir takes a pen from his field jacket and marks crosses on the map. "I was thinking about these spots here."

Caleb taps a different area. "Here too, sir. It's farther out, but they can move back and forth behind cover, and that way they'll have more than one firing position."

Amir considers this for a moment. Staring at the map, he imagines the impending battle. Would the men be able to move about in the thick desert dust and dense smoke? He shakes his head. "True, but I want to keep them within reach of the stranded tanks in case we have to evacuate. We'll have to decide. Either we evacuate the tanks and their crews, or the crews only." Looking at Caleb, he asks, "Can we tow the tanks while under fire?"

"We'll be exposed to enemy fire for too long. I say dump the tanks."

Amir says, "I agree."

Ethan looks at the unit around them. "It's a miracle we got here in the first place."

Caleb smiles. "I like miracles in battle. It means *Adonai* is watching."

Amir gathers his soldiers, showing the commanders their position in the terrain recesses. "Machine gunners: be careful about shooting at troops in the open because they could be our own crews evacuating. Make sure of your targets and shoot at preset ranges whenever you can. Limit yourself to your own cone of fire. We don't want to be shooting every tank twice.

"Crews in disabled tanks: no heroism. I want to put Bravery Medals on beating hearts only, you hear? If an enemy tank has a range on you, evacuate, and leave a demolition charge in the tank. Everyone: know all our positions so you know how and where to move. It'll be easy to get lost in the smoke and dust." He points to a lean redhead. "David, since you're not driving, you know your job?"

David's look seems as deadly as his scoped and camouflaged sniper rifle. "Drivers, to panic the crews, and officers to panic everyone else." He casually flips the safety on and off, eager to put his gun into use.

Amir continues, staring at David, "And any infantry that comes near. Anti-tank teams are your top priority, should they dismount and take positions. Spend your free time on radio operators and the rest; they don't have any support element nearby anyway."

He glances up at the ridge. A sentry is signaling.

Caleb studies the signals. "Enemy armor. Three clicks up the road."

Amir stands. "We have five minutes, not more. Try not to raise too much dust."

Ethan says, "They could be ten times our strength."

Amir remains calm. "It doesn't matter how many there are as long as we have enough ammo. We have the advantage of terrain, cover, and the training of our gunners." He points to the pass. "It's a bottleneck. They can't get out all at once."

Ethan says, "We're all set, sir."

Amir climbs aboard his tank. "I'll be the first to have a target, so wait for me to fire. Take as many as possible with the first volley. Once it starts, we coordinate by radio." He raises his fist. "Follow me!"

---

Through the narrow streets of East Jerusalem, Ameer leads his platoon toward *Bab el-Amoud*, Damascus Gate of the Old City. He can hear every footstep, every rattle, every curse from his tired men. Ameer's mission is to set an ambush for the enemy that Tarek and his unit would push toward him.

Faris' group would flank Tarek to prevent the enemy from spreading the fight. They carry anti-tank weapons and machine guns, as well as ammunition and demolition gear. Tarek signals for a halt and calls Ameer and Faris for a meeting.

"Our reconnaissance says they're alone. We don't see any armor and, even though we're roughly the same in numbers, we should be able to take them."

Faris says, "They must be waiting for reinforcements. Our scouts have spotted logistic units staging fuel for tanks."

Tarek nods. "True. It looks like they're going for a major push into our part of the city, and this is probably just a reconnaissance, together with a local defensive unit. We need to move as quickly as possible. By the time their armor gets here, our Jordanian reinforcement should be here, too, with tanks and infantry. Then we'll finish them off."

Faris twitches in eagerness. "What do we do now?"

"Stay calm. We move as planned. No surprises, no room for mistakes. If we get too excited or lose sight of our objective, we'll compromise the mission. Clear?"

Ameer and Faris reply in chorus, "Yes, sir!"

"Stick to your mission and listen to your sergeants. I put my best two men with you. They know the rules, and they know the game. When in doubt, ask for their opinion, even in front of the men."

Ameer says, "We're all eager to move, Father."

"I know, but don't forget what you have to do. Faris, stay calm, and keep in mind the tactical situation. Your job is the most crucial. You're protecting the entire unit."

"No one will go through us, sir. We'll kill them all."

Ameer adds, "Leave some for me —"

Tarek scoffs. "You two talk like you're going to wipe the Jews from Palestine in one swift move."

"At least we'll try. Don't spoil our morale, Father."

"It *will* get spoiled if you are unrealistic. This is one fight, in one battle, in one war, among many. It is a long conflict, and it will not end today. Today, we stay alive, and finish our mission. This we can do, and we'll do it well if everyone does his job."

Faris shifts his weight impatiently. "My sergeant is signaling. The men are deploying."

Ameer looks up. "Mine, too. We're in place. The ambush is ready."

"Keep an eye on the men, and maintain awareness," Tarek cautions one last time.

Ameer notices tension on his father's face. Taking your son to war surely is a hard thing to do. He tries to reassure him. "Don't think of us as students any more, father. We'll do the job, and retreat in safety, just like you taught us."

"Ameer, wait for them to come to you, ok? Faris, your job is trickier because you have some freedom of movement. Contain the fighting. Unless I order you to, don't move up, or we'll end up shooting at each other. The Jordanians should be here soon, and then we can regroup and get ready for the second assault."

"God bless you father, take care of yourself."

"Watch your backs and keep a lookout. This is the demarcation zone, and they may have people sniping from any of the homes around here."

Faris snarls, "I hope they do. We'll go in and wipe out their whole families."

Tarek shakes his head. "If you get caught up in killing civilians, you'll never know when someone is sneaking up on you. These civilians may be occupiers, but keep your focus on military targets. Harming non-combatants is absolutely forbidden. Clear?"

Faris salutes. "Yes, sir!"

"Let's move out. God be with you!"

Ameer moves swiftly, his aides following him in silence. They have all wrapped their *keffiyah* on their heads. No sounds of footsteps, no rattling equipment. Ameer thinks his heartbeat is probably the loudest thing around. His men are all in place.

A voice crackles on Tarek's walkie-talkie. He listens in and turns back to Ameer and Faris. He looks confident. "It's as we planned. The Israelis are concentrated in that large municipal building."

Some of Tarek's men are from the city and have given him crucial information. Once firing erupts, the Israelis will have two choices: they can choose to die in their compound or rush out through the only available exit gap . . . right into Ameer's ambush. Faris' unit would keep the Israelis from finding another way out.

The plan is for Tarek to start with an intense barrage of fire to give the impression of a much larger unit, enveloping the enemy and leaving him only one way out and right into their trap. Ameer is counting on getting his share of the fight.

He isn't scared, but there is a new trepidation he has not felt before. He longs to confront the enemy. He wants retribution for all the death and poverty in his life, and the long suffering of his people. He wants retribution for the thousands of dead children, victims of bombs, malnutrition, disease, and despair.

Ameer goes back to his sergeant, who is supervising the men as they dig in. He whispers in his ear, "Everyone behind hard cover. Check them out from the enemy's approach route while we can, to make sure they're well concealed."

The sergeant points to the scattered men. "Nearly done, sir. Yes right away. We have covering fields of fire and supporting positions. No one will get through."

Ameer claps his sergeant on the shoulder. "Good man. Happy to have you with me."

"We're proud to serve with you, sir. *Insh Allah,*" — God willing, — "We'll give them hell."

Ameer turns to a large fellow holding a PKM machine gun and his assistant, carrying belts of ammo. "I want the machine gun in the house. Keep alternating between the first floor windows; you will sweep the whole street." Looking back toward his sergeant, he orders, "I want our snipers on the roof, Sergeant. Keep the bazooka team close. Tarek may send for it." Ameer's bazooka team is one of the three that Tarek's company was given. The RPGs that Tarek requested, which can penetrate the frontal armor of the Israeli tanks, were not available.

Ameer looks around him. He shouts his last orders to his NCOs, non-commissioned officers, "Stay with your squads, and hold your positions."

His sergeant's squad has built two sandbag bunkers up at the street corners near the Damascus Gate, each facing where the enemy will come from. "*Raqeeb*," he says to the sergeant, "We'll stay there, with our reserves and the ammo." He points. "You take the left side, I'll handle the right. We don't know where the pressure will come from. I expect it to come from both sides."

"Yes, they'll probably spill out both ways."

"*Insh Allah*. Faris is ready."

The sergeant glances towards Faris' men. "Let's hope Faris doesn't get too excited." Looking back at Ameer, he says with confidence, "Your father has lectured him enough. I think we'll be all right."

Bursts of machine gun fire and scattered rifle shots come from beyond the buildings.

Ameer says, "First contact." He identifies the whooshing sound of a bazooka rushing through the air. "That's our bazooka. Father's hitting them!"

The sergeant says, "He'll go after their machine gun nests and fortified positions first, then circle around them to open a gap towards us. Soon they'll be running our way." The sergeant points toward the street ahead, where the enemy is expected to come from.

Ameer nods and looks back at his men. He motions his men to cover, then silently brings his rifle to his heart, pounding it twice. The men emulate his gesture and exchange stares of resolve, as they take their positions. They are eager for action. He looks at his sergeant. "I don't know what's coming our way, but I can't wait to face it. *I feel it.*"

# CHAPTER 13

An urgent dispatch has diverted Amir's armored platoon to the streets of Jerusalem. They had barely recovered from their clash with the enemy at the pass, which had been a crushing victory. Now their weary minds and aching bodies are once again bouncing around the cabins of their equally strained machines. Their scheduled 8-hour break before heading to the Golan Heights turned into an emergency rescue mission, as an infantry unit in downtown Jerusalem was surrounded by Arab fighters. Approaching their destination, the Mandelbaum Gate, Amir, in his commander's seat on his tank's turret, bangs his fist against the heavy armored top and yells in his intercom to his driver, *"Maheir, Maheir!"* — Faster, Faster!

His tank's tracks tear into the asphalt, and every turn in the tight city streets makes the tank moan and skid. The other tanks can barely keep up. In a blur, sympathetic faces appear in an apartment window. He waves to them. He would soon leave "their" side of the city — the Jewish side — and the smiling faces will be replaced by hostile looks and, eventually, enemy soldiers eager to kill. The faces wave back and he feels a chill — he is writing his nation's history.

Through the screech of tracks and roar of engines, Ethan's yell comes from the radio. "Amir, we can't keep up! My tank is going to throw its tracks! We're still on the sand pads!"

"We have to hurry. Even if only a couple of us make it there, we can turn the tide of the battle. The dispatch said those poor bastards are trapped in the municipal building. Some have scattered and are being run down."

Ethan says, "It also says the enemy has bazookas."

"Radio all machine gunners. Stay alert; keep an eye on street corners and rooftops. Stay head-on to them. They're still using the old ammo. It won't penetrate our front armor."

Caleb crackles through on the headset. "They can still knock out our tracks."

Amir's men aren't used to urban fighting. He addresses all tank commanders. "After first contact, get up on the machine guns. Gunners, use the co-ax. Try to locate sources of fire and suppress them until the infantry closes in."

Ethan's voice comes through again, with an urgent tone. "We need to stop and check the map."

Amir struggles against the wind to hold his map steady. "I'm checking it now."

Amir's gunner comes out of his hatch. His expression is grim. He takes off his headphones and shouts, "Sir, command says our people have been overrun."

Amir yells back, "There must be survivors still resisting. We need to get there now!" He gets back to Ethan. "Ethan, where is the infantry I ordered?"

Before Ethan can answer, a stranger's voice comes over the radio. "Captain Levi here, infantry. We're in trucks, five minutes behind, and trying to catch up. The halftracks are another five minutes behind."

"Captain? How come you're under my command?"

"Those are the orders, sir, and I'm not complaining. We're eager to give you a hand. You'll need it with all the Arab infantry on the loose."

"Ok, you focus on the upper levels and rooftops and fill in our blind spots. Try to locate any anti-tank teams. I'm afraid we're going to be too late for those poor bastards."

"Don't go in without us. Command says we're facing hard-core, well-trained, and well-equipped *Fedayeen*. Not like what we've seen before."

Amir hates the idea of slowing down, but the captain is right. "I'll wait for you, unless we have an emergency."

The captain continues with a more cheerful tone. "Command says we don't have to worry about the Arab's reinforcements."

"Because?"

"Vaporized. Our air force took care of an entire armored Jordanian unit that was on the way."

Ethan's eager voice comes through. "They should have left some for us!"

Amir asks the captain, "Levi, does the enemy have anything in the air?"

"No sir. Nothing. No planes."

Ethan jumps in again. "Our Air Force did its job."

Sergeant Caleb's voice interrupts. "Sir, we got a distress signal. I think it's from the municipal building. Our people are still fighting in there!"

That was all Amir needed to hear. Tossing the map inside and wiping the sweat from his forehead, he yells into his microphone, "Can you answer them?"

"I'll try."

"You know what to say." Amir is going to save those men from certain death. He knows he will. Every nerve in his body twitches in anticipation. Unlike the stress of the previous battles, his eagerness is mental as well. *Amir feels a creeping sensation that overwhelms his mind and numbs his senses. He's never felt this way before — was he nervous? — and for a fleeting moment it consumes him, controls him. And then, it's gone. But it leaves Amir certain of one thing: he has to get to that municipality building.*

Captain Levi cuts in. "Lieutenant Amir, wait for us. This isn't open desert."

"I'm sorry, Captain. Every second counts."

"What's the plan?"

"I'm going in; you too, Caleb. Ethan, you're in command, wait for the infantry, but stay ready if I call you in. Caleb, we go in with strafing fire, we must draw attention. We can relieve the pressure on the guys inside and divert fire until our boys can go in."

Ethan's angered voice comes through. "Why only two tanks? I want in!"

"I want to surprise them. Be ready to outflank."

Caleb asks, "Aha. You're not letting them flee. You'll send the other tanks to cover their escape routes and finish them off!"

Amir nods with a satisfied smile. There is no way he can fool his sergeant. "Any objections?"

Ethan shouts, "Save some for me."

The sergeant says, "No, we won't!"

Amir needs his men to focus. "For now, we save those poor souls. Focus on that. Levi, where are you?"

"Your rear tank is just in front of me. You have to slow down."

"Sorry; those Arabs won't wait. I have to surprise them. Now is the time."

Caleb is jubilant. "Tell them we're coming, and Hell is coming with us!"

Amir scans the road ahead. They would soon reach the fighting. On his map, he had noticed a house with a fenced garden on the block that stood between them and the enemy's advanced units. He decides to go through the garden and then the house, bursting into the battle scene to surprise the enemy. Amir hopes the fighting has already driven out the house's inhabitants.

Amir yells to his sergeant, "Caleb, I want you on full alert!" He breathes in relief when he spots the house — heavy smoke is streaming from its windows. It should be empty. He looks back at Caleb, perched on his tank and bouncing around like him. The other tanks are slightly behind. He points at the house and signals Caleb to follow him right into it. Amir then climbs down into his tank and closes his hatch. He orders his driver to drive straight through the smoking house.

"Through it, sir?"

"Yes. They won't expect us there, will they?" He grabs his microphone. "Caleb, cover my back. Use your main gun on hard targets. Look for infantry and use that co-ax. Face any bazookas head only. *Tnuah Ve'esh!*"

"*Tnuah Ve'esh!*" Caleb shouts.

The two tanks break through the walls of the house and come out the other side with a loud, long crash, and a cloud of dust, falling and bouncing over debris. "Keep a fast pace. Watch out for bazookas and Molotovs."

Caleb shouts, "The Arabs are everywhere!"

Caleb's main gun fires. Amir watches through his porthole as the shell sends the bunker and the two gunners in it into the air. He gives the order to fire at another enemy trench. He smirks when his shell blows it apart. No enemy personnel in this one though. Vacated already? Instead, he can see the enemy regroup in a calm and orderly fashion that he has never seen before.

Amir barks, "Ethan, get ready. Is the infantry all set?"

Levi cuts in. "About to deploy, sir."

Amir relaxes a bit at the force in Levi's voice. *So far, so good.*

Amir yells into his microphone, "*Seren*, don't mix with the Arabs, they're uniformed like us."

Levi confirms the order. "Understood. We're two minutes out. I'll send a unit to support your tanks, another to guard the flank."

Amir is now in the eye of the storm. He and Caleb have neutralized the initial threat and dispersed the enemy from the front. But to get to the front of the municipal building, they still have to go across another street. It could be swarming with a waiting, well-entrenched, and determined enemy.

Amir and Caleb are now sitting out in the open, exposed to any anti-tank team that has a clear shot, so Amir decides to move. He grabs his microphone and gives a quick round-up of the situation. "I'm behind the building where our guys are stuck. We've dispersed all enemies in the back so far. Caleb and I are just around the corner, but the enemy seems to have redeployed their antitank guns to the other side. We haven't taken any direct hits yet. Levi, we need infantry!"

Caleb says, "Let me go in, sir. We may take a hit head on, but it won't go through. You can get them before they reload. We'll probably be out for a few seconds, from the shock and smoke."

"No. I'll go in, and you take their gunnery team."

"Too late, sir. We're past you. Pray for us." Amir looks on through his tank's port as Caleb's tank cuts into his path and turns around the corner and into the street. He watches as it goes over a smoking road barricade. As the barricade crumbles under Caleb's tank, Amir can see a huge tree trunk under the sandbags. He shouts in his microphone, "Caleb, don't climb that rubble! It's a trap! There's a huge tree trunk! You'll show your belly! Caleb! Stop! Caleb!"

A shell bursting through Caleb's thin undercarriage armor cuts off

Amir's plea. His sergeant's tank lifts in the air, its turret hatches flying off. It crashes down violently to rest on its tracks, smoke pouring out of its slots, and Caleb's radio goes silent. Amir angrily orders his driver to push past, hoping to get the antitank team before they reload.

Caleb's tank is a lifeless block of metal, consumed by a raging fireball. Amir keeps going like a robot. His instincts take over as he shouts orders to his crew. He directs his gunner toward the puff of smoke from the antitank gun. *As he focuses on his target, the sensation fills him again, insurmountable. Amir's perceptions transcend the gap to his target, and morph with his enemy's senses. Amir can see and hear what the enemy senses. He even feels it. It makes no sense, and yet, somehow, Amir knows that he is inside the enemy's head. He feels the trepidation of the enemy, as he sees his own tank, gun pointed at . . . himself. The sensation numbs his body, stalls his mind.* A flash from the enemy bazooka, the hurling fireball . . . he shakes back into himself. He watches in horror, his mind racing with thoughts of Debbie, his father's lectures. Death is about to hit.

---

Ameer hops over his barricade, his sharp eyes looking out from behind the *Keffiyah*, and he peers anxiously down the street. He can hear Israeli tanks about two blocks away, near where his father stands. The tanks are jeopardizing his father's plan. He breathes in relief as his father and his men finally come into view, rushing back toward them.

Ameer turns to his men and raises his hand. "Don't shoot!" He signals the machine gunner in his barricade. "Stand by to cover their retreat!" He whistles to his sergeant on the other side of the street and gives him the hand signal for covering fire.

Ameer watches his father run toward him, his head low to avoid flying fragments from light mortar fire, and sporadic shots from the

Israelis who, only minutes before, they had cornered in the scarred municipal building.

When Tarek reaches Ameer, he makes a quick status check. Most of his men are okay, and his bazooka team is just behind him. There is no enemy infantry in sight. Turning back toward Ameer, Tarek catches his breath and looks at his son. Ameer can see the disappointment in his father's eyes as he shakes his head. "They overran us with tanks. They came right through a house." He is quiet for a moment as he listens. "They're moving again. Get ready!"

Ameer helps his father behind his barricade.

"Where is Faris?" Tarek asks. "Is he covering the perimeter? They can overrun us from the sides!"

"He's in place, ready to cover us."

Tarek points to two of his men, the last ones to arrive. "I'll send them to him. He needs to prepare for withdrawal."

Ameer puts a knee to the ground, next to his tired father. "Can you feel that? The tanks are coming!"

Tarek puts his hand on Ameer's shoulder. "They have tanks all over the place, and a large number of infantry. Our situation isn't good. We'll be surrounded in no time. Two of the tanks are just off this corner; they'll be here any second."

"Where's our reinforcement?" Ameer asks, wiping the sweat from his forehead. He can feel his anger toward his Arab allies rising, and he feels betrayed. "They should have been here an hour ago. We were promised a full armored battalion!"

Tarek shouts 'Mortar' as he pushes his son's head down, and bends over him to cover him. The shell hits nearby and a cloud of dust envelops them. He coughs. "They're not coming."

"Did they run away? Are we supposed to fight tanks with rifles? We don't even have enough ammo for the bazookas."

"No, the Israeli air force knocked out the Jordanians. My spotter saw them, about ten miles out."

"And what about the Arab air forces? Isn't there a single plane left? And the *Yahoud*, God damn them, how many planes do they have? They're covering three fronts! Don't they ever need to *land*? Or refuel? You were so right about our Arab brothers. We're on our own in the fight."

"Concentrate on what's happening right now, Ameer. We need to pull out and minimize our losses. I have a diversion ready. We'll make a single push, all together, out of here. With infantry supporting their tanks, we won't be able to make any countermove. Spare the anti-tank ammo for our retreat, and only use it if necessary."

Ameer points to the walls of the once grand municipal building across from them, now pockmarked by bullet holes. "They're here to rescue the men trapped in that building."

Faris appears behind them. His face is covered with sweat and his uniform shows bloody signs of close contact with the enemy. "We got those who ran towards us. Now let's finish the rest of them off before they can escape, or get reinforcements."

Tarek pulls Faris behind their barricade as a volley of small arms fire from the municipal building whizzes by. With a stern voice, Tarek orders, "Get your men ready to protect our flank. They have infantry moving in from your side to cut our retreat. Did you mine the street? We must slow them down."

Faris nods. "Our booby traps are ready. Demolition charges too."

Ameer points to the building where the trapped Israelis are hiding. "Are we going to finish those bastards? Their reinforcements will be on us as soon as they regroup, and it will be too late, Father."

Tarek has a sadistic look. "We're not going to finish them off. Just keep pressure on them, keep them yelling for help on their radio."

Faris says, "Our first battle won't be a full victory if they survive!"

Tarek points at his head, inviting them to follow his reasoning. "You don't want your first battle to be your last, do you? Those survivors are our way out of this mess."

"What do we do, Father?" asks Ameer. He is certain that his father's experience would get them out, somehow. What can Tarek come up with, and what was that diversion he was taking about?

Tarek has a wicked look. "My demolition team rigged the building from two sides, to collapse on them. That'll keep them all busy for a while."

Faris protests. "Some of them might survive. They're in the basement."

Tarek snaps back at Faris, "*We* will survive! That's what counts for now." Looking at Ameer, he orders, "You stay with me and my platoon, we're organizing the delaying action."

Giving Faris a harsh look, he goes on. "Faris, you're in charge of the retreat. We'll escape through the narrow streets where their armor can't maneuver. Gather up the men, I want a full count. Check our transports. Put the ammo and gear in operational trucks. Make sure they have full gas tanks." He waves Nabil, his trusted sergeant in, and tells him and Ameer, "Keep only the weapons we need to hold them off."

Ameer says, "We have a bazooka and some ammo left, a Dragunov sniper rifle, and a couple of machine gun crews with PKMs."

Tarek looks at Faris, grabs him by the arm, and jabs his finger at his chest. "Our lives depend on you." Pointing at the corner where they built their sandbag barricade, Tarek goes on, "We're going to hold that corner and force them to focus on it. When the building blows, they'll have their hands full. Eyes too, from the dust and rubble. We'll take advantage of the chaos to double back to you. Be ready, and have a Jeep ready for me —"

A burst of firing from the building opposite interrupts Tarek's orders. A man comes running, crouching to avoid shots. Ameer recognizes Tarek's demolition expert. Tarek directs a burst from his machine gun toward the building and the shooting stops.

The soldier runs in, panting, covered with dust and dirt. "The building is ready to go down!" He hands Tarek a contact breaker, wires stringing from it. "Just press this. I have a backup with a delay in case the wire gets cut, but I'll have to go back in."

Tarek smiles and claps his man on the back, raising a puff of dust. "Don't worry. You've earned your pay, my friend. Saved the day, too. Go with Faris to the rendezvous point, we're going home." He nods to Faris and waves them to go. Faris and the soldier trot away.

Ameer listens to the rumble of the tanks. "They're on the move again, Father. Shall we deploy?"

Tarek puts his hand on Ameer's shoulder. "You're in charge."

Ameer doesn't waste any time. Waving to one of the two machine gun teams, he yells, pointing to the top of the building next to them, "Up on the roof!" Then he directs the other machine gun team inside the same deserted building, but at ground level. "There's a long corridor inside, keep switching positions." Ameer shouts to the two scrambling teams. "We retreat to the trucks at the whistle!"

Ameer looks around for the sniper and the bazooka teams. They are nowhere to be found. Instead, his father is standing behind him, holding both weapons. Nabil and two more of his men stand near Tarek, while the rest are heading to the rally point.

Tarek tosses the sniper rifle to his son. Ameer watches as his father sits behind their sand barricade and throws the bazooka nonchalantly onto his shoulder. Without looking back, Tarek orders one of his men, Ramez, to squat next to him, by the ammo pile.

He signals Nabil and the other soldier to go to the bunker across the street. "You'll be able to retreat when you blow the building at my signal." Pointing to the switch, Tarek says, "Here's the contact, with plenty of slack. Make sure you don't cut the wire."

He gives a calm order to Ramez, as he points to Bazooka shells. "Put one of those pills in, I can feel the earth shaking." Tarek jolts slightly as his man shoves the projectile in, and then taps his shoulder to let him know that the weapon is ready.

Ameer settles next to his father, wipes the sweat from his face, and checks his rifle, adjusting the scope. He looks through a firing port between the sandbags and checks his field of fire. He feels a rush through his veins as the world seems to stand still. Enemy mortars go silent, meaning the tanks are close. The trapped Israelis have stopped firing. The air trembles with metallic groans and the earth shakes as the roaring death grows louder and closer, echoing across buildings around them.

Ameer takes a deep breath, and then exhales slowly. He remembers his father's lessons: both eyes open while sighting, maintain a wide field of view. Critical threats first, essential ones second . . . Ameer is startled by an enemy tank as it rounds the corner just ahead of them. He shouts to his father, "Look!" Ameer aims his rifle at the tank.

Tarek's reaction is swift. As his target climbs over a destroyed barricade, Tarek aims his bazooka. "It worked. He's climbing on the tree trunk. Stupid. I'll get him in the belly!" He presses the trigger. The three men watch the shell hit the enemy tank's thin-skinned bottom. Fire flashes from its vents. Hatches fly in the air. The turret is dislodged. Secondary detonations sound as ammo blows in the raging fire. The sight reminds Ameer of the UNRWA boxes of canned food, the ones with the "not for sale" logo on the side. As kids, they used to blow up those cardboard boxes with firecrackers, sending their flipping tops wide open. Faris liked to trap insects inside, and the images of burned and mangled soldiers inside, like those blasted ants, brings a grin to Ameer's face.

Tarek barks to Ramez, "Reload!" A quick tap on the shoulder soon follows: *weapon ready*. A second tank appears from behind the burning one. The main gun is already trained on them, and the coaxial machine gun can open up any second. Tarek fires, and his round strikes the tank's turret.

Ameer looks around him, barely hearing anything as the sound of the anti-tank weapon resounds in his ear. Except for his father, no one has fired yet. The two tanks are isolated, for now. He can see the second tank creep forward through the settling debris. He shouts, "It's still moving!"

Tarek hollers to Ramez, "Reload!" Ramez fumbles with the scattered ammo. Tarek shouts, "Now!"

Nabil aims his machine gun at the tank, spraying it with bullets, hoping to distract the crew. The loader finally gets a round in the bazooka. Tarek fires. Ameer covers his ear to protect it from the blast and bends down below to his firing port. Tarek shouts, "I got him in the tracks! He can't move anymore!"

Ramez shouts, "Finish him off, sir, he can still use his gun!"

Tarek focuses on the smoking beats of steal and hollers, "*Ehchee!*" — Reload!

Ameer motions the soldier to stop. "Wait, they're bailing out. The bottom hatch is opening. We don't have many rounds left."

Two more tanks appear, stuck behind the first two. They hesitate to round them and expose their sides, but rounds from their turret smoke canisters fill the air with a fast-growing cloud. Tarek changes position to get a better view. Ameer shouts, "Father! Wait, they haven't seen us yet!"

Tarek points at the municipal building. "I'm giving the order to blow it!"

Peering through the smoke, Ameer sees the crew from the second tank evacuating. He shouts to his father and points at them, then at his sniping rifle. *I'm going to shoot them.* Tarek nods his okay; Ameer shoulders the rifle, shoving it into his firing port, yet making sure the muzzle doesn't protrude, to avoid disclosing his position. He peers through his scope, takes a deep breath, and then exhales slightly, steadying his aim.

The enemy commander jumps to the machine gun on top of his turret and starts spraying bullets to cover his crew's evacuation. A burst hit next to their sand barricade, raising a cloud of dust and throwing splintered bits all over.

Ameer raises his head; he can barely make out the brave machine gunner through the smoke. He is obviously blinded by the smoke and dust, shooting haphazardly, not knowing where his enemy is. He looks distraught. *Ameer feels it. A sensation fills him instantly, as he tries to make out the enemy's face in his scope. The sensation transposes him into the enemy's mind. Ameer can feel his distress. As if a sensory tunnel has bridged the two minds, Ameer can see through the eyes, hear through the ears of that face. The sensation numbs his own senses, slowing him down.*

Two tanks have moved up and now stand dangerously close to his position. Ameer shakes out from his daze. The tanks are less than a hundred meters out. The evacuating enemy crew is preparing to rush back toward them.

His father, one knee on the ground next to him, leans over and speaks into his ear. "*Shwai, Shwai.*" — Slowly, slowly. — "They can't see us because of the smoke. Start with the last so they don't notice they're under fire."

Ameer focuses intently on his scope and says with a flat voice, "I'll take them all." He squeezes his trigger and sees his target fall to the ground. He takes aim at the next man and puts a bullet in his chest.

Ameer sees the man topple, mortally wounded. By now, the first two men are aware of the sniper, and scurry back to take cover behind their tank.

Ameer sees a face emerge, and, as his crosshairs settle on it, he squeezes his trigger. The enemy's head explodes. The fourth man is still hiding behind the tank. Looking under the tank, Ameer can see his enemy's feet. He takes a shot. When the man falls, screaming with pain, Ameer puts another bullet in his chest. He watches as his body spins violently then comes to rest. Ameer grins victoriously, and feels his father tap him on the shoulder.

Tarek points at the enemy commander now hopping off his tank. He whispers, "Don't miss him!"

Ameer looks through his scope, locking onto the commander's head. He still cannot quite make out the man's features, yet as soon as the scope settles on it, *the sensation comes back, and Ameer's numb mind is tunneled again to the enemy's. Ameer can feel his shock and despair. He can see, through the enemy's eyes, the bodies of the tank crew he just shot. He can see his own rifle, pointed . . . at him! One of the dying men points a pleading hand towards him. Ameer can even feel his cry.*

"Ameer! Shoot! Shoot now! Ameer!" Tarek's orders flush the sensation out.

Ameer leans back into his rifle. Through his peripheral vision, he senses danger. He looks around and sees one of the two rescuing tank's main guns turn into a perfect black disk as it aims at their position. He points towards it and turns to his father, who has already detected the danger. Tarek grabs him and shoves him into the building near their barricade. Before disappearing inside, Tarek turns toward Nabil, and gives him the signal to blow up the building. Ramez pushes both of them into the second room of the floor they rushed into.

The three men throw themselves on the floor, covering their heads with their arms, as a shell from the enemy tank blows their bunker apart, along with part of the wall of the building they've taken cover in. Dust and burning powder fill the air, and the three men huddle on the floor.

Ameer opens his eyes. He can't feel a thing. "Are we alive?" he asks.

Tarek checks his son with his hands, then his assistant gunner. "Not for long, unless Nabil blows that damn building right now!"

A thunderous explosion shakes the earth, followed by a steady rumble and a shrieking sound. Ameer peaks through the broken glass of a windowpane. The municipal building collapses as concrete slabs, broken columns, and falling blocks of stone entomb everyone inside. A thick wave of smoke and dust rolls up and away from the rubble, quickly enveloping the street in a long wave of man-made agony.

Tarek tugs at Ameer's arm as the dust penetrates broken doors and shattered windows. "Let's get out while we can. Whistle for the men to retreat."

Ameer blows long blasts on his whistle. As they rush out of the building's rear exit point, the machine gun teams and his sergeant's team join them. Dust puffs from their clothes with every step and the men are struck with nervous laughter as they run to the rallying point.

Faris greets them with a large smile. He coughs as he hugs Ameer and pats him on his back, lifting a cloud of dust. "Thank God you are safe. You made it. We're ready to go."

Tarek looks anxiously at Faris. "What are the scouts saying?"

Faris answers with a smile. "It looks like your plan worked. The tanks are converging on the collapsed building. They probably have survivors inside, and the roads out of here will be free!"

Faris and Ameer congratulate each other with another hug. Tarek says, "Keep sending scouts ahead. We'll move east, one street at a time." He pauses for a second, then asks Faris, "What's our count?"

"Four dead and twelve wounded, two badly."

Tarek gazes away for a moment, towards the inferno they have just escaped.

Faris looks at Tarek with admiration. "You just saved all of us from certain death. We've killed many. You should be proud. We're all proud of you!"

Amid the deserted streets and empty homes around them, Faris shouts, "*Ya 'eesh Tarek!*" Long Live Tarek! Long live the PLO!" The men repeat his words, echoing the cheer as they push back toward their trucks.

———

Ameer sits in the passenger seat in the first truck, which had its battle-mangled roof cut off. Tarek leads the convoy in a jeep. He stands up and turns towards his men in the back. "We did well today. We were let down by our Arab friends, again. But we did well. We will do better from here on! With the PLO, we will decide what to do and when to do it! We will control and lead as we should have, from the start! *Tahiya felasteen!*" The men stand in the bouncing truck and echo his shout in unison.

# CHAPTER 14

It is the first quiet evening since the war began. Joint efforts by the US and the USSR finally yielded a ceasefire, and most of the neighborhood has gathered at Ely's place for a barbecue. Most of the guests are out in the garden, while the children play in the backyard. Many have come for a firsthand account of Amir's brave actions.

Amir, on the other hand, is looking forward to some quiet time with his parents, and some private time with Debbie. His feats of arms, his saving the lives of what turned out to be a large group of reservists, the commendations and admiration of everyone far and near . . . could not fill that deep dark pit inside his chest, numbing his mind with denial: Caleb and his men were gone. His crew, his trusted friends who told him they'd go anywhere with him, were . . . gone. But he wasn't. Amir felt ashamed to be alive.

Amir was in a guilt and sorrowful mood, and the victory of Israel against all of its neighbors was nowhere near enough to alleviate this. Nor could anything explain that haunting feeling, which was still flashing back. That enemy sniper who killed all his men, yet spared him. And what was that blurred vision when they were face to face across the battlefield? Why did it feel like he saw *himself* through the scope of the sniper's gun? Why is this "thing" haunting him? What is this "thing"?

Amir walks into the kitchen and watches children play through a window overlooking the backyard. That is where he played as a child. Back then, the place seemed big enough to hold all his fantasies. Now he couldn't find a single secluded spot for a little privacy where he could ponder upon his anxious thoughts. Make some void in his mind. Across the fence, a short distance away, stands Debbie's house. Amir looks at it with yearning, wishing he could just step over and hold her gently in his arms. Would she understand what he feels? Can he talk to her about death, the loss of brothers in arms, knowing her own orphaned heart will never heal?

Amir overhears Sara excusing herself from her friends and walking towards him.

She puts a hand on his shoulder, and whispers into his ear, "She should be here any minute. Put aside your grim thoughts. You know they're *groundless*, and now you know what your elders have already learned. We call it *war*. We each do our part, and pay a price. From grieving mothers and orphaned children to the men who gave their lives, and their brave companions. You did more than you had to, and you saved many lives, Amir."

Sara's blunt but comforting logic brings Amir's mind back to the cacophony of his house. He nods a still unconvinced understanding and says, "She's late."

Sara smiles and pulls him into the living area. "She called. She needs ten minutes."

"Maybe I should go to her place . . ."

"That would be rude to our guests, now wouldn't it?"

Amir takes a deep breath and goes on with an intense voice, "I should be going back to the families of my crew, may their memories rest in peace. They are in deep mourning and in very bad shape. And we are here, celebrating victory."

Sara looks him straight in the eyes. "Any and all deaths are regrettable, but we wouldn't be here, celebrating, if it wasn't for the sacrifice of some brave men. You did your duty and more, and you're only here by miracle. A gesture from God. Many, many homes are *celebrating* today because of your actions and the sacrifice of you and your men. *Never forget that.*"

Amir acquiesces, and Sara continues, "Maybe one day our neighbors will understand that we can live together. Enough war — time for peace!"

Amir grins. "Not the guys we fought in Jerusalem. It was them or us."

"And so it was you. Now forget about those Arabs. They're not ghosts."

Amir mutters, "Maybe they are. Ghosts . . . I wonder . . ."

Ethan and Dina are coming through the backyard gate. Amir starts for the kitchen door, but Moshe's voice catches him. "*Shalom*, Amir, running from your guests?"

Moshe walks toward Amir with open arms. "That was quite a stunt you pulled at the pass, ambushing and destroying an armored unit four times your size. I'm proud of you."

Amir steps back. He is a little embarrassed. "Well, we took advantage of the terrain, and —"

"Yeah, right. It was a miracle you got there in the first place. And in the city, you saved a hundred guys! You went through a house!"

"How do you already know all this?"

Moshe gives Amir a look and points up. "My friends upstairs, remember? I read your report and debrief. Your father has, too."

Amir hears a familiar thump. His father has returned and thrown his bag into a corner. Amir rushes to him. Although he knew his son was ok and home, Ely has an expression of sheer relief as he sees Amir. "My heart and soul. I'm so happy to see you." Ely lifts Amir off the floor in a tight hug, indifferent to the people around them.

Amir pulls his father aside, away from curious friends. Facing him, gripping both his hands, he says, "Everybody is telling me I am a hero. But my whole crew and my sergeant's crew are all dead! I am sick of this. I want to go to their families, *Aba*."

Ely shakes his head. "I know you did that already, and you will again, tomorrow. You lost some good people, but you also saved many more. There were tens of soldiers in that basement. Young volunteers who needed you. You saved *all* their lives."

Winking at Moshe, Ely adds, "Besides, your victory had a far reach. Our intelligence units immediately broadcast the news of their routing. That was one of their toughest guerilla units, and our message sent all the other Arab units into hiding. Even the Jordanians quit the fight."

Amir nods his acknowledgment. "Yes, they were tough. They took my tanks head-on and stopped us. I haven't seen such skill and determination before."

Moshe slaps Amir on the back. "Determination? *Them?* You drove your tank through a house and right into the middle of the fray!"

Moshe's enthusiasm doesn't make Amir feel any better. "I should have stayed put and waited for the rest of our units. I went ahead and it cost me my crew." Amir hesitates as he mutters. "My whole crew . . . except me. I'm . . . ashamed."

Ely pats him on the back. "I read the reports, son. Not just yours. The other tank commanders' too. You did what you had to do, and everything you could have. You stayed in the open, covering your crew with your machine gun, under fire. They fell to a shrewd, well-trained sniper. There is nothing you could have done. I wouldn't have done things any differently either. It's a miracle the sniper didn't get you. Perhaps the smoke . . ."

The thought of the sniper makes Amir's thoughts drift. He closes his eyes and takes a deep breath as he feels the presence of his enemy again, as if it is a personal encounter with a shadowy ghost invading his mind. "There was something strange about that sniper."

"You saw him?" Ely frowns.

Amir lowers his voice. "I could almost make out his face. The strangest thing is, I think he was watching me, instead of shooting. He could have shot me, but he did not. He looked, or I'd rather say he felt, like someone I know, someone close, even intimate, but I can't explain it any better than that. It was like I could almost see myself in his place, like a hallucination. This sounds crazy, but I could *feel* he had the same sensation. I *know* that he felt the same as I did. What do you make of this?"

Moshe shrugs. "That's weird. I'm glad you didn't put it in your report."

Ely puts a hand on Amir's shoulder. "Don't worry. That's what we call *zazoua*." — The fog of war. — "Strange things happen. I wouldn't worry about it."

Moshe jokes, "Ely always has an explanation and a moral for us."

"Well, we did have a clear victory on every front, we pushed them back in the west, we took the East Bank, and we have the Golan Heights. Now we have secure natural borders, and we have the best army. We won on all accounts!"

"So where's the bad part?" Amir asks.

Ely looks at Moshe as he answers, "There is no bad part. It's just . . . well, the unfinished business of peace is now laid out before us."

Moshe raises his eyebrows. "Where are you going with this, Ely?"

"We've won a war, but the conflict is far from over. There's a lot of anger outside our borders. If we don't have a breakthrough towards an understanding with the Arabs, the next one will be harder."

Amir has a shocked look. "The next what? The next war?"

Moshe nods. "Yes. They'll be better prepared, and we might not, that's what Ely is trying to say." Moshe looks at the concerned faces around him, and claps his hands as he cranes his neck toward the dining room. "Enough of this. I suggest we have a minute of silence in memory of our dead soldiers. We'll think about the next war another time."

Ely asks everyone inside, and they gather around the dining table. Under his guidance, all the visitors become silent. Some close their eyes, and concentrate on his blessing: *"Yeye zichram baruch."* May their memory rest in peace.

They all respond in unison with heavy hearts and some with moist eyes, "Amen."

They return to their seats, and Amir slides away towards Debbie, who has just walked into the kitchen. Her beautiful chestnut hair falling over her shoulders, she holds a large, steaming chocolate cake, the kind she knew Amir loves so much. Amir takes the cake and stashes it on the kitchen counter. "Debbie! At last!"

Debbie has a shy smile as Amir hugs her tight. "I baked your favorite cake ... don't spoil it." She giggles as he squeezes her against him. "I was so afraid when you were away. Now you're here, all of you are here, and we're all so glad."

Ethan raises his drink in a toast. *"Mazel Tov.* Here's to the two of you." He winks at Amir and adds, "You should have seen how the men shouted when our army took the Temple Mount. Everyone was cheering triumphantly: *Har Habait be yadenu!"* Ethan takes a sip from his drink and goes on. "The men were crazy. They all wanted to go there, even the wounded!"

Debbie sighs and tilts her head onto Amir's shoulder. She pulls him away and out toward the garden. Amir is happy she made the move. Ethan can go on for hours.

Ely laughs. "Good, no more talk about the war. If anyone else wants to hear more war stories, well, Ethan will be all too happy to comply." Dina grabs Ethan by the hand and leads him away. Ely smiles again, "Or maybe you'll just have to wait."

Debbie tows Amir through groups of friends and out, under the open skies and between the trees to the far end of the garden. Dina follows with Ethan, and they sit on the ground not far away, with their backs on the fence and the clear sky for shelter.

A small distance away, the neighborhood celebrates their victory, their great army, and the newfound safety of their homes. But Amir's mind is somewhere else. It's with someone else: the enemy sniper. *Where is he right now? What is he doing? Preparing for the next encounter? WHY did he not shoot? WHAT did HE see? Feel?*

———

It is late in the afternoon, and the camp is like a termite's nest on fire. Fear and anger linger in the air, as families rush to gather their belongings, pack their tents, dismantle whatever they can carry from their homes, and toss them haphazardly on crumbling trucks, for yet another hastened trip . . . in the wrong direction. Yes, again.

In Tarek's place, the atmosphere is one of cold death. Moaning and muffled cries despoil the air, as Tarek, sitting on a chair, holds Rabih's body as tightly as he can. Beside him, Ameer grips Layal's hand, and holds his dead brother's limp hand against his heart. Sami stands in the corner, next to Samar, who is holding Rima, doing her best to keep the shocked mother from collapsing. Tarek's eyes are filled with tears. His mouth opens and his head turns toward Rima, but no words are uttered, no sound comes out, only an agonizing moan. His drowned eyes keep searching for clues in Rima's blank face. She hasn't spoken a word since *it* happened.

Rima's eyes are as dead as her son's. If not for the dripping tears, one would swear that no life inhabits her body. She sits, her clothes red with blood, staring at her lifeless son in his father's arms. He was in hers when life finally slipped from his body only two hours before.

Samar looks at the gathered men. "Those Zionist bastards entered the camp, hunting for the men. Rima hid Rabih in the closet and made him swear not to move. We only know what we guessed from overhearing, and what we heard the Zionist officer say to his men as they withdrew from the camp. Three of them came inside here and started slapping Rima around, asking questions. Then one of them ripped her dress open." Samar pauses and breathes deeply, in an effort not to choke. "Rabih burst from the closet and charged them with the hunting shotgun. He shot the two who were slapping his mother. He couldn't reload in time to stop the third soldier from shooting him. He took bullet after bullet but kept charging until he was upon him. Rabih killed him with his own bayonet." Samar pauses again. "The Israeli officer came into the house. He saw Rabih dying. His soldiers, dead. And Rima with her clothes torn off. He didn't let his men inside to see, to avoid a massacre. He called his lieutenants and ordered every-one to move out . . . Rabih was left in a pool of blood."

Gathering his strength, Tarek gets to his feet, lifting the riddled and bloodied body of his son, oblivious to the weight, his torso rocking back and forth as he hums in despair. His voice is soft and sad. "Your name is Rabih, like the spring. The spring of our lives. The spring *in* our lives. Where did you go? Why did you go? How can there be no spring any-more? Why you? It should have been me defending our home, not you. What does Allah say about this?" He raises his wet eyes to the heavens.

"*Ya Allah.* Is it punishment, is it a test, or is it just Your will? Are You happy, *Allah*? Satisfied? What have You done? What has Rabih done? Defend his mother? Her honor?" Tarek falls back to the chair, Rabih still cuddled in his arms. "What have I done to deserve this?"

Faris intervenes. Eyes swollen, he holds both Tarek and his dead son. Slowly, Faris eases Rabih from his father. Turning toward Ameer, he signals for help. Ameer helps him carry Rabih, and gently presses Tarek into his chair, as he tries to rise again towards his dead son. Faris carries Rabih, kisses his forehead, murmurs to his ear, "*Shaheedna el batal. Akhouya.*" —Our martyred hero. My brother. — He turns to face the door, adding, "The Sheikh is here." Rima raises a trembling hand toward her dead son, but she can't move, her empty eyes following as Faris takes him from the house to prepare the body for burial. Ameer, despite his own reluctance to let go of his brother, gently keeps Tarek from following.

Tarek lets out an incomprehensible moan, and his tear-marred face is frozen with pain. Ameer swallows his pain as he watches Faris carry Rabih away. His empty chest is ready to burst with anger and desperation. His brother, his lifelong companion, his *spring* is dead. Ameer can feel his own soul trying to seep out and into his brother's lifeless body, trying to animate it, to bring it back to life. Make a miracle. Ameer would share his soul if he could. He would give it away, if he could. If it went back into Rabih's body. How could life go on without Rabih? Maybe it couldn't, maybe it was impossible, or maybe it was all . . . not happening. Ameer looks at his father, then his mother, both distorted with pain. Both living dead. They look like their souls *did* manage to exit their uninhabited bodies. Reality kicks in as Ameer realizes he has to help.

He kneels beside his father, embracing him and urging, "Let him go. Let him go to Allah. It's best for him." Whether or not Tarek can hear, or understand, he does not know, but he tries to steady his voice and says softly, "*Yaba*, we have to be strong. You have to take care of mother."

Tarek puts his arms around his son, and rests his head on his shoulder, moaning, "Why him? Why not me? All my life, everything I did, was for you two. To make you happy, to make you proud, to make you safe." Tears run down his cheeks. His face is pale as if he was himself amongst the dead. Raising his head, he goes on, "He wasn't ready. I knew he couldn't be put in harm's way. And now he's dead, and killing the entire Israeli army wouldn't bring him back." Tarek turns to Rima and puts a hand on her shoulders. "Rabih is gone. It's all my fault!"

Ameer cries, his voice choking, "*This* is God's will. We all die with Rabih today. We don't challenge Allah's will."

Tarek stamps his foot, his whole body shuddering. "Death, cowardly Zionist death, has no business knocking at my door. Not while I was out. And don't tell me it's Allah's will to take life from an innocent boy trying to defend his mother!"

Ameer nods. "I don't have an answer. We never will have an answer. I do know that mother needs you. Rabih was her dream, her joy in life. You have to stand on your feet, so that she can lean on you." He then adds, his own voice breaking, "We all need to lean on you. Rabih . . . Rabih was *everything*. For all of us. He was . . . *Rabih*."

Tarek shakes his head and takes Rima's limp hand. "Coming at them with a shotgun. My poor son, my brave son." Tarek lets go of Rima, slips from the chair and falls to his knees. He points to the blood-stained spot where it had happened, right in front of him. "Right here!" He puts his hands onto the blood, swirls it around, and then brings his bloodied hands to his chest. "This is where he died. This is his blood. *My* blood. *Lahmee wa dammee* . . . My flesh, my blood, *rouhee, albee* . . . my spirit, my heart. My Rabih."

Ameer takes both his parents' bloodied hands and squeezes them. "Rabih is at peace now. By God, I can even hear him. He's saying, 'Don't consider those killed for Allah as dead but living with Allah in heaven. Don't be sad, don't cry for me. I'm happy here, I have found my home, and it's a beautiful home. There are no Zionists here, and no death.' I can see him there. In the house he always dreamed of."

Tarek joins his hands to Rima's. "Rima, talk to me, come to me, let it out!"

Rima rises slowly, her face that of death itself, her pale lips barely moving, her flat voice rising to anger as she says. "What's there to say? There is nothing. Nothing. My son, my soul, my Rabih, is gone. Those bastards ripped my boy apart. Just a young boy, a child defending his mother. I wish they would all burn in hell!"

Ameer stands. "They are! Rabih sent them there. He's in a better place."

Rima looks up at her son, her voice still dead. "He was too young. Even for paradise, he was too young." Rima falls exhausted and wailing into Tarek's arms. She lets out, "You should have seen him, my Rabih, my proud and angry Rabih. He charged them! He took out two and was trying to reload as the third one shot him. He wouldn't die, he just wouldn't die . . . not until he made sure I was safe, and they were dead." Looking up at her husband's face, she goes on, "He kept going. They riddled him with bullets but he kept going. He took this devil's bayonet from its sheath and killed him with it."

Tarek hugs his wife, and says, choking, "Our brave son. My Rabih. My hero."

Rima's voice is detached and full of pain. "He looked at me with his sparkling eyes, and told me 'It is ok. I am at peace.'" Rima takes a deep breath and adds, "His last words were for you and Ameer. He said, 'Tell them to be proud of me, tell them to keep fighting, tell them to take care of you.'" Looking at Ameer and Tarek, she goes on, "He also said, 'Be strong mother, and they'll have to be strong too.'" Pointing to where Rabih had fallen, she adds, her eyes soft and sad, "Then he smiled at me and coughed up blood. He said *'Raje'e a'al beyt, akheeran'* I am going home, finally. And then he closed his eyes."

Faris and the sheikh are at the door. The sheikh declares, "He is a martyr. May God have mercy on his brave soul. We have to give Rabih a proper burial. Let's take him to the pray parlor, then bury him in the cemetery of our village. Time is running out."

Tarek says with a broken voice, "Thank you, Sheikh Ahmad. What do you mean, time is running out?"

"The Israelis are kicking people out of their homes. They'll be especially vicious to your camp because they lost men here."

Ameer cries out. "We have to pack? Again? I won't do it. I refuse. Rabih hasn't died in vain!"

Tarek says sorrowfully, "Ameer, my boy. If we stay, and die when the Israelis come, *then* Rabih will have died in vain. Dying for this camp won't win the war. We have to live to fight another day. If not for us, then for Rabih. His last words were to keep up the fight, remember?"

Faris steps forward and grips Ameer's arm. "Your father is right, Ameer. There's no point dying here. They'll call an air raid on us, and decimate us from the skies."

Tarek mutters like a robot, "We pack and that's an order."

Rima straightens. "God knows, I could kill with my bare hands right now. But we have to listen to Rabih. He asked us to continue the fight, not just today, but until we win. We shall keep our strength, to fight another day."

Rima pulls at Ameer's arms, gazing into his eyes. "You hear me, Ameer? You hear Rabih, talking from above? Would he want you to die in this place, to die in vain? No, Rabih wants more. Rabih wants victory! He wants a home for us, a proper house, and our land back. Can any of that be done by staying here and waiting for death to be thrown at you from the sky? My son, you'll do the enemy a favor by staying here." Walking toward the corner where they stored their suitcases, Rima pulls one out. "I say we pack. We pack and go as soon as we give Rabih his ceremony."

The sheikh says with a warm gesture, "Everything is ready. I took care of it."

Tarek nods. "Then let's get on with it."

At the burial grounds on the outskirts of the sheikh's village, the families of the men fallen in combat gather. They quickly read the *Fatehah* — the Opening verse of Koran — bury the bodies in a hastened ceremony, and rush away. Sounds of sporadic fighting can already be heard in the next village.

Tarek, broken and worn down, resumes his command. He shouts orders to his men, who have gathered in his house. "Leave the military trucks here. Faris, booby-trap the equipment we leave. We'll only use buses and civilian vehicles. I don't want our convoy bombed."

To Ameer he says, "Check our list. Every family, every person. We don't want to lose anyone. Check food and water supplies with Nabil. Load our livestock in the last trucks. We leave in half an hour."

Tarek rallies the men around him, and attempts to put some rationale into their action. "We're joining up with the main Palestinian force. We're going to join the PLO, become a real army. We lost this battle, but we'll fight the rest of the war on our terms. The Palestinians don't need help from anybody."

The men around Tarek cheer, taken by his charisma and fortitude. As for Ameer, the prospect brings a glimmer of hope in his despairing heart. He gnashes his teeth, and says to Faris, "I can't wait to avenge Rabih."

Tarek turns toward his son. "From now on, we will decide when and how we die, where and how we fight."

Faris shouts, rousing the men with another cheer. "*We will* avenge his death! Rabih's blood won't go unpunished. We'll fight until we win. Until they all die!"

Ameer says, sadly, "Our own liberation army. Rabih would have loved that." Looking at Faris, he adds, "He'd have made a fine soldier."

Faris puts his hand on Ameer's shoulder. "Rabih *was* the best soldier. I can see him, as your mother described it, charging those bastards. Rabih is a hero. I'll think of Rabih every time I go to battle."

Ameer looks at his friend, spitting death and hatred with every word, and says, "Me too. We lost a battle, but not the war. This is not the end of it. Rabih is watching. He is waiting. I won't disappoint him. We *will* take them all. For my dead brother. For all our dead brothers and sisters. By God, all of them! This I swear!"

# 1970
# Wed to War

# CHAPTER 15

Tarek sits on a bench on his bedroom balcony, overlooking the camp, baking in the mid-September sun. He turns 40 this year, and right now his thoughts are back in Dar Moussa, his *home*. Tarek can see himself working in his fields 22 years ago. The memories are a painful wound buried deeply in his chest. The passing years have brought a heavy psychological toll, which falls on him all the more because of his position as a leader. *Twenty-two years. Twenty-two* long *years,* Tarek thinks to himself. Rabih, his younger son, has been dead for three years, three months, and seven days. He and Rima as well, in a way...

Their latest camp is one outside Jordan's capital, Amman, but it is more like a small, crowded village, albeit a poor and derelict one. Narrow, dusty streets wind between haphazardly mushrooming houses, none of which are completed. Most have barely plastered cinder-block walls and tin roofs. Those who arrived first, such as Tarek and his unit's families, moved into the concrete houses that formed the nucleus of this refugee camp. It was about two years ago, after almost a year of nomadic life. Their souls are still in their last camp, where Rabih was killed, but their minds are fully focused on the offensive, on military action, on getting back to their country, to their villages and homes. They are still refugees, but they have now become fighters. Freedom fighters, for their country, for Palestine. Patriotic songs blare from radios, filling the air with a constant reminder of their unfinished business with the enemy—a solid anchor for every daydreamer and a morale booster for everyone else. *Al-ana al-ana wa layssa ghadan, ajrass al a'wdati fal tukra'h.* Right now and not tomorrow, let's ring the bells of our comeback. The vibes of Lebanese singer Fayruz had become both a chant and a prayer, even an anthem for freedom.

The camp is built around a main UNRWA complex that houses the school, the administration building, a couple of barracks where food supplies are stored, and a doctor's clinic. These improved buildings even boast occasional rudiments of civility such as electricity and running water, and even a sewage system. New families, as they join the community, live in tents on the outskirts of the camp. Thanks to Tarek's effort to build proper latrines and showers, the stench of stagnating sewers is fading, and with it the disease-carrying mosquitoes. Tarek says they are lucky not to be in an arid part of Jordan. A small measure of agriculture in fields outside the camp contributes to their supply of food. They now have their own community and society, and this is a true morale booster for Tarek. They are getting organized, they are acting. As part of the PLO, they were now acting under one leader—a *Palestinian* leadership for their struggle. They no longer have to depend on the help of any unreliable Arab armies. This is the sole glimmer of hope in the dark tunnel of their lives.

Tarek watches his son, Ameer, walking around, calling out for Layal. He rolls his eyes at his son's casual civilian clothing. What a contrast from when he dressed for battle! Ameer's curly hair appears like a halo around his head. His loose shirt hangs baggily around his waist and his wide-bottomed jeans fit loosely around his legs. Tarek thinks to himself, "at least it's better than seeing him in battle fatigues, no matter how more manly these were." A smile adorns Tarek's face as he sees Layal, just as casually dressed, catching up with Ameer. Of course, it suited her perfectly, with her long, black silky hair. Now the two are getting married, and Tarek's only wish for them is to live through peaceful times, and not suffer through the harrowing experience of outliving their own children.

Layal seems serene, but outside the camp, the atmosphere is not so calm. The Jordanian kingdom is in a major confrontation with the PLO, and the two have already clashed over influence and authority. The increased presence of the Palestinians, their mounting arsenal and their military agenda cannot possibly cohabitate with the Jordanian Kingdom's own aspiration for sovereignty and self-determination. Last June saw serious battles between the two, right in the center of the capital, Amman. Tarek knows that the PLO's leadership is plotting against Hussein, the Jordanian king, who just today reacted to the many clashes between the two forces by announcing the formation of a military government. Egypt and Syria are helping Palestinians with weapons and training. Tarek and his unit, now under PLO control, have been raiding Israeli targets in the occupied lands. Tarek is in charge of a full battalion, and Ameer is serving as a young lieutenant under his command. His units are armed with Soviet weapons and gear. Unfortunately, Tarek fears that their war potential was not enough to bring about significant military gains, let alone political ones, at least not in a conventional confrontation, but he keeps this opinion from his soldiers, for fear of hurting morale. He does, however, try his best to instill in Ameer a thirst for knowledge and reason, in his mind a much stronger weapon than all the hardware they could acquire.

His greatest wish is for Rima to get better. Whenever Ameer would come home after a mission, he would directly go comfort his mother. Losing Rabih had been more than she could bear. The constant fear of losing her other son is, in her words, a daily dose of poison. Every mother in the camp with a son old enough for combat, or a husband, is drinking from that poison cup. Some, like Rima, have already been sickened by it. She only finds comfort when Ameer and Tarek are both near her, and in the company of her best friend, Samar, who has also known the enduring pain of losing a loved-one to the Israelis. Besides being best friends, they found comfort and peace by working at the camp in the women's charitable society. They help the most deprived in their daily struggles, providing them with care, food, clothes, and whatever useful items they are sent by charities. Most importantly, their mere presence around the needy was beneficial, and that worked both ways. In their free time, if they had any, they would sew and sell Palestinian embroidery, in order to bring in some extra money.

Tarek shakes his head to disperse his morose thoughts, in order to concentrate on the imminent event: the whole camp is helping to prepare for Ameer's wedding. A much-admired emerging leader is getting married, none other than the son of their beloved and trusted commander. His beautiful bride is the daughter of a distinguished martyr.

Layal is busy resizing an old wedding dress for her taut figure. Rima was extremely delighted to have found such an appropriate use for her never-used dress. Ameer is planning to enjoy a week away with his bride. The wedding is a God-send, a short escape from their miserable reality.

Tarek rests his body against the balcony rail, remembering his own marriage on the run. The radio is airing their favorite songs of "returning" *ajrass al-awdah* — the bells of return, and his mind rides the waves, returning into the past. He shivers back to the present, as Rima steps behind him and wraps her arms around his chest. It brings him back to Dar Moussa, near the brook, where he and Rima used to sneak out for a romantic afternoon together. Rima whispers softly in his ear, "Where have you drifted, *habibi*?

Tarek turns and bends his head toward her, breathing deeply and closing his eyes as he feels her lips graze his ear. "*Sakhrat al O'shaq.*" — I hope *they*'ll get a better life.

Rima rests her head on his shoulder. "At least they're getting a ceremony and a decent wedding night." She adds with a wink. "He has a surprise for the honeymoon."

Tarek takes her by the waist. "This wedding certainly suits you. You look gorgeous. How about *we* go on our honeymoon?"

Rima snuggles against him. "Nothing would make me happier." She pauses for a second, and gazes away.

Tarek gently runs his fingers through her hair. "Some things are not for us to decide. I, too, would have wanted for Rabih to be with us. Today, and every day."

Rima raises her hand, pointing at an imaginary scene. "I can see him. Tall. Proud. Handsome. Standing next to Ameer . . ." She shakes her head. "We must not torture ourselves, or feel guilty about happy moments. This is not what he'd want. Rabih would forbid it."

Tarek holds Rima's cheeks with both hands. "You are right. Let's not spoil things for Ameer. Let's do what Rabih would have us do. For both of them."

Rima looks heavenward, her voice cracking. "And for us. Rabih, *Allah Yerhamo*, would want us to be proud and happy on this day. He would." She forces a smile. "Let's get busy and prepare for Layal's *henna*. It'll keep our minds busy too."

Tarek asks, "Is the bedroom ready? Did the carpenter finish putting the new bed and closet together? He should be done!"

"He has. It's like a dream! New sheets, fresh flowers . . ."

"I'm jealous. When will you do that for me?"

Rima's face is radiant. Tarek feels happy just to look at her, her beaming eyes . . . He raises an eyebrow and tilts his head slightly. "Not tonight, I know. We're sleeping on the couch."

Rima shakes her head. "*La!* The whole house is theirs. We're sleeping at Samar's."

"Good. So, what about the rest of the preparations?"

Rima says, "The living room is ready for the sheikh and the guests, and the party's all outside. Even the stage is ready. We're rushing to finish the food, and then we'll be all set." She puts her hand on her chest and says, "Part of me is very sad, but that's the part that will always be sad. That dark, hollow, part." Before Tarek can reply, her voice firms up. "But the rest of me, the part that's still living . . . I'm happy, very happy, Tarek. This will be the happiest day of my life. I want you to know that."

Tarek holds her tight. "Me too. I'm so glad this is finally happening."

"They'll have a better wedding than we did, on the run in that carriage."

Tarek shrugs. "I hope for them to have a better life than us."

Rima sighs and squeezes Tarek's hand. "They'll be fine. Everybody is more hopeful now. Except you, of course, the eternal pessimist."

"I am not a pessimist. But the road to our dream is long and full of sweat, blood, and . . . bugs!" Tarek smashes a spider dangling from the roof overhang.

Rima grins. "Can't we forget it for a day?"

Tarek shakes his head. "I'm sorry.  I'm just worried about our Jordanian friends."

"I know." Rima steps back, her face showing her concern. "Some of our people have gone too far. You think they will try a coup?"

Tarek lowers his gaze and takes Rima by the hand and leads her down the stairs to the living room floor. "The world has gone crazy. When they can't kill the enemy, they go for their own. The Popular Front for the Liberation of Palestine has blown up the four airplanes they hijacked, right on the tarmac of Amman's airport. That's an affront to the King. I just don't know. I only hope we'll get through this wedding in peace, and then I don't care . . ."

Rima frowns. "That doesn't sound very much like you—"

The front door opens and Ameer strides in. He looks tired, with sweat on his face, and his clothes dusty. Taking a sip from the drinking jar by the door, he greets his mother with a kiss on her cheek. "What's the secret? You stopped talking but you forgot to hide the looks on your faces!"

Tarek frowns. "I'm angry you still haven't cut your hair! I don't care what the latest fashion is: it's not right for a wedding day!" Tugging at a curl in Ameer's mane, he goes on, "This will be frozen on your head for eternity. We have a photographer coming."

Rima gently pokes Ameer in the ribs. "So, where are you going on the honeymoon? I heard you were planning to put your leave to good use. The money you saved too."

A tease sparkles in Ameer's eyes. "I have plans. It's my secret, though. I got a camera, and I'll show you pictures when we come back." He shoves his hands in his pockets and sighs deeply, half-choking on his words. "*Allah*, I wish Rabih was here. That's the only—" Ameer gazes into his mother's eyes. "Is that what you two were talking about?"

Seeing Rima's mouth tighten, Tarek cuts in. Putting his hands on his son's shoulders, he reminds him. "We miss him like you do. But tonight is your night, and Rabih is watching and enjoying with us. The only question is, are *you* ready?"

"Ready? Yes. I think. How was it between you two? Were you 'ready'? I bet there was no romancing allowed back then."

Rima laughs and slaps her son on the shoulder. "Ameer! That's none of your business . . ."

Ameer catches her hand and pulls her in. "Mother, I'm just comparing notes."

Tarek laughs as he remembers his and Rima's ordeal. "You know how we were married." He gazes at Rima's glowing face as she hugs her son. He points his finger to his son's chest. "We were just as lucky as you in knowing that we were made for each other. That's one thing we have in common."

Tarek snatches Rima from his son's arms and swings her around, a happy smile on his face. "Absolutely! We knew it when we were kids, didn't we?"

Putting her back on the floor, he walks to the radio and cranks up the volume, and then grasps his son by the shoulder for a *dabké* dance, his feet moving to the rhythm as he adds over the music, "And now it's your turn! Layal and you were also made for each other. It's going to be a perfect night, son. We're going to dance until dawn!"

---

With colored lights, strobes, and spotlights shining everywhere, and huge speakers blasting away, Ely's garden is more like an open-air dance floor, with the star-filled sky as a roof and an evening breeze for freshness. The religious ceremony has finished — the Rabbi chanted a moving wedding prayer and the bride and groom broke the ceremonial glass together — and now cheerful friends are dancing and singing to the band's music, circling around Amir and Debbie as the two struggle for balance on chairs held high in the air. Most of the neighborhood — friends, schoolmates, fellow soldiers — are here on this joyful September night. They spin around as they dance the *Shirele* — wedding dance, and, as the circle tightens, they lower the couple to the middle of the floor, and the newly wedded couple joins the *Hava Naguila* ring.

Ethan looks up to his dear friend Amir. In the last three years, Amir has grown from an angry teenager into a mature, determined young man. Over the loud music, Ethan shouts, "You still haven't told us where you're going for your honeymoon."

Amir leans out of the circle of dancers, nearly falling, and yells, "Are you serious? Knowing you and the guys, you'd probably meet me there. This is my *honeymoon*, not a *Gadna* camp!" Amir taps his friend on the head. "This time we're on our own."

As Amir and Debbie retract from the circle, Ethan probes, "Somewhere sunny?"

Amir laughs. "Yeah, right, we're parachuting into the Negev, that's why I took her jumping the other day." He glances lovingly at Debbie, who flings herself onto Amir, and wraps her arms around his neck. "I'll go anywhere with you!"

As Amir swings Debbie around then puts her back on her feet, Ethan isn't giving up. "Come on, Debbie. Tell us where. We'll set up a little room service, breakfast in bed, all those good things."

Debbie shakes her head. "I can't tell you what I don't know. I only know about our first night — tonight — which is from *aba*. We're staying at the King David. A whole suite! After that, I don't know anything."

Ethan feigns shock. "He's kept it even from you?"

Debbie playfully pulls Amir's ear. "Would you believe we haven't even started our life together and he's already keeping secrets from me?"

Amir has a sneaky smile. "You always say you like surprises."

As the DJ switches to disco music, and turns up the volume, Debbie has to yell to be heard. "I just hope you aren't taking all your guns with you."

"Relax, I'm not taking my guns. Well . . . maybe just a couple." Amir laughs. "We'll call you from the airport on our way back, then you can hear all about where we went."

Moshe steps in behind Amir and takes him by the shoulders. "So you're hush-hush about the destination. Just send us an 'all good' sign, will you?"

Ethan forces a heavy frown. "Do you really trust this guy with your daughter?"

"You mean for the honeymoon?"

Ethan laughs. "No, I mean for *life!*"

Moshe has a serious tone. "A man who can lead a unit to *Gehenom* and back, I trust with my daughter. I'll trust Amir with anything and everything that matters to me." Taking Debbie's hands, Moshe says with a soft voice, "Come and dance with your father."

---

As he awkwardly tries out some new disco moves, Moshe says, "Your mother, God bless her soul, would have been proud. You look so much like her. I wish you, my heart, all the good things in life, everything you need, and everything you want."

Debbie says sadly, "I wish she was here. I miss her today more than on any other day."

Ely, having sneaked from behind them, throws his arms around the father-daughter duo, bringing them to a stop. He takes Debbie into his arms. "Now it's my turn. I want the pleasure of dancing with the bride, too!"

As they dance away from Moshe, Ely eyes Debbie head to toe. "You look stunning. Amir is a lucky man. You take care of each other now . . . as you've been doing all your lives."

Moshe, left empty-handed in the middle of the dancing, spreads his arms, and calls out loudly, "What about me, am I supposed to dance with Amir?"

Dina lets go of Ethan's hand and takes her father's. "No. You dance with me, Dad."

As they leave Ethan stranded for a partner, Moshe says, "One day soon it's going to be you, my girl. Are you thinking about it?"

"You know I am. Ethan and I have been together for ... well, always."

Debbie and Ely circle near them. Dina grabs her sister by the hand and pulls her close. They both say, as if it was a rehearsed chorus, "We'll always be with you, *Aba*. Married or not, we'll always be with you."

Moshe pulls both his daughters in, hugging them tightly, and clears the knot in his throat. "My main concern has always been your happiness. I think you've already found it. Now you have to enjoy it, with moderation and good sense, so it can last you a lifetime."

Debbie punches Moshe with her elbow. "*You?* Talking about moderation and good sense?"

"Well, Debbie, the lessons of life are sometimes very hard, and thinking twice about major decisions can't do you any harm. I learned that the hard way."

Dina reassures him, "We're going to be fine, don't worry about us, *Aba*."

"If you want me not to worry, then *you'll* have to do the worrying."

Dina puts a kiss on her father's cheek. "We're not going to war, we're getting married."

Moshe shakes his finger at her. "Not you, little one, not yet. Until you're formally wedded, I'll still call the shots for you. Besides, everything in life is a mini-war, a fight or a struggle to get something done."

Ely interrupts. "Are you going to stop blabbering and get back to dancing?"

Amir barges in, giving Debbie a sip of *Rishon Le Zion* wine from the glass in his hand as he puts his arm around her neck. He winks at Moshe. "Are you trying to change Debbie's mind, Moshe? It's too late for that."

Moshe laughs. "I'm too anxious to get rid of her!"

Amir laughs. "I just asked the DJ to play one last song before the buffet starts, so enjoy it. Then we'll cut the cake."

When the music starts to fade, the DJ calls everyone to go to the buffet. Amir and Debbie, surrounded by friends and relatives, head for the long tables filled with salads, cold meats, seafood, spicy vegetables, and a large variety of tasty pastries.

Moshe's pager buzzes and he rushes inside to make a call. He returns two minutes later and heads straight for the DJ's microphone.

The crowd turns to Moshe as he taps the microphone to make sure it is on. He knows they expect a tearful goodbye to his daughter, but, to him at least, he has better news for them. He has wonderful news for them actually. He announces proudly, "I have great news! I was just on the phone with our HQ, and guess what?" Moshe is unperturbed by the shocked silence. "The Arabs are killing themselves. They're doing our job for us!"

Ely steps forward, his expression both puzzled and angry. "What are you talking about, Moshe? This isn't the time for playing games."

"I mean what I say. The Palestinians tried to assassinate the king of Jordan, and they failed, and now the king's entire army is chasing them."

Ely says, "And where does that leave us?"

"We're on high on alert, just in case. Effective immediately."

Amir steps forward, Debbie at his side. "We must report back to our units? Now?"

Ely rushes towards Moshe. He is furious. "You damn fool! You could have at least waited until our children had taken off. Or we could have told them to leave early. You *never* think!"

Amir is unshaken. "I'd hate to cancel my honeymoon, *Aba*, but you know that I will never run from duty."

Moshe's joy at the plight of his enemy vanishes. "I'm sorry," he says lamely. "I really didn't think." He looks at the reproachful faces gathered around him and the reality of what he's done sinks in: he's just ruined his daughter's most important day. Moshe tries to soften it. "Well, it's mostly the air force, you know. Some planes are already in the air, just in case."

Debbie protests. "In case? In case what? You said they're killing *each other*. It's my wedding day. *My day!*"

"Well, the Jordanians are doing too good a job. They're even bombing their refugee camps."

Ely's voice is harsh. "And HQ thinks we should give the Jordanians a hand? Is that it?"

Moshe tries explaining with a guilty voice. "No, but now the Syrians are moving against the Jordanians with armored units. And the Egyptians are on alert too."

Ely can barely contain himself. "Syrian armor on the move? Egypt on alert? And you're saying 'just in case'?"

Amir puts a hand on his father's shoulder. "Relax, father, it shouldn't be more than a couple days on alert. We'll be back in no time."

Ely shakes his head. "It's different when it's internal. Besides, HQ won't rule out the possibility of using this as an excuse to gather troops along the borders. Perhaps try something."

Moshe nods. "That's an option, but HQ doesn't seem to think so. There were no preparations made. This will be a quick one."

Ethan and a group of hot-headed friends are eager for action. They gather around Moshe and drill him with questions. "Are we going to engage the Syrians?" "Has the Syrian air force scrambled its planes?" "Have the Egyptians moved?"

Moshe is relieved to see someone else enthused by the possibility of crushing the Syrians, but he downplays the likelihood. "If the Syrians cross our red lines, yes. But it won't go that far. They'll back off, don't worry."

Ely's voice betrays his concern. "I hope you're right. I hope it doesn't escalate."

Moshe takes Debbie's and Amir's hands and presses them together. He feels terrible about his behavior. "I'm sorry. I forgot myself. I . . . I don't know what to say . . ."

Debbie lets him have it, her eyes filled with tears. "You didn't forget yourself, this *is* yourself. You forgot *me!* How could you, Dad?"

As Amir nods an "it's all right" sign to Moshe and wraps Debbie in his arms, Ethan shouts to everyone, "Well, the party was nearly over anyway. Could we at least have a quick bite before we go? I'd hate to leave all this good food."

Moshe picks up the microphone. "Please, listen up, everyone! What I've just told you, I haven't told you yet. Go, enjoy your dinner . . . just, do it quickly. That's an order."

The young men of the Israeli Defense Forces, don't need to hear that order more than once. They converge on the long line of tables, piled high with abundant food, and gulp it down in mere minutes, as if it were the last meal they'd have in weeks.

Moshe reaches for Debbie, wondering how he could fix this. She spins away from him. He cries out, "*Sliha* — I'm sorry, Debbie. I'm sorry."

With burning tears in her eyes, she pouts. "You spoiled the most beautiful day in my entire life!" And she turns her back on him.

Later, after the young men have returned to their homes to dress for battle, the news arrives that the Palestinian camps are being shelled and attacked by the Jordanian army. Meanwhile, Syrian tanks had started to move in, to help the Palestinians, but the Israeli air force circled overhead and drove them back. Without firing a shot.

Standing in his bedroom, Amir tries to explain the insane situation to Debbie. He quits his equipment check and takes her by the waist. "You know I'll be back in a couple of days, at most. I'll probably be back tomorrow. Relax, everything will be okay."

Debbie glances out the window at the garden below and says between tears, "Your father's already dressed, web gear and all. He's on his radio already. Ethan, too. The wedding night is ruined. Even the cake was done in a minute. No blessings, no sending of wishes, nothing."

Amir pulls her against him. He feels terrible. For a moment, he feels weak, and Debbie's wet eyes are a challenge he feels unable to resist, or ignore. Her desperate gaze is a call he *has* to answer. He wants to stay with her just as much as she wants him. Like her, Amir has been anticipating that night for a long time. Their eyes lock into each other's, closing the bond of their feverish bodies. Amir cannot turn his eyes away from Debbie's face. Her expression turns into one of yearning. She speaks softly, as her lips touch his, saying, "This was going to be our night. And they took it away from us."

Amir kisses her, then kisses away a tear on her cheek. "They took our wedding night away from us, but we still have a few moments, together . . . right now." Amir leads his bride over to the bed, gazing into her eager eyes as despair turns into romantic lust, and the adrenaline of desire is compounded by the one of fear. Debbie stifles her tears and, breathing heavily, begins to unbutton his shirt, while Amir tears clumsily at her dress.

A loud knocking sounds at the door.

Ethan's voice comes through the closed door. "I hope I'm not interrupting, but, there's a Jeep waiting for us downstairs, and a chopper at the base. We have to go . . . now. Sorry."

Debbie closes her eyes and sighs deeply. "Our moment in time . . . gone before it started . . ." Opening her eyes in horror, she pushes Amir and springs to her feet. "A Jeep . . . a chopper . . . You're not just reporting for duty, you're going on a mission!"

"Probably surveillance or reconnaissance. Don't worry." Amir is torn. He itches to go and answer his country's call. But how can he leave this bed?

"But there are Syrian tanks on the move!" Debbie protests.

"They're headed for Jordan, not here. Besides, our planes have already scared them off."

Debbie turns around and cries, "Promise me you'll be careful."

Amir squeezes her in his arms and whispers in her ear, "Of course I will." He looks into her eyes. "I thought you were used to this by now."

"I'm Moshe's daughter, and so, yes, I know. But with you—it's not the first time I've seen you go, but now it's different. I hate it. It's like a bad omen." Debbie lowers her head into her hands and hides her tears.

Amir kisses tears off her cheeks. "We'll get our *moment* back, and make it up tenfold, I swear. A hundred fold. As soon as I get back . . ."

"I thought we were finished with those horrible battles." Debbie's tone turns to anger. "That's what everyone said after the last one. Our borders are now secure, our army is invincible . . . all nonsense!"

"We have to do this, Debbie, so our children don't . . ."

"That's what our fathers said!"

"We still have to do it, until we reach a permanent solution."

"You still believe that?" she asks tearfully.

"Debbie, if you don't believe in it, you can't work toward it." Amir takes Debbie tenderly into his arms, and she smiles sweetly at him through her tears. He slowly lets go, kisses her one more time, and heads for the door, grabbing his gear along the way. The soldier in him took over.

---

Ameer is sitting in the back of the truck with his back resting against the cab, his body sore from the steel bed. They have been on the road for hours and are now entering Lebanon. Layal, half asleep, is slumped to his left, her head resting on his shoulder. Ameer's whole family and several friends ride along, baking in the sun, bouncing and hurting with every bump, wincing with every engine moan, every missed gear change. Ameer looks at the men around him, haplessly clenching useless rifles, their angry eyes challenging only the dust that blows into their faces.

Ameer looks back at the long convoy of trucks stretching out behind him. It all seems unreal. He thinks back to the young men dancing the *Dabké*, and himself as the solo dancer, hopping and jumping in the middle of their circle . . . when all of a sudden their camp came under heavy fire. The first rounds clearing the tanks' tubes were mistaken for the sound of the *tabble*, the wedding drum. A second later, the shells landed, and the ground started to shake under the advance of tanks. As men took up guns, a sentry ran in shouting, "Jordanians! It's the Jordanian army!"

Tarek immediately raised a white flag. The attackers were the troops of Zeid Ben Chaker, a staunch officer loyal to his king, and a bloody battle was guaranteed. Unlike other Palestinian leaders, fighting fellow Arabs was not part of Tarek's plan. He went to the Jordanian officer, and the two soldiers, who had high mutual respect, negotiated the withdrawal of the Palestinians, out of Jordan, with whatever they could carry.

This is how Ameer came to spend his wedding night in the back of a truck with his bride and her family. He couldn't even steal a moment away with Layal, as the trucks were already waiting . . . They carried their weapons, and their essential personal items, like clothes and documents. Layal managed to pack the new blankets and bed sheets which were meant to adorn her bridal bed. If there's any virtue to moving constantly, it's being particularly good at packing. The most important item everyone carries is the refugee registration card, the only proof that they "exist." Some still have a rusty house key, a cold souvenir, enduring the years just as poorly as its owners. Ameer lets out a yelp. "Our luck is cursed."

The proverb *Ejat el-hazeeneh tatefrah ma lakat matrah* was on everyone's lips. — The sad woman came to celebrate but never could. The *henna* Layal had worn was meant to deter evil, but it could do nothing to deter armored vehicles.

Tarek puts his hand on Ameer's knee, saying with a sad smile, "You know, son, in a way, you're better off than me."

Ameer raises an eyebrow. "How can that possibly be?"

"Well, on our wedding day, when I was running away from death with your mother, we drove a carriage. At least we're in a truck now."

Faris holds a plate of ribs. "And we managed to salvage some food." He takes a bite, and adds, "But we'll get back at them one day, trust me!"

Tarek says, "Remember, we drew first blood when we went for their king, Faris. If their policy doesn't suit us, that doesn't mean we should kill them. Remember who the real enemy is."

Samar snaps, "Look at us, packed in like sardines in a can! What kind of a life is this? Thank God Wassef is not here to see this."

Rima puts a hand on Samar's arm. "Relax, things will be better. We never got along with the Jordanians anyway. Lebanon will be different."

Tarek agrees. "We have some guarantees and some promises. The political climate in Lebanon is better for us. It's a nicer place to be, anyway."

Samar parses her lips. "In another camp?"

"Yes, a camp, but with real houses, and electricity and running water. Ameer and Layal will have their own place, I'll make sure of that."

Ameer hugs Layal and whispers to her ear, but it is loud enough for everyone to hear it, "Lebanon was our destination anyway."

Layal sits up, a sparkle in her eyes. "That's where we were going on our honeymoon?"

Ameer smiles. "Yes. And it still is. Let's hope we make it there in time. A UN officer I befriended helped me book a room in a hotel. It's the best and most expensive. It's on the beach. The booking starts today."

"Can we come and visit?" Faris asks, perking up. "They must have good food."

Ameer mimics a diving motion. "They even have a swimming pool."

Tarek slaps his son's knee. "Son, why do you need a swimming pool if you're on the beach? You're getting spoiled."

Samar says, "Oh Tarek. It's okay to be spoiled on your honeymoon. And no, Faris, you can't visit. Let someone have some peace and happiness sometime in this life. Wow! A hotel on the beach. I wonder what it would be like—"

"I wonder too. That's why we should visit." Faris insists.

Layal says, "We'll be more than happy to have you all as guests." Ameer opens his mouth to protest, as she adds, "But, perhaps not all at the same time."

Sami breaks his hours-long silence, a wide smile adorning his face. "I wouldn't mind a dip in the pool."

"We'll be more than happy to have you, brother," Ameer says. "But you need a bathing suit, okay? This isn't the river, it's a hotel, and your underwear won't do."

Layal punches Ameer with her elbow. "You don't have a bathing suit either."

Ameer sighs, and then stares at the long convoy behind them, filled with comrades and their families. He drifts back to the many times they had to pack and leave. This last time, they're being pushed away much farther than before.

He says, "You people did notice, that this is the wrong direction, as far as Palestine is concerned."

Rima snaps at him. "Ameer! We were doing fine, and you had to bring that up?"

"There's no reason to see this as a bad move," Tarek says. "We weren't getting anywhere, left in camps to rot. Now we'll be allowed to continue our fight from Lebanon, and we'll have autonomy. Think about it as a stop along the way, a decent stop. We need to get organized, to sort out who is on our side. It's for the best."

Ameer sits up a bit and asks, "But for how long? It's *our* homes we want, our real homes, and our land, our Palestine!"

"Things couldn't go on the way they were. We have to sort out our problems with the Arabs. Inter-Arab fighting is Israel's dream come true. The Israelis must be having one hell of a good time right now."

Ameer says, "I heard the Israeli air force flew over the Syrian tanks that were sent to help us, and drove them away. They sent the new plane, the Phantom. Four of them were enough. They didn't even have to fire."

Faris puts his head between his hands and sighs. "What a crazy world we live in. The Israelis helping the Jordanians against the Syrians, who were helping us against the Jordanians."

Tarek says, "Israel has all the reasons in the world to turn Jordan into a peaceful neighbor. Imagine if they had no reason to fear from that side. What a relief to their military."

Ameer clenches a fist. "And that's what we should take advantage of. Israel is cornered. We have to keep it that way, overstretch their resources, and coordinate our attacks —"

"What attacks?" Samar lashes at him. "We're running away in a truck, we barely have clothes, and we don't even know where we're going. Even *Abu Ammar* — Yasser Arafat — had to flee to Cairo disguised as a woman. What a disgrace!"

"Relax, mother," Layal says with a soft voice. "Let's wait and see what happens when we get there." She turns her eyes toward Ameer. "Can we talk about our honeymoon again, please? Tell me more about the hotel."

Ameer takes out a worn brochure and shows it around. "Well, it's a large building on the beach, with rooms overlooking the sea. They have a swimming pool and three restaurants."

Layal snatches the brochure from him as Faris asks, "*Three* restaurants?"

Ameer rolls his eyes. "I'm actually more anxious to see the new camp. If father is right, it shouldn't be such a bad place. We'll be spending more than a honeymoon there."

Rima laughs bitterly. "That's great, that's just what we need."

"What do you mean?" asks Ameer. "I thought you wanted a decent place."

"*Our* decent place, not some nice camp in someone else's country. I want Palestine!"

"She's right," Samar says. "Listen to yourselves. Hotels, nice camps.

Before you know it, you'll abandon the fight. Why kill and die for something when what you have is almost as good? If the soil here is just the same as it is there, then so what?"

Tarek nods. "You're right to think that way, just one more generation and Palestine will be completely forgotten."

"That's exactly what I was thinking," Samar says.

Tarek has a stern look. "Resilience, my friends. It's up to us to keep the fire burning. The desire has to stay alive in our children."

Ameer bangs the butt of his kalash against the truck bed. "None of us will settle for anything less than our own village! Your village, father, Dar Moussa, where you came from."

Faris shouts, "They are our villages, all of them. By Allah, we will get them back!"

Tarek says, "That's the spirit! I wish we could raise a toast." He stands and looks at the long line of trucks following them. He leans over to his rucksack and takes out a folded Palestinian flag and a pole. He fixes the flag on the pole, and holds it aloft in the wind, waving it and yelling, "Palestine, *ard al joudoud.*" — Land of our ancestors. Soon truckloads of men, women and children are waving flags and shouting war cries along the empty road.

Suddenly, two Israeli jets shriek overhead. Ameer leaps to his feet and snatches the flag from Tarek. He climbs up on the cab, waving the flag from side to side, his strong figure standing defiantly over the truck, shouting and cursing at the warplanes in Hebrew. Ameer had learned to speak, read and write Hebrew as part of his military training.

The two Israeli jets fly low over the convoy, as if they were going to attack, but they do not fire. They spread terror instead. Ameer and his group are still alive thanks only to the good mood of the Jewish warrior flying overhead.

# CHAPTER 16

Face and hands smudged with dark camouflage paint, Amir moves swiftly to take cover behind a large rock. He looks at the other side of the river with his binoculars and signals for Ethan to join him with the rest of their platoon. They are about to ambush a group of Palestinian terrorists. Jordanian sources have warned them that a small number of rogue *fedayeen*, about half a dozen or so men, are preparing to cross the Jordan River that same night into Israel. It was a thank-you tip for having scared off the Syrian tanks two days ago. Thanks to that, Jordanian forces had completely routed the armed Palestinian guerillas. Most Palestinians either fled or were in the process of leaving. Still others, already absorbed by the local population, were joining civilian life, becoming Jordanian citizens. But a handful of guerillas remained, and the Jordanian forces, in an effort not to alienate Arab public opinion even further, thought it better to let the Israelis handle them. Allowing these small incursions to depart from their territory is a smart political face-saver for Jordan. It shows they haven't given up the fight for Arab rights.

Amir's mind isn't totally focused, though. It travels through the fading light, gliding across the river's peaceful murmur. Through the darkening waters, Debbie's tearful face looks back at him. Amir had indeed been assigned a mission. Out and away, without a phone anywhere near. Stealthy movement on the opposite river bank triggers Amir out of his thoughts. He peers through his binoculars. What he sees is not a half-a-dozen guerillas. It looks like an entire enemy company preparing to cross. Was it a bad tip? A trap? He turns to Ethan. "Troops coming. A lot of them."

Ethan asks, "How many? Anything heavy?"

"About three platoons. Machine guns and RPGs. Heavy rucksacks."

"Son of a bitch! That's a raiding force, not a terrorist group."

Amir lowers the binoculars. "The sun is down. It'll be pitch dark soon. I think they'll wait for that. They can spot our regular patrols and will try to cross between them. They obviously don't expect us to know about them."

Ethan takes the binoculars and searches. "Your orders?"

"We're outnumbered three to one. We'll never get reinforcements in time. Not without them noticing it. But we can't let them get away. Nor through."

"Right. Neither is an option. Tonight we have the element of surprise. Let's make them drive into us. We can wipe off a full platoon before we even start, and —"

Amir shakes his head, interrupting. "And we'll be left with two more to deal with. Still outnumbered and outgunned. We have to set a multistage ambush. We must minimize our casualties, and maximize theirs."

Ethan lowers the binoculars. "We have mortar back-up on stand-by. Six tubes."

Amir nods and turns to his sergeant, signaling for him to close in. "We need the mortars ready for immediate action."

"Airburst, sir?"

"Airburst, and flares. I'll give the coordinates soon."

Ethan looks puzzled. "You know where you want them?"

Amir is still figuring it out in his head, but he relents and tells Ethan what he has in mind. "Here's the plan: Loaded with equipment as they are, there are only two places in this area they can cross — right in front of us, which seems to be their intent, and about two hundred meters downstream. The crossing here is better concealed, with the bushes they can use for staging, so it'll probably be their primary route. We wait for them to get deep in, and then one squad opens fire to cut their front formation. It'll be easy — they'll be neck-deep in water."

Ethan raises the binoculars. "Let me see."

As Ethan scans the river, Amir goes on, "The others will try to help. Hearing only three or four guns, they won't be careful. You know how excited they get when the shooting starts. Darkness and a couple of overzealous sergeants mean they won't resist the temptation to try to bring back some Israeli bodies. Especially after what they've just been through."

Amir points at a cluster of rocks below them. "When they counterattack, the squad that opened fire should take cover behind those rocks and stay down. They won't be able to immediately retreat without being exposed to fire from the enemy on the far bank. So instead, they stay under cover until the mortars hit, then fire on anyone who makes it ashore here. Put the corporal in that position, as squad one, and tell them I want back-up weapons, grenades, and spare ammo at the ready."

"Okay, I get your drift. Now the other guys open up, from different positions."

Amir nods. "Once a large part is in the water, not before. They will cover them from positions on the bank. That's for our mortars to handle. I want two squads spread out here, downstream from Squad One. They have to be scattered and not present good targets for crew-served weapons, and to confuse the enemy. At this point, the Palestinians will realize they haven't just surprised a couple of sentries, and they'll try to outflank us."

Ethan turns the binoculars towards the other crossing point. "From over there . . ."

"Exactly. They won't expect us to be there as well."

Ethan aims his finger towards the other crossing. "Can I have the honor?"

"Yes. You're squad Four. You'll lay claymores with manual triggers just below the top of the river bank and upstream from the crossing, then take covered positions downstream from it. Your mission is to let them cross, and then close the trap."

That surprises the sergeant. "Let them cross?"

"Right." Amir has a cold look. "I want to annihilate that force, not push it back to fight another day. Squad Four will wait for them to cross and head toward us as they try to outflank squads Two and Three. You wait for them to enter the minefield, then go for the claymores and open up with small arms. Don't let anyone through. The river bank exit downstream is an absolute priority. Remember, we don't really know what they're up to."

The sergeant asks, "When do we call in the mortars?"

"When they're in the river. Against their support positions on the bank first, then the rest. Our airburst rounds will shred them to pieces. The other coordinates for the mortars will be the second crossing point, in case Squad Four has to open up early. Flares will go above the river, and on the bank behind it."

Ethan looks jubilant. "We'll have them in a half circle of fire. That's genius, Amir."

"I don't want us to shoot each other. I'll lead squad Five and act as reserve, with the radio. I'll be scanning the frequencies for any transmissions in Arabic, just in case they have radios, too. Three squads are enough for the initial contact, then Four will join in at the end. My squad will stand back and move along the arc as needed. Everything clear?"

"Yes!" The sergeant is clearly pleased. "I'll distribute the ammo, the mines, and position the men."

Amir looks at the men around him. "Sergeant. You're squads Three and Two, corporal, you're One. Ethan, as I said, you're squad Four."

Ethan itches in anticipation. "I'll be in position, with the minefield set-up."

"I thought you like to blow people up. Don't forget, we have to surprise them. If they send a scouting team in first, don't engage. Wait for as many as possible to commit to the water. Use your judgment. Those men are heading for our homes: they must not get through. We can't let them live to fight another day either."

Ethan rubs his hands together. "I don't mind fighting another day."

Amir shakes his head. "Think about it this way, my friend: as long as we're fighting, it means we haven't won, and our homes aren't safe. That's what my father taught me, and Ely is always right." Amir pauses for a second, then turns deadly serious. "Now let's prepare to unleash hell."

# CHAPTER 17

Ameer stands on his balcony, overlooking their new camp. Called *Burj al-Barajneh* — tower of the towers — it overlooks the southern outskirts of Beirut, not far from Beirut's International Airport. From what he can see, the camp 'scatters' rather than 'towers.' They have been here for a couple of months now, and he has just finished fixing up his new house. He is quite satisfied with it, and Layal loves it too. With its plaster facade and primitive windows, it looks like most other houses in their camp, albeit slightly larger. Amir has two bedrooms upstairs, and a full bathroom, while the living space, kitchen, and dining room are all on the ground floor. Their lives are now starting to take a relatively steady pace.

In the distance, the modern buildings of Beirut glitter in the afternoon sun, and Ameer wonders if his people will ever get their own city, their own country. Tall buildings, wide streets, cozy restaurants, crowded cafes, beautiful beaches . . . their own! Ameer had never seen anything like Beirut before. It looks like a dream. Ever since arriving, Ameer has been awed by the city's many havens. He went running a couple of times on the warm beach of *ramlet el bayda*, or "white sands," which, unlike their camp, is actually true to its beautiful name.

He took Layal to Hamra Street — discreetly, since the Palestinians are still seen as temporary guests — and they enjoyed a dessert at the Café de Paris. Ameer wonders what Paris itself must be like. That was only the Café de Paris, in Beirut, and it was heaven. Even the flies have a better life here, Ameer had joked as he pointed to one that had landed in his ice cream bowl. *'Where we live, they eat shit.'* For the first time in a long while, Ameer and Layal both feel like real human beings. The only thing that bothers Ameer is how people always seemed shocked whenever his handgun showed from under his shirt. *What? I have a permit for it! No, not from the Lebanese Authorities, from the Palestinian Authorities.* Nobody argued . . . Palestinian rule is starting to prevail. Lebanon had signed up to it, actually, with the 1969 Cairo agreement. Their attitude and their violet influence were starting to prevail too. In the Café de Paris, Hamra Street, Beirut.

Ameer's gaze returns to his derelict camp. The scorched streets down below are in a constant state of tumult. Noisy workshops and busy supply stores are mixed in amid the houses. A car electrician is right next to the butcher shop, while the grocery store also doubles as the bakery. The clamor of traveling merchants, shouting mothers, barking dogs, and clucking chicken fills the air. Children are constantly dashing back and forth, wooden rifles dangling around their necks, their hardened bare feet more like those of cavemen than those of kids.

Layal joins him on the balcony and scans the camp. Ameer takes her hand and tries to smile. He notices her 'You don't fool me' look as she gazes into his eyes and gently asks, "What's bothering you now? What's wrong?"

Ameer shakes his head.

Layal persists. "What is it, really? You've been promoted, you have a good salary, and we have a decent house, a real house, with our own bedroom. All the comfort we've dreamed of! Just like your father promised."

Ameer sighs. "That's exactly the point. We're being bought. We're living better, we have homes, we are paid soldiers in our own army, most of us have enough, and everything we need."

"So where's the catch?"

"We have all that we need. Nobody's willing to die for what we *want*. Not anymore. Just look at those cases of fruits. Back in Jordan, one of those would have to feed the whole community for a week. Now every family has a case of their own . . ."

Layal looks out at a group of men playing cards on a table in front of the fruit and legume shop. They are smoking from *nargilas* and playing backgammon, right there between cases of tomatoes and cucumbers. "It's killing the men's fighting spirit?"

"Not *my* men, but I am not sure about some of the rest."

Layal shakes her head. "I don't think the men are getting soft, at least not yet. Going home is still on everybody's mind and in everybody's dreams. You train your troops every day. They're as eager as ever for action."

"They're going to have some, pretty soon. We'll have a mission very soon."

"A mission? We've barely settled!"

"That's exactly the point. The PLO wants to make it clear to the enemy that we haven't lost our willingness to fight, or our commitment to the cause."

"Does anyone know what the mission is?"

"No." Ameer squeezes her hand gently and smiles. "I couldn't tell you anyway."

Layal frowns, but it soon turns into laughter as she points her finger to the street. Faris is running, wearing his track suit, and waving his *kalash* up and down with both hands, singing military tunes. A dozen boys follow him, doing the same with their toy guns, echoing back his cries, each elbowing the others to be the first one behind him.

"Faris!" Ameer waves him to come up.

Faris runs in place and shouts, "I'll be right up!"

Ameer decides that if they're going to discuss the mission, he wants Tarek in on it, too. "Actually, I'm coming down. We'll go for a walk." Faris stops and claps his hands to dismiss the boys around him. *"Yallah yallah bi kaffeh lyom!"* Come on, enough for today!

Ameer gives Layal a kiss and trots down the stairs. He peeks into his father's house across the street from his. Tarek is reading a newspaper in his sitting room. "Yaba, will you join us?"

Tarek promptly puts his paper aside and nods a 'yes'. Although he wouldn't be part of the operation, he is in charge of the entire outfit, operational planning and procedures included. This will be Ameer's mission, to set a standard for young officers to follow. Tarek joins Ameer and Faris, and they walk up the street, greeting and saluting friends and comrades along the way. They head for Tarek's office, near the training ground on the outskirts of the camp.

Tarek asks, "How are your men doing?"

*"Tamam!"* — Perfect. — "They're in training now. We can go take a look."

"They're going to be happy to learn about the operation," adds Faris.

Tarek looks at Faris—he is practically salivating at the prospect. This could be a problem. "Not a word to anyone, and that's a strict order. We can't risk compromising security."

Faris has a concerned look. "You think they have spies among us?"

Tarek nods. "No one knows for sure, but there are many new faces in the camp. If there aren't any spies yet, there will be soon. I'm sure the Israelis already have girls working the neighborhood, searching for information. And then there are all the traveling merchants. They go in and out, unhindered, unquestioned, seeing every corner and every street in the camp, and talking to everyone. Security is a nightmare. Even inside Beirut, we have put a number of suspected people under surveillance."

"Inside Beirut? What do they want from the Lebanese?" Faris asks.

"Any information on us or our allies. We think we're close to catching one of them. An owner of a restaurant on Hamra Street. That's top secret. But remember: we have to be careful. Everything is on a 'need to know' basis from here on."

"Father's right. Don't give any specifics to the men."

Faris is frustrated. "It's not like we even have any specifics. When do we get orders and plans?"

Tarek puts a hand on his shoulders. "Right now, Faris, right now. But son, learn to relax and start thinking about military operations as missions, and not as a way to unleash your personal hatred."

Faris has a sadistic look. "Just mixing work with pleasure."

"Faris, from now on, we act as an army, and we follow strict orders from the top. There will be formal debriefings after every mission, and full reports from all officers."

Ameer clenches his fist in excitement. "We're part of something big now. Don't you see, Faris? *Nahnou awlad al thawra*. We are the sons of the revolution.

Faris' gaze settles on the training ground as they approach. "It's what we dreamed about."

Ameer waves to his sergeant, who is busy running the men through the obstacle course. Tarek taps Ameer on the back, and motions for him and Faris to enter his field office on the ground floor of the administration building, just off the training area.

Inside, Tarek opens a small safe inside a closet, takes out a map, and unfolds it on the metal desk. They sit on wood chairs. "We're going for a military target, and our main objectives are maximum damage and proper withdrawal. Ameer, you've been chosen for this operation, with Faris as your second in command. We want to bring all of our boys back with us, remember? All eyes are on us, and we should set a good example."

"We're the *crème de la crème* of the liberation army," Faris whispers in a skewered French as he peers at the map. "I learned that on the French news broadcast on the Lebanese TV, *Canal Neuf.*"

Tarek points to an area in the occupied territories and removes some photographs from an envelope. "This is the target."

Ameer says, "It looks like a military compound."

"It is. These are military barracks, housing one of their border patrol units. They've been coming down hard on us lately, and we want to hit them where it hurts. Intel says there's about fifty men in total, with roughly half of them in there at any time."

"What are we supposed to do when we get there?" asks Faris. "Go in and start shooting?"

"Exactly. Of course, you'll prepare an escape route, and you'll mine and booby-trap it to delay pursuit. We expect the borders to be under close surveillance after the hit. If our border guards tell us security has been increased and the alarm has been given, then your contact will take you to a safe place to wait until it's okay to come back."

Ameer feels a rush of energy swell his every vein. "What will our strength be? We need a full company for this. We need mortars and explosives."

Tarek puts a hand on his shoulder. "It's your call. Do the full planning."

Ameer focuses on the map intensely, and then examines the photos. His mind is racing. It is his mission. Finally. He knows his father would keep an eye on the details, but still, once they leave Lebanon, he will be the one leading. He is a full-fledged officer now, a *mulazim* — a lieutenant — with two stars on his shoulders. It's a good feeling.

"I figure about twenty men should go in, and head in small groups to the sleeping quarters and sentry posts." Ameer says, confidently, "While another twenty or so stay on the heavier weapons around the exits for fire support. They'll have RPGs, machine guns, and light mortars. Whatever we can carry. We'll go for ammunition depots and fuel tanks too. That will add to the confusion and casualties."

"Twenty? Is that enough?" asks Faris.

"Yes," Ameer says. "I don't want the men to shoot each other. We'll establish fire zones for each team, and coordinate the extraction." He looks at his father and goes on, "About five four-men teams will work best. With belt-fed PKMs and lots of grenades, we can hurt them bad."

Tarek nods. He takes a paper and a pen from a drawer. "I agree. We need to plan exact objectives and circulation once inside. How many other men?"

Ameer already has this figured out. "I'll need a third platoon to prepare the exit route, mine it and set ambushes, take care of any wounded, and carry extra logistics. More than that will ruin our stealth going in."

Tarek seems satisfied, and hands his son the paper and pen. "How do you deploy inside the barracks? How do you withdraw? Show me point-by-point, with a timeline, and an abort plan. The way back to the border is your most critical part."

Ameer first makes a list of essentials for the mission: reconnaissance, infiltration, assault, extraction and withdrawal to safety. Ameer has learned his lessons well. With his father watching, Ameer sketches rapidly. "We'll have predetermined targets inside the camp for each team. I see three sleeping quarters; one team each. Just a quick hit and run, from the entrances and all through to the exit." He points to the auxiliary buildings. "The other two teams handle the security posts then do cover and support where needed. They'll start with the guards in the towers as we first open up. Once we're retreating, they'll have a go at the ammo storage and fuel tanks, here and here." He pauses for a second. "And we need to consider the possibility of the whole thing being uncovered before we get in."

Tarek's face changes to dead serious. "Abort immediately and withdraw. That's an order. You'll have predetermined meeting points with the locals."

Ameer realizes the danger. "We will do that."

Tarek has more advice. "Do not forget, you need to keep track of any unit that is outside the barracks and may come back. You cannot risk having them all over you before you retreat."

Ameer approves. He still has a couple of questions for his father. "What do we use for transport, once we cross the border? Do we go in as *fellaheen*?"

"There's a major construction site not too far from the compound. We have people on the inside, and they'll help us. Once past the border, your cover will be as construction workers. You will use pickup trucks for your transport and escape. We'll assign a strike team to help you break back through the border. They will control and secure one of the pre-assigned crossing points."

Tarek points at different spots on the map and says, "We'll also create a diversion at another point along the border. It'll confuse them, and they'll think it's you trying to make it back and they'll converge there. That should give you some breathing room. And in case you have to stay, they'll probably think you made it back. Since it's at night and at close range, don't worry about their air support. But the mission has to be swift, and over before sunrise." Tarek puts the map back into the safe and motions for Ameer and Faris to head outside. "Let's leave it for now. Think about it tonight, and we'll meet again tomorrow."

Ameer puts the paper he has scribbled his notes on into his pocket and walks out with Faris, his father just behind them. His thoughts are on the mission. Soon he will face a major test, and a chance to get back at the Israelis.

———

Amir and Debbie have been enjoying married life for two months. But today, Debbie is having something of a breakdown. One of their best friends, Jason, and many other members of his unit, were killed the night before as they slept in their barracks. A Palestinian assault team had infiltrated their base, fired on everyone, and vanished into the night.

Amir stands in his bathroom, nervously sweeping his face with a razor blade as he tries for a perfect shave. Debbie is dashing back and forth between the bathroom and the adjoining bedroom. She clenches her fists, cursing and muttering as she gathers a pair of black corduroy pants and a silk shirt to wear at Jason's funeral. As Amir peers into his bathroom mirror for a last touch on his shave, Debbie startles him as she shouts practically to his ear. "My God! Is it an exchange market for death? We take out some of their soldiers, then they kill some of ours? Is it ever going to end, Amir? How long do we have to go on like this?"

Amir winces as the blade nicks his skin, marring his efforts. He wipes the blood with his finger and looks at Debbie in the mirror. "This is a war of attrition. They cause us minor damage; we cause them *more* minor damage —"

"Until it's you who gets killed, and I get to be the one everyone feels sorry for?"

"This has nothing to do with you and me. We're just two people; maybe soon enough we'll have a family. We're striving and sacrificing to achieve peace over the land of Israel, secure our borders and, one day maybe, achieve peace with our neighbors."

"You think that's possible?"

"There's no other choice, for both of us. Soon, the Arabs will have to see that we are here to stay, in *our* land. We have to make them understand that hard ways won't work with us. They will *have* to talk with us."

"In the meantime, more people will die." Debbie collapses on a chair in the bathroom.

Amir kneels next to her. He is about to bury a friend and isn't in the mood for making up rosy outlooks. "As I said. More people will die, until one side yields to the reality. Not us. We *are* reality, and we are prevailing. We will keep on killing them until they understand."

Debbie is not convinced. "Our borders are supposed to be safe. Look what happened."

Amir has an angry tone, as he buttons his jacket. "We — well, they were complacent. Thank God half of them were absent without leave. But no one was manning his post, and even the sentries were killed where they stood. Or probably slept. Those poor bastards. I can see them waking up panicked and screaming, only to be riddled with bullets in their beds. *I can see it as if I were there myself.* Those Palestinians knew their job, and knew it well." Amir pauses before going on, "We never thought they could attack a hard target such as this. The surprise was total."

Debbie puts her shoes on. "I feel deeply for them. I feel what all the wives, mothers, and children feel . . . As if death had stricken our home, as if death will strike our home . . . like it did with mother years ago."

Amir snaps his belt on. "We have to stay strong. Our fathers created our nation from nothing, and now it's up to us to make their effort permanent. In the meantime, more good people will die. We must make peace with that hard fact."

Debbie sits on the bed and puts her head between her hands. "I don't want to think about it. I cannot bear the thought of losing you. I wouldn't want to live without you."

Amir sits beside her. "If that happens, God forbid, you can't think about your loss. Think about what it brought to our nation. We don't die for nothing. Our blood is the nation's blood, and when a soldier dies, it's for a purpose and a reason."

Debbie looks up, her face full of tears. "None of that will matter the day your commanding officer shows up at the front door, not knowing how to knock..."

Amir pulls her in, kisses her gently behind the ear and whispers. "You have to be strong and brave, and we have to..." He shows her the time on his watch. "We have to get ready. We can't be late for a funeral."

---

A crowd of children, women, and teenagers watches Ameer, surrounded by some of his men, and still pumped up by the success of his military mission just a few days before, as they explain and role-play various parts of the operation that made every headline.

A small group of unfamiliar men and a lone woman approach Ameer's training area just outside the camp. With their mixed civilian and military clothing, and strange weapons, they appear to be hardcore mercenaries. A tough-looking, uniformed Palestinian officer leads the way. Layal dashes past the mercenaries and trots to her husband. She grabs him by the hand and pulls him out of the training arena.

Ameer shouts, "Take a break!" and signals for his sergeant to give the men ten minutes rest. Glancing warily at the strangers, his troops head for water jugs.

Ameer watches the group approach. He recognizes the uniformed leader as a high-ranking PLO officer named Abu-Raad — *Father of thunder*. Abu Raad is in charge of special training for their crack units. He'd taken part in many aggressive operations, going deeper into enemy territory than most, and causing significant damage to a number of Israeli communities. He is also known for losing many of his own men in the process. Palestinian civilians have always paid dearly for Abu Raad successes, since they are usually the victims of Israel's retaliatory attacks.

Layal asks, "Who are these people? They look like uncouth monsters."

"The officer is PLO, Unit Seventeen. It's Arafat's Special Forces. I don't know about the others. They want us in with their units. They did approach us a couple of times."

Ameer nods towards Tarek and Faris as they approach from the opposite direction. "Father must know what this is about."

As the strangers draw closer, Layal studies them. "They look European. Look at those tall, blond ones, maybe they're Russian? That short one looks Chinese."

"Or Japanese. I can't tell the difference. Must be here for training."

Tarek and Faris reach them. Layal squeezes Ameer's arm. "Mercenaries? Since when? We don't need people to fight for us. We have all the men we need."

Tarek says, "She's right, Ameer. I hope they don't impose outsiders on us. I wouldn't bet my life on someone who's fighting for money."

"I don't think they're mercenaries. The Unit Seventeen officer, Abu Raad . . . I think it's about training and Special Operations. They must come from resistance groups like us."

Tarek nods. "Let's talk to them. We aren't being good hosts."

They head for the group, who has stopped in front of the office's closed door, waiting for them. Tarek salutes. "*Salam aleykoum*, Abu Raad, You're welcome here."

Abu Raad bows his head, his battle-scared face trying for a pleasant reply. "*Aleykoum as salam*. Tarek, right? Lieutenant colonel, in charge of the camp?"

Tarek salutes and extends his hand. "Right, I am. And let me introduce you to . . ."

Abu Raad reaches out for the handshake, and Ameer notices that his hand is just as scarred as his face. "I know, your son, Ameer. Soon to be captain, I hear."

Tarek proudly smiles. "He's going to catch up with me."

"Not today. You're a full colonel as of now. I have the papers with me, as well as the insignia." He turns to Faris. "And you must be Faris."

Faris nods. "I'm Faris, indeed. How come you know so much about us?"

"Well, I've seen your files and studied your cases. You're being promoted as well, Faris, to lieutenant, as soon as Ameer gets his captain's third star, which shouldn't be more than two or three days."

A promotion is always a good thing, but Ameer suspects there must be something behind it. Promotions do happen fast during wartime, but still, he's far too young for captainship. And his father hasn't taken part in military action for months now. His next promotion wasn't due for a year.

Tarek is thinking the same thing. He looks Abu-Raad in the eyes, and says, "What are you going to ask us to do in exchange for these early promotions?"

Abu Raad smiles. "You don't have to put it that way, colonel . . . I'll explain, but first let me introduce you to our advisors. They come from all over the world. They're here to assist us in our fight against the Zionists."

Tarek says, "Let's go inside. We'll have a drink, and get to know each other."

"Please, after you."

Ameer glances toward Layal and shrugs. "Go on home. We'll talk later." He follows the group into the office.

———

Tarek, suspicious of Abu Raad, leads the way to his office in the center of their camp. The upper floor contains a radio room, an observation room that overlooks the camp and facilities for him and his personal guards. The ground floor, besides his own office, consists of a room for on-duty guards, an office for his secretary, a filing room, an office for his aide, and a sitting room, which is where Tarek invites the entire group to sit.

Tarek's aide and secretary greet the visitors cordially, while the guards salute.

Tarek asks, "Would you prefer cold drinks, or some Arabic coffee? We have tea as well . . ."

Abu Raad looks at the sweaty faces of his men. "I think I speak for all of us by asking for cold drinks, thank you, colonel."

Tarek nods to his secretary to bring the drinks, and she responds with a raised eyebrow and a complicit smile—she must have noticed the 'colonel' part. Abu Raad hands Tarek a small wooden box. "Everything is here. Of course, there will be an official ceremony later, but I thought I'd hand this over now."

Tarek's secretary is all smiles as she walks back in with a tray of ice-cold soft drinks.

With everyone served and seated, Tarek says, "Okay, comrade Abu Raad, why don't you introduce us?"

"Of course." Abu Raad points to the Japanese sitting to his right. The young man stands and bows mechanically. "This is Akira, from the Japanese Red Army. They recently split from the Japanese Communist Party. Akira is a martial arts specialist, as well as an expert in exotic assassination methods. Poisons, gases, darts, arrows, you ask for it, he knows it." He puts a hand on Akira's shoulder and smiles. "And they work; I've seen it first-hand."

Tarek is skeptical. "These are very particular techniques you use, Akira. May I ask how they fit into our military context?"

"They don't," Abu Raad says, answering for the Japanese fighter. "Akira isn't here to help us shoot down raiding Phantoms; he's here to teach you how to kill a Zionist general while he sunbathes in the Cote d'Azur, or skis in the Alps. He will also teach you to kill with anything at hand — ropes, blades, or even just your bare hands."

Tarek's mouth tightens. He doesn't like what he's hearing. "Why? We don't need those skills for the kind of missions we have. Is there a change of methodology?"

"Let me go on." Abu Raad turns toward the two stone-faced blond giants. "Hans here is from the Baader Meinhof Group. He's also a close-combat specialist. Together with Ralph, our weapons specialist, he'll teach us the best techniques for using all sorts of guns under every conceivable circumstance. From contact range to a kilometer away, silenced twenty-two's to anti-tank rifles. When it comes to firearms, they know best. They'll also teach you how to customize and fine-tune your weapons."

The two Germans barely nod as their names get mentioned. Their stature and their expressionless, confident features impress Tarek and his entire group.

Ameer mutters, "We'll turn into mechanical killers."

Faris whispers back with a cruel smirk, "It's about time."

"Speaking of custom solutions, this here is my friend Tony." Tony stands and smiles to everyone around, nodding to Tarek. He is thin and fair-skinned, a big nose adorning his smiling face, but Tarek can see the shrewd killer in his eyes.

Abu Raad goes on. "Tony is from Italy. Believe me when I say, gentlemen, Tony walks into your kitchen, Tony comes out with a bomb. Let Tony into your room, and there will be nothing left in it that is safe to touch, use, or even look at. Tony is our demolition, booby-trapping and bombing expert. He will also teach you how to make single-use non-metallic guns. He also knows more than you can imagine about electrical systems, detonators, and timers. He always has a surprise for the enemy."

Still wondering where Abu Raad was leading them, Tarek gestures to the man and woman who sit together on the small couch in the corner. "And the gentlemen here? The lady?"

"Rafael and Maria are a husband-and-wife team. They're guerilla warfare experts, straight from Uncle Fidel. Rafael has the best collection of cigars in the world, and it's constantly replenished. They'll organize our structure and enhance it for guerilla warfare. They'll also complement our knowledge in communication and signaling."

Tarek is relieved to hear about something he can use, something more down to earth. He smiles as he points to the two Abu Raad hasn't introduced yet. "And the good looking athletes? They're here to pick on our women?"

Abu Raad has a thin smile. "These two boys, as we like to call them, are Nicolas and Alexis. They're elite troopers from Russia. Besides being Olympic champions and top soldiers in the Spetznatz, they'll teach us . . ." He bends down to the men. *"A shoto vi budeti nas utchet?"*

"*Bce!*" they reply simultaneously.

Abu Raad laughs. "They said they're here to teach us everything." He goes on, "Besides teaching us *everything*, there's no one like them when it comes to infiltration techniques. They are trained for sabotage missions deep into NATO lines. They'll teach us how to go in, accomplish the mission, and come back."

Faris declares, "We're already doing that."

"We're going to improve your ways of getting in so you can hit targets that the enemy thinks are safe. You're going to do it not just by land, but also by air, using hang gliders, and by sea, using small craft and scuba tanks. You'll go deeper, hit harder. We won't leave any places where they feel safe. We'll turn their days into dark nights, and their nights into hell."

Tarek says, "There won't be many such missions if we go as deep as you say." He scrutinizes Abu Raad, searching for a clue to his real motives. Did their commanders just want to turn them into 'one mission' men? Train hard, go in, maximize damage, and to hell with coming back? Or are they just supposed to increase the lethality and reach of their troops?

Abu Raad lowers his gaze and changes the subject. "We'll meet tomorrow morning, if that's all right, for an in-depth introduction of the training schedule. We'll show you everything we'll be doing, as well as the changes in structure and organization that are coming. Training with heavier weapon will take place in the Bekaa valley, and more advanced training will follow, almost certainly abroad."

"Abroad?" Tarek is surprised. His fears are materializing. The groups these men came from were not the kind of influence he wanted for his son and his men.

"Eastern Europe and Russia. Top elements only."

As everyone departs, shaking hands all around, Tarek remains in his office. He is deeply perturbed. Sure, he wants to win the war. The sooner the better; and the more damage done to the enemy, the better still. If they could hurt them more with special training, then okay. If they could become better fighters, he definitely wants in. The conflict is becoming international, and if that means international attention, then Tarek would be all for it. But it could also mean incessant manipulations for other causes, and he can't shake the feeling that things are getting out of hand. These new guys are fanatics, killing and maiming randomly, spreading horror among civilian populations. Being aided by hired fanatics wouldn't help them enhance their image. Is their fight moving toward such extremism? Assassinations? Shameful, even upon a hated and ruthless enemy. What if they were assigned civilian targets, as many others already have? Tarek had always insisted on military objectives only—he is not a killer of women and children.

As a matter of fact, that is exactly his grievance with the Zionist enemy. Men like Abu Raad like to use this as a rationale, but Tarek knows how to respond. The Palestinian cause is a just one, and that's what makes it worth fighting, killing, and dying for. Tarek also knows that there are many, amongst the 'enemy,' like his old friend Samuel, who care about the plight of the Palestinian people and want the conflict to end in just peace.

Tarek will have to have a serious talk with Ameer and Faris about this new turn of events. The whole purpose of their fight is to go home. How could they achieve any gain, political or military, using these methods? Tarek fears Ameer's generation is being steered in the wrong direction. Ameer's potential, as well as that of his peers, will be put into ineffective and immoral use. Can Tarek's common sense prevail?

# CHAPTER 18

"What is this place, a giant gym?" Amir wonders aloud, as he enters a large hangar with Ethan. The place looks like some sort of converted indoor training facility, with a scarred wooden floor, benches along the walls, and stacks of mattresses and odd training equipment. On one wall, a solitary basketball hoop still hangs by a couple of bolts. In a corner, wooden crates with army markings betray the true, new nature of the facility.

Ethan says, "Yeah, right, a 'firing range' gym." He points at paper targets and steel brackets stacked in the far corner.

Moshe stands a few feet away, talking with Ely and several other officers.

"Meet the CO," Ely says, pointing to Moshe.

"This is Moshe's doing?" Ethan's eyes widen with surprise. "He never tells us anything. What are we supposed to do here?" He looks at Moshe. "*Shalom*, Moshe. What is this place?"

Moshe turns around and steps towards them. "Welcome. Here you'll train for your new missions. It's not entirely my doing, but I had the privilege of working on it from the start. Many of the programs were developed by me and experts I've gathered from our troops."

Amir points to pallets of assorted military hardware. "What kind of missions do you have in mind? What's in those crates?"

Ethan asks eagerly, "What are we going to train for?"

"We've assembled the very best trainers we could find to prepare you and your new teams for specific missions. Very specific missions."

Amir is suspicious. "What kind of missions?"

Moshe says, "Our sources say the Palestinians are getting ready for new kinds of terrorist action. They could happen in Israel or abroad."

Ethan is puzzled. "They're stepping up the terrorism? Despite all the bad publicity?"

"To them, bad publicity is still publicity. Getting their names in the papers is what they want, to draw the world's attention. They're getting serious foreign support, and they want to put it to good use. They target everyone, everywhere. No rules, no limits."

Amir frowns. "I guess it's not going to be the usual reprisal raids?"

"Oh, no, that's regular army stuff."

Amir cannot hide his impatience anymore. "What, then?"

"Basically, it's counter-terrorist action. In some cases you'll carry out specific, punitive or preventive raids, some of which will take place abroad. And then there's the long-term project — the infiltration of enemy ranks."

Ethan steps back in horror. "We're going to pretend we're Palestinian?"

Moshe shrugs. "Why not?"

Amir mutters, "Me, a Palestinian?"

"A select few will undergo extensive training to improve their language skills, especially Arabic. But other languages, too—you might pose as a foreigner. And there will be fighting and survival skills."

"Who's been selected for this job?"

"Once you pass your training, the ones who are eligible will remain in the program, and believe me, you may not want to do this. This is strictly on a volunteer basis."

"Why wouldn't I want to go ahead?" Ethan asks.

"For one thing, it's extremely dangerous. But also the job requires the utmost in mental, psychological, and physical skills." Moshe gives Ethan a serious look. "Patience, for one thing, is at the top of the requirement list. Strict obedience to orders is another." He watches their reaction carefully. "And you also may be required to 'allow' the killing of innocent people. You think you can do that?"

Amir raises a hand. "That's a very high price to pay. What's the catch?"

Moshe explains, "We will be saving many more lives, by retracing the small groups to the brains behind them. Those hiding in the shadow, not just the known leaders. This is a new doctrine in the application of force. We're building a force dedicated to the eradication of new threats. This force will rely on intelligence gathered by deeply embedded agents. We will thwart, preempt, respond to, and destroy all of their terror attempts."

Ethan and Amir are in full sync. "We're in."

———

A large group of soldiers enters the gym. Some of them are from Amir's unit. They're telling jokes and laughing loudly. One of them dashes to the basketball hoop, pretending to dribble a ball. Another follows, and they mime dunking imaginary balls to the cheers of their mates.

Moshe shakes his head. "Call the guys over, Amir, and wait for me here. I have to get something from the office."

Amir takes a deep breath and whistles loudly. The strident noise echoes across the hangar walls and all the men turn towards him. He circles a pointed finger above his head, the signal for gathering up. The men put out their cigarettes and adjust their uniforms as they make their way toward him.

Amir motions for them to stand in front of him. "All right. I'm glad you're all here. Moshe, whom you all know, has something special for us—"

"He sure does," Ethan says, his jaw dropping, along with most of his men's.

Moshe emerges from his office with his 'something.' An athletic-looking gorgeous woman. Amir stares at the tall beauty as she and Moshe approach them. She is wearing tight jeans and a snow-white sweater, with trendy canvas sneakers on her feet. The men are all somewhere between mesmerized and disturbed by her beauty. Her eyes go from one of them to another as she too scans the outfit, getting them hooked in turn.

Ethan's elbow in his ribs brings him out of her spell. Ethan whispers, "She looks like someone out of a movie."

Moshe stops in front of the men. "This is Anouchka, our director for the program. Anouchka comes from Leningrad, Mother Russia, our second homeland. A top teacher, top agent, with extensive field experience, from diplomatic circles to the trenches. She will supervise the curriculum of your program, and your entire training."

Ely is skeptical. He asks, "*She's* their teacher?"

"Top of her class, multiple field deployments and assignments. *All* successful."

Ely shoots back, "Fine, but unless we inject the boys with tranquilizers, how do you expect them to concentrate?"

Moshe laughs. "She's not exactly their teacher. She'll just follow their progress, take notes, and report back to me. She's in charge of individual dossiers."

Ely looks straight at Anouchka. "She's going to be with them *every* day?"

Moshe answers, "Think of it as an extra test. We'll find out who's impervious to distraction. I'll keep an eye on things, I promise."

"You'd better. Your eagerness has always blinded you. You're the first person I know who would fail this training."

Moshe looks back at Ely and muses, "Thank you for the hearty compliment."

Anouchka looks at Ely with a disarming smile. "Sir?"

Moshe steps in. "Anouchka, this is colonel Ely, Paratroopers."

Anouchka asks in perfect English, "Will you take part in the training, Colonel?" Her tone is friendly and confident. She returns Ely's gaze with a charming stare.

Amir watches with amusement as his father fumbles for words, and then finally says in a stern tone, "Some of these boys come from my unit, or units I closely supervise. This one here is my son, Amir, and next to him is Ethan. 'Like' my son."

Anouchka looks at them, lingers on Amir, and then back at Ely. "You don't approve of my presence, but I am certain that experience has taught you not to trust appearances."

Ely straightens up and clears his throat. "I'll be blunt, Anouchka. I don't think someone like you should be put in charge of these men, training for worst-case scenarios. Whatever you train for, the environment should duplicate it as closely as possible. And these guys are going to *Gehenom*, not to Russia, and certainly not to Hollywood."

Amir looks at Anouchka. He knows his father well, and he knows that it wouldn't be easy to stand up to him, especially not for a girl surrounded by fighting men.

She responds with a small bow and another bright, engaging smile, her compliant attitude and good looks giving extra meaning to her words. "A woman, foreign or not, could be the most dangerous thing they'll face. I know that first-hand, from missions of my own. That's the reason I was selected. Not every job is going to consist of dark, muddy infiltrations, and rapid-fire attacks against terrorist camps. We'll get into that later, but I thank you for being honest with me."

Ely catches Amir's smile and puts on his serious face. "All right. But I'll be watching."

Moshe declares, "Anouchka will record your progress, your weaknesses, and your skills, should you have any." He laughs. "Make no mistake gentlemen — Anouchka can take anyone of you in mental challenges and language training, not to mention physical combat."

Ethan laughs. "You mean she can kick my butt, sir? I wouldn't bet on that!"

Moshe has a wicked look. Amir knows it too well. Moshe turns to Anouchka. "Could you confirm my statement please?"

Anouchka turns into machine mode. "Yes." She steps toward Ethan, who prepares to defend himself, and punches the man next to him in the belly. As Ethan laughs, Anouchka, still facing her first victim, jabs him in the throat with the inner edge of her hand. Ethan drops to his knees, holding his throat, gasping for air. His eyes grow bigger and fear replaces surprise. Anouchka kneels and massages Ethan's throat, gradually restoring his breathing. The men all stand in awe. It took her less than two seconds to put both men down.

"This is no Krav Maga. It's not what we learned in the army . . ." Ethan mutters as he struggles to breathe.

Moshe has a satisfied look. "I think everyone's got the 'distraction' message. Gentlemen, where you're headed, it will be strictly low blows, preferably from behind."

Anouchka stands up. Amir watches the look in her eyes change from honeyed charm to lethal arrows. "Gentlemen," she says slowly, "I want

you to give your full, undivided attention to every minute of your training. Each and every discipline, even things you've studied previously,
will have new techniques and new methods. Your goals are different, so
your training will reflect that. We will do extreme physical condition-
ing. We will teach you aggressive driving techniques. We will teach you
how to kill, and how to do it without being noticed. We will teach you
how to hold a champagne flute. How to pretend to be someone you're
not. Every detail counts. And remember, counter terrorism or infiltrated
agents, only the best of you will be selected at the end of the course."

When Anouchka is finished speaking, Moshe leads the men on a
tour of the new training complex. He introduces them to the rest of the
teachers and their assistants. The chief instructor, Isaac, goes over the
specialties they will cover: close combat, hostage rescue, counter-terrorism, bomb disposal, emergency field medicine, foreign languages,
mental skills, resisting and inflicting pain, interrogation techniques
from both sides of the equation, navigation, communications, signal
and electronic intelligence . . . social skills . . . everything that could
possibly be needed. And everything will include real tests. "The training itself will be dangerous," Isaac adds ominously. "And some of you
might be seriously injured before even leaving this facility. If you don't
follow our instructions, you will pay the price; now or later, but better
now, so we don't ALL pay the price."

---

At the end of the tour, Ely follows Moshe to his office. They sit on
wooden chairs next to his desk, and Moshe pours glasses of cold water.
"So, are you happy? Isn't the program great?"

Ely is not happy. It seems to him that he and Moshe would never
have the same goals. "You'll be turning these young men into killing

machines. I only hope there will still be some humanity left in them. What would be the point, otherwise? Don't forget our ultimate goal. A decent nation, for decent people ..."

"Don't worry about that. They'll have plenty of free time to enjoy themselves and their families. Don't you feel better about Anouchka? She's the best. Anywhere."

"Well, I'm still worried."

"Anouchka's only here because she doesn't have an assignment. The way things are going, she'll be back in the field soon."

Ely knows that Anouchka's charm had already worked on Moshe. "I hope you're right. I am beginning to warm to her. But I'll wait before making a final opinion."

"Where she really shines is in espionage and intelligence. She's learned quite a few tricks working for Russian intelligence."

"I realize she can be a tremendous asset. You shouldn't compromise her safety."

Moshe slaps his hand on his desk. "No names, no photos, no records ... she *is not* here. She's in disguise every time she steps outside."

Ely nods and says, "We do have a lot to learn from her. How did you manage to find her, not to mention recruit her?"

"She was raised by a Jewish Russian family. She's only twenty-five. She was born in a German death camp, and her mother died giving birth to her. The women in her mother's bunker hid her from the Nazi guards and took care of her, until the camp was liberated. Her father had died in forced labor as well, so she was picked up by the Soviets, and sent to a boarding school. Later, she was enrolled and trained by the KGB. One of our agents contacted her. He didn't even have to flip her, she actually wanted this."

Ely says, "You're investing a lot of time and manpower in your intelligence and counter-terrorism units. What's the point?"

"This is going to be the next war, Ely. Not all-out battles, just hit-and-run terrorist attacks, and psychological and media warfare. Knowledge is going to be our best weapon. We have to penetrate their organizations and strike at will, where it hurts, before they can hurt us. We have to learn from their methods. Anouchka trained with the people who are now training the enemy. Now she trains them. She's there whenever she's not here, gathering info for us. She's our most valuable deep cover agent, an information treasure trove. Her people trained . . . no, *built* our enemy . . ."

Ely couldn't disagree more. "No, no, and no! The Arabs are reorganizing their armies; they're rearming their units, changing tactics, getting new, modern weapons. They're rewriting their doctrines and training for large-scale maneuvers every day. They've learned their lessons, and they'll put that knowledge to good use in the next conflict. Terrorist incidents are a plague, but they don't threaten our *existence*. It's Arab armies that do. You're in *intelligence*, you should know that!"

Moshe points around the training area. "Times are changing, Ely. Tactics evolve, and we must adapt. That's the new thinking. Our leaders worry that all-out terror will drive people crazy and stop the influx of Jewish people our country depends on."

Ely is impatient. "Are we dismissing conventional threats?"

Moshe stands up and walks with him out of the office. "We're not dismissing conventional threats. We're just adjusting and preparing for new ones. God knows what lies ahead."

Ely responds, "You have to assume it will at least be both. Terror and conventional warfare. But we have to give the negotiations a chance." He shrugs and takes a peek into the hangar before leaving. The men are all gathered around Anouchka, as she demonstrates physical drills. Amir stands out amongst them, leading in both questions and answers. He seems to stand out in Anouchka's eyes as well, as she gives him much more attention than she does anyone else. Is Moshe doing the right thing? Are these young men ready? Would Amir and his friends cease to be high-moral soldiers, and turn into killing machines? How will these young men, how will Amir, be able to go on as sons, husbands, fathers? Will they not somehow be destroyed as well, just like the enemy they intend to annihilate?

———

Weeks have passed. Amir and his mates have gone through grueling training. Many have failed or quit along the way, but a handful remained. From the original two hundred men gathered from various units such as Amir's, about twenty made it past the physically demolishing, mentally breaking, intellectually challenging series of trials and tryouts. It is late at night, and Amir knocks at Anouchka's office door, having received the order to report to her. Her firm voice echoes through the thick door. "Enter."

Amir walks in and stands to attention. Anouchka is at her desk, going through files and photos of the applicants. She remains focused. Amir looks around. A small table nearby has a full stack of files. Amir recognizes photos of friends who didn't make it. He peers at her desk, where only a few portfolios remain. She is looking at his.

Amir speaks first. "Sir, you sent for me. Sir."

Anouchka looks up, lowers the file she holds, "Relax. Yes I did. You're on time. I'm reviewing your results here."

Amir prods his neck toward the file. He still stands to. Anouchka has a soft tone, for the first time. "Relax. You're not on duty."

Amir eases up his posture. "The results are out? Final?"

Anouchka surprises Amir with a wink, "Yes, results are out. You have decent scores." She waves him to her side.

Amir obliges and draws near, bending over the desk. "Decent? I have top scores!" Amir keeps peering into the numbers. "Weapons skills, team leadership, languages, navigation, comm —"

"Yes you do." Anouchka interrupts him. "Ethan did well too." She notices Amir's gaze towards another pile of files on the corner of her desk. Photos of Palestinians in keffiyah and battle gear are within each file.

Amir is mesmerized. He points at the enemy's files. "What are they like? The Palestinians, you've lived with them. Trained them. You know them."

Anouchka shakes her head. "They're a poor people on the wrong side of history. They think they have the sympathy of the Arab leaders. Of the Soviets. They think having a cause is enough to win it." Her gaze turns hard as she adds, "Some would wipe us clean off the earth if they could. They would not hesitate to kill and die for their cause." She pauses for a second then goes on, "Our job is to prevent the first and facilitate the second."

Amir is still gazing at the photo, lost in his thoughts. "Kill. Dead. Our job."

Anouchka gives Amir a stern look. "Yes. This you will do. I was saying you have good scores. Indeed the best. The unit is yours. It's your command. About twenty of you made it from this first batch."

Amir is taken aback. "The unit. My command? Did Moshe—"

Anouchka puts her hand on his shoulder, interrupting. "Moshe doesn't even know yet. It was my call."

Amir seems oblivious to the hand on his shoulder. He looks at the other files. "But why me? The others have top scores too."

Anouchka pats him on the cheek. "They all have top scores. Otherwise, they wouldn't have made it. But leading is not for all. Leading is for the select few. And you are the one for this." She pokes her finger at his chest. "Some qualities cannot be objectively measured. Human qualities. Man qualities. The right stuff." She ends her sentence with a deep gaze into Amir's eyes.

Amir fumbles with his words, disarmed of speech. "And I am —"

Anouchka confirms before he can go on. "You are. The one to head this unit. I know that, deep in my heart."

They gaze into each other's eyes. They both seem entranced with the other. Amir tries to speak, but Anouchka says, "We'd better stop this right now. You're married. Happily married."

Amir acquiesces, "Yes. I am. We should stop this. You've mesmerized me from day one. We must stop. I have never even looked at another woman."

Anouchka puts her finger on his lips. "Amir. I'm the one who's mesmerized. And I've never been."

---

Hours have passed. It is late at night and Anouchka is sloped in Amir's arms, in her bed. He caresses her hair, runs a finger down her face. "Now you tell me about you."

Anouchka lowers her gaze. "What about me?"

Amir gently lifts her face towards his. "Why do you do this? You have the looks and smarts for everything. Anything. With your contacts, you could be a Hollywood star. Why this?"

Anouchka lowers her cheek on Amir's hand, hesitates a bit. "It . . . it needs to be done. I'm good at it. I think of what I can do to the world. To my people. Not what I can do to me . . ."

Amir puts his hand on her chest, feels her heart pounding. "What about the little girl inside? What's her story?"

Anouchka seems touched. She seems to be a different person. She fumbles for words. "There never was a little girl inside. That little girl never . . . never was."

"Maybe you never let her." Amir kisses her neck, rubs his lips behind her ear.

"I'm letting her now. I'm letting her like I never did."

Amir goes on kissing, gently moving over. "You should do that more often. The little girl wants her life too."

Anouchka teases him, avoiding his kisses. "So you prefer me as the little girl?"

Amir firmly grasps both her hands, pulling them towards the bedhead. "Let's see what Krav Maga and Kama Sutra can do together. The little girl and the spy. At once."

Anouchka breathes deeply, manages a joke as she clutches his waist with both legs, in a ground grappling technique. "So there's four of us now. Soldier and lover, little girl and spy."

Amir resists her shove to swivel him around. "I'm gonna have to earn top score here too."

Anouchka has a mischievous smile. "You already have."

# 1973
# Sharing Death

# CHAPTER 19

Ameer stands in his backyard garden, trying to make out his wife Layal through the haze of the window glass. He can hear his newborn daughter, Nidal, requesting her milk — screaming for it. It has been a tough night, and Layal must be exhausted.

Behind Ameer, a silent killer approaches, his face hastily smudged in mud, with makeshift greenery camouflaging his head, advancing on all fours. Hiding a smile, Ameer looks the other way. He pretends not to see his son, little Tarek, sneaking up on him.

Summer is gone, and it is now the end of September. Little Tarek, his pride and joy, has been the sunshine of his life for the past few years, and now his newborn sister has only added to Ameer's fatherly pride. The past three years in the camp have been good. Not good enough though — because they are still there in a camp, for one thing, but also because growing tensions with the Lebanese government had led to occasional armed clashes — but good nonetheless. Thanks to the overwhelming political support of Lebanese Muslims and their political leaders, who strongly opposed Lebanon's western-oriented Christians, the Palestinians were becoming what they couldn't in any other Arab country: a political and military force to be reckoned with. Morale is high — the Palestinian resistance now has worldwide reach, and they have ties with every revolutionary movement in the world. Money and equipment are flowing in, from oil-rich Arab countries and from the Soviet Union, and it reflects in both their training and their operational tempo.

There are some, like Ameer's father, who disagree with the 'open warfare' policy of Palestinian leaders. Tarek approves of the armed struggle to regain their lost land, and the national charter of the PLO, but he abhors the killing of civilians. He claims it only serves to depict the Palestinians as heartless villains, when they are actually the victims, and that the blood of innocents only adds more fuel to the fires of hatred on both sides of the conflict. As for himself, Ameer leans towards the tougher stance, if only out of frustration from conventional methods and the ineptness of the Arab countries. For many of his fellow soldiers, the open resistance is the only thing they have left. No one else listens, and no one else cares . . . and the years are passing by. Tarek and his family have been on the road for a quarter century . . . And for what? Ameer firmly believes the only way to get anything done is through tough military action. There are no other options. He is now dedicated, heart, mind, and soul, to their fight for freedom, and he volunteers for every operation that he can.

Of course, their campaign of attacks is greatly outmatched by the enemy's raids — in ferocity and in cruelty. And yet, no one questions the legitimacy of Israel's indiscriminate air bombings and commando raids, not to mention the killing of innocent Palestinians, young and old.

Little Tarek jumps out at him. *"A'aleyhoum!"* Unto them! He sputters a full burst from his wooden kalash, and declares Ameer dead. The gun is a close replica of a real Kalashnikov that Ameer spent hours carving from a block of wood. He even painted it like the real thing.

Along with a carved handgun, it is his son's favorite toy. Ameer hears Layal laugh.

She stands at the back door, and has witnessed the attack. Ameer laughs to his son and says, "*Tayeb, Tayeb Tarek, ana mayet* — Okay, okay, Tarek, 'I'm dead!'"

But little Tarek insists, pointing to the ground. "*La', La', mayet a'la ard, a'la ard* — No, no, dead on the ground. On the ground!"

Ameer has no choice. He appreciates how his young son snuck up on him without making a sound. Little Tarek really could have surprised him. Ameer cries, "Aaah! I'm dying . . ." and pretends to gasp his last breath of air as he collapses to the ground, eyes shut. He wonders if his son's preferred game would one day turn to real, as it unfortunately did with him.

Little Tarek isn't satisfied. "Open eyes. Open eyes!" He nearly tears off his father's eyelids trying to pry them open. He then tries to curl Ameer's right leg under his left. Ameer helps, since Little Tarek couldn't lift his heavy limbs. But when his son tries to snatch his arm and pull it away, Ameer raises his head and asks, "What are you doing? I'm dead on the ground. What else do you want? I can't be more dead than this!"

Tarek shakes his head. "Dead . . . on ground. Open eyes!" Putting his finger on Ameer's lips to silence his 'dead' father, he says, "Shh. Hand over there. Like Jamil."

Ameer realizes his son is trying to copy the death of one of Ameer's soldiers. Jamil was killed during an air raid on their training grounds, and his severed arm was thrown several feet away from where his body was found. He had been caught by flying fragments as he dove for cover. Ameer's training sessions were Little Tarek's favorite show, but on that specific day, the young child had seen firsthand what would cause an adult to throw up in horror.

Ameer tries to explain things in as rational a way as he could, to his young child, so he could understand, and hopefully forget. But little Tarek's memory had taken an enduring snapshot of the awful scene. Was this the reason he's begun wetting himself again at night? How deep into his fragile mind had the horror cut?

Ameer decides to tell Layal about it. He stands up, sweeps his boy into his arms, and heads for the house. He wants to change his son's mood, as well as his thoughts. He holds Tarek in his right arm, gazing into his eyes. "Who's the strongest soldier in *al-Asseffa*?" — Storm troops?

Little Tarek bangs on his chest with a fist. *"Ana!"* — Me!

Ameer tries to rationalize Jamil's death. "You know what happened is an accident. You know it is not something that happens to others."

His son's mind is in a world of its own. "Jamil was hurt. Poor Jamil."

"Yes, but that will never happen again. Not to anyone."

"The planes will not come anymore? They will not bomb us?"

Ameer knows better than promising what he can't deliver. "We have sirens now, and if the planes come, we can go hide in the shelter."

"The shelter is safe?"

Ameer presses his boy against his chest. "Yes. Nothing will happen to you there. Now let's think of something else . . . how about reading a book, learning the alphabet?" His heart fills with a father's joy, a feeling unmatched by any other, as his son starts reciting a famous alphabet song by Lebanese TV comic *Shu-shu*, ('What-what') *"alef beh, bu beyeh . . ."* Ameer hugs him tighter. "That's my good boy. Who's going to give a big hug to *mama*? And a gentle kiss to his sister?"

Little Tarek scrambles down and runs to his mother, who carries him inside to kiss his sister in her crib. After she sets him on the floor to play with his favorite blocks, Ameer tells Layal about the incident in the garden.

Layal nods. "Well, it doesn't take a genius to figure that one out.

We're going to have to deal with it. Any ideas how *not* to give him a 'killer's' education at that young age? Who knows? *Insh Allah* he won't need it. I'll call the doctor and ask him about it later." She pauses, and then says, "Speaking of giving people nightmares, are you really going to go to that training camp?"

Ameer feigns surprise. "You mean in Russia? Sure. Only the best go. It's an honor."

Layal shakes her head. Her expression is troubled, as it usually is when she voices objections to Ameer's extremist opinions. "It's all anger and destruction. That's not like you; it's not what you've always wanted. You're a real soldier, not one of those fanatics."

Ameer waves her worries aside. "It's training, serious training. We should do anything we can to become better fighters."

Layal doesn't let it go. "Right. Fighters Ameer, defenders of your family, your people, and your land, that's what you are. I think those fanatic foreigners have had too much influence on you in the last three years. You used to dream about our country, our land, and our home. You would dream about our children's future." Stepping closer to Ameer, Layal looks into his eyes and says with a pleading tone. "These cruel foreigners are messing up your mind. Now your dream is to kill, just that, to kill. It's not getting us any nearer to our Palestine, to our homes. You've changed, for the worse."

Ameer takes her by the shoulders. "For the better! We're better now. You have to understand, I've told you over and over. Defeating their military isn't an easy thing. It'll take time. And new means of fighting. We'll never win a direct confrontation."

"Now everyone thinks *we're* the bad guys, not the Israelis. What do we gain from that? Will it bring us closer to our land, to our Palestine? Every military operation, every war takes us further away from Palestine."

Ameer is taken aback. "You've been talking to my dad."

Layal rests her head on his chest. "Is that a bad thing? He's the wisest and smartest among you all. Better yet, he knows the enemy more than all of you."

Ameer snaps back at her. "We tried the wise man's ways. They don't work."

Layal looks at her son. Little Tarek's face shows signs of despair, his lips pouting as he tries to keep his tears back. "Look now, Tarek is about to cry. Fear at home as well?"

"That's enough, Layal. I make the decisions around here, or do you want to do the fighting while I sit at home?"

Layal puts her hand on his cheek, saying with a soft voice, "That's not what I mean. Nor do I mean to upset you. I just wanted to talk some sense into you. You said yourself that your father is against this new approach. Don't you respect his opinion?"

Ameer hesitates, takes his wife's hand and admits, "I do respect his opinion, and I'm not saying our approach is the best. But we have to try! When the conventional doesn't work, we have to try something else. What's your problem with that? Can't you see we're making progress? One day, *their* civilian population will get sick of this, and ask for a solution."

Layal shakes her head. "They're getting back at us a thousand-fold."

Ameer answers, his voice harsh. "We're soldiers, all of us, young and old. We have to fight for our nation, our lives, and our rights. Whatever means we have, we must use."

Layal tries another approach. She puts her fist on Ameer's chest and knocks on his torso. "I hope that deep inside, you'll remain the loving man I know. Not a killing machine."

Ameer smiles. "Rest assured. That man is intact, and so is our dream. Palestine, our homes, our villages . . . and a peaceful life." He hesitates before going on, "I'll be leaving soon. We'll be gone for a while. And that bothers me."

Layal raises her eyebrows. "Something bothering you? How could that be?"

"I've never left you for so long. How are you going to manage?"

Layal smiles sadly and replies, "We'll be fine. Don't worry. But how are *you* going to manage without *us*? Not a day goes by without you spending hours with Tarek. And now Nidal is here! Will you take her picture to look at, every day?" Layal has a sorrowful smile. She points toward little Tarek, now snoring on a soft pillow, a peaceful smile adorning his face, his head resting on his hands, and Nidal in her crib, fists clenched, lost in her dreams. "Wouldn't you rather have the real thing?"

Ameer sighs. "I'm going to miss them like hell. And you, too."

Layal leans closer, in a sexy and inviting move she knows he couldn't resist; she swiftly wraps her arms around his neck, pressing her chest against his. "You will? I do already. The kids are asleep . . ."

Ameer lifts Layal up, pulls away the bed covers with his foot, and slides her between the sheets. She turns to him. "You're covered with sand!"

He is quick to come back at her. "And you smell of milk!"

"No I'm not! We've been on bottled milk for a while now." Tapping her finger on his chest, she goes on, "Besides, it's only on the shirt. Unlike you."

Layal removes her shirt and Ameer reaches for her. He sniffs her gently, from her navel to her upper neck, just below her ear, the tip of his nose and his lips barely touching her skin, then he whispers in her ear, "The smell is gone. Now you're all mine . . ."

Layal smiles as she sneaks in her last move. "Now, about that training? Isn't home a better place to be?"

Ameer hasn't lowered his guard. "Later. Now you have to load me up with good memories, nice memories, which will make me long for home. I already miss you and the children," he says, kissing her neck and massaging her bare chest. She shivers and breathes heavily. Ameer goes on, "Duty calls, and I'll have to go . . . but later. Now let's enjoy these moments. *Our* moments. Our communion."

Layal breathes deeply, shivering and closing her eyes as Ameer goes on. They're both immersed in a long rehearsed physical harmony that reflects their unicity in love. Layal finally opens her eyes again, as they both breathe deeply. Ameer locks her face in his hands, "There's this divine light coming out of you . . ."

---

Amir rushes to his children's bedroom. His daughter's loud blabbering is her way of letting the whole house know she is awake. Yet her new-born brother, *Areih* — Lion cub — needs to finish his sleep. Holding her in his arms, dazzled as always when he looks at her, Amir points to his son and whispers, "Shh . . . We don't want to wake the baby."

"Shh." Liz puts her finger on her lips, leans close to her dad and says with a mischievous look. "Boo!"

Amir walks to the window and peers outside, through the closed curtains. A ray of light shines through. It looks like a beautiful morning. The last day of September, and from now on they could expect the milder, less humid days of October. He looks around the bedroom. He has a 'full' family now. Liz is two years and two months old, and baby Areih has just brought a fresh breath of air, and many sleepless nights, into their lives. Amir whispers to his daughter, "We have to get a new room for your brother. Those pink-painted walls and all these Barbie dolls aren't for boys.

Liz voices her protest of the tiny invader. "Barbie for me, only for me."

Amir glances at Areih. Dark curly hair like his own, long lashes, eyes gently closed, fists tight, a sweet purr coming from his nose.

As he walks into the living room of his apartment, he sees her expression change to concern. Liz points at his partially filled rucksack in the corner and asks, "*Aba holech*, father go? *Aba holech*, go again? Come back?"

Amir smiles. "Of course. Aba will come back. You know that, *boubati*, my dolly."

She squirms with laughter. "Liz *bouba, aba* kiss *bouba*!"

Liz needs not ask twice. Amir buries his face in her tummy, kissing and gently nibbling at her.

Their laughter brings Debbie rushing in, shushing them with a finger to her lips and hastily closing the bedroom door, after a quick glance to Areih's crib.

Amir sits on the living room couch with Liz on his lap. Liz says, "*Aba* go fight?"

Amir nods. "Yes, *Aba* is a soldier.

"Why *Aba* go fight?"

Amir looks to his wife for help.

Debbie shakes her head. "Good luck. I need the answer myself."

Amir tries to reassure them both. "*Aba* is only training now. There's no fighting."

Liz isn't letting go. She has heard the training explanation dozens of times, but this time she has some questions. Looking up with a worried face, she asks, "If Papa no fight, Papa stay with us?"

Amir peers into her eyes. "We have a big army and we have to train for when there's a fight, against the bad ones. *Aba* always goes to train, very hard, to be strong and ready."

Liz spreads the fingers on both hands as if she was getting ready to count. "Are there many 'bad ones'?"

He makes a serious face. "There are plenty of bad ones."

"More than nice ones?"

Amir doesn't have time to change his logic. "More than nice ones, but —"

Liz bangs her fists on his chest. "No, I don't want! I want many nice ones! Many more."

Amir struggles to put his own logic and warring tactics into simple terms, and he says, "We're stronger, and smarter than the 'bad ones', and so we'll win."

Liz calms down. "Like before? Like even before I was born? When you won, and mama was so happy?"

Amir nods. "Exactly, like before, when we won. You see, there's no point in being afraid."

"You killed all the 'bad ones' before?"

"Yes, we did. And we won."

Amir has underestimated her smarts. "Why are there *new* 'bad ones'?"

Amir scratches his head. "This is getting complicated. Listen to me, *bubba*, there was a war, and we won. Now, there may be another fight, and we'll win again. We'll kill all the new 'bad ones'"

"Some 'nice ones' will die too?"

"Sometimes they do. It's *God's* will—"

Liz cries, "Why God want nice ones to die? Not you. I'm afraid. I want you to come back quick quick! And stay with me and mama and Areih."

Amir rests his forehead on his daughter's. Softly, confidently, he says, "*Aba* will always be right here beside you. I won't let any harm be done to you, or anyone else in this house. There's no reason to be afraid, my little one, papa will always be by your side."

Liz says, "And baby Areih, and Grandpa Ely and Grandma Sara, and Moshe and Dina and Ethan, and—" Liz goes through all her beloved "good" ones. She wants to make sure God knew the entire list, and would not neglect to keep them all alive.

"*Koolam*." Amir says. Everybody. "No one will be hurt, I promise, and certainly not you, the one I adore." He seals his promise with a strong hug and a warm kiss on her curly hair.

The front door opens and Ely comes in, followed by Moshe and Debbie, just as Amir says, "Now let's play with your toys. What do you want to play?"

Ely says, "I think she wants to play with her mama." Amir sees Debbie cringe. The two of them barging in with these looks can only mean something is wrong.

Liz is unmoved. "No, I want play with papa. After, I eat with mama."

Considering the sleeping baby in the other room, Amir decides it would be better if he kept his daughter busy while they talked. "Okay. Get a puzzle."

While Liz scampers to the toy basket, he looks up at his father and Moshe. "We can talk. Is something wrong?" Liz comes back with a wooden jigsaw puzzle of Little Red Riding Hood. She dumps the pieces out on the floor, and Amir joins her. He said, "Where does Little Red Riding Hood go? Can you find her place?"

Amir looks to Ely, who motions Moshe to speak. Moshe says, "You'll be on a mission soon. We wanted to get some feedback from you before we finalize operational planning."

Debbie's tone betrays her shock. "*Elohim!* How can you talk about this as if it were a trip to the supermarket?"

A knock at the door interrupts Debbie. Amir says, "Come in!" Dina and Ethan step inside, followed by Sara.

Dina goes to Liz and gives her a kiss. "How's my little niece?"

Liz says, "I'm doing a puzzle." She places Little Red Riding Hood in the right spot. "Little Red Riding Hood is going to *Savta's*" — grandma's — "house, so the big bad wolf will not eat her."

Ely waits while Sara puts a grandmotherly kiss on Liz's soft and rosy cheek, then says, "Debbie, years ago, we set out to establish our country. We were a few bands at first, and now we're the most feared army in the region. This is very unfortunate."

"Very unfortunate?" Amir asks.

"That it has come to this. In the war of independence, we achieved great military victories. But we've been winning battles, not the war. The war isn't over. The war can only be over when we have a full, comprehensive peace with our neighbors."

Amir says, "What, peace with Egypt and Syria? With Jordan? Why? We'll squash them whenever they lift their heads."

Ethan adds, "And the Palestinians?"

Ely nods. "Yes. Peace with everyone. On fair terms, or the peace won't last."

"What difference does it make, as long as we're winning?" Ethan asks, not pleased with Ely's logic.

Ely frowns. "We can't guarantee a win every time, and people are dying. This land is our land, but we should enjoy it, not spend our lives defending it —"

"But how can we think of peace in the climate we live in?" Ethan interrupts.

Moshe says, "Let him finish, Ethan, he's getting there." Amir is surprised by his unusually compliant attitude.

Liz says, "Your turn, Daddy. Do the big bad wolf."

While Amir pretends to have trouble figuring out where the wolf belongs, Ely goes on. "We're going to stay in this game of fighting and talking until someone decides that it doesn't make sense any more, and agrees to some compromises. I'm talking about peace between the people, not just governments."

"We still don't know how this concerns us." Ethan falls back in his chair.

Dina knocks him on the head. "There's going to be more fighting. Are you happy now?"

Ely looks at Moshe, who nods in agreement. Ely goes on. "Debbie was asking us how we could deal with war as if it were a trip to the movies."

"I said supermarket." Debbie retorts.

"Whatever. We always knew it was only a matter of time before death would strike home. But death hit the wrong place in the past. It took Liz. Not me, not Moshe."

Sara lets out a long sigh. "We all died, in a way, that day." Everybody eyes Moshe, who, silent as ever, nods at Ely to go on.

"From the day we lost Liz, Moshe and I decided that, as long as the war was raging, if our children were to grow up before we saw the end of it, and if they were to take part in it —"

"Tell them why, Ely!" Moshe insists, clenching his teeth.

"Liz was killed while on a secret mission. Our own, uncalled-for counter-attack drove the enemy upon her unit's concealed position. If we'd known where she was, her life could have been spared. The point is, if fighting is going to be your way of life, Amir, then we want to have as much scrutiny as possible concerning your missions."

Moshe adds, "We're not giving you safe missions in the office, but at least we know where you are, and we study your missions ourselves. We follow your every step."

Debbie asks, "Doesn't anyone complain about preferential treatment?"

Ely smiles as he replies, "No. No one does, not with a hunting list like theirs. Their unit is one of our best, and some of these men are among the most decorated in the army."

Debbie's voice trembles. "I feel sick when I think Mother's death could have been avoided."

Moshe raises a hand and starts to speak, "What happened is that—"

"What happened is that we didn't have the proper information to make the right decision." Ely interrupts. "That happens in a war. The way we're doing things now, we can hope to avoid that sort of situation. There's no point talking about the past."

A baby's cry turns all heads toward the hall to Areih's bedroom. Ely says, "Besides, I think my younger self is waking up. Can I hold him?"

Debbie stands. "Certainly, but I think he needs some cleaning up before."

Ely rolls back his sleeves. "I'll give you a hand."

Sara exclaims, "You never did that with your own!"

Ely hunches as he starts towards Areih's bedroom. "Better late than never..."

Amir asks, "Can I play with my Liz now?" He tousles Liz's glistening curly hair as she cozies back against him.

Liz says, "I put *Savta* in her bed. But the wolf wants to eat her." She mimes pointing a rifle at the wolf and shouts, "Bad wolf! *Aba* shoot the big bad wolf. Boom boom!"

Moshe says, "Look how she points her gun. Truly a gifted girl. I wonder what the boy will do." He goes on with a more serious tone, "Your unit's been training well. You are our best men. You are the best man. You will be given sensitive missions."

Ely points out with a worried voice. "Sensitive, but well planned. Carefully planned. With you as a leader."

Amir seems lost as he mumbles, "Yes. Sensitive. Best man. Leader..."

# CHAPTER 20

Guided by the bus driver, his female colleague, and a Russian officer named Raslan, who is fluent in Arabic, Ameer, Faris, and other
groups of ten or so Palestinian officers tour their new training facility. It is a large compound, with a main building, a couple of dormitories, an indoor training facility, and an open-air training arena.
To the center of the facility is a large, warehouse-like structure, with
plain windows and white facades. A high wall surrounds the entire
compound, with over watch stations positioned every few hundred
meters or so along its length. There is a lot of wild greenery inside,
with tall pine trees between the buildings. Behind a thicket of high
bushes, beyond the built-up area, Ameer notices a strange collection
of abandoned vehicles. Cars, buses, a wagon, and, oddly, a wingless
plane fuselage.

The flight from Beirut to Moscow had gone smoothly, and all of
them were processed quickly at the airport, as they were part of a military mission. But the four-hour bus ride to the facility was tiring and
cold, despite the small glass of vodka they were offered. Arriving at
their destination, Ameer's group is given thirty minutes to freshen up
before their introductory meeting in the training hangar just before

supper. He can see groups from other countries there as well, although he can't tell yet where they are from.

Half an hour later, Ameer is sitting on the cold floor of the gym, wishing for a comfortable chair and an extra layer of warm clothing. The early October sun in Lebanon feels much warmer than the one in this frigid and isolated place. Faris and the rest of his men spread out around him, observing the other groups as they join them. They are all waiting for Alexandar, their chief instructor and the man in charge of the camp. Ameer had heard Raslan during the bus trip saying that Alexandar had taken part in every conflict on the planet in the last couple of decades. Southwest Asia, Africa, Latin America — you name it, he's been there. Now he is in charge of the camp, where he would help produce more soldiers like him. Alexandar finally appears, accompanied by a strikingly gorgeous, svelte blonde in her twenties who draws everyone's attention like a car-sized magnet. To Ameer, the smoothness of her skin and the tightness of her figure suggested a mature girl rather than a young woman. The men whistle and cheer. The presence of a female among the instructors would be a definite boost to the few women in the group, although she is certainly prone to steal the show.

The trainees all get to their feet.

Alexandar doesn't so much speak as bark, in Russian, when addressing them. The Arabs are gathered as one group. Raslan handles the translation, as Alexander bellows, "Gentlemen, ladies, freedom fighters of the world. I welcome you here, where you will learn to be better fighters. Raslan will be your coordinator, and Anouchka here" — he points to the beautiful blonde — "will be in charge of supervising the program, and your individual files, from training to mission orders and post-operational debriefing."

"Her?" Faris asks, incredulous. "She's in charge of us?"

Alexandar answers in English, "Yes. Make sure you behave around her, and don't be deceived by her looks. She can take any one of you in hand-to-hand combat. She has her way of doing things, and trust me when I say she knows what she's doing. She will keep track of you during and between missions, and she may be your contact once you graduate, depending on where you operate. She will provide us with continuous updates on you, so we know exactly how you perform. Any questions?"

The questioning looks did not translate into questions, so Alexandar goes on, "She speaks Arabic better than any of you, by the way. She answers to our chief of operations in the middle-east, from Beirut, and she will brief and debrief you on every assignment."

Ameer looks at Anouchka. She is looking around the room, at the new trainees, and when she spots Ameer, it seems to him that her eyes widen briefly, but the moment passes quickly. Ameer listens with intent as she speaks in a soft, yet forceful, tone. "We believe that the fight for the Palestinian people, or the Chilean people, or any other of our oppressed brethren, can be simpler if we break the backs of our oppressors, instead of just their fingers. Our main enemy is capitalism and the governments that embrace it and impose it. We believe that our cause is everybody's cause, and that our fight is a universal one. The main enemy is SASHA — the USA and its allies — and we have to wage a full-scale war on them."

"You want us to attack the USA?" Faris raises his hand after asking. "How do we go about doing that? Bomb New York City?"

Alexandar looks at Faris and booms, "Why not, Mr. Smart?"

Anouchka smiles. She has an answer for everything. "Attacking the USA is the problem of the all-mighty USSR. As for bombing New York City, or Washington, well, why not? If it suits our purpose, we do it, as simple as that. Disseminating independent cells within

their population is easy. Obtaining or building weapons is not difficult. The only thing we need is an order from above, and when we get
it, we do it."

Anouchka sweeps them with her gaze. "Most of you are Palestinians,
mainly from the PLO. The Middle East is on fire, and for now, you will
operate there, and focus your efforts on missions against Israel. I will be
personally responsible for all missions against Israel and Israeli inter-
ests. Even outside the Middle East."

Faris asks, "Like blowing up their embassies? Like the Munich
attack against the Olympic sportsmen last year?"

Anouchka punches a fist into her palm. "Yes, exactly! That operation showed our determination and capabilities, proved our willingness
to die for our cause, demonstrated their inability to respond adequately,
and, most importantly, got serious media coverage. That is what we
want. People are asking questions, sometimes the wrong ones, sometimes the right ones. But at least they're asking them."

Anouchka's eyes keep returning to Ameer. He, too, is fixated on her.
He fumbles for the words, and then says with a loud voice, "In other
words, we're trying to get the world's attention. To our cause."

"Exactly, young man," replies Alexandar. "As long as our attacks go
on, they can't turn a blind eye to our cause. And their governments,
one day or another, will have to follow their population's will. You
all know how divided American society is on the Vietnam issue. The
Vietnamese people will prevail; you can see it happening. You can also
see the American people rioting in their streets. That's going to happen
everywhere. The myth of the almighty Americans is just that: a myth.
We're the people, and we make the decisions, *our* decisions."

Alexandar gazes at them, hands on hips, as if waiting for more questions. When none comes, he points to a table with a stack of file folders
on it. "Take a file on your way out, go through it, study the program,

and I'll see you at the mess hall for supper. Don't forget to work on your reading material and language skills. You're dismissed."

As the students walk out, Anouchka's glance lingers on Ameer.

Faris elbows Ameer. *"Mu'ajabeh —* she's enamored, my friend."

Ameer does not answer. *Anouchka's short gaze seemed to stall his thinking, and the effect lingers on.* He does not move either.

Faris gives him a shove in the back, shaking off his daze. "You too my friend! I cannot blame you, I am too! But Layal told me to take notes, so you'd better behave."

Ameer tries to keep his tone casual. "It's not the girl, you know me better than that. Although there *is* something strange about her—"

Faris claps his hands. "It *is* the girl. Oh, I know, you've always been devoted to Layal . . . but this is something else. Plus, she does seem to be interested in you."

Ameer is perturbed, in a way he can neither comprehend nor control. He asks, "In what sense? Have you noticed anything particular about her? You found her strange too?"

Faris slaps his friend on the back. "Are you kidding? I've never seen anything even remotely so beautiful. This is the Russian Brigitte Bardot . . . trained to kill. Pheew! Paralyzing. But of course, for a handsome guy like you —"

Ameer shakes his head. "That's not what I meant. It's like I've seen her before, I get that . . . sensation. And I think she felt it too. There was a bridge, a mental bridge."

Faris puts his hand on Ameer's shoulder. *"Physical* you mean. Physical bridge. You've seen her in your dreams Ameer. OK, I *am* taking note, you're overwhelmed. I haven't seen you lost like this before."

When they get to their room, Ameer tries to change the subject. He throws his file on the only chair in the room and points at the two beds on either side of the single window. "Which one do you want?"

"It doesn't matter. I'll take the one on the left."

Ameer notices the sparkle in his eyes, and he tries again to end the conversation. "It's not what you think, so cut it out. I'm not picking on our trainer, ok? Besides, as Alexandar describes her, she'll probably knock me out."

Faris laughs. "You mean beat you up? Or 'knock' you out . . ."

"Neither. And stop this! I mean knock me out of the program. She's in charge, remember? Imagine everyone's reaction if my file reads, 'expelled for hitting on teacher!'"

Ameer gazes around the room. Through the window, he sees nothing but tall trees and another dorm. Inside, there's one large closet for both, a small table, and a public address speaker above the door. The walls are bare, painted white. "It seems strange that all the hardline campaigning is okay by everyone. I don't mind killing soldiers, or even civilian men. The Jews are all reservists anyway. But why kill women and children?"

"Because ours are being massacred, for one thing, and because it's the policy. Civilians will get more TV time than the military."

Remembering Layal's words, Ameer says, "I know, but it will rally people against us, not with us. We'll be terrorists not freedom fighters."

Faris shrugs and says, "Let's hope we won't be assigned to hijack a plane out of Japan, or Argentina. I wouldn't mind hijacking an El-Al plane, though."

"Anything that gets us closer to freedom, and closer to our homes, is fine by me, but I would stick to military targets. I'd feel like a coward with my gun to some woman's head. Or a hopeless fanatic. And I am not that. I am a revolutionary, a freedom fighter."

Faris gives him a shrewd smile. "You can start with the husband, if you prefer." He points to the folder he's holding. "See? It says here that women and children are much better when it comes to getting the attention of the media. Military targets, especially in war zones, aren't interesting."

Ameer shakes his head. "I don't know. Actually, I do know. That's not what Tarek taught us. I definitely don't like it. It will ruin our cause, make it something that it's not."

"Your father is still fighting old wars. We lost those wars, remember? Times change, tactics change, and the battlefield changes. We have to adapt. That's why we've been selected for this program."

Ameer corrects his friend. "Our records and experience are military. We have no experience doing this kind of work —"

"That doesn't matter. We're still at the beginning of our 'careers', and we can learn new things. The older generation is, well, the old generation."

Ameer is not convinced. "They want to wipe out everything we know and rebuild us from scratch. To free Palestine is our purpose. Wanton killing is theirs."

"And that's what's going to happen, we will destroy Israel, like the PLO charter says, and we will regain the whole of our land and rebuild our homes. We've been using the wrong methods, that's all. It's time for a drastic change, for new ideologies, new strategies, and new tactics."

Ameer reminds his friend of his father's teachings. "I'm not sure what to say. I am a soldier, and I will kill in combat, as I have done before. But I cannot execute women and children in cold blood. Not even you can."

Faris says, "Strategy is the crucial point. Our old strategy did not work. We're not abandoning the old-fashioned way of fighting; we're just leaving it to lesser fighters —"

Ameer has a disdainful expression. "Lesser fighters — you mean like my father and the boys back home? They're not good enough anymore?"

Faris backtracks. "Let's just say that they're better at what they're doing, while we can do better here."

Ameer sighs. "Only time will tell who is right and who is wrong. What's on the program for the coming days?"

Faris checks the file in his hands. "Physical fitness in the early mornings. Infantry weapons and drills, basic and advanced. There's a special course on demolition using household material and equipment — check out this diagram." He holds the folder for Ameer to see. "Nails and steel balls around the explosive charge! We have live trials on this one, to check the pattern and density of hits. Then there are ingress and egress techniques for special vehicles." Faris nods to Ameer. "There's a school bus, a plane, a train . . . and a boat."

He looks up at Ameer, laughing. "I haven't seen a boat in the back yard, maybe we get to cruise around." He reads on. "We'll learn how to go in, how to control people and where to confine them. There are also infiltration and ex-filtration techniques. We learn how to fly a small plane." He flips to a picture of a tiny plane that looks more like a dragonfly. "Well, it's not a plane. They call it an ultralight."

Ameer smiles at the thought of the ultralight. "I can see why. It's probably good for landing past their borders. Is it noisy? I wonder how much weight it can carry."

Faris lifts his shoulders. "I don't know. That comes at the end of the training. There are also navigation techniques."

Ameer shrugs. "Don't we know most of this?"

Faris goes on, "Look, a booby-trapping course. Then physical fitness again, marksmanship, small unit tactics, and then your turf: history and military doctrines."

Ameer points to the papers. "What's that diagram?"

"That's a school bus. The school children have been moved to the back, and gathered around a hidden bag, which contains a bomb. The device is remotely operated by one of our guys, in front, next to the driver, holding him at gunpoint. Personally, I'd kill the driver right away and do the driving myself."

The thought of killing children angers Ameer. "*Allah Akbar!* Putting children around a bomb? That will give us back our country?"

Behind him, at their bedroom's open door, Ameer feels a presence. He turns around and sees Anouchka standing there. Her stealthy sneakers masked her approach. She must have heard what they had been talking about.

Anouchka's voice is strict. "Your name is Amir? Or am I wrong?"

Ameer is taken aback. The sight of her, her voice . . . his mind grows cloudy again. Her eyes engulf him in a paralyzing net. He is aware of his heart beating. He barely manages to answer, as he slowly raises his eyes. "Yes sir . . . ma'am."

---

Anouchka looks straight into his eyes. "Use 'sir' when you address me. Are you trying to reverse-indoctrinate our soldiers?"

Ameer stands to attention. Anouchka is amazed at how well he avoided showing any sign of recognizing her. She is just as amazed by her own stamina at holding back. She wonders what would give in first, her weak knees, or her pounding heart. She gazes at Ameer. His bright eyes, his handsome, tanned face, his muscular body . . . she knows so well. She wishes she could send this Faris guy away on some assignment. Ameer says, "Yes, ma'am, I mean, yes, sir! No, I'm not trying to reverse indoctrinate anyone."

Anouchka takes a deep breath, pretending to be angry, doing her best to maintain a severe tone. "We show the slightest weakness and the whole policy fails. You have to understand the strategy. Hitting their military only gets them more military support." She jabs at the file Faris is holding. "Those diagrams, turned into real pictures in the front pages of every Western newspaper, are our best tools. We force the world to recognize us, fear us, and deal with us. A few civilian casualties here and there are of absolutely no concern, even if they are women and children. You understand?" She looks Ameer straight in the eyes, trying to read them. "Am I clear enough? Have your people not suffered any civilian casualties?"

Faris's words — "We've had our share, sir." — are lost as she studies Ameer.

She says, pointing to the diagram, "Is a child killed by napalm any different from a child killed by *this* bomb? They kill a hundred children for every one we kill. Are their children dearer to you than yours?"

"No, sir. We'll follow the program."

Anouchka keeps at Ameer. "Next time you have a problem with putting a bomb aboard a school bus, you talk to me, not to your mates." She sees an opportunity and decides to seize it. "I'll see you later about this. During the dinner break, in my room."

Anouchka fears that 'Amir', with his chivalry, would give himself away. She also wants to see him again, alone. Thoughts of their last 'training session', as they called it, fill her mind. It was in her bungalow in Israel, a hot, out-of-control game of passionate love and irresistible lust. She'd been attracted to him since the moment she laid eyes on him. She is taken out of her thoughts by Ameer's reply. "Next time there won't be any problems with putting a bomb in a school bus, sir. You can count on us."

With a strict tone and an aggressive look, Anouchka orders, "I still want to see you during dinner break, in my room, down the hall and to the right on the ground floor in the administration building. My name is on the door. Eighteen hundred sharp."

"Yes sir." Ameer stands to attention, imitated by Faris.

Anouchka looks straight at Ameer, glances at Faris. "You're dismissed . . . For now."

———

Later in the evening, wearing clean clothes and having taken a good shower, Ameer heads for his meeting with Anouchka. Although he feels apprehensive about it, *a sensation he's felt before drives him forward. Forward and ahead, to something he feels he already knows.* As he reaches the last room down the corridor on the ground floor of her building, he tries to rationalize. He considers going back. But that would be disobeying. He is about to knock when Anouchka opens the door and looks at him. Her eyes are piercing. Friendly. More than friendly. Mischievous. Inviting. She's a 'different' Anouchka. She peers out and checks down the hall, whispering, "Alone?"

Ameer nods "yes" and decides not to lower his eyes. Or maybe it wasn't his decision. Even her strangely softer tone has a grip on him. "Faris is at the mess." Ameer is entrapped in the drowning glitter of her eyes. He feels a rush in his body, and all his mind can do is freeze. Mesmerized, itching to close the gap between them, yet unable to move. He stands at her mercy.

Anouchka seems similarly confused. She says something Ameer can't make out, takes one more look down the hall, grasps Ameer by his belt and pulls him in. She shuts the door, pushes him against the wall, and pulls herself so close that their faces are touching. Ameer can feel her heartbeat. Or is it his? He can feel her body heat, through the frustrating barrier of clothing. *He can sense it.* Ameer shivers when her warm lips touch his ears and she whispers, "Are you real?" His lips touch the side of her bare neck, and she writhes in eager anticipation.

He runs his lips up her neck, driven by an uncontrolled impulse. He whispers heavily in her ear, "I will show you." Ameer takes Anouchka by the hips, squeezing her against him.

Her voice trembles, and her breathing stutters, as she whispers, "You fool. What are you doing in this shit hole? How did you end up here?"

Ameer gives the only answer he can give, as he runs his hands underneath her shirt, in a firm grasp from her hips to her armpits, clutching her torso, then squeezing her breasts. "Learning to kill."

"You *are* killing me."

All that seems to hold them collapses at once . . . Anouchka rips his shirt up and off. Ameer frantically pulls hers away. Anouchka pauses as their eyes meet, a short lock where the eyes confirm the passionate lust tearing inside. A knowing-of-what's-ahead look that no new lover can give, as the two immerse in a frolic play of love that lasts well past dinnertime and into the early night.

In the midst of it all, through a brief moment of tenderness, as they lay on her sofa by the window, Anouchka holds Ameer's face with both hands. Staring at him, she asks in Russian, "*Kto ti Amir?*" — Who are you, Amir?

Ameer salutes. "I am Ameer, freedom fighter —"

She shakes her head. "You're really good. You're better than me." Her thoughts stray for a moment before she asks again, "Are you real?"

He moves a lock of hair off her forehead and gently runs his fingers down the smooth skin of her face. She shivers. "I know that you're real, right here with me. I'm not sure about the rest . . ."

Ameer gazes into her eyes, drowning in them yet again. "I don't care about the rest. Right now . . . there is 'no rest' . . . there's nothing else."

Anouchka smiles as if his response has quenched her fears. Before they can resume their lustful romp, the camp alarm goes off. A man's voice comes through the public address speakers. "*Srotchnaya cvedanya!"* Immediate meeting! "Everyone is requested in the mess hall, right now." Ameer hears footsteps coming down the hall.

Anouchka seems to panic. "It must be Alexandar, you have to leave."

Ameer jumps into his trousers, shoves his shoes on, grabs his shirt, and dashes for the window. He turns back hastily to Anouchka, kisses her, and jumps out onto the backyard.

---

In Maalot in the Galilee, a Jewish-Arab village, some Palestinian *fedayeen* have captured a school bus full of children. Using blinding floodlights, wailing sirens, and overzealous, fake reporters as diversions, Amir's entry teams make their way to crouch beside the blue and white primary school bus. Amir assembles his four-man-strong Team Blue at the rear, while Ethan's Team Black waits near the bus's front door. Two more teams are on immediate standby. Amir squats with his back to the bus and peeks through the rear window with a pole-mounted mirror to locate the terrorists. Three are going up and down the aisle. A fourth, right near Amir at the back, seems to stand guard by what could be an explosive device.

The handle on the rear side door is broken, so Amir decides to let Ethan's team go instead of his. Amir gives the "GO" signal to Ethan's Number Two team member.

Ethan tears open the driver's door, his number two pulls out the dead driver's body, and Ethan leads his team onto the bus. They rush towards the back. Ethan shoots two terrorists in the aisle, putting double taps directly into their faces, an arm's length away, their skulls bursting under the impact of the powerful rounds. He pushes their limp bodies to the floor, not waiting for them to slump down, and stamps on them as he races to the rear.

A hijacker tries to hide behind a frightened child. Ethan's Number Two crouches slightly and empties the whole clip from his handgun into the man's chest at contact range. He then shouts "stoppage," signaling a clip change, and moves to the side. Number Three in Ethan's team takes over. Not taking any chances, he blows the lifeless terrorist face again with a three-shot burst, before proceeding behind Ethan. Number Two, now reloaded, puts more rounds into the terrorists Ethan killed already, looking them up for any bombs or grenades. Number Four in their team stays behind, covering the bus lengthwise from the driver's position, shouting and waving for the children to stay low, and stay calm.

In full sync with Ethan, and avoiding Team Black's cone of fire, Amir and his team have moved to the side of the bus, where he stands by a rear side window. As his Number Two puts his back to the bus and squats, and Amir climbs onto his mate's knees, Number Two hugs him around the legs to stabilize him. Amir's Number Three violently cuts and pulls the plastic window pane out of its frame and Amir shoots the fourth terrorist, putting half a dozen rounds into his chest and then another three rounds right into his frozen, astonished face. He tosses his near-empty pistols out and draws another, fully loaded one, from his chest holster, ready for more threats. There are none.

Screams from the children fill the air but, amazingly, they all respond to the verbal commands and screams quickly subside. Some gaze at their rescuers, frozen with fearful admiration. Others hide their heads under their hands, covering their ears from the deafening sound of the shooting, or try to hide under the benches.

Ethan pushes the rear side door open. "Well done, Amir. He had his hand on the detonator." He turns and says to the children, "Don't be afraid, children, *Hakol B'Seder*" — It's OK now. — "Stay calm and seated, you're going home." His men check for hidden weapons, then give Okays. They check the terrorists for signs of life and any surprises concealed on their bodies. Ethan's men declare the bodies clear and move them out of the way. Amir, who is watching from the back door, signals Ethan to check the device.

"Make sure there's no secondary firing mechanism on it, no wires."

Ethan reports, "There's nothing here, I guess the wire was the only way they had to detonate."

"Stay close to it, and don't let anyone get close. We'll evacuate from the front." The operation has so far gone textbook perfect, but it isn't over. The bomb disposal unit streams through the rear door.

Ethan addresses their leader. "Don't touch anything, we're moving the kids out."

"Yes, sir."

Ethan and his first two team members go out through the front door, while his Number Four carefully guides the shocked children to follow them. Inside the bus, Amir's men, in from the back, make sure all the terrified children get out safely and calmly. The men from Ethan's Team Black stand outside in a line and rush the children into a smaller evacuation bus. It has a large gate at the rear and a low step to make it easy for the children to hurry onto. Amir posts one of his men, Nehemiah, at the rear gate of the evacuation bus, so he can help the children in. Thankfully, none of them freezes with panic or has any trouble following the instructions. Amir wonders if the daily threats they live with make it possible for them to deal with the situation in such a brave way.

One of Ethan's operators, Naphtali, snatches a five-year-old boy from the line. He says, "*Elohim! Benny*" — God! my son — "What are you doing here? Why are you on that bus?"

"I was going for lunch at my friend's, Shimon." The boy turns to his friend Shimon, standing by his side, and then to his mates racing around, and shouts proudly, "Look, everybody, it's my father! My father is a commando! My father killed the terrorists! Look! It's my father!"

The running children look back in amazement. Benny and his father are the heroes of the day. Nehemiah rushes Naphthali, the father, into the bus with the children—there was no time to dally. Amir gives the thumbs up to the decision and shouts, "Move it!"

Amir's team moves forward with the last boy. Amir checks that all the kids are out, and signals "all clear." He hurries with the last child to the evacuation bus, where thirty students are packed into twenty seats. He closes the rear door and gives a double knock for the go ahead, and the driver takes off with a screech of tires.

Amir addresses his teams. "You did well, everyone! Ethan, you were perfect!" He looks at Ethan's team buddy, "Nice job spotting that third guy." He shakes his head. "Too bad about the poor driver."

Ethan grins. "I wouldn't worry too much about the driver. He's an Arab. They killed their own."

Amir retorts, "He was a brave man, he tried to stop them. He was going for their leader's gun. He was protecting *our* kids."

"I still couldn't care less. Perhaps his children will hate the Arabs who killed their father, instead of us. How about that, for a change?"

"We're not going to talk about that now. I am not shedding tears either, just recognizing the facts. Let's go back to HQ for a debrief. We have the operation on film?" A team member nods, and points to two of the reporters. Amir says, "We'll review it today, while it's fresh, and take notes. I want everyone's report first. Ethan, stay with me."

"I thought we were clear now."

"We still have a bomb to defuse."

"Defuse? Why don't we blow it up? The bomb crew is here . . ."

"What's the matter, you don't enjoy the job when there's no one to kill? We have to learn about the bomb, see how it's made."

Ethan taunts his friend. "Are you trying to impress someone?"

"We may have to deal with a bomb someday in a situation where we can't evacuate." Amir realizes what was behind Ethan's question. "Impress someone?"

"You know whom I am talking about . . ."

"She's not even here; she's on a mission somewhere . . ."

"Too bad . . . I saw you sneak into her bungalow at night. *Many* nights."

Amir is shocked. "That's impossible."

"Don't worry, I'm not taking note of that. Actually, I'm a little jealous."

"How do you know we weren't just discussing tactics?"

Ethan says shrewdly, "You just admitted it. It seems you haven't been studying the interrogation course, my friend. I believe I caught you with your pants down. Pun intended." Ethan grins. "What's my silence worth?"

"How about I cut out your tongue?" Amir is deeply disturbed. He had hoped no one knew. Anouchka has made him fail in his most devoted duty.

Ethan claps Amir on the shoulder. "I'm just teasing you. I realize the damage that could be done. No one will ever know about this, I swear."

"I love Debbie, and I love my children. Never, in my whole life, have I even *thought* about anyone other than Debbie. Not until *she* came along."

Ethan's thoughts seem to drift as he gives Amir an understanding look. "I know you too well to think otherwise. She's mesmerizing . . . I understand that it happened. But if you care about your family, make sure it stops right there, or you'll be head over heels before you know it. She has you under her spell, but I can tell she's taken by you, too. Don't underestimate *your* effect on her." He pokes his finger on Amir's chest. "Careful Amir. Maybe *she* won't let *you* go. She's not someone who would take no for an answer!"

A few feet behind them, a world away from Amir's mind, the bomb squad carefully lifts the shielded explosive from the rear of the bus. Ethan slaps Amir on the shoulder, "Look, they got the bomb out. Let's go dig into it."

Amir is still worried, and it isn't about the bomb. "Subject closed?"

"You have my word." Ethan points to the bomb squad. "Come on, time to focus. You've got to be ready for the debriefing."

Amir says, "It was good, it was perfect . . ."

"The operation or the girl?"

Amir is irritated. "Hey, we have a deal. I mean the operation."

Ethan shrugs. "I was too excited to let anything stop me. *Momentum*, as you say."

"Use of violence should always rely on momentum. Conventional or counter-terror operations. I'm just glad none of those children were hurt. They are the real heroes, all of them."

Ethan says, "I remember what you said when you gave your demonstration on hostage rescue. Bus, plane, building . . . As long as we're on the move, as long as we're pushing forward, they're deprived of any initiative. They're forced to withdraw or die; they have to submit to our tactical will, and we control the situation. No offense, but that's when I noticed Anouchka had some feelings for you."

Amir lets his mind drift. "I wonder where she is right now. She told me she was headed for Russia, to some sort of terrorist training camp."

As they approach the bomb squad, Amir says, "Enough of this now."

"Yes. Let's learn about this explosive device. For next time around . . ."

# CHAPTER 21

Ameer is driving his Jeep up the mountainous road, with Faris at his side. It is dusk, and cold mountain air blows through the open windows, yet Ameer wouldn't notice for he is burning with anticipation. It is October 6, and the first phase of Operation Badr is under way. At two o'clock this afternoon, a combined Egyptian and Syrian force will unleash a rolling wall of fire upon Israeli positions, and move in from several fronts. Badr, named after prophet Muhammad's first determining victory, which culminated in the taking of Mecca, will mark the Arabs' first victory against Israel. Just like the prophet, they will victoriously enter their enemy's cities and take them. There will be no failing this time. They *will* go home.

Ameer is leading his company on a raiding mission. Their target is an Israeli observation outpost in the occupied Syrian Golan Heights. He checks his rearview mirror and notices the dust raised by the three trucks carrying his men. On the isolated mountain roads, that cloud of dust can be seen from far away, even in the low light, and Ameer is concerned about giving away their mission.

"I'm going to stop earlier than scheduled, at the first landmark," he declares. "I'm dumping Anouchka's plan."

Faris has a satisfied grin. "Perfect. Yours is better anyway." He turns to the back seat and reaches for his rucksack, piled up amid the weapons and other gear. He pulls out a map, unfolds it, and looks out the windshield. He points at a location on the map. "This is it; we're almost there."

Ameer and his team have heard about the foiled bus hijacking. The plan seemed to have been thwarted from the minute it began. Ameer looks at Faris. "Had those *Fedayeen* followed my plan, they'd have made it." He bangs a fist on the steering wheel. "It was our mission, and we should have taken it."

Faris gives Ameer a devious look. "Perhaps she thought it was too dangerous for you."

Ameer spits his words out. "They were all rookies. With those children as hostages, just think how many of our friends could have been freed from jail. And we'd release the kids after —" Ameer notices Faris's look. "Too *what?* Dangerous?"

Faris widens his eyes as if innocent of any sarcasm. "I saw you two had a thing. You'd be in logistics if she had it her way."

Ameer slams on the brakes, squeezing the wheel furiously. Dust puffs into the car as it comes to a stop. "Are you crazy? Imagine if someone hears you! Layal would be destroyed!"

Faris looks behind him, squinting in the cloud of dust, and shouts, "The trucks!"

Ameer yanks the Jeep into first gear and gets it back up to speed. His mind is somewhere else, though, racing between the soothing love of his beloved wife and the irresistible lust for his lover. Layal's eyes against Anouchka's. The warmth of love against passionate heat.

Faris turns back to Ameer, "But it's the truth. You're going to lie about it?"

Ameer smiles at his friend. He always admired Faris's head-on approach to life, and he wishes he could just confront his wife about this the way Faris would. He confronts his friend instead. "Look, something happened, I don't know why. We just couldn't resist it. Now it's a thing of the past, never to be revealed to anybody, do you understand me?"

"Mmm . . . Yes, of course." Faris has a sly look. What happened, *exactly*?"

Ameer answers with a laugh. "*Exactly?* That's none of your business. She asked me to her room for the dinner break, remember? I knew there was something about her. I had this . . . *sensation*. I think she did too. We were both out of control."

"Go on, it's getting interesting. You were there for a few hours . . ."

Ameer shakes his head, and the lingering emotions that fill it. "The rest is private. It's in the past, and it's never happened. It never will again. I pledged it." He points to a large, rounded rock on the side of the road. "That's the landmark." He pulls his Jeep over, gets out and waves for the trucks to stop behind his car.

Faris joins him. "I recognize the terrain, just like on the map." He points to a snaking footpath forking away from the road just after the rock, going straight up the steep hill on the right side. "Damn. Is that the path you want us to take? It's too steep. Some of the men are fasting!"

"Fasting?"

"Well, it is Ramadan. Not that you were exactly restraining yourself, flesh-wise —"

"Never mention that again. Understand? NOT EVER!"

"Okay. I'll tell the men to dismount and get ready to march."

As Faris gives his orders to the sergeants in the trucks, Ameer peers at the map. He taps Faris on the shoulder, to get his attention, and points to the footpath. "Faris, look. We'll go up from here, and then split into three groups."

"You're changing everything!"

"I just don't like the kind of intelligence she claimed she had, or her plan. Sentries sleeping, our entire force moving in single file, with me in front and ahead, taking point . . . it doesn't make sense."

Faris agrees. "Not at all. It's good you changed everything." He takes the map from Ameer and spreads it on the Jeep's hood. "You said three units. The footpath seems to split in two before reaching the target —"

Ameer cuts into his friend's guesswork by opening up the back door of his Jeep and pulling out his rappelling gear. "My platoon is climbing." He lifts a heavy bundle of rope to his shoulder and points on the map to an area behind the target. It is a sheer cliff.

Excitement lights up Faris' face. "That's more like it. That's more like *you*. You and your crazy plans. They won't expect anyone to climb those walls. They must be fifteen meters high. More actually. We'll squeeze them from three sides."

Ameer moves his finger along the map, showing Faris his intended route. "My unit will be the most exposed. I'll climb the cliffs immediately behind the bunkers, and then we'll get on top of the two bunkers. Remember, we have to take these positions intact, and get the logbooks for their radio transmission. We have to broadcast at least once from there, pretending we're them." Ameer has a brief smile. "I hope my Hebrew will do."

Faris says, "It will. Tarek made sure of that, all these years. Now let's hope this Arab offensive goes down as planned, and we finally bring Israel to its knees."

Ameer has a worried tone. "I believe we can win . . . except for one thing."

Faris punches him in the shoulder. "There you go again. What's it going to be this time? We win and then die of the plague?"

"I think it's pretty obvious the Arabs are starting this war for themselves, and not for us. They're not interested in Palestine being free any more. They just want to wipe out the insult of the last war and get into a better bargaining position, for *their* land."

"So, what? You don't think they'll continue on to Tel Aviv?"

Ameer has a cynical laugh. "The real question is, why would Syria or Egypt shed blood for us? Especially in a scenario where total victory probably can't happen anyway. Neither the US or even the USSR will allow for a total routing of the Israeli army."

Faris sighs and looks at the path up the hill. "Well, we'll do our part."

"Yes, we will." Ameer stares into Faris' eyes to make sure he fully grasps his next words. "I will fire first, Ok? You wait for my signal. I only want snipers on the bunkers' openings. Otherwise, we'll shoot each other. We're in our own crossfire. Your men will handle the small buildings next to the bunkers." He pulls out a black-and-white picture from his inside pocket. It clearly shows their target.

Faris is surprised. "Where did you get that?"

"It's a Russian satellite photo. I got it from Anouchka's file. I did my job, without telling anyone, even her. I had a hunch about this operation. Something wasn't quite right about the Israeli set-up."

Faris raises an eyebrow. "You think it's a trap? But Anouchka planned it . . ."

"I don't know. But my instinct tells me there's something wrong." Ameer points back to the map. "Now, you can see the two smaller buildings next to the bunkers. They're for the generators and the radar station. Be careful not to blow their fuel tanks. The explosion would be seen from a long distance." Ameer points to highlighted areas. "Minefields."

His sergeant, Khalil, approaches. He points a thumb toward the men behind him with their assault vests and backpacks on, rifles in hand. "*Jahzeen.*" We're all set, sir. "Three platoons, as ordered."

Ameer glances at the men. They are stretching out and lighting up cigarettes. Ameer isn't fasting, but he can't help to remark with sarcasm, "*Ramadan Kareem*. I see none of the men is fasting. So no moaning on the way up then. Let's move! And put out those cigarettes. I can smell them from a mile away, and so can the enemy. I've changed the initial plan, and I'll brief you along the way."

Faris faces Khalil. "You heard him. Quiet, and no smoking." He signals his next order with a cutting motion of his hand at his radio antenna and a back-and-forth movement with his finger followed by a fist. "Keep radios off, hand signals only."

Ameer's sergeant comes up, followed by the rest of the platoon. Ameer pulls another bundle of climbing rope from his Jeep and tosses it to him. He has one last look at the men, at their determined, eager faces. Commitment shines on every face. They don't need any speeches. Ameer smiles to his sergeant and gives the marching signal.

Two hours of hard marching and climbing later, Ameer's platoon is in place, just behind the bunkers. Faris' and the sergeant's teams are in position as well. The three teams form a triangle around their target, with Ameer's team on slightly higher ground, Faris and Khalil's teams are lower than the bunkers, invisible to their occupants, approaching directly from the fields, avoiding the mined sectors, and avoiding the exposed footpath.

Ameer climbs to a vantage point on top of his target and sees five enemy foxholes a few meters in front of the bunkers, invisible to anyone coming up from the front. He raises his fist, signaling Faris and Khalil, who are about to walk straight at them, to freeze.

There are two soldiers with machine guns in each foxhole. Some of the men are dozing in the sun. There is no activity coming from the bunkers. Ameer makes a circle with his thumb and finger then flashes the number five to tell Faris and Khalil about the foxholes. Ameer signals that he'll take care of them. He turns toward his men and sig-nals the corporal to send him five of them. He assigns one to each of the foxholes, explaining with hand signals. The men rush away to their positions, and at Ameer's commands, they toss grenades into the fox-holes, followed promptly by rifle fire. The foxholes and their occupants are turned into mashed soil and burning flesh. Ameer jumps down the side of the bunker and moves his team, hugging the wall of the building. His corporal's team is assigned to the other bunker, while Faris' men would handle the auxiliary buildings, and Khalil's team takes covering positions. Ameer signals Khalil to his side, to join his entry team.

The heavy steel door is ajar, and Ameer quickly pushes it open. In the familiar chaos of smoke, sound, and dust, Ameer plunges inside, his trusted Khalil and the rest of his squad right behind him. Ameer comes face to face with an Israeli soldier. The soldier squints into Ameer's face, as he stands backlit by the door.

Ameer can hear him stutter, "Amir . . . Amir? Is that you?"

Ameer freezes, his kalash leveled at the soldier. How does this man know him? Why does *he* seem to know him? The Israeli's expression changes as he goes for his rifle.

Khalil cuts the man down with a burst from his AK. *"Allah Akbar!* What the hell are you waiting for, sir? He nearly got you!"

Shaken, Ameer says, "I don't know, I thought I—"

"Don't think. Push ahead and kill. Your own words."

Ameer wonders if his mind has played tricks on him. He is tempted to ask his mates if they'd heard anything, but they are already past him, fanning out through the narrow hallways, clearing rooms in the bunker with bursts from their AK's. Ameer stands, scratching his head, looking at the soldier's corpse. Did that really happen?

As the firing subsides, both inside the bunkers and out, Ameer hears a burst of fire come from a room below, then silence, and Khalil emerges. He hands Ameer a pack of papers. "Are these the logs you want?"

Ameer takes the papers and nods. He starts reading the papers. Faris bursts in. "You were right, they were ready for us. The path is mined, with manual triggers. They have them in the foxholes."

Ameer orders, "Give me a quick report, take care of the wounded, and establish a defense perimeter. They may have patrols up here. And have someone clear all signs of fighting — if they send reconnaissance planes, they should think we're Israelis. They're going to call us soon if anyone heard the firefight. I need to figure out these codes." Ameer looks down at the logbook, goes through its pages.

Faris stands to attention. "Right away. You think those logs could be fake?"

"They're real. They didn't expect us to prevail." Ameer shakes his head. "If they knew we were coming, then someone sold us out. Who could have done that?"

Faris' voice turns angry. "Why don't you ask Anouchka about that? She must look into this. It was a 'need to know' basis operation."

Ameer shakes his head, wondering aloud, "There is a leak somewhere. I wonder. She must be stranded somewhere with no comm."

———

Amir and his unit race through the mountain pass through the Golan Heights, their Jeeps bouncing off rocks and boulders. They heard about the war, an all-out Arab assault, on the radio, and immediately rallied their units, eager to get in, do their job, and stop the enemy. Not all his men are with him — they couldn't wait for everyone to join up. All he needed for now was a small strike force. Even though it was Yom Kippur, the enemy's attempt at surprising them had backfired since many of the men were gathered at synagogues and heard the news quickly. The IDF ranks were filling up quickly.

Amir and his unit are supposed to meet up with Moshe's army intelligence team, at an advanced military post, where they'd get instructions on their mission. Their country was under attack on two fronts. The Egyptian army had crossed the border from the west, along the canal, while the Syrian army was gaining ground in the Golan Heights, to the Northeast. If the invaders kept up their momentum, the very existence of Israel would be at stake. Thankfully, and inexplicably, the Egyptian army's deployment didn't show signs of going deeper past the Canal and towards Israel proper. The IDF decided to concentrate on the broken Golan Heights fronts, an immediate threat to their nation, as the Syrian army was progressing fast, and Israeli units were ridiculously outnumbered. Both invading armies are deploying a new arsenal of weaponry — a new set of surface-to-air systems — and are effectively putting them to lethal use, wreaking havoc on the Israeli Air Force.

After an hour of their frenetic driving along the rough roads, Amir's unit reaches the outpost. It looks like a vision from hell. A Syrian force had overrun it, before an Israeli counter-attack snatched it back. Both sides had paid dearly — burning vehicles litter the ground, and scores of bodies, covered with plastic sheets, are lined up on the ground, near the main building. Wounded soldiers gather at a makeshift field hospital. The air is filled with the smell of dust, burnt powder and smoke.

Moshe isn't difficult to find. His Super Frelon helicopter is right in the middle of the landing square of the base; a pair of Cobras, with menacing teeth painted on their noses, stand guard on either flank. Moshe is by his chopper with some officers, peering over a large map spread on a small metallic table. Amir stops his Jeep a few meters from

Moshe. He signals for his lieutenant in the Jeep behind him to get their two platoons and vehicles out of the way, and to give the base commander a hand while he talks to Moshe.

As Amir dismounts, Moshe dismisses his men and rushes to him, with a concerned look on his face. He looks him over. "*Mah schlom-cha?*" — How are you?

Amir is jumpy. "I'm fine. Just give us something to do."

"Patience, young man."

Amir nods and stares Moshe in the eyes. He doesn't seem to be hiding anything, but then again, with Moshe, who would know? Amir is worried about his father, who is on a special mission on the Egyptian front. They don't have proper air support, because of the efficiency of the Egyptian SAM systems, and the Egyptians were also wielding new man-operated Anti-Tank missiles that were causing massive casualties in their armor divisions.

Moshe seems to be reading his thoughts. "Ely is okay, I just spoke with him on the radio. You can do that later on if you want. I know *he* wants to talk to you."

Amir sighs in relief. "I'm afraid they're getting butchered out there. Is he ... careful?"

"I know he is. At first, the Arabs broke our backs. We took heavy casualties. Those new anti-tank missiles, the 'Saggers,' are deadly, and our air force can't provide close support because of the new SAM missiles they have, not to mention the Shilkas." Amir raises an eyebrow. "They're deployed in combination?" Moshe goes on, "Yes. Twenty-three mm anti-aircraft quad guns. Self-propelled. Radar-guided. They're shooting down all our low-flying planes. The SAMs are shooting everything at medium altitude. They have those new SAM Six." He points to his sensor-laden chopper. "I've been on a listening mission to learn about their radars, their frequencies, and their homing technologies. I have a full team of electronic specialists with me, working on a solution."

Amir says, "Good. But where do I fit in? How can my troops help? I have a fraction of my men here, Ethan with the rest of the unit is still behind."

Moshe pulls Amir toward his field table, and points to the map, showing present Israeli positions as well as those of the enemy. "Special teams will be inserted at critical points into enemy territory, where their jobs will mostly be reconnaissance, and also—"

"Why don't we go for their SAMs? Their radars?"

"They have good security around them. It would be next to impossible. We're out of direct fire range."

Amir studies the map. He notes enemy troop positions as well as those of suspected SAM units. "Moshe, if your maps are correct, then I have an idea. Look here, the SAMs are slightly behind the front units so they aren't threatened by our troops. But on the flanks, where they don't expect any attacks because of the terrain, they're exposed. We can mount flank attacks, hit and run missions on both missiles and mobile radars. We can use our own missiles, or spot for our artillery. Our one-seventy-five's can reach them from these locations." Amir traces an arc from the side and with arrows straight through the enemy's advancing division, showing how he would outflank them, and how their artillery could move into range.

Moshe's face lights up. "We'd be opening a path for our air force, right into their belly."

"Exactly."

Moshe bangs his fist on the table, a sadistic grin on his face. "What do you need from me?"

"Comm. gear, TOW missiles, and portable SAMs for choppers. We'll need to break away quickly after each engagement — their SAMs are not far from their main units, and that's a lot of firepower to run away from. We could use anti-tank choppers as well. I'll need direct communication with the pilots."

"You've got it," says Moshe, showing him selected frequencies on the radio. "I like your plan. But how do you expect to reach firing spots so far in?"

"How heavily loaded are you?" Amir points at Moshe's helicopter. "We're ready to go."

Moshe is taken aback. "HQ would kill me if they knew I compromised that chopper. It's loaded with sensitive material."

Amir replies, "By hugging the ground, we can avoid detection."

Moshe is still concerned. "What about extraction? You'll be pretty far in."

Amir shrugs. "We won't need it; we're staying there. We'll hop from one position to the next, once Ethan links up with me by land. I'll need close air support, plus resupplies in ammo." Amir's look is full of intent. "We'll see you in Damascus, my friend."

Moshe nods his okay. "It's a good plan, but what if you have someone seriously wounded?"

"Don't worry about us. Actually, we can do more, if you find me the resources."

"What do you need, and what for? We're stretched thin . . ."

Amir's excitement builds. "We'll do exactly what I just said, but on a larger scale. A company-strength force, increasing to battalion-strength, as more troops arrive, mounted on light vehicles, can clear up the full flank for our air force." Amir takes a pen from Moshe's shirt pocket and puts crosses on his intended destination points. He shows Moshe how he could neutralize the vulnerable enemy SAMs on the entire enemy flanks.

Moshe gives him the thumbs up. *"Be seder.* What will you need?"

Amir says, "I'll need eight to ten Jeeps with TOWs, six to eight with medium mortars, and about ten with heavy machine guns for defense against soft targets, and as many with recoilless guns as you can. Lots of ammo and logistics for two intense days."

Moshe looks shocked. "That's a lot!"

Amir shakes his head. "I'm talking about opening a full corridor in their flanks for our Air Force. If our airplanes help with the land battle, then we can redirect our armor against Egypt sooner."

Moshe stays calm. "I'll see what I can do. You'll need your cars to be equipped with communication."

"One radio for every four cars will do. We'll drive the Syrians crazy. We'll destroy every SAM position in our area, and we'll clear the skies for our boys." Amir has a cruel look. "We'll make them pay. I swear it."

Moshe looks at Amir with admiration. "That's the spirit. I'll get you all you need."

Amir insists, "Don't forget the air support. How about . . . your Cobra escort?"

"My thoughts too. They are the best."

Amir is satisfied. "Thanks. Send them as soon as you can."

"My mission is in the same area you'll be operating in. I'll drop you and stay on standby, the cobras too. Do not engage larger units, just tickle their flanks so we can go in."

"We're good to go?"

Moshe nods. "I guess you are." He steps back. "Take care of yourself. Brief your men, then saddle up with me. I'll have Ethan join up with the main force, once I get it together for you."

Amir says, "I'll leave instructions for him."

Moshe takes him by the shoulders. "I can see you're on top of things."

Amir is confident. "I am. Let's save our country. And teach them a lesson, once and for all. When we're done. They should not *want* to attack us anymore. Ever."

Ameer is gathering his men outside an Israeli position they have just overrun. Following their success at their first objective, Ameer decided to use the intel from the satellite photos, and the available Israeli trucks, to attack yet another position. They overran the enemy, but got bogged down in the process.

It is very late in the afternoon, and the Arab attack is already well underway. Khalil is driving back from a scouting mission Ameer had sent him on; before they can return to their trucks, and commit the troops to the fight, he needs information on any enemy that might be in the vicinity. He also needs to know about friendly forces in the area, since they were driving undercover, in Israeli vehicles. Just in case, Ameer had both Palestinian and Israeli flags ready to fly on the vehicles.

Khalil screeches to a halt in a cloud of dust. "There's an enemy force heading our way. More than twenty Jeeps with TOWs, Guns, mortars, and heavy machine guns. Two minutes out."

Ameer looks at Faris. "Status?"

"The wounded and all the gear are loaded. We can leave within seconds."

Ameer shakes his head. "Yes, but we're slow, with the trucks. They'll catch up."

Faris and Khalil try to speak at once. "I can—"

Ameer interrupts, putting one hand on each of their shoulders. "No. You cannot. I can. I will stay behind with my platoon and the Jeeps. Faris, you're in charge. You take the entire company back to our trucks. And wait for me. The Israelis cannot follow us too deep in, we control the area." He looks at the approaching cloud of dust. "Go. Now!"

Faris and Khalil look at each other.

Ameer insists. "Every second counts. I have the advantage of surprise. I will only delay them for a few minutes then break contact."

Faris and Khalil reluctantly nod, quickly shake hands with Ameer, then turn around and rush towards their troops. They climb aboard the trucks and drive off. Ameer orders his men to bring the captured Jeeps.

Ameer sets up an ambush for the incoming Israeli force. From the South-East, where the Israelis are, a single dirt road leads up to their position, snaking through small terrain mounds. He sets four of his men, in their Jeep, behind the last of those, directing one of them, Nemer, to climb the mound and observe the enemy. With three more of his men, he remains next to his Jeep, flying an Israeli flag, in the open, a few meters ahead of the bunkers, where the rest of his men have scattered, manning heavy machine guns and RPGs. With two of his men standing next to him, he opens the hood of his Jeep, pretending to fix an engine problem, while the third sits at the wheel. The men are ready. Ameer is not. *That sensation is back. He hasn't felt it in years but the feeling is unmistakable. It takes ahold of him, yet again.* Enemy vehicles appear, about two hundred meters away. They come to a sudden stop, and all the cars disappear in a cloud of dust. A mortar round explodes near his men at the last mound, and the sentry they had posted on top comes rushing down. They hop in the Jeep and rush back. One of them shouts, "They have gone off the road, they are coming on foot from everywhere! The Jeeps you see are empty!"

Ameer shakes out of his daze. "Everybody in my Jeep." The men quickly pile up. Ameer points to Nemer, and the Jeep he's in. "Do as me!" Ameer quickly takes out the two spare fuel jerry cans hanging on the back of his Jeep, and shouts to his driver, "Go!" The Jeep takes off in a cloud of dust.

Ameer shouts to Nemer, who pulls out the two jerry cans from the back of his Jeep. Mortar rounds are exploding around them, and machine gun fire pocks the ground, dings the car. His men are firing back as well. Ameer and Nemer are caught right in the middle. Ameer opens one of his jerry cans and tosses it inside the remaining Jeep. Nemer does the same. They both throw the remaining cans on either side of the Jeep, after pouring some of the fuel on the ground. One of Ameer's men dashes back towards him, an RPG launcher on his shoulder. "Go Sir! I'll cover you!"

Ameer looks at the launcher, follows its aim. There's a small flash of light. Is it a sniper scope? Binoculars? *Ameer feels the sensation back again, stronger than ever. It controls him. It guides him. Ameer motions his man down and bellows, "No! Back! Take cover!" Ameer stands motionless, squinting towards the light.*

Nemer throws a grenade inside the Jeep. He takes Ameer by the shoulder, and rushes him back to the bunker, amidst a hail of bullet and shell splinters. The grenade explodes. The burning car, doused with fuel, fills the air with dense smoke.

---

Amir knows the military outpost he's heading to, like many others, is in enemy hands. They have failed the non-written duress code interrogation when responding to their HQ's request to acknowledge their status. He orders some of his men off their Jeeps, leaving only a driver-machine gunner team, and into the others. The two-man Jeeps proceed towards the objective, raising as much dust as possible. The rest of them swerve off the sand road and onto the rocky trails leading to the top of the mounds surrounding the bunker. They set up their TOW missiles and their mortars. When they are within view of the seized bunker, the two-man Jeeps raise so much dust that they disappear in it, and mask the entire area around them. Then they assume firing positions, aiming their machine guns at enemy positions, and wait for the signal to fire the first mortar round.

Amir gives the order to fire. The first mortar shell is immediately followed by a hail of fire, which is returned in kind by the enemy. The desert sand and battle smoke prevent any exact assessment of the situation, but the enemy seems concentrated in the bunker or running towards it. In between, there is this strange group pretending to fix their Jeep. Amir calls his sniper, Shimon, to go prone next to him. He points him to the two men with jerry cans, rushing around the Jeep. "Wait for my signal."

Shimon checks through his scope, turns the focus ring, then adjusts the distance turret a few clicks. He looks back into it, following the moving targets. "Ready."

Amir is peering through his binoculars. *The sensation he's felt before overtakes him again. He looks at the stranger, tossing jerry cans into the Jeep. Amir feels his body go totally numb, and he is unable to move or speak. He has to give the order. He can see himself, from the target's viewpoint, giving that order. He can see the bullet zipping through the air, blowing his own head off. He is paralyzed. Still. He can feel the target equally lost, and he even stops his own man from firing a rocket at them.*

Shimon cuts through. "Sir, they're about to light up the fuel. We will lose them."

Amir throws his binoculars, snaps the rifle from Shimon. "You're zeroed?"

"They're two hundred meters out. I just need to squeeze."

Amir puts the rifle to his shoulder, looks through the scope. He can see the enemy tossing a grenade into the Jeep. He knows he only has a few seconds before the smoke turns accurate fire into spray and pray. He cannot take the shot. The enemy turns towards him, stops for a second, before his mate grabs him by the shoulder and pulls him back, as an explosion wrecks the Jeep apart, and a burning fire fills the air with dense smoke.

Amir insists on peering through the scope. He wants to see that enemy. His face. The sensation is slowly fading, and Amir wants to know. He wants to know what it is, and why it's happening again. Who is *that* enemy? Is *he* causing that sensation? Like in Jerusalem, in '67? Why did he pause? Why did he, like him, stop his man from firing at *them*?

# CHAPTER 22

Approaching the maze of refugee houses he calls "home," Ameer pushes his Jeep to go faster on the last stretch. Faris sits in the seat next to him. It's mid-October, and the weather is still hot, but a gentle breeze makes it more tolerable. He veers onto the road leading to the camp. The upscale suburbs of Beirut and its airport, with their patches of greenery and modern buildings, yield to a web of narrow dirt roads that meander around protruding house corners and bulging walls.

Ameer imagines the smell of his son's freshly washed hair, as he'd sit on his lap for dinner. He's been shuffling between training and battle for so long now, and he misses his family badly. He is eager to see Layal. He has decided against telling her about his affair. It was best for everyone. Even if she understood it like he did, as a one-time mistake, it would probably still mar their relationship forever. Nothing good could come from talking about it now. He only ever knew Layal, and he wished he hadn't spoiled that.

But now the war is over, and he is coming home. He decided to take a long break, at least a couple of weeks, to enjoy his family. No more missions on faraway lands, or training on other continents. And no more 'fog of war' . . . that overwhelming sensation he had while confronting the enemy. Snapshots of that last encounter on the Golan Heights were still flashing in his mind. For a brief moment there, just like in Jerusalem in '67, that sensation took hold of him yet again.

But now, Ameer is dreaming about his wife, about taking a bath, perhaps together — if the kids give them a break. And if the neighbors, whose own bathroom window is merely three meters away from theirs, also give them a break. Fresh sheets, Layal's soft skin, the sweet smell of home cooking. Even more, he has one fixating thought: Little Tarek. Ameer can't wait to hold him, until all the feeling of missing him is dispelled. Right now, he'd say it never will. And he misses his daughter Nidal, and wonders how much she's grown. Is she sitting upright by herself? Has she added any new sounds to her babbling? Will she remember her father? Faris always laughs at him when he tries to talk about these feelings. How could Faris understand what it was like to be a father? Ameer is a different person when he's inside his house. The fierce fighter morphs into a warm and tender family man, who can spend the whole day blabbering a secret language only he and Little Tarek understand.

"Stop daydreaming," Faris snaps. "We're almost there."

Ameer says, "I miss them like hell."

"*Relax.* There'll be a reception committee. The men want to celebrate. We'll dance the *dabké* and sing 'til morning."

Ameer smiles in anticipation. "I can only imagine my father's reaction to our victory. He'll probably downplay everything."

Faris is defiant. "He can't downplay what we did. Of course, then again, we're going back to a camp in Lebanon, not to our new villas in an upscale Jerusalem suburb."

Ameer laughs. "Does that even exist? An upscale Jerusalem suburb?"

"I don't know, but I'd settle for an apartment."

Ameer nods. "Me too, just take us back to that land we don't even know. Tarek still shows us mother's family pictures. It's all she has left. Black and white pictures and an old brass house key."

"He wants to keep the flame burning." Faris pauses a second. "Why wouldn't he approve of the war's results?"

"He's always said that the Arabs have other objectives than ours, and he's right. He always is."

"Kind of disturbs you, doesn't it?"

"Not a day goes by without me having more admiration for Tarek's wisdom."

Faris says, "He'll be proud of you. We're all disappointed for not having gone in and taken land. But we achieved an important mission. We broke their myth of invincibility. Now they'll be forced to make concessions. They can't afford another war like this one, but we can go on forever."

"You got that right. The real fighting can begin now." Ameer turns into the road that marks the entrance to his neighborhood and drives past the new medical center, the only construction in their camp with a relatively clean look, with a painted façade and modern windows. The guard at the door, whom Ameer knows well, turns his head away when Ameer salutes him, and doesn't return the salute, pretending he hadn't seen him. Ameer is too excited to think twice about it. "Look, we're home! I miss it. *Al-hamdu lellah*."

Faris frowns as he looks around. "I don't see a welcoming committee. No banners, no crowd? What's the matter with these people?"

Ameer is equally disappointed. "The men will feel let down . . . they're merely an hour behind us."

Veering into his street, Ameer sees that windows are closed and that the only banners are purple. Everywhere. Ameer sighs. "All those purple banners. Someone young died; someone very young."

"Maybe one of the younger trainees."

Ameer sighs. "I hope not. I pity his parents. Losing a son. It's so devastating."

Faris points ahead. "There's your neighbor coming out of your house. Look, there's your father and Rima. They're waiting for us. They look . . . What's happening?"

Ameer sees his father with the same face he had when Rabih died. He brings his Jeep to a screeching halt and jumps out. His mother Rima collapses when she sees him and Tarek has to ease her to the ground, as he waves another woman in for help. Women all around start showing up at their windows, dressed in black, wailing. Men, emerging from their houses, fire guns in the air. Young boys wave Palestinian flags. He hears some of them shout, *"Allah Akbar!"* but he is focused on his father. For only the second time in his life, Ameer sees tears in his father's eyes. Despite their wet coat, Tarek's piercing eyes are riveted into his. Ameer notices his father take a deep breath. His heart pounds like a drum. The neighbors look at him with evasive looks of guilt. Ameer grabs his father's shoulders. *"Shu sar?"* — What happened? — "Where's Layal? Where's my boy? Where's little Tarek? Where's Nidal? What happened?"

Tarek mutters, "Layal is okay, I think. And Nidal. You have to be brave my son. *Macha' Allah, Allah Akbar.*"

Ameer is overcome with a rush of despair. "Little Tarek! It's him! It's my little Tarek! What happened? Is he sick? Where's Layal?" He pushes his father away and heads for his house.

Layal appears in the doorway, her face swollen from crying. Ameer rushes to her. Holding her by the arms, he cries, "What happened to Little Tarek? *Ebnee . . .*" — My boy. — "He's behind the house, playing in the garden? He has to be there, that's where I left him. I promised him I'd be back. I promised him he'd be safe. I *swore* it!"

Layal's pale, dried lips hardly move. "Little Tarek is playing in

*Janneh*" — paradise — "now. Our boy, our little boy ... left us two days ago ..." She falters to a stop.

Ameer is in shock. "What do you mean, playing in paradise?"

Tarek approaches. With a broken voice, he explains. "Little Tarek was playing in the field. He found an unexploded cluster bomb and was tossing it around. He died ... was killed."

Ameer shakes Layal, screaming. "*La*! I don't believe you. I want to see him, and I want to see him now! I know he's not dead, he *cannot* die. I promised him I'd keep him safe. I am his father, and I will keep, *my boy*, safe! Forever! I will not let *anything* harm him ... *ebnee* — my own son."

Tarek takes him by the hands. "Take it easy on Layal, she's under sedatives. Nidal is sleeping at the neighbors. You have to take care of them now."

Ameer lashes back. "I want to see little Tarek. Now! If he's dead, I want to see his body. Take me to my son! He wants to see me too." Ameer's voice starts to break. "My dead son needs to see me ... my little Tarek ..."

His father answers with a soft voice. "Little Tarek is with God now."

Ameer looks his father in the eyes. "Has he been buried?"

"He's in the hospital. We weren't sure when you'd be back. He's in the hospital's mortuary, waiting for you."

The reality begins to penetrate Ameer's numbed mind. It hits a wall of denial. He shouts with outrage, "*The mortuary?* Alone? But he's afraid of the dark! Let him out; let my son out of there now!"

Tarek looks at Faris, who steps in to help, disbelief on his face too. Faris takes Ameer by the shoulder. "Ameer, you have to be brave, like you've always been. Allah is taking care of your son now."

Ameer shakes his head. "I need to see him. You have to understand. I have to see his face. His body. I want to ... my son, my own, my flesh and bone, *he* is *me*! Nothing can exist without him. Nothing. There is nothing. Do you understand?" Ameer pulls frantically at his own skin, as if, by some miracle, he could revive little Tarek out of his own flesh.

Tarek says, with a firm tone, "Come with me son, I'll take you there." He takes Ameer by the arm and walks him toward the hospital, near the entrance to the camp.

Ameer lets go of his father's hand and dashes all the way to the hospital, pursued by Tarek and Faris. He hurries inside where the shocked and tearful faces seem to have been dreading his arrival. The mortuary is down a flight of stairs, which Ameer takes in a single bound. He glances left and right and then frantically pulls on the lever of the only closed cell, pulling it out.

The sight of his son's remains, his wooden kalash and handgun next to him, will be Ameer's companion for the rest of his life. Ameer stares at the peaceful face, poked by the burning powder of the bomb. He dares not touch it, at first. He moves his hands above Little Tarek frozen face, then his body, as if he'd expect him to rise up and jump into his waiting embrace. Little Tarek does not move. Ameer looks at the wooden pistol next to his son's body, then the kalash. Without turning, he hands the kalash to Faris, behind him. In their war games, little Tarek would always hand Ameer the heavier kalash and Ameer, in a gesture that only a father can understand, has decided to keep it, so he can continue playing with his dead son, wherever he was. He knows he'd never accept his son's death, and only upon their reuniting, through his own death, could he achieve deliverance from this maddening reality.

Finally, Ameer wraps his arms around the cold, inert body of his son, and lifts him up, as Faris takes him by the shoulders, trying to stop him. With a long wail of agony, Ameer falls to his knees, clutching his son as tight as he can. *"Albee inta, rouhee inta."* — You're my heart, you're my soul. *"Inta a'ayesh, bi albee, bi dammi, inta ma bet mout."* — You're alive, in my heart, in my blood, you cannot die. — *"Abadan ma bet mout."* — You can never die. Ameer lifts and cuddles his son, pressing him against his chest, choking as he hopes for a miracle, for an awakening from this nightmare. But Little Tarek does not stir. He does not breathe. His body, his beautiful face, remain burnt. Cold. Limp.

In Ameer's mind, little Tarek laughs and plays, but in his hands, he is a lifeless, limp corpse, his head dangling from his neck, his innocent face martyred by the blast that took away his life, his skin marred and blackened by the explosion. Ameer is slowly becoming aware of this. *"Wallahi sa antaquim lak!"* — I swear I will avenge you. Ameer swears revenge before Allah, before his dead son.

His father tries to calm him down. *"Bi kaffi yabni,"* Tarek says softly, *"Bass, bi kaffi."* — Enough son. That's enough. But Ameer is in a different world. In a world where there's no talking, and no listening, and no life, either. Ameer's world is one of death, and only death. It has no earth and no skies. It is a red ocean forever floating in blackened, hollow space. With a long wail of agony, Ameer howls his anger and his sorrow. He swears to drown his enemies in an ocean of their own blood. Their most cherished blood, the blood of their children. All of their children, all of their blood. A whole ocean of it.

---

In their living room, Amir and Debbie stand stoically silent on a mattress next to the wall, as the tradition bids in such circumstances. A breeze gently sails through the open windows, refreshing their dead faces with a futile breath of cool air. Cool and air have just been banned forever from their lives.

One by one, people walk by them, mouthing words of sympathy. Amir isn't aware of the faces, the words, or even the presence of their friends. One after another, people approach, shake hands, mumble a few words, sometimes giving a glance. Looks of compassion, looks of courage, firm handshakes, long handshakes, sweaty handshakes, two-handed shakes, they are all the same. They all drown in his flooded mind.

His thoughts go from blurred visions to focused snapshots, mixing memories of smells, sights, and sounds from their lost life. Instant, yet distant memories . . . of his daughter Liz. Now and then, Amir and Debbie are roused from their abyss by a close relative or, worst of all, a friend who has suffered a similar nightmare. Amir clutches Ron, a friend and comrade-in-arms who lost his son a year before in a terrorist attack on a school. Seeing Ron pushes away the denial that was Amir's refuge. Ron's ordeal had been the talk of the neighborhood, of how real it seemed to everyone but him. Now it is Amir's turn, and his own dead child is as dead as his friend's, and that is a fact. A friend like Ron brings in a surge of reality. Ron means reality. Ron *is* reality. Ron means: Liz *is* dead.

In those few moments of devastating truth, Amir tries to follow a vision of her as she walks through the door, holding her doll tight to her chest; he tries to hear the sound of her crying out from her bedroom. It is all true and real, right there in his mind, locked up and under guard, with nowhere to go, bouncing back and again against the inside of his skull.

But it is only in his mind. With a broken voice, he manages to say, "She was just here, Ron, my Liz was just here. I came home, I'd been dreaming about her all along the way. Dreaming and dreaming . . . I could smell her, I could see her, I could even feel her. Now they tell me my Liz is gone!"

Ron replies, choking on the words, "Liz is in good hands now Amir, you have to believe it. She's fine. This is *Elohim's* will."

"I kissed her good night before leaving. I said, '*Sweet* dreams,' and she said, 'I'll dream of you, coming back home...'" Amir's voice breaks.

And so it goes, mourners by the dozens, coming to show their sympathy. The whole Rehavia neighborhood, all of their relatives, friends, and military personnel, everyone is here. They come every day for the *shiva* — the seven mourning days that follow the burial. The overwhelming traffic of people grants Amir's family a transitional period. Being surrounded by so many people, all here to ease and share their pain, is supposed to take their minds off the most horrible thing for Amir and Debbie, if only for a few moments. They lost their beloved daughter, Liz, and she will never come back.

Then the friends leave, one by one, with pitiful, shamed faces, returning to their lives, and Amir and Debbie are once again alone, facing their ghost. A lonely little ghost, wandering around the house, smiling in her white, glistening sleeping gown. The grandparents are there nearly all the time, as well as Ethan and Dina, together with a few close friends. They help with the daily chores, and Ely takes special care of his grandson. At bedtime, Amir and Debbie prepare themselves for the inevitable mix of nightmares and hopeless dreams.

Rest is a pill-induced coma, wrestling with unwanted reality. They cannot accept the impossibility of turning back time. There is an unbearable weight on Amir's chest, as he lay on his bed. An unbearable weight of emptiness, hollow grasps, and helpless denial.

Amir lies on his back, looks toward the door of his bedroom, and extends his hand to the empty door frame with a smile. That is where Liz would be every morning, trying to guess whether or not her parents were awake, and whether she could sneak in. Amir would then turn toward the empty space between him and Debbie, where they'd pretend to fight over whom would get to cuddle Liz first, much to her delight. This memory soon became a regular morning ritual, his daily reminder of the perpetual black hole in his life, his chest, and his mind. Amir himself has become one huge black hole.

Being the head of the family forces him to stand tall. Even if he has to fake it. He has to keep going, for the sake of the others. Just like Amir, Debbie tries to escape reality, and when that doesn't work, she denies it.

Every day, Debbie would go to the door of Liz's bedroom and make sure everything is in order. In the evening, Debbie would tidy Liz' toys, clean up the bedroom, and make sure her clothes for the next day were on her chair, ready for her to wear. Amir has to force her to stop washing Liz's clean clothes again and again. He cannot stop her from fumbling with her toys since he was doing the same. He keeps her favorite in his pocket. A metallic toy soldier that Liz had decided was her father. She kept it with her for protection, in her pocket, at all times. It was there when she died.

It didn't work.

Amir sits on his bed, his head resting between his hands. He glances at Areih's crib, and decides to give it a small push to lull him into sleep. Debbie comes in and gets behind him on the bed, putting her arms around his neck.

Amir tries to comfort her with a logic he didn't believe in himself. "Things happen, and this is *God's* will. You have to stop blaming yourself. How could you know there would be a bomb on their path to the birthday party?"

Debbie cries, "Liz was the only one hurt. Just one tiny bit of steel, straight to her heart . . . She was so happy going to the party!" Debbie can't hold her tears back.

Amir tells her, "I would have sent her with her friend as well. Liz is in *God's* care now. The best care she can get. But life goes on, and we have to take care of ourselves, as well as our Areih." He nods toward the crib, "We have to make up for her absence."

Debbie sniffles. "Poor Areih. He knows something's happened. Whenever someone approaches his crib, he looks out, hoping to see her face. He misses her just like we do."

Amir confesses, "I've always feared such a moment. Death always hits where you expect it the least. Ely and Moshe always feared for us should one of them die. Instead, it was your mother who was killed."

"There's an evil eye on the name Liz."

Amir shakes his head. "No. Let's not get superstitious. I don't believe in that. When dealing with life and death, we have to go back to our faith in God." He hesitates then goes on saying, "Of course, you can always look up to Moshe, his stoicism, and learn from him."

Debbie recoils. "Learn what? He's not so tough. He keeps it all inside, and then takes it out on someone else. I know how brutal he can get. That is *not* strength."

Amir shakes his head. "There are no gentle ways to wage war, Debbie. There's no chivalry in it. War is deceit, treason, and killing your enemy in a big bloodbath." Amir stutters, "War is your children, murdered on their way to a birthday party . . ."

Debbie cries out, "I miss her! I want to hug her, and all I get is emptiness. Empty bed, empty room, empty . . . clothes. I won't see her until I die. How long before I do? I want to die now —"

"*Chas ve Chalilah!*" — God forbid!

Debbie says, "I want to be with her. She needs me. She wants me to sit next to her. She needs me to comb her hair, to dress her, to cuddle her. *I* need to cuddle her."

Amir clenches his fists, fighting back his sorrow. "Not a minute goes by, not a second, without me thinking the same thing. But we have to face our reality and bow to His will. Get ahold of ourselves and get back to our life. We have no choice."

Debbie holds him by the shoulders. "I see how you struggle in bed at night. Maybe you should take some medicine yourself. There's no shame in that."

Amir shakes his head. "I like to stay sharp, but I'm having a hard time, just like you. You think I'm carved out of rock?"

Debbie touches Amir's face. "No, not you. Not when it comes to children."

She pushes away from him, dismay in her voice. "We have to stop it, Amir! The killing, this madness, this non-ending war . . . it has to stop!"

Amir turns away. He doesn't know how many times someone can die, how many more times *he* will die. But he knows that there is no other way. Not for him. To him, now more than ever, the killing *has* to go on, even if just for the sake of revenge. Until the end of time. They would all pay. Mothers, fathers, and yes, children. Every last one of them: for his Liz, they would pay with their blood, their best blood. Their children's blood.

# 1982
## No Winner

# CHAPTER 23

Ameer sits on the carpet in the middle of his sitting room, thinking about the tragic events of the past few years. Nine more years of battles, almost exclusively over Lebanese turf, against their Lebanese hosts. And that is where they still were . . . Lebanon. Now it had become a destroyed and ruined Lebanon, the exact opposite of the one that originally welcomed and sheltered them. Ameer reaches for the pod-mounted electrical fan behind him and turns it on. It is early summer and soon enough there will be two or three fans working around their house, desperately pushing the heat and the mosquitoes off their sweating bodies. His son Laith, –Lion cub – born after Tarek's death, and now seven, sits on his left side; his daughter Nidal, a perfect copy of her mother when she was nine, is in front of him, by her sister Roula's side. The five-year-old needs all of her elder sister's help to keep up with the game. All four are deep into a card-matching game, which Ameer likes to use to train and test their memories. He loves spending his spare time with his family; these moments are the most precious in his life.

What his family doesn't know, however, is that despite the nine years that have passed since little Tarek died, the fire of his memory still burns in Ameer's mind, and as far as he is concerned, the young boy also plays with them. He can see his boy as vividly as if he were there. Little Tarek's wooden *kalash* still hangs on the wall, next to a picture of him in which he wears a *keffiyah* on his head, and has a real kalash dangling from around his neck, pulling on him, as he holds a small Palestinian flag. A portrait of their leader, Yassir Arafat, is there too, with his own *keffiyah* and *kalash*, and the Palestinian flag in the background.

The death of his son has turned Ameer into a ruthless fighter with no qualms about the terrible damage he inflicts. He had been gradually promoted and has taken part in all of the heaviest fights. He is known as a fearless soldier and a daring officer who would stop at nothing to get his target. Their blind quest for retribution's main victim, the Lebanese population, was paying a heavy price for its welcoming attitude toward their refugee brothers. Their "territorial" behavior, growing ranks, and swelling supplies of heavy weapons, have, together with the support of part of the population, turned Lebanon, the Switzerland of the East, into a new Cambodia. The PLO was eating up the beautiful image of Lebanon, and regurgitating a country deserted from humankind.

As he keeps the children busy, Ameer has one ear tuned to the TV news and the other to Layal as she fills him in on the details of her brother Sami's return.

Sami was studying in the USSR, courtesy of a PLO scholarship, and is finally coming back, to settle down. He is now a full-fledged surgeon thanks to the People's Friendship University in Moscow. Among their circle of friends, Sami is the only one who hasn't chosen the warrior's path. But he's earned respect and admiration by achieving a higher, more difficult goal. Was it Sami's revulsion towards war after his father's death that drove him? Or was it his mother's constant efforts to 'get him out of here'? Probably both. Dr. Sami's purpose on earth is to save lives, not terminate them, and Sami made his mother proud.

Ameer is excited about Sami's return, and has to help coordinate the evening's event. All the friends and relatives are invited over for dinner. The whole house is busy with preparations. They have not spared any effort, or cost, in order to make this a memorable evening.

Samar's emotions are at an all-time high. She hasn't seen her son in a year, and he's achieved what she's always dreamed for him — he's kept away from the war, alive and sane, saving lives, not destroying them. That point is another victory for her. Her son is 'doing good.'

A knock is heard at the door, and Ameer calls, "Come in!" over the chatter of his children. Faris, Khalil and Tarek walk in. Tarek smiles when he sees the game Ameer is playing with his children; it took him back to their days at that first refugee camp, when he used to play the same game with Ameer and Rabih.

The children rush to the new guests, arms thrown wide for their usual welcoming acrobatics. As Faris, Khalil, and grandpa Tarek indulge in their pleas for airborne pirouettes, Ameer complains, "That was a learning experience you interrupted. It's not just a game."

"No problem, let's start over." Khalil suggests.

Roula pulls Khalil by the arm, saying, "You help me."

Faris squats next to Laith, and Nidal hops back to Ameer's side.

Ameer reaches out and turns the volume up on the TV, switching to Channel 7, the Lebanese government's official station.

The familiar face and voice of Hejazee, the news anchor, comes through. "Today, June Fourth, Nineteen Eighty-Two, an assassination attempt was made in London on the Zionist enemy's ambassador to the UK. There's new tension along the Israeli-Lebanese border, and war seems imminent."

Ameer switches off the TV. He looks up to Tarek. "We're on our own in the next one. And it's going to be a big one, trust me."

Khalil raises an eyebrow. "So what, Egypt has turned its back on us and has signed a Peace Treaty with Israel. That doesn't mean we're alone."

Samar says softly, "Perhaps we should learn from Egypt —"

"And get a patch of desert to pitch our tents in?" Ameer retorts, "It's *our* land we're fighting for, Samar. Palestine! All of it. We're not beggars in need of charity."

Tarek watches from his corner, nodding empathetically at Samar.

Faris immediately sides with Ameer. "We cannot be defeated. We are an entire people fighting for a just cause. The Syrians will fight with us, too. They have to."

Ameer looks at his father, motioning him to join the conversation. Tarek shakes his head and gets back to his newspapers. He flips through three of them in turn. He reads *al-A'mal*, to get their Christian Phalanges opponents' outlook, *as-Safeer*, for its leftist columns, and *An-Nahar*, for its unbiased and thorough reporting. Ameer says, "The Syrians may be willing to fight, but for their own land, not ours. Our men tried an operation from the Golan Heights, four years ago. They are still rotting in Syrian jails. Besides, haven't the Syrians waged war upon us here in Lebanon? They killed more of us than Israel in the last few years."

Faris asks, "What about all the help the Arab countries give us?"

Ameer has an angry tone. "What help? Some cash, so we shut up? A few mercenaries from far-away villages in foreign countries no one knows about? It's only for propaganda. The Arabs are traitors. What about the weapons we *really* need? Like sophisticated SAM equipment, secure radios, or anything that can actually make a difference?"

Faris slowly nods. "You have a point. We get a small push here, a speech there. That won't get us anywhere. The Israelis are colonizing our villages, bringing in people by the thousands from all over the world, while we're stuck here with a scaled-down society."

"Scaled-down country, my son. Country. *Al Watan al Badeel.*" The alternative homeland." Tarek shakes his head. "You wanted my opinion on this mess."

Ameer exclaims, "Of course we do. You mean Lebanon, and the plan for settling in? None of us will go for it." Ameer stares at his father defiantly.

Tarek has a bitter smile. "Perhaps you won't, but your children will, one day. Look at it as a long-term objective. Our people in Jordan have already done that. Do you think the Zionists are going to give up their land, or even part of it? All our fighting amounts to a mosquito bite for them. A mosquito bite for which they get tons of medicine. If you *know* something doesn't work, why would you keep trying it? You're not looking at things with the proper perspective."

Faris looks at Tarek. "Why don't *you* look, Abu Ameer, and tell us what *you* see."

Tarek tells them, "Egypt is out of the game. We haven't been able to do anything from there since the infamous Camp David Treaty."

Faris slaps his knee in outrage. "Cowards! That treaty left us out entirely. Imagine, turning their backs on us after all the talks and speeches. We should fight them, too."

Ameer says, "I say anyone not with us is against us, starting with our Arab friends."

Tarek goes on, "Sadat tried to include us in his deal, but Begin left everyone out so he could take his opponents piecemeal, just like they do at war. Doesn't that bother you?"

Ameer knows what he means, and it does bother him. "You're

talking about us being left out, in the end, after each of them has made his own separate deal."

Tarek nods. "Precisely. But we, the Palestinians, are the heart of the issue." Tarek bangs on his chest. "It's *our* land. What should we do? What *can* we do?" He glances at the faces around him. "Lebanon has been disintegrating for the last few years, mostly thanks to our actions, and my guess is, at least until the incident in London, we're being prepped for a permanent stay. The *Kissinger Plan*."

"Yeah, absolutely," Khalil says. "Everyone has been fighting everyone else. The Syrians came in pretending to maintain the peace when all they wanted was to break *our* backs and use Lebanon for their own agendas. Now they've turned against everything they pretexted to enter the country for and are starting fires only to put them out themselves. That's why they allowed us in Lebanon, so they can follow us in. That help-the-Christians rumor is their own creation."

Tarek says, "The Syrians have to keep the pressure on Israel, and they need indirect means."

Ameer snaps, "Great, we're indirect means now."

Faris seems unhappy. "So, nobody cares about us?"

Tarek is unperturbed. "Nobody. We have to rely on ourselves. The last war proved that Israel is untouchable. Let's face facts."

Khalil looks baffled. "What are you saying, Tarek?"

Ameer is equally struck. Tarek is not only admitting that Israel is there, but there to stay. He even *names* it without the usual spitting face. "Yes, what you are saying, father?"

"I'm saying that both the USA and the USSR seem to agree on one basic point — everything that happens here is subordinated to the security of Israel."

Khalil objects. "But the USSR is helping us, training us, equipping us!"

"Don't forget that the USSR voted for an Israeli State at the UN in November of Ninteen Forty-Seven. It has done everything it can to help establish the state of Israel."

Ameer says, his calm long gone, "All this we know. But so what? We will win anyway. Justice and Allah are on our side."

Khalil is dismayed. "So, we're not going home? We stay in Lebanon and the Zionists keep our land?"

Tarek responds, "We don't have to stay, and no one can force us to. We're a fighting people, and we'll keep fighting until we reach our goal. It's as simple as that."

"So, what's the catch?" Khalil asks.

Tarek frowns at him. "We have to adjust our goals. We have to admit *essahayeneh* won't spontaneously disappear."

Faris clenches a fist. "Where is your *Thawrah hatta al-nasr,*" — Fight until victory — "Huh, Abu Ameer?"

Ameer raises his hands. "Just tell us what you think we should do, father. Israel is gathering troops according to Soviet sources."

Tarek replies, with a calm smile, "We have to keep the pressure on the enemy, but at the same time we have to signal that we are ready to talk about an acceptable solution. I don't think targeting civilians is doing us any good. It ruins our image, and worse, makes them seem like the victims. We have to reverse that, and show the world the truth. That we want a fair and just solution. Peace."

Ameer has no answer. All he knows is fighting, it is the main thing he has been taught, and now his father wants him to choose another 'path,' one that he is neither prepared nor ready for. He has lost sight of the true goal: peace, not fighting just for the sake of killing.

---

It is the 4th of June, and it is a beautiful morning. But for Amir, it is just another morning. The last few years have brought more bitter fighting, many terrorist actions, and a lot more violent reactions. Many in Israel have grown disconnected from the 'war', and simply go about their daily lives. Amir, on the other hand, is part of a famous commando unit, and he is always on active duty. He has to be. He wants to be. Every mission he takes part in is now a personal mission. It won't get his daughter back, he has long acknowledged, but it does help get *him* back. *At them.*

Lying on his bed, sunshine through the window is nothing more than a bright irritation. He holds a steel soldier, which Liz used to pretend was him, her protector. The one that *failed.*

His sons Areih and David, now nine and seven years old, are brimming with energy, and full of questions. Ethan and Dina are now the proud parents of Ben, seven and as eager as his father, and Eve, four.

Debbie steps into the bedroom and says with a soft tone, "Good morning. The kids are downstairs, waiting for you, to play basketball. Ethan is here too, can't you hear them?"

Amir stands and hastily puts the toy soldier into his pocket. "I'll be right down, I just need a minute."

Debbie takes his hand and tugs at him. "Come on. Ethan and the kids are waiting. Go have some fun, enjoy your children. They need it. You need it. It's . . . allowed."

"You're right. Let me tell them I'm coming." Amir walks to the window. Sure enough, all of them are there on their basketball court—a part of the driveway with a basketball hoop on one side.

Handsome, sturdy Areih, his younger brother David, and Ben, are passing the ball. Ethan is spinning his daughter Eve up and around.

Ethan looks up at Amir. "Come on, Amir, the kids are waiting! We need you to start."

Amir acquiesces and races down the stairs. Outside, he runs past David and Areih, and grabs the ball from them. He dribbles around the children until he reaches the basket. He tosses the ball in and turns to them. "So, what's the score?"

Areih laughs. "There's no score, we haven't even started! We're waiting for you!"

Amir looks toward the ornate iron gate. Ely and Moshe are on the way over. They look anxious, their faces making an odd match for their sports clothes.

Amir walks toward them. "You look tense. Both of you. What is it?"

Ethan is more direct. He looks at Moshe. "What's going on? How big?"

Ely frowns at him. Keeping the war outside their homes is impossible, but he always tries to keep it away from the children. Or keeping their children away from it if he can. He plays it down. "We just might respond to their provocations." Ely grabs the ball and tosses it to the children. "Why don't you children try some penalty shots. We'll be right back."

The foursome walks away from the children, who take turns shooting the ball into the hoop. Ethan can barely hold his eagerness. "We're going in. Right? We're going in!"

Amir itches in anticipation. "When? What's our objective? Tell me!"

Ely motions him to calm down and lower his voice. "Let's keep it quiet for now. There's no go-ahead yet. Some people are against it."

Ethan snaps, "You mean *you're* against it!"

Ely says to Ethan, "I'm against going in and destroying the country. That won't bring peace, only more enemies."

Ethan disagrees. "What's wrong with going in and mopping the country clean of terrorists?"

"And putting in a strong, friendly government?" adds Amir.

Ely shakes his head. "Lebanon is a quagmire. We shouldn't get involved there. It's a mixture of tribal and feudal warfare, and there is no one reliable enough for us to stake our security on."

Moshe turns to Ely. "The Lebanese greeted us with flowers in 'Seventy-Eight, Muslims, especially the Shias, and Christians. They'll do the same today."

Ely has a serious tone. "As long we get rid of the Palestinians for them, it'll be okay, but this time we'll have to stay to help establish a friendly government and avoid any political voids, or else we'll become the enemy."

Amir is afraid they might succumb to his father's logic. He knows the Lebanese problem all too well. "As long as we kick the PLO out, we're good."

Moshe is adamant. "We can mop the area clean."

Ely stops walking, waits for them to do the same and turns toward him. His face stiffens as he tries to control his anger. "Why would we need to do that?"

Amir is oblivious to his father's emotions. "They keep raiding us. They'd be right here in Jerusalem if we let them."

Moshe grumbles. "Our settlements. They keep bombing our settlements, up north."

Ely grumbles, "If the settlements get us killed, then we should review our policy about them." Ely notices the aggressive looks around him. He backtracks a bit. "We should get our priorities straight, that's all I'm saying. Security first." Ely tries to build on his argument before anyone interrupts. "You're forgetting the long-term problem of Palestinians inside Israel." He goes on, "A few years down the line, and that will be a huge issue. They'll outnumber us, and given that we're the only true democracy in the region, that's trouble. It's not a matter we can settle with our army."

Moshe says, "In the meantime, the terrorists are stepping up their operations, and we can't sit by and watch. We'll handle internal issues later."

Amir agrees. "Yes, we go in, mop it up. First their armed forces, in Lebanon, then here."

Ethan adds, "We can establish a security zone, if not a friendly government, manned by an ally, like the South Lebanese Army. That will stop the attacks."

Ely answers, shaking his head, "Get back to your history books. Show me one case where a foreign nation could impose itself and win."

"Us!" shouts Amir. "We haven't budged since 'Sixty-Seven, and we're not going to!"

"Right." Ethan clenches his fist, looking at Amir, who responds with a thumb across the throat. "We'll butcher them." He has that callous look his father hates to see.

Ely tries once more. "We can't just go in like that. We don't have a clear post-war strategy for governance, and making permanent of our results." He looks at Moshe and adds, "Our government isn't exactly known for its reasonable thinking!"

Ethan responds, "There's no reasoning to do. We go in and finish it."

A crackling sound comes from inside Moshe's jacket, which he had hung on the fence. It is his walkie-talkie. Everyone gathers around Moshe.

He answers and listens, then says, "Thank you very much for the heads-up." He turns to the men. "Someone tried to assassinate our ambassador in London. He is badly hurt, and is now in the hospital. They don't know if he'll make it. This is it, the excuse we need to go in."

# CHAPTER 24

Ameer is feverishly running up and down the stairs inside a large building. He is charged with preparing the entire neighborhood to resist the Israeli army's assault on Beirut. The Israelis have overrun them in the open fields and on exposed roads, but now they are approaching the city. Yasser Arafat has promised that Beirut would be another Stalingrad, and has issued the order to resist to all armed factions of the PLO. Although a large number of their fighters, along with thousands of innocent civilians, have already been detained and shuffled off to prison camps, the majority has managed to retreat into Beirut for the final confrontation. Beirut would be a demonstration to the world of their urban fighting skills and sheer determination.

Ameer's building is a large commercial center on the southeastern edge of Beirut, right in the likely path of advancing enemy units. The building has held its own against the incessant attacks and counter-attacks of the Lebanese civil war, becoming a main strongpoint on the west side of the Green line that separated the belligerents. Now the Israeli army is coming, with air power, main battle tanks, and heavy artillery. It is a new kind of war, requiring a new kind of defense.

Ameer rushes through crowded hallways, patting the dusty backs of his men to cheer them. His encouragements, together with the orders he barks, are answered with equally upbeat reactions. The air is alive with anticipation. Ameer can feel it in the building itself, as if it has taken sides with them and joined in their efforts despite the wounds of seven years of civil war. The general feeling is all the more enhanced by the loudspeakers Ameer has placed in select parts of the building, blaring out patriotic songs. The men all hum along with Fairuz as her songs play continuously. *'Al-ghadab a-sata'eh aten wa ana kullee eeman.'* — The striking anger is coming, and I am full of faith. It is one of their favorite songs. *Zahrat al-mada'en.* — Flower of the cities, Jerusalem.

The morning sun doesn't penetrate the darkened hallways and stairways. Littered with piles of ammo boxes, rucksacks, and building material, the building is like an obstacle course for Ameer and his men. In full battle gear, they rush about in all directions, burdened with ammunition, sandbags, heavy weapons, and a plethora of equipment.

Despite their setbacks in the south, they have inflicted serious casualties to the enemy. Faris is in charge of delaying tactics, engaging advancing enemy columns with hit-and-run attacks. Their approach is to ambush the smaller units the enemy sends on side patrols, and avoid the firepower of the main attacking force. Then they vanish into the countryside before the enemy's assets can be brought in as support. Still, they are helpless against Israeli warplanes, and are equally powerless against their fast-reacting and quick-advancing self-propelled artillery.

As far as Ameer is concerned, nothing matters but the task at hand. Besides their experience fighting the Israeli enemy, long years of fighting in Lebanon have honed the Palestinians' skills in urban warfare. They have the potential to make the city impregnable. Should the Israeli government insist on trying to take Beirut, the price of that task would be excessively high.

Meanwhile, Israel's indiscriminate use of force, resulting in thousands of dead civilians and a flattened nation, has brought the sympathy and support of reporters, even foreign ones, to the PLO. News of atrocities and summary executions are filtering out, some of it thanks to disgruntled and disillusioned Israeli soldiers.

The PLO's fight, including their *fedayeen* suicide attacks, is wreaking havoc on enemy morale. But the last hope of survival is resisting in the cities. Although delaying actions are being intensified at a great cost of precious lives, the enemy is now closing in. Ameer is worried about Faris, about his own family, and about his mission. The enemy is in too deep to go back empty-handed. Despite all this, Ameer has some inner satisfaction, for he is now confronting the 'real' enemy, instead of their Lebanese substitutes. He is looking forward to every possible face-off, every encounter, and every ambush that the upcoming days will bring.

In the meantime, he is putting his accumulated skills at waging war to good use, preparing their static position for resisting the enemy's advance, and planning ambushes along the avenues of approach. Most importantly, he is preparing their defense and communication lines to resist air attacks, a game changer in the upcoming battle. His mind never rests, his nerves twitch even as he sleeps, which he doesn't do much.

Ameer shouts into his handset, "Where's the engineer? I asked for an engineer."

A man comes panting. "I'm right here sir, I came as fast as I could."

Ameer eyes him top to bottom. "What's your name?"

"My name is Ayman. I'm—"

"Good, it means blessed. We need some of that here." Ameer looks at the man again. "Do I know you?"

Ayman nods with a large smile. "Jerusalem, sir, Nineteen Sixty-Seven.

And I still serve with Tarek. He sent me here." Ayman pauses for a second, "You were just an angry kid then." With a wink, he adds, tongue-in-cheek, "You're a very angry man now."

Ameer gives him a hug. "My father's sergeant! Where have you been all these years? You blew that building where the Zionists were trapped. Are you still that good?"

"I've since trained in Eastern Europe. I trained in demolition, entrenching and digging techniques, and—"

Ameer raises his hand. "Perfect! That's exactly what I need. You're the man."

"What are the instructions, sir?"

Ameer pulls him to his map table and points out a handful of features. "This is our street, this is our building, and this is the enemy's most likely avenue of approach." Ameer points to the wide street that leads to their building. "We want to make it very difficult for them to come in from these narrower streets. We can move through the sewers, going in and out the manholes, pop out from window to window and door to door, and disappear. We're mining everything, and we have linked minefields."

Ayman frowns. "I saw the men laying them on the way in. So my job is inside? I don't have the structural drawings."

Ameer smiles. "That's why I asked for an engineer. Can you figure out the layout?"

Ayman nods. "The partition walls are thin; I can locate the columns and beams. What's the job?"

"I want holes in the slabs large enough for a man with full gear to go through. We'll put ladders in them. They'll have to be centrally located, to avoid direct fire, and I want at least two or three on every floor. Don't weaken the building's structure as you cut through!"

Ayman says, with a confident grin, "That shouldn't be too hard."

"I also want sandbag pillboxes inside the building. They have to have clear views of their fire zones." He hands Ayman a sheet of paper. "Here's a drawing of the zones we need. You may have to pull a couple of walls down." He points. "I want to fit in some of our recoilless guns here, B-Ten's and One-oh-Six's. They generate a lot of blast from the back."

"Do we have electricity? Water? The Zionists have cut them over the entire city."

"I asked for a generator, it should be here soon. Diesel fuel for it as well. We have two large water holding tanks underground, but still no pump."

Ayman looks relieved. "Perfect." He points back to the map. "The holes in the slabs, if we make them large enough, I can put a winch on top, to bring ammo up and down."

Ameer is delighted. "Perfect! Do it. I also need some openings in the walls; one of my guys is marking them for you with spray paint. And I need an opening through the fence to the building behind us. It's protected from direct fire, and we'll use it for ammo storage."

Ayman asks, "How about the building we're in. You want it rigged as well?"

Ameer shows him more points on the map. "No. We'll be mining the approach and the immediate vicinity. As for the building, we don't plan on evacuating."

Ayman insists, "We can still mine the columns, at the lowest level, just in case. I can give you a remote trigger. I will also shore up the underground tunnel for evacuation."

"Okay, but only when you're done with the rest." Ameer adds with a smile, "You like this, don't you? Blowing up things . . . buildings?"

Ayman laughs. "Is that all sir?"

Ameer nods and shakes Ayman's hand. "For now, yes. Don't waste any time, we have many more buildings to prepare. If we have time left, later, we'll prepare a few more surprises for our friends. A few tricks I learned . . . you'll love it."

Ayman salutes and says, "I have a few tricks of my own, sir. I'm sure you'll like them too."

Ameer is satisfied. "Good. There are two truckloads of sand bags in the street. Distribute them to all floors and around the perimeter walls."

Ayman says, "We'll be done before nightfall, sir."

Ameer salutes and dismisses Ayman. He turns back to his map, takes a chocolate bar from his pocket and munches on it.

Tarek's sarcasm echoes from behind. "You blasphemer, it's Ramadan! What kind of example are you setting for your men?"

Ameer is surprised to hear his father, yet he is still locked on his map. He points out the window to the sound of artillery shells. "The cannon has fired!" A normal fasting day ends at sunset to the sound of a cannon firing. It is still morning, but cannons are firing. Ameer turns toward his father to greet him, and his surprise doubles — Tarek is standing there with Laith. "*Yaba*, are the roads safe!?" Ameer says to Tarek.

Laith rushes to his father. "Father, we were bombed during the night! But then it stopped. I wanted to see how you get ready for war!" Ameer still remembers how he used to ask his father the same questions. How he's always wanted to go with him, and take part in his wars.

Tarek is confident. "We were shelled during the night, when the men were moving ammunition out. They must have agents everywhere. Layal and the girls are safe in the shelter, they won't budge. Any news from Faris?"

"He's okay . . . I think. Should be back after dark. What's it like out there?"

"Chaos. The psychiatric hospital has been bombed, and the doctors have all fled, so we're trying to find someone to handle the orphans and the elderly. We're out of electricity and water. People are fighting at bread lines. The enemy is dropping leaflets urging everyone to leave. To make matters worse, every single newspaper has its front page full of announcements from all embassies urging their citizens to do something, go somewhere, or call someone. It's a full pandemonium out there." Tarek produces *Felasteen al-thawra*. "Of course, there's *our* paper, which is more optimistic." The front page reads: "*Fashala al-aduw fe hujumehe a'la sayda.*" The enemy's assault on Sidon has failed. Indeed, the city of Sidon south of Beirut was surrounded but not taken by the fast-moving Israeli troops.

"*Insh Allah* all their assaults will fail. We'll make sure of that." Ameer says.

Tarek taps Laith on his back. "*Yallah* — come on, boy! You've seen your father, now let's go back home. Your mother must be worried. I'll show you some things on the way out, and we head back home while it's quiet. Ameer, I forgot to tell you. The only fruits we have in the city are coming from the Zionists. And they're good."

Ameer slouches haplessly, and looks at his son, so much like he once was. "Boy, I hope you never know what it's like to have your son standing next to you, on the frontline, waiting for all hell to break loose."

Tarek says, "I did, and I didn't much like it. Now let's see what we can do for his generation. Maybe they won't have to fight anymore. Maybe the madness will end someday. Maybe Laith will have the satisfaction of knowing that his legacy to his children won't be a life of killing and dying." Tarek looks at the busy men around him. "We'll have our land back someday, and the nightmare will be over."

"First, we break their backs, and send them to hell! *Felasteen tabka hurra! Thawra hatta al-nasr!*" Ameer shouts. Palestine stays free! Revolution until victory! A wild cheer spreads through the building, echoed by each man as he hears the cries and adds his own shout. Tarek walks out, hand in hand with Laith.

In his makeshift office overlooking the Palestinian side of Beirut, Amir sits on a wooden chair, hidden behind curtains of netting and canvas. He is in an abandoned living room in an abandoned apartment atop an abandoned building, overlooking an abandoned street. Abandoned by all, except rats, inbound shells, and the occasional bullet whizzing by with death as its aim, ricocheting around, puncturing nothing more than empty air.

The Lebanese Forces soldiers, who have been resisting the Palestinian and Syrian onslaught for years, have agreed to let them use the building. They showed the Israeli where they had to crouch or bend, or, for exposed stretches, simply run, in order to avoid enemy snipers. Amir is on the tenth floor. The stairway between his position and the ninth floor is exposed, entirely shorn of walls. Ladders have been put up between shell holes in the slabs for passing through. Amir has posted sentries at the back entrance of the building, to prevent anyone from coming inside without his approval. Any sound or light or movement in their dwelling would trigger a volley of fire from the enemy. Amir only uses his 'office' for surveillance, and planning covert missions. One advantage to the many holes in the building is the constant breeze. A light wind cools the heavy night of June as Amir, Ethan, and some of their men take turns behind the binoculars and their night scope, a marvel of electronic light-intensifying technology that turns the black of night into visible, yet greenish, scenery.

Amir peers through his binoculars, and then switches to the night scope. His main interest is a big building opposite their position, towering over the area. Between the two positions was the 'Green Line', as the Lebanese called it. It is a chaos of neglected and wild vegetation that grew along the demarcation line between the two opposing forces. But there is nothing hospitable about this 'green' space. It is more like a maze of sniping corridors, machine guns firing cones, artillery zones, minefields, all in the ghostly setting of shorn buildings — with their dangling slabs, shelled and bullet-pocked facades, and fire consumed plaster. Wild greenery has overtaken it all, turning it into the ultimate urban jungle, inhospitable for all except the local wildlife, which includes some humans. These smelly 'jungle rats' as they're called: dangling AK's, shabby clothes, dirt-baked skins, and overgrown hair — blend naturally with the environment. Their job is to guide friendly forces through the Green Line during raids. Most of them are men who lived or worked in that area before the war, and so they are extremely well acquainted with it.

Amir looks at his men and points to the building opposite. "They're humming around like bees in a beehive. Aerial reconnaissance shows that they keep bringing weapons and material into the building, reinforcing positions — they must be anxious for a battle." He scratches notes on a pad, using a beam of moonlight that shines through what he called their sunroof, a gaping hole through the roof courtesy of a 160mm mortar shell. "I think they're building bunkers *inside* the building! They're impregnable. We can only flatten them . . ."

"Do you think they're scared, sir?" asks his sergeant, Ron.

"You mean *you're* scared, don't you?" Amir smiles.

Ron nods. "I guess I am, sir, if that's okay with you."

"It's OK. We all are. Don't fight it. Live with it. We've done this before."

"We're fine sir, in our unit. But the regular army boys are having stress problems, especially the reservists."

Amir answers as he looks into his scope, "They'll soon be in for a treat. If we have to go in, it will be hand-to-hand, house-to-house. Those bastards will never give up." He looks up as Ethan pops in. "Those are some real warriors over there," he declares.

Ethan mumbles, "You sound like a fan."

Amir replies, "Just happy they're giving us a chance to slaughter them. All of them. But you have to admit that they're putting up a fight."

Ethan sits beside Amir. "They are. Their *last*."

His sergeant Ben asks, "You think it will be settled by the end of this campaign?"

Ethan and Amir reply with one voice, "Yes."

As Amir gets back to his maps, Ethan guesses his thoughts. "Whatever you're planning, I'm in it with you, my friend. Don't you dare think otherwise!"

Amir smiles. "I know. We'll need reliable locals to guide us."

Ethan has a wry smile. "Waiting downstairs. We're good for tomorrow."

Amir looks up in surprise. "You sneaky little devil." He grins. "All right. I'll get my unit ready for support in case we have to withdraw under fire. No one else will know. We'll take two men."

Ron and Ben stand to attention. Ethan is beaming. "We're ready."

They are interrupted by a Colonel entering their position. They stand up and salute casually. He returns the salute and calls in to someone behind him, still outside the room, "Anouchka, come in."

Amir tries to hide his surprise as Anouchka walks in. Ethan is equally surprised. Anouchka has a stern look as she walks in and nods to them, with reprimand. "I've learned you're planning an insertion."

Amir acquiesces. "Yes. A quick recon. We have local guides."

Anouchka shakes her head. "Saw them. Not reliable. We have no intel on these street rats. They have no commitment to anything. You have to be very careful. Not go in too deep. I want to see your mission plans before you commit. You must push at least three days until we corroborate the intel."

Ethan is taken aback. "Three days? But they are already here. Downstairs. They know the area well. We're set for two days from now and they're staying here till then. It's best we minimize the risk of any leaks by postponing, and letting them go."

Anouchka is firm. "Then we cancel."

Amir is quick to respond, and points to the maps on his desk. "We are only going one street in, past the green line. To a vantage point overlooking the access routes into Beirut. We'll take photos of their defenses."

The colonel steps up. "Ok, you can do that. But you must avoid contact, take as many photos as you can." He designates points on the map, "We need photos of the defenses here and here. We need a street perspective to augment aerial recon."

Anouchka looks at Amir. "I want a step-by-step plan of the mission. Before you go."

Amir is prompt to respond. "Agreed. Right away."

---

Ameer and Layal are enjoying a relatively fresh morning, indulging their ice cream cups at the "Café de Paris" in Hamra Street. Layal forces a smile. "You see, it wasn't so hard. Just a one hour break for you. For us."

Ameer looks worried. "Yes, I know. And I needed it. But every minute counts."

Layal lowers her gaze as she fumbles with her treat. "Every time we come here, there is a reason to regret it. Let's just have our ice cream."

Ameer teases her. "You begged to come here. It's the best café in the city!"

Layal approve. "Yes I know. It's like a different city. There's no war preparations here. People are living almost normally."

Ameer corrects her. "Almost yes. But they are under siege same as us. This is probably the last batch of ice cream. Their electricity is cut, same as ours." Ameer glances at a group of reporters, walking up the street. Three men and a woman, with foreign looks and attire. He signals Layal to stay put and walks up to them. He nods towards a newspaper shop as he crosses eyes with Anouchka. She follows him inside.

Anouchka whispers as she takes a newspaper off the stand, "Are you fucking mad? What are you —"

"So happy to see you too," Ameer interrupts. "Are these cameras or missile launchers your crew is carrying?" He looks at her shirt, it reads 'Beirut siege 1982' and goes on with a mischievous look, "I like that too. Should I liberate you from it?"

Anouchka dismisses it and reprimands him. "You are crazy! You will compromise your safety. You must exfill at once. What are you doing here anyway?"

Ameer jokes, "Exfill? Huh. Yes, as soon as we finish the ice cream."

Anouchka is nervous. "So much for fasting. Not that anyone seems to follow Ramadan anyway. I have to leave, but know this, as I am stuck here with no comm."

Ameer asks, "Know what?"

Anouchka comes closer and whispers, "Insertion. Tonight, at ten P.M. Just behind the museum, from the hollowed building. Single squad plus the locals."

Ameer looks perplexed. "Insertion. One squad. Behind the —"

Anouchka takes her newspaper to the cashier, pays for it, and leaves the shop.

Ameer returns to Layal, who's in full inquisitive mode. "Who . . . what the hell was that?"

Ameer is nonchalant. "Intel officer, Russian. She just informed me of an infiltration attempt. Tonight. We must leave."

Layal is taken aback. "She's . . . Russian? Intel? An infiltration attempt? Was this planned?

Ameer remains calm as he requests the bill. "No. Just fate."

---

It is pitch dark on the front line, that infamous green line. Amir, Ethan, Ron, and Ben follow their two guides, men from a local street gang. In some places, they have to wade through thick, shoulder-high vegetation that hides the ground underneath. Trying to focus on and follow the guides' exact footing to avoid tripping a mine, all while secondguessing the dark environment for living threats is nerve-wracking.

Amir crawls under a dangling concrete slab. Bombs have shattered the building, and the columns have been completely blown away by the force of the blast. He is third in a line of six. The two guides who lead them wear ragged shoes and ripped shirts over denim trousers that look like they could be family heirlooms. Or scavenged wear. Their sanitary condition is deplorable. Amir pinches his nose and whispers to Ethan, right behind him, "The Palestinians may not hear us or see us, but they'll certainly smell those guys."

Ethan doesn't smile. "They told me these guys are the best. This is where they lived before the war, and they've been fighting in this neighborhood since 'Seventy-Five."

"At least we know they're popular with the fly community."

Ethan goes on, "They're the eyes and ears of the Christian militia."

Amir shows his surprise. "They're part of that outfit? These dingoes?"

Ethan says, "No, not really, not regulars. Just some sort of local hired hands."

"Hired!? That isn't what you told me."

Ethan pushes his friend forward. "What do you care as long as they get us in?"

"I'm worried about getting out. These guys work for money, and we're worth a fortune if we're caught."

"It's too late now. But I'm sure they're OK. See how good they are? They know every inch of the way."

Amir says, "What scares me is that the guys on the other side are probably as good . . . we're blind here."

Ethan sniffs in disgust. "Should they come our way, we could still smell them."

Amir hides a smile. "From far. We're downwind."

The lead guide signals them to keep silent. Amir regroups his men in a narrow ditch that runs parallel to an old building, partially covered by the building's fallen facade. He reiterates the orders for total silence. He has the men double-check their equipment for anything that can rattle. Even the tiniest metallic ding can be heard in the tense silence of the night. He sips from his canteen and passes it around until it is empty to avoid the slosh of water. They are well into no-man's land, and could easily stumble upon an enemy patrol, doing the same kind of covert reconnaissance.

Amir whispers, "Weapons ready, cover your sectors, and keep silent. Don't shoot unless you have to."

"We enter building, sir," the lead guide says in his broken English. "When get out, other side *Fatahland*." That was the name used for Palestinian territory. "Very careful, very silent. Full silent. Don't shoot if see someone." The man points to his lips. "We talk."

"Talk? You meet your enemy and talk to them?" Amir cannot hide his surprise. "You mean you negotiate?"

"Trust, trust, sir. We good. We know area. Only shoot if us shoot."

The two guides exchange a few words in Arabic. They don't realize Amir and Ethan are fluent in Arabic.

Still, Amir can't make out the words of the two men's whispers. He does detect a note of sarcasm, which could be the two men joking at the amount of equipment Amir and his men are packing. They are probably boasting of their superiority to the 'rookies'.

Turning to the rest of his group, Amir says, "Keep your eyes open, guys; cover all angles. Don't stare at specific points, use your peripheral vision. You know the drill."

Ethan says to Amir, "Try to catch what they're saying — I don't trust them."

"Great. I thought they were reliable."

"I thought so too. But there's something weird. And then that smirk on their face."

Amir agrees. "I was hoping to get some intel on the terrain, and compare with our maps. Instead, we're sneaking in like rats, and hoping to avoid a trap."

Ethan glances at the guides suspiciously, several meters ahead. "There's definitely something fishy about them, and it's not just the smell."

Amir points a finger at Ethan, then at the guide in front, meaning: 'he's yours if something goes wrong.'

They enter the ruined building through a large hole in its sidewall. The four men stay in a close two-plus-two formation, Amir and Ron leading. They don't lose sight of each other, and keep all sides covered. Should anyone be wounded, his buddy will be within arm's reach.

In the dark innards of the building, they move one pair at a time, with each buddy keeping a hand on the shoulder of his partner, as the other group provides cover. In the surrounding obscurity and ever present danger of mines, trip wires, and ambushes, forging ahead is an exercise in self-control, or rather, environmental control. They approach the opening leading out of the building. The door is flanked by a pair of windows on either side, with moonlight pouring in from all. There isn't much left of either the door or any of the windows. They'll be in the clear in just a few meters . . . as in, in the middle of an open firing field.

The leading guide turns back and whispers; "Out, *Fatahland*. We climb building, and see all defenses. *Very* close. This what you want?"

"Absolutely. This is perfect. We head back after that?" Amir plays the inexperienced officer while probing his guide's eyes for clues. He senses a feeling of satisfaction in the man. Shouldn't he instead feel uncomfortable if their 'guests' were inexperienced?

"We go out, and you follow us," the guide answers.

As they approach the opening, Amir realizes that their guides have suddenly extended the lead distance between them. They will be well out of the building by the time Amir and his men reach the exit. He points toward Ron and Ben and then at the second windows on either side of the opening, directing them there.

As he faces the doorway, *Amir is taken by the sensation he's had many times before. Something strange is about to happen, and he feels as if he isn't in control. The invading presence he's felt more than once is again in him. It controls him. Through it, he can see himself, from the 'other side'. The sensation builds in him, stronger than ever.*

The chilling clicks of the guides' AK rifles' safeties coming off pull him out of his daze. Amir needn't say anything to Ethan, who is already aiming his rifle at the guides as they clear the doorway. Amir puts a hand on Ethan's gun barrel and motions him to the windows directly to the side of the door. Ron and Ben have already moved to the outer windows, to provide flanking fire.

Ethan nods. They are expected to exit from the door, and they need to surprise their enemy. Somehow, Amir doesn't even think about doubling back. He *has* to go.

Amir mimes his plan. He points to himself and Ethan, then motions a jump through the first set of windows on either side of the door, and covering the area directly in front. Ron and Ben would handle the flanks. Amir points to the smoke grenades on his chest, meaning they'd be part two of their plan, while part three is rushing back where they came from and ex-filtrating the area.

"*Be seder?*" He whispers.

They all check their weapons and furtively whisper back: "*Be seder.*"

---

It is a calm night. Ameer sits on a concrete block on the second floor of a two-story building right in the middle of the Green Line dividing Beirut into the Lebanese controlled East and the Palestinian controlled West. He waits for all hell to break loose. He can hear the quick, clicking claws of rats running in a blown out ventilation duct. Distant thumps of explosions south of their position bounce off from one charred building façade to the next. He breathes slowly as he glances through a shell hole in the wall at the street below. Mangled carcasses of cars, scattered bits of sidewalk, broken glass, and fallen debris from ruined buildings compete for space with a collection of empty shells, fragments of bombs, and rubble piles, with wild greenery jutting out everywhere, trying to cover it all, as if nature could find a way against war and destruction. A once majestic old tree stands decapitated, humbled, mocked and overtaken by wild outgrowth. A true image of the entire nation . . . Ameer's thoughts drift to the peaceful streets of West Beirut, which he likes so much. Even the spared parts of the city where he goes to escape their dirty camp now look more and more like an extension of their camp. Hamra Street, the Corniche by the sea — they all were littered with the clustered tin shops of thousands of refugees selling cheap clothes, stolen goods, knock-off articles and whatever else they can lay their hands on.

Ameer shakes his thoughts away and looks around him. The early century buildings are now ghostly bunkers and crumbling strongholds. The lovely gardens evolve into an ugly overgrowth that envelops everything in its menacing tentacles. It is his turf. It looks like hell, and he has personally contributed to that. He is at home. Ameer always wished he had the Zionists at the opposite side of this Green Line, instead of his Lebanese enemies, and now, the Zionists have come. They have come, and now he can shoot them right here. They are not hiding behind their borders, behind impenetrable barriers. They are right there for *him* to shoot and kill.

Ameer shoulders his HK SG1 sniper rifle and peers through the Zeiss scope. He turns the magnification down to the lowest level, one and a half, to have the greatest field of view. He marvels at the clarity of vision offered by the German optics in the bright moonlight. Whenever he can, and mostly for specialist equipment, he'd equip himself and his men with Western weapons. They offer much better accuracy, and quality accessories were available. Thanks to that and his intensive training efforts, his unit was a superior combat force, with a substantial tactical edge, succeeding where others failed.

Ameer is worried by Faris' latest scheme. Two local militiamen from the opposite side had been handsomely paid to lead an enemy squad, including two officers, into an ambush. He couldn't participate because he was busy with preparations. Anouchka's message suddenly changed everything. It didn't matter how she knew, and besides, after Faris left, *he suddenly had the feeling that he had to go. It was that unexplainable sensation again, and he could not resist.* He left his engineer Ayman, in charge, and followed stealthily, taking along his long-time friend, Khalil. Ameer took a position in a building overlooking the ambush spot, where he could lay supporting fire. He and Khalil prepared several firing positions so they could quickly switch from one to the next in case they were spotted.

Ameer doesn't like what he sees. The two hired guides have crept out of the building across the way, just as Faris said they were supposed to, but the enemy is not showing up.

Ameer whispers to Khalil, "Can you see anything?"

"No," Khalil whispers back. "Faris' men are in place. No sign of the Israelis."

Ameer is eager. "They must be just behind them."

Khalil shakes his head. "This is taking too long." Indeed, seconds feel like hours when waiting for the enemy to pop out.

Ameer trusts the instincts of his friend. He anxiously focuses into his scope, *but the sensation is back. Ameer is numb, paralyzed.* He takes his eye off his scope and wipes his sweat, trying to whisk the feeling away, getting some control back. *Instead, the sensation literally tunnels him to the enemy's mind. He is in the enemy's mind. He is the enemy. And he's coming out of the building. Not as planned.*

Khalil is impatient. "They have to come out, now!"

*As if he's given the order,* two enemy soldiers jump out of windows flanking the doorway. They cut down the two traitors, rush ahead a few meters, and converge right in the middle of the Faris' men, denying them the ability to shoot without hitting each other. Two more men appear on the adjacent windows. They have Faris' men lined up from either side, and they are quick to open fire, forcing them to crouch and hide for cover. Faris' men have no target, despite the close distance, unless they are willing to expose themselves to the deadly flanking fire of the two Israelis posted at the windows.

The only ones who have a chance to make a solid hit are Faris and his teammate, right in the middle of his unit. Faris raises his weapon at the enemy, from a few meters away, but doesn't fire. Faris then motions his teammate's weapon down. *Ameer can see it. From the enemy's side. Ameer tries to whisk the sensation away. He tries to get the lead enemy soldier in his scope. The sensation puts him next to the enemy soldier. It puts him in the enemy soldier. He has his crosshairs on his face. It is the face, and it is in control. Ameer sees through it, and hears through it, as if all perceptions were tunneled straight to his mind. Ameer cannot fire. He cannot understand either. He sees Faris, in front of him, gaping with awe, motioning his mate's rifle down, then getting riddled with bullets. Bullets from his own machine gun. Ameer feels as if he himself shot Faris.*

Ameer takes his eye off his scope and stares in disbelief at his rifle. He hears Khalil shout, "Open fire!" Ameer's battle senses quickly shake him out and get him back into action. He tries to recapture the enemy soldier in his scope. Alerted by Khalil's shouting, the Israeli glances at Ameer, but he too doesn't shoot. He fires instead in the direction of Faris' men.

Smoke grenades which the enemy must have tossed envelop and cloud the scene with an impenetrable screen. Ameer immediately switches his scope to one of the soldiers firing from a window. He puts his crosshairs at the dark mass behind the muzzle flash and fires three shots in quick succession. The target stops firing, and Ameer quickly switches to the other window. He shoots again, with the same result. He even hears the enemy's rifle crash on the ground.

But he can't bring himself to shoot at the two soldiers in the middle, as they retreat in a hail of fire and thickening smoke. He tries convincing himself that he has no shot, but he knows it's that dreaded sensation again. Some of Faris' soldiers, having escaped the few seconds of inferno, are now emerging from behind cover, as the smoke still envelops the scene. Seeing that they aren't chasing after the Israelis, Ameer realizes they must be waiting for an order. No order means Faris is badly hurt. Was his vision true?

Ameer drops from his position on the second floor to a balcony below, then lands on a sandbag bunker, pulling some of the bags down with him. Khalil follows. Ameer signals to Khalil, who tosses two grenades into the building the enemy has vanished into.

The smoke is now settling, and the men look for enemy bodies, but can only find the two guerillas they have bribed and Faris, his upper body riddled with bullet holes, his blood, like his life, pouring out. Two more of his men are seriously wounded, others have lesser injuries. Ameer approaches his friend in horror; it is a miracle that he's still alive, but he won't be for long.

Faris coughs up blood. "*Alhamdu lellah*. Thank God, you're here."

Ameer kneels next to his dying friend. "Of course I am. I followed with Khalil." He points to his previous position overhead. "We were up there. Did you really think I'd let you go alone?" He adds, "We saw the whole thing. I got the two at the windows."

Faris slowly shakes his head. "That isn't what I meant . . . Who was the *other* one? He looked —" Faris coughs up some more blood and struggles to breathe.

Ameer says, "Stop talking; we'll get you to the hospital. Khalil, get the stretcher from the car. We can't carry him by hand.

Khalil nods to one of the men. "Right away. Do you want to send someone in pursuit? The Israelis must be carrying their wounded."

One of Faris' men says, "We can put a squad together, sir. We'll take pursuit."

Ameer glances at the smoke-cloaked darkness inside the building. "It's no use."

Khalil says, "We can try sir, for Faris' sake. There must be a blood trail."

Ameer nods. "Send a small team, but you stay with me. Watch for booby traps. We don't need more casualties. We'll go to the American University Hospital."

"Too late for the hospital . . ." whispers Faris. "Allah is waiting for me, I can feel it. Ramadan is a good time to die. I have even done my *zukat* — charities — for the first time . . ."

Ameer smiles at him the best he can. "Don't be silly. The doctors will patch you up. Stop talking, you need your energy." He puts more dressings on Faris' wounds, looks back to Khalil. "Keep the pressure on the wounds." Facing back at Faris, he jokes. "Since when are you such a believer, huh?"

Faris mutters, "A couple of minutes. I think . . . we all have to . . . before we go to Him. I thought it could be my turn . . . *maktoub*." It's all written.

Faris' face seems to relax, and Ameer asks, "Why didn't you fire?"

"I thought I saw . . . I saw . . . " He points at Ameer, but then drifts off.

"What?" Ameer leans close. Maybe Faris has an answer for Ameer's predicament.

Faris grasps his hand. "I'm going to see little Tarek. I'm going to see your boy. I'll take care of him for you. You can stop worrying now. You can sleep at night now . . ."

Khalil's eyes are wet. "He's out of it, sir . . ."

Ameer hasn't lost hope. "Not yet. Faris, stop talking, we have a car. We'll be in the hospital in no time. Have no fear. We'll take care of you."

Between grimaces of pain, Faris says, "Fear? Huh . . ." Faris coughs out a bloody laugh. "Damn it, I'll miss the World Cup final . . . Go Brazil . . ."

Ameer cannot help a sad smile. "Will you just shut up? You're going to bleed yourself to death if you keep on talking."

Faris puts a limp hand on Ameer's arm. "I'm already dead. Just floating now . . . It was good to be your friend. You've always been my only family, my brother . . ."

The car screeches to a halt in the street behind them. Ameer says, "There's our car. It won't be a comfortable ride."

Faris mutters, "I saw. I think I saw, something weird, very weird . . ." He winces a smile and drifts away. "I wish I could die in *Felasteen*. After victory. In my home, in my land. Maybe you can bury me there, one day? I don't want to be buried here . . ."

"I will try my hardest, my brother." Ameer felt the same — he wanted to be buried in his homeland. But what had Faris seen? The mystery is greater than ever, now that Ameer knows there is something *real* about it. Who is the mysterious man, and why does he have power over him? Does *He* feel the same? None of them could shoot the other . . . Again! His mind swirls as he watches Faris, gasping with his last breath, a manly smile on his dying face, a tough look in his eyes, exuding strength until the very end.

# CHAPTER 25

As Debbie walks into the kitchen, she notices Amir's slumped silhouette on the living room couch. Outside, it is nearly dark, the early setting September sun hinting at the upcoming fall season. Amir hasn't turned on any lights. Nor the TV. He is just there, a dark figure in the darkness. He has been fighting in Lebanon for months, and is now on a break from duty. He seems to have brought back some of Lebanon's hell with him, locked up in his mind. Debbie tries to ask him about it, and he reluctantly replies, "We are drowning in there. Ely was right. Good men are dying . . . and for nothing."

Debbie is adamant. "We have to pull out of Lebanon. People are dying on both sides. Our poor soldiers, and all those civilians, by the thousands . . ."

Amir stays silent and does not answer. He is trying to understand that *sensation*. Back in the Beirut ambush, it was stronger than ever before. This time, it lingered there for a while, taunting him. What was it? Why could he not shoot? What was this out-of-body experience? As in Jerusalem in '67, and again in the Golan in '73, Amir could feel and sense through his enemy's mind. He was *in* his enemy's mind. Was *he*, for those few yet eternal seconds, the enemy?

Debbie quietly sits next to him. She slithers into the narrow space between Amir and the armrest of the couch, asking with a soft voice, "What's bothering you?"

"Everything . . . so many people dead, not much achieved. What a disappointment."

Debbie tries to cheer him up. "You routed the PLO. And now it is time to get out of there fast, before we fully drown into the Lebanese swamp."

For the first time ever, Amir seems to be rethinking his ideas. "When we do the things we do, we hope and pray that we're doing the right thing, that it's the only option that we have. For our country, for our families, our children, our future . . ."

Debbie says, "You are making our dream come true. The sacrifices aren't going to waste. We may be nearer to our dream of peace in Israel than ever before."

"I know. It's the price we have to pay for our freedom and our very existence."

"So what's the problem?"

"This war wasn't about survival. We just went in there, wreaked havoc on the country, destroyed everything, and didn't achieve a permanent objective. We piled military mistakes upon political mistakes, and we made new enemies. There was so much we could have done, and yet it was all handled so badly. It started as a good thing, and now look where we are."

Debbie puts her arms around Amir's neck. "It isn't so bad. Our borders are safe now."

"Yes, but for how long? If we really want peace with our neighbors, we have to make peace with their people. We just added another entire people to our long list of enemies. Look at Egypt. A useless piece of paper between governments, and their people would be glad to jump to our necks any time. Do you see any Egyptian tourists in our streets? Or us in theirs?"

Debbie frowns. "You used to enjoy this. It is the first time I hear you talk like this. What happened back there in Lebanon? Is it Ben's death?"

Amir puts his head between his hands. "Yeah . . . no . . . I don't know. Everything. Everything and nothing."

"Try talking to me, for a change. Or just think out loud." Debbie puts her head against his. "Anybody in there?"

"We kicked them out, but their organization is still in one piece. They've just been relocated. The Palestinian problem hasn't been solved."

Debbie squeezes his hand. "They're off to Greece, Tunis, wherever . . . they have no access to us, and that should do it. Now the Palestinians will perhaps develop a peaceful leadership, and we can talk to them and nego-tiate a peace treaty with them too."

Amir muses, "We should have bombed the evacuation boats. That would have been good. That's what we should have done."

Debbie is shocked. "I don't believe my husband would talk like that."

Amir hunches. "We'd get some bad publicity for a while, a use-less UN resolution, or something . . . Someone might take a fall for it, but then everyone forgets about it. The world wouldn't be too sad that we got rid of one of the largest, worst terrorist organizations in the world. There's no middle ground in war. We either are at war with those people, or we're not. At least then we wouldn't have lost all those men for nothing."

Debbie says, "Ben's wife called. She wanted to thank you for stop-ping by. I spoke to her son too; what a courageous young boy."

Amir has a bitter smile. "Just as tightly wound as his father. I guess they feel like he's still out there, somewhere, and coming back. He's still out there, in a way, but he's not coming back."

Debbie's voice trembles as she remembers. "They were with him in the hospital when he died. I was there too. They lived through his agony. Every minute of it."

Amir's voice wavers as well. "He should have died in Lebanon, his wounds were so bad . . . He just hung on until he could see his family. He was dreaming, hallucinating about his son, all the way back to the evacuation chopper."

Debbie says, "Let's pray his death will not be squandered."

Amir is skeptical. "I am certain the Syrians will find someone to replace the Palestinians. They never liked Arafat, anyway; they always tried to rein him in."

"So you think the Palestinians might come back to Lebanon? After all this?"

"Palestinians, or someone else. Now we have to stabilize Lebanon, too. We created a void and we didn't fill it."

Debbie is dismayed. "So it was all really for nothing? Our government is about to collapse, our image is ruined, and peace is even farther away."

Amir seems to drift again. "You know in that clash when Ben was hit?"

"Yeah?"

Amir mimics firing a gun. "I had that sniper right where I wanted him, but it was very strange, I just couldn't shoot. As if my body wanted me to avoid engaging him. I could almost say I spared him, but I also know that he did the same for me. I'm sure he had me in his sights, for a long while too. He switched to Ben and Ron instead, hitting them. Ron was lucky that he got hit in his rifle, because the sniper was a good shot. And he *spared* me. I just *know* that. It was like . . . it was like I was right there in his mind."

"Is this the feeling you talked about before? Like it's your own life you're sparing?"

Amir shrugs. "Yes. It is. Maybe, you never know. But this time, I know it wasn't any 'fog of war.' It was real . . . he was a good soldier. Calm, precise, deadly. I'm surprised how well-trained they are, but this one was something else. Outstanding soldier."

Debbie sits back and looks at her husband's eyes. She reaches for the light on the side table and turns it on. "What do you think it is?"

"It's very uncanny; it's as if it was the same guy, all these times. And he has such an influence on me. Not influence, *control*. I just can't understand." Amir looks away, waving his hand to dismiss the subject. "Never mind. Let's eat something, I'm starving."

Shouts and squeals come from the bedroom one floor above. Debbie says, "The kids are hungry too." She points to the sound of footsteps running down the stairs, punctuated by giggles. "Did you know they're bathing and dressing all by themselves now? Even David."

"Well, it's about time, he's seven. I did that when I was . . ."

Debbie punches him with her elbow. "You did nothing, you old bum. Sara told me you were pampered all the way."

Amir feigns shock. "I might have been pampered, but I did help in the house. I even did the dishes and set the table."

"How come you've suddenly forgotten how to do those things, now that you have your own house?"

He stands. "OK, I get the hint, I'll set the table." When they enter the kitchen, Areih and David are already there waiting. Amir starts putting plates on the table.

He whispers to Debbie, pointing at the children buzzing around the kitchen, "This is what we fight for. Peace and a decent life in every home. If we're not going to find it, then there's no point winning all the wars."

David asks, "We won all the enemies?"

Areih adds, "And no one can kill us anymore?"

David says, "*Aba*, you won't have to go to war anymore?"

Areih has more. "What about us? When we get big? I want to go to war! I want to kill all the enemies, like this —" Areih pretends to spray bullets all over the place.

Amir declares a cease-fire. "There won't be a need for that Areih. No one can attack us. This *is* why we wage war in the first place. To secure our borders."

---

Ameer rests on the bulwark at the boat's stern, gazing into the turbulence of the propellers. The "Sol Georgios" has already left Lebanese waters. The Palestinian fighters are evacuating Beirut, under the supervision and protection of the French Foreign Legion. Yasser Arafat has joined them too, coming to the harbor in the Lebanese prime minister's bulletproof Mercedes. A massive crowd had seen them off, waving flags, throwing rice and flowers, crying and screaming for revenge. Once again, every one of them had to pack everything he owned into a single suitcase.

Layal slides by his side and whispers into his ear, "Bigger than the truck we took out of Jordan, no?"

Ameer has a stern look. "We have to stop. Assess. Think about other ways. We have to look forward. We've been doing the wrong things the wrong way for a long time."

Layal raises her eyes to her husband's. "What do you mean?"

"Look at us. A couple of planes could send us to the fishes and no one would care. We're getting help from Tunis, from Greece, but nothing from our alleged Arab friends."

"Let's go sit with your parents and the kids. They need your support right now."

"*My* support . . . My best friend, my brother, is dead. His body is rotting over there."

Layal says, "I know. He was part of our family. His last wish was to be buried in Palestine. Go, talk to Tarek."

"I lost my brother in 'Sixty-Seven, I lost my son in 'Seventy-Three, and now I've lost my best friend, my other brother. Who else is left to be killed?"

Layal takes his arm and moves closer to him. "We're alive and well, and we're going somewhere else. We've been in worse situations, or have you forgotten? Things can only get better, think about it that way."

"I'm not so sure . . ."

Layal holds his face with both hands. "Don't give me this wretched look. It is not you. Sad is ok, angry is fine. But not this. Not miserable. How would Faris want you to be, right now?"

Ameer lights up a bit, reinvigorated by the thought of his friend's undying spirit.

Layal softly goes on, "Can I ask you something?"

"Sure."

"Why didn't you shoot that Israeli officer? You told me you had him in your sights and just couldn't shoot."

"I don't know." Ameer smiles thoughtfully. "Something inside of me said no, and I couldn't squeeze the trigger. It was overwhelming, so strange, I was like . . . completely overtaken. At one point, when I opened up on the others, I thought . . . I *know* he looked at me, or . . . or *from* me almost from inside my head. He could have shot at me, too, to cover his people, but he didn't." Ameer's thoughts drift as he remembers. "Maybe I'm going crazy, I don't know. In the smoke and dust everything was so blurred. The strangest part is that this isn't the first time it's happened. The same thing happened in 'Sixty-Seven. And also one time in 'Seventy-Three, in the Golan Heights, when we hit that post. It's like a hallucination. And it's haunting me, and getting inside my mind. It's getting *me* inside *his* mind."

Ameer pauses, and Layal smiles. "Go on. For once you're talking."

"The only thing that stays the same is that *sensation*. When I think back, it's like I've always had it. It is the same sensation, and it's the same face. The same man. I get inside his mind. I know that isn't possible, but that's how I feel . . . As if part of me were there, right where I was aiming. I was with this guy. I *was* this guy. I thought . . . I *felt* like I saw through him. It makes me freeze. Him too, obviously." Ameer sighs and shakes his head. "For now, though, Faris is dead, that's all I know. Maybe Faris would be alive and with us, right now, had I pulled the trigger."

Layal gazes into her husband's eyes. "This . . . sensation. It scares me."

Ameer forces a smile. "Come; let's go ask father what he thinks of our ordeal."

They stroll down the deck to where Tarek and Rima are sitting. Tarek's long-time friend and aide, Nabil, is with them. The three are trying to keep a bunch of children entertained. The girls, led by Rima, are playing hopscotch. Tarek and Nabil are passing a ball around with the boys.

Layal looks back toward the stern of the boat. The Lebanese coast is now disappearing. Oblivious to the girls' pleas to join in the game, she mutters with a shaky voice, "*Ya Allah*, I hope my mother is okay."

Ameer pulls her close. "She'll be fine, don't worry. Sami's home is in a safe neighborhood. He's a doctor with a fine reputation, and all the neighbors adore him."

"*Insh Alla*h. I hope you're right."

Ameer nods. "I'm positive. Now let's take care of the kids." He walks over to Laith and grabs him from behind, growling and munching at his ears. "How's my lion doing? Taking care of your grandpa?" He bends down again and grabs Nidal with his free hand and lifts her up. "And my big girl, watching over your sister?"

"Is it true we're going to live in tents in a dirty camp in the desert, Father?" Nidal seems horrified at the thought. "What if there are snakes and bugs? And where will I bathe my doll?"

As Ameer settles them down, Laith thumps his chest. "I love camps. Like you when you go to war. I want to go to a camp. I'll stand watch every night. When the Israelis come, I'll shoot them! Tatatatatata..."

Nidal, elder and wiser, snaps back, "When the Israelis come, they'll be in a jet plane, they'll burn you and all your friends with napalm, and you'll be dead before you even see them, so stop bragging. We lost the war, we are running away."

Layal reprimands her daughter. "Enough honey, that's no way to cheer us up."

Nidal's voice trembles. "But that's what everybody says. Don't lie to us. We lost, and they're taking us to a prison camp. They're going to do with us what the Nazis did to them, a long time ago." She starts to cry.

Laith follows with a pout. "And Uncle Faris is dead..."

Layal says with a soft voice. "We did lose a battle, but we didn't lose the war. The war won't be over as long as we live. And we're not going to a camp. We'll have our own house, just like before. It's a different place, with a different school, but many of your friends will be there too."

Laith pipes up. "What are we going to fight with? The men say we only have our rifles left."

Tarek raises his fists in a boxing stance. He too is obviously overwhelmed by the events, and their dramatic routing. He has warned about it many times. But still, he has an answer for every scenario. "We'll use our fists, young lion. Our minds too... We'll use everything we have but, by Allah, I promise I shall see my land again, and I'll see you there with me. So keep your faith. The next fight will be where we choose, and how we choose, and that's the way to win."

Nabil speaks up. "Well said, Tarek. That's the spirit! We need more like you on board this ship to keep morale up." Nabil lost his son in the fighting, but the most bitter tears he shed were when he was forced on board and made to leave. The fighters felt that it was their entire cause they were leaving behind, and many saw it as a betrayal to their martyrs and years of struggle. It took five able men to force Nabil on board. Only through Tarek's wisdom did Nabil finally agree to abandon the soil where his son was buried.

Tarek puts his arm around Rima, who has been seasick ever since the ship set off. He gives her a slice of lemon to chew on. She smiles at him. "Thanks, *habibi*. Where did you get that?"

Tarek smiles back. "My usual bag of stuff. You know . . ."

Rima looks at the fading shoreline in the distance and says sadly, "Here we go. On the move again."

Tarek shakes his head. "I know. What can I say? We're trying, and we're trying hard. There must be something else we can do."

"There *has* to be something else we can do, Father," Ameer says. "Did you talk with Abu Ammar? What's our course of action? Any ideas?"

"Our leaders are a mess. They still can't believe this is happening. They can't believe the PLO can be routed while the Arab world watches and does nothing."

Ameer says, "But they must have plans! Something to look forward to."

Tarek puts his hand on Ameer's shoulder. "The old man is a fighter, more than anyone I know. And a very shrewd one. Personally, I don't think anything can bring him down, but we have to admit that we took a knock out . . . blow." He adds, "We have to find something more fruitful to do than just sending young men to their deaths. Besides, what we've done so far has never achieved anything. They still hold our land, and we're on a boat . . . in the wrong direction, yet again."

Ameer groans. "We're in the middle of the sea. Things can't get much worse than this. This is exile from exile, deportation from deportation. *Nakba fi nakba*. A Catastrophe within a catastrophe . . . How can we keep up the fight from our next destination?"

Tarek gives his son a confident smile and adds, "We'll find a way. We just have to admit there isn't a lot we can do in a conventional, military way."

Ameer agrees. "I realize that. We have to find something that gets results. Waging wars like we've been doing is obviously the wrong answer."

Rima says, "The children are doing fine." She nods at Layal with approval as she runs around with a bunch of smiling children.

Tarek shakes his head and gazes out to sea. "We have to admit total victory isn't possible. We should change strategy."

"How? What strategy?"

"Direct confrontation failed miserably. We've tried guerilla warfare with no real results. You tried, against my advice, a years-long terror campaign. That was our worst mistake. We were seen by all as evil men, killing innocent people. All the while, our own civilians and our camps were bombed with cluster bombs, napalm and white phosphorous. Why do you think the world did nothing about the *Israeli* terror campaign? For years, decades! Against civilians!"

Rima cries, "They were happy to get rid of us. If only the world could know what our people have been through."

Ameer says, "I think Tarek is on to something, mother."

"I'm not on to anything, really. We should get our ideas from what has worked historically."

"Like what? I have to admit I haven't done much reading lately." For the first time in a long while, Ameer is eager to listen and learn from his father. Tarek had been right all these years . . .

"Well, Gandhi chased the English out without violence. The Vietnamese, the Algerians, the Americans against the British . . . every nation had to fight for itself, somehow, at some point. Peacefully or otherwise. The only common point is that it has to be done from within. You resist an occupying force from within, not from across its own borders."

Tarek catches his breath and looks at the curious eyes and waiting ears around him. "We should take the fight where it belongs. Back to Palestine. We use our land, and the people still living there. We fight from *within* our land. You can go on shooting, as long as you target their army, or you can go on a hunger strike, as long as you do it in front of international television, or you can hand out leaflets. I don't care what we do, as long as it's from there. We can just throw stones at them, for all I care. David didn't go against Goliath in a wrestling match, he used a sling. Why don't we?"

# 1989
## Akhee - My Brother

# CHAPTER 26

It is December 1988. It has been a year since Palestinians in the Occupied Territories began engaging in what they call the "Intifada." This civil uprising is their latest and, so far, best weapon against the Israeli state. There are neither strategies nor tactics and certainly no standard operating procedures in the Israeli army manuals for teenagers and children charging them with stones. The Israeli army is at a loss. It has been this way for more than a year now. In this latest fight, the Palestinians have managed to impose what Israel has always successfully avoided: they brought the fight back *into* their lands. For the very first time as well, the Palestinians are clearly depicted as the victims by the international community. The media is now able to tell about the systematic daily humiliation, segregation, and mistreatment they are subjected to at the hands of the Israeli occupiers.

Amir pulls his Jeep to a screeching halt in front of his house, jumps out and heads for the front gate, grumbling about how *it's the middle of the day, on a Saturday,* and *everyone's going to be at home.* He'll have to be in and out — and, at all costs, avoid Areih, his sixteen-year-old pack of dynamite. His noisy approach, however, brought out more than one curious neighbor. Debbie rushes to the door, wearing her workout outfit.

She takes one look at him, and her eyes widen. "*Ma kara* — what happened?"

Amir explodes. "*Kharah!* — shit! A bucket of shit! Dumped on my head. All the men are laughing. I need to take a shower, now."

Debbie holds her hands up to block him, a distance away from his chest, too disgusted to touch him. "You're not coming into this house."

He glances at the staring neighbors. "And just what do you suggest I do?"

Debbie points to the corner of the garden. "The hose." Amir heads for it, realizing he cannot possibly enter the house in his condition.

Debbie has a sadistic grin. "Wait, I'll call the boys, they'll have a blast hosing you down."

"Keep them away. I don't want them to see me like this."

Areih barges out the front door. Debbie taps him on the back, "Areih, hose your father down. He's just come from the front line and needs a little, ah, cleaning up."

Amir hurls a shout at his son: "Go back to your studies, and leave me alone!"

Areih scowls as he seems to realize what the matter is, and stomps back into the house, giving his brother David a shove when they cross at the door. Amir realizes he hasn't made things easier with his angry reaction. Areih is a bundle of angry energy, and Amir has always feared his boy would someday act on those urges. His son was eager to shoot the 'damn Palestinians', and his fanatical friends from a nearby settlement weren't helping him tame his anger.

David, on the other hand, looks amused. Grabbing the hose, he blasts away. Amir decides to give up protesting and strips to his underwear, turning under the stream of water. He shivers at the contact of the cold gardening water, and kicks his uniform away.

Debbie looks at him with disgust. "Those clothes aren't going into my washing machine. Just throw them into that garbage bag behind the gate."

"We could —"

"We could not. Just toss it away, the whole uniform; you have so many others anyway."

"Will you get me some soap? I might as well do things properly . . ."

Ely and Moshe walk into the garden. Ely takes one look at Amir, and laughs. "Which hurt more, the shit or the bucket?" he asks.

"I was wearing a helmet and full armor, thank God, and the old woman held onto the bucket. She just tossed its contents on me and two of my soldiers from her window. The guys wanted to shoot her."

"You should have let them!" Areih barks, from his upstairs window. "You should have killed her yourself!"

Amir faces his son. "We have our orders, son. We can't fire unless our lives are in direct danger. That's what they want, to be shot. They want us to get violent in front of every TV camera in the world." He sighs and turns to his father as David sprays his back. "I miss the true wars. Now we just run after kids throwing stones at us. This isn't what we trained for."

Ely nods. "They're smart, those Palestinians. They're changing everything. They brought the battle here, bringing us back to square one." Ely leans against the fence. "Then they changed the rules of engagement. We're not fighting a real war anymore. We can't go after them with what we have. We'd be doing exactly what they want."

Amir asks, "What do we do, Father? Just let them stone us to death?"

"The army is giving it back to them tenfold, using sticks and clubs on all those we catch, which is neither right nor very clever. The smart thing would be to play it down. The more violent things turn, the more attention they get. They will get tired, eventually."

"Maybe you should say that to our generals and their ridiculous orders. That's how this happened: a bunch of kids were throwing stones at us, as we were trying to save two cornered settlers who went in and shot a young Palestinian guy. We backtracked against a wall and pointed our guns at them, and that's when I heard a splash and felt the impact of..." He pinches his nose. "I can't tell you the smell."

"You don't have to." Ely grins. "The whole neighborhood stinks of it..."

David laughs. Amir frowns at him and goes back to scrubbing with soap. "Very funny." He gnashes his teeth. "I wish they'd fire on us, just to —"

Ely looks alarmed. "Is that what you want to show the world? Israeli crack units killing boys?"

"Which side are you on, *aba*?" Amir growls. Amir waits for his father's retort. Like many others, Amir, too, has grown weary of the perpetual fighting. The dead are dead. They are not coming back. Not his daughter, not his friends. Violence is finding new ways to impose itself and its deadly toll, and there is no solution in sight. Amir never shied away from battle, but this time, they have lost the initiative. They are reacting, and the whole fight seems pointless. Unlike earlier battles, there doesn't seem to be anything to gain from this one. They were on the defensive, and their only objective was for "hostilities" to end. Perhaps his father had better ideas about this form of confrontation.

Ely looks around. "Don't be silly. I was there when we took those streets. All of us were there." He shakes his head. "But things are different now. Force won't work. We are living here in violation of UN resolutions. The world has been willing to turn a blind eye to our actions, but if we behave like criminals, if we maintain our presence in the West Bank and Gaza, that could all change."

Amir asks, "Are you saying give them back the land? Good people died taking it. My own —"

Ely says, "We paid for it in blood, yes, and I don't think we should give it back just like that. But if we can't use our firepower, maybe it's time for something else."

Amir says, "Like a blockade, or economic sanctions? Or do you mean compromises?"

"We're going to have to talk with them. And yes, until we do, we have to keep the pressure up, so we have a better bargaining position."

Moshe has been holding it in for too long. He erupts, "Bargaining?"

Debbie puts her hands on her father's shoulders. "I think Ely is onto something. Besides, I think we're all tired of fighting and living in this daily nightmare."

Ely spreads his arms wide. "There are a couple million of them. You can try to kill them all, or you can talk. Which is it going to be?

Moshe grins. "Kill them all."

Amir thinks Moshe must be insane. He used to think and act like him, but the last years have taught him otherwise. Israel has managed, over the years, to impose its will through military power. They have fought their opponents as they gathered under the banners of Pan-Arabism, communism, and terrorism. Yet their military victories have failed to provide a permanent political solution. There was something inherently wrong in that principle he has lived by so far: systematic, yet blind application of force. It will certainly not work against fear-ignoring, death-defying youngsters armed only with stones.

Amir replies to Moshe, "I thought moving them was the plan. It was working."

Ely shakes his head. "Well, they aren't budging, and we can't kill them all." He points to Moshe. "Not even you, Moshe. This isn't Nineteen Forty-Eight. They have CNN and ABC covering the situation; a Reuters cameraman even filmed soldiers systematically breaking the bones of two young Palestinians with clubs. It turned out those soldiers were following orders. Do not forget, the Palestinians techni-cally have the legal endorsement of UN resolutions . . ." Ely raises his eyebrows. "That leaves only one option."

Moshe's sarcasm is blatant. "Talking. Right. And what shall we talk about?"

Ely replies, "Don't you think some concessions are a worthwhile price for peace? Don't you think it's about time we started worrying about normal aspects of civilized life, and not just survival?"

Debbie slaps her father's shoulder and stands behind Ely. "I'm with you Ely, all the way." She returns her father's angry look and goes on, "Does every family need to lose a child before you realize that there's something terribly wrong with your attitude? Don't you always say, *aba*, that what really matters is results? Well, forty years on, FORTY years, all I see is more death, more anger, and then more death . . . and no solution."

Moshe mutters, "Well, I suggest you both join the peace movement, Peace Now. You'd be most welcome over there. You've just denigrated our whole lives' worth of effort, and the blood of our martyrs."

Amir agrees with his father's logic. It somehow confirms his own impulses, although he'd balk at saying that aloud. What he says is, "We're not going to give away vital concessions, but haven't we been fighting for a final political solution? I think it's worth a try." He looks at Moshe. "The ultimate objective of war is a lasting *peace*."

Moshe shakes his head in disbelief. "They'll always want more, and if we show weakness by talking with them, that's the end of us. They'll never be satisfied."

Amir takes the hose from David and flushes the soap clean off his body. He turns to David. "You can turn off the water now. Can you get me a towel, please?"

As David scrambles back into the house, Ely says, "We're talking about an agreement. We give some, they give some, and they can establish a Palestinian state, under international auspices. Most Israelis agree to that today, whether you like it or not. We are a democracy, aren't we? This will put them under one authority so we can control them better, and we can hold that authority responsible. If that authority fails, we send in the troops. Hard and strong." Ely looks at Moshe with a challenge in his eyes. "If we're wise enough, it's for the best of everyone." As Moshe reddens with anger, Ely continues, "We'll be putting a leash on them, and that's more than all our tanks can do."

Moshe is fuming. "You're fooling yourself. A leash on a dog will stop him from biting others, not his own master. You're talking about millions of 'dogs'!"

Amir's thoughts waver between the two sides. He is still upset by his recent encounter, but overall he leans toward his father's logic.

He says, "Those people who are rebelling, they've never fought us before. They've lived under our rules for years, and I think we can talk some sense into them. They've shown that they can be reliable, if allowed to live decently." Amir turns toward Moshe. "I've just seen them, and they aren't the terrorist groups we've fought for years. All they want is peace, dignity, and land. We can give all that. They're a people we can deal with."

"And they won't be so understanding forever," Ely adds. "Just give them more hard times, and see what happens."

Moshe won't hear any of it. "They want us dead, that's all I know. A good Arab is a dead Arab. That's what they say about us anyway."

Ely shakes his head. "Yes, some of them do. Because of the position we've put them in. But there are people we can work with. We have to, because we can't go on the way we have. We either have to absorb them, or give them their autonomy. Those are the only humane choices, and if we want to be a democracy, absorbing them isn't an option because they'll soon outnumber us."

Moshe gnashes his teeth. "We should absorb them into the sea, that's what I say. Into the sea . . ."

Amir points to his pile of filthy clothes on the ground. "Those people were rioting because settlers had just destroyed their crops, their whole work, a year's effort, and kidnapped some of their men, beating them halfway to death. For no reason. You should have seen their mangled faces. Then two more go in and kill another one. What should we expect them to do? Nothing?"

Moshe looks at Amir and Ely defiantly. "Those settlers should be decorated. We should destroy everything those Arabs do; break every bone in their bodies."

Ely puts his hand on Moshe's shoulder. "*Enough*, Moshe. They are humans like us. Let's use our brains and put our hearts in it too." He raises a finger. "This is how it goes: there's one and a half, soon two million Palestinians in the West Bank and Gaza —"

"Judea and Samaria." Moshe throws in.

"Whatever . . . the territories," Ely goes on, "Either we wage war against them and push them out, into the nets of the PLO, and the even more fanatical terrorist groups that are popping out every day, or —"

Amir guesses his father's logic. "Or we bring the PLO in. Into a peace settlement. They'll be contained forever. They're already getting established here."

"Won't work," Moshe says. "Some of them might go for it, but most won't. They want us off the face of the earth, plain and simple."

Ely has a thin smile as he nods to Moshe. "Some of us want them all off the face of the earth, too, so I guess we'll have to compromise, and take our chances with the less-radical elements. Let's offer them a seat in the room next to us, and see if they take it."

Moshe is still unyielding. "They'll want your room too."

Amir laughs. "Dad is right. It makes sense to me." He has a somber look. "I don't want to lose another child, and going on this way isn't getting us anywhere. We've tried the hard approach. We tried to get them all. But the situation got only worse, and now we need something that works. An agreement that satisfies both our people is the only way for a long-term solution. Years and years of war . . . It has to end with peace. It has to . . . end."

Moshe disagrees. "They won't abide by any agreement. Security can't be guaranteed, and they aren't even united. Do you really think the PLO has any control over the extremists?"

Ely switches to a more friendly tone. "Yes, if we strengthen it and give it credibility. One thing is sure. The solution must be long-term, and it's not military. Peace has to come from the people. Not just something politicians sign. If it's to last, it has to be wanted and accepted, not imposed and unfair."

Moshe reveals another aspect to his fears. "If our people hear someone like you two, both war heroes, talking like this, they'll listen. That's a problem. People will become soft. That's dangerous to our long-term survival . . ."

David comes back from the house with a towel and Amir's robe in hand. He has a sour face. Amir dries himself quickly and puts the robe on. He glances at his son. "Thanks. What's wrong?"

David hesitates for a moment, then says nervously, "It's Areih . . . He's gone."

Debbie's face stiffens. "Gone? Where?"

David lowers his head. "I think he's with Dan. He took his *gear*."

"*Gear?* What gear?" Looking at the frightened expression on Debbie's face, Amir snaps, "What do you know about this?"

Debbie shakes her head. "I don't know about any *gear*! But his friend

Dan, from the Wolf's Hill settlement, promised Areih that he would take him on patrol in Ramallah. I think the sight of you when you came home was all Areih needed. After that last incident, when Dan and his friends provoked a big scuffle and had to call you for help, I made Areih promise me he wouldn't go with them."

"My son is on *patrol!?* He's grounded. For a year!"

David says, "They're loaded with guns, *Aba*. He got so mad when he saw you."

Debbie clutches Amir's arm. "You've got to find him. Those kids from the settlement are sick. They are nothing but trouble."

Amir looks at Moshe, feeling angry. "Indeed. To us and the whole country." He turns to David. "Do you know where they might be heading?"

"I know where they went last time. I can show you."

"Just tell me. I'll find him." Amir dashes inside to put new clothes on, get his gear, and alert his unit. On the way upstairs, Amir is unnerved by *that familiar sensation seeping in — in his own home? Scattered and fuzzy feelings mix with his own perceptions, clouding his mind. Yet . . . it pushes him forward. Inexorably.*

———

Ameer is in his living room, watching TV. It seems funny to watch live coverage of what is happening just a few blocks away. The windows of some of his friends' houses could offer a better view.

Layal is busy running around her new house, trying to get everything to work the way it should. She's moved one vase five times before she finally puts it on a table near the front door. It has only been a couple months since they have moved from Tunis. While there, Ameer and his father became even closer friends and advisors to Arafat. They have settled in the West Bank city of Ramallah, after the Israeli Civil Administration had approved their *jama'a shamil*, family reunification permit, which relatives of Layal had applied for years ago. Ameer is hoping to get a closer look at the Intifada, and, admittedly, a better grip on it. Layal has just finished buying furniture, using the morning hours before the shops close at noon, as all shop owners systematically abide by the self-imposed strike. Ameer could tell from her radiant face that she is pleased with her purchases.

She points to the bare windows with a smile and says, "All we need is some curtains and a couple of pictures to hang on the walls."

Ameer smiles back. "You can't expect to have this house exactly the way you want it right away. We spent years putting together our home in Tunis."

Layal frowns. "Those Israeli bastards wouldn't let us bring anything. I'm sure that the customs officer's wife is having a ball with my things. Now we have to buy —"

Ameer pats his thigh and waves her over to sit with him. "It's a small price to pay, don't you think?" He shouts, "We're home . . . in *Our* country. Screw the furniture!"

Layal hops into his lap and wraps her arms around his neck. "We're home indeed. In Palestine. After all these years. What does your father say? Isn't he eager to join us?"

Ameer shakes his head. "He's jubilant, of course. But we're still in occupied land."

"What does Arafat say?"

"He likes our experience, especially father's. We're trying to move things the right way. This is a turning point." He gazes into her eyes and pulls her closer, smelling her hair. He kisses her. "What's for dinner tonight? I'm starving."

She snubs him. "I thought you wanted to cuddle."

Ameer is distracted by his worries. "Hmmm?"

Layal seems to read his mind. With a worried tone, she asks, "How are things going outside? Where is this going?"

He points to the TV set. Palestinian youngsters recklessly charge menacing *Haras Hudoud* — Border Police jeeps, throwing stones at the steel beasts. Israeli soldiers have caught some who had ventured too close and are dragging them away for a ruthless beating, with clubs and rifle butts. "Every stone they throw carries off a little bit of anger. After more than twenty years of occupation, it's going to take a lot of stones . . ." He scratches his head. "The Israelis can't control them. And that beating is making people even angrier."

Layal looks at her husband with concern. "Can anyone control them? Can you?"

Ameer doesn't want to talk about this. "I found a place for Tarek and Rima, so you can relax, they won't be staying here. It's a two-story house, so I booked both floors in case Sami wants to settle here. I am working on his papers. We need doctors like him."

Layal says with a sad tone. "It's worse than war. All the victims are children . . ."

"The Israeli blockade is hurting. The hospitals are overwhelmed, and they don't have drugs or even basic medications. International phone lines are cut and in some areas, the electricity is cut."

"What will the future bring? You don't seem so positive now. You were excited at first, but now . . ."

Ameer sighs. "I just wonder how many boys will have to be killed and mutilated before we get there. I'm tired of the sight of all the victims. They're all kids." He lifts his chin. "Proud boys, hiding their tears, swallowing their pain. I bow to every one of them."

"You still believe this is the ultimate battle?"

"I think it's what we should have been doing from the start. For once, people all around the world can see the truth. We are the victims and they are the criminals. I just brought two French TV reporters into the hospital. It was sickening. I'm used to people dying, but with these kids it's different. I hope we can get somewhere before there's too much hatred on the streets."

"It'll be the inferno the extremists want," Layal says. "Can you control our people?"

"Not really. Many are loyal to us, and we're recruiting more every day, but some join up only because they need the income. But we've been away too long. I'm not sure how many we control. Some organizations were already set up when we came. Some, like Hamas, will be impossible to control. They have a different agenda than ours."

"What do they want?"

Ameer points a finger to his head, circling it. "They're crazed fanatics. They want to destroy Israel, wipe it off the map."

Layal feigns surprise. "And *you* find that crazy? You've certainly circled around!"

Ameer motions her to calm down. "We've learned our lesson, and we paid a dear price doing that, over forty years of struggle and sacrifice. I do not like the Israelis any better, but I do hate them less. And I am also realistic. Our means should define our objectives. Some things we just have to accept, and the time of hapless heroism is gone."

Layal puts her hand on his chest. "Well, is *my* hero popular, at least?"

"The real heroes are those kids." The sight of the daily battles waged by children is particularly humbling, especially for a veteran of real battles, who would think twice before engaging the enemy out in the open the way they do. "There's still a lot of allegiance to extremist movements. So much hatred has built up, so much pain has been inflicted. They intend to spread terror by any and all means. Other countries finance them to create leverage against Israel. They have well-trained officers who are skilled at exciting their followers and throwing them against the Israelis. They've managed to take the fear out of their hearts. I can't find a single person, boy or girl, young or old, who's afraid."

Layal gazes into his eyes. "*You* never were afraid —"

Ameer shakes his head. "This is different. Different and strange. To me at least. Watching the Israelis from up close, without shooting at them . . . we used to dream of the opportunity to line one up in our sights. Living right next to them is a creepy experience."

"But a possible one, right?"

"Next to them, maybe. Not under their feet. Thanks to their daily humiliations, the Israelis have managed to raise the worst foe they could have possibly imagined: an army of fearless teenagers seeking to avenge two generations' worth of vile occupation."

"But they don't carry weapons, right?"

Ameer is categorical. "No, no one is armed. Wouldn't the Israelis love that? Anyway, we're trying to infiltrate the extremists, bring over as many as we can, and have some eyes and ears inside, too. We can't allow them to escalate things into warfare, or, even worse, terrorist attacks which would just bring more armed retaliation."

Layal sits up, alarmed. "More death, more hatred. Pretty soon, there won't be any innocent people left. People will *have* to take sides."

"That's exactly what the extremists on both sides want. More death and more hatred. Otherwise, they'll be out of job. The real problem for all of us is controlling them."

Layal looks surprised. "Are you becoming a pacifist? Have Tarek's wise words influenced you? How I hope this is true . . ."

"Maybe. Yes and no. But I've learned my lesson, and I can see the way now, clear as the day. We're fighting for our land, in our land. Everybody is fighting, not just soldiers. Nobody's scared of going down to the streets, picking up stones and throwing them at the enemy, even if they might eat a bullet. The pressure of the uprising is huge, and the Israelis will have to make a move. They'll have to make some concessions." Ameer sighs. "Just like us, many among them are tired of this never-ending conflict. We have to start negotiations with the Israelis. It's the only way for us to get our land back."

"Our own *Palestinian* land? Jerusalem? Like in the UN resolutions? *Insh Allah!* It seems like a dream." Layal checks her watch and stands. "Dinner is ready. Will you call them?" She smiles. "They listen to you."

Ameer calls up the stairs, "Dinnertime, children! And I'm starving!"

Nidal and Roula cheerfully rush down the stairs from the upper floor where they were playing. Ameer can sometimes hardly believe his daughters are already sixteen and twelve. Nidal dresses like a young lady, and Roula emulates her every move.

From the kitchen, Layal says, "Who's hungry?"

Roula shouts, "I'm starving!"

Nidal is quieter. "Me too. What's for dinner?"

"What you like: *kabab, hommos*, salad, and chips."

"Great!" Both girls answer enthusiastically.

Ameer says, "Where's Laith?"

Layal asks nonchalantly, "Would you call him, Nidal? He must be in the backyard. His friends Imad and Karim dropped by."

Ameer says, "Bring them all in. I'd like to meet his friends. The new generation."

Nidal looks at the floor, guilt in her eyes.

Layal spots her, and asks, "What's with the face, Nidal? Where's your brother?"

Nidal confesses, "He's gone, again . . ."

Ameer springs to his feet. It is too dangerous for his boy to be outside, and Ameer knows all too well what Laith has in mind. Ameer's son had inherited all of his impetuousness. Ameer is red with anger. "And you didn't tell us?"

Nidal tries to defend herself. "He promised he'd be back for supper. He said he only wanted to watch."

"Why didn't you tell me? Or your mother?"

"He trusts me, papa, and he said he wouldn't be in danger."

"I have to find him. He's a child. He can get in trouble without realizing it. The Israelis are getting trigger-happy. Two boys were killed today! Sixteen and fourteen, and another by the settlers!" Ameer bangs his hand on the table. "Nidal, where is he?"

Nidal avoids her father's stare, muttering unintelligible words.

Ameer is angry. "He didn't even say where he was going? That's clever."

"Karim didn't go, but he must know."

"Run!" Ameer yells. Nidal bolts. He looks at Layal. "So, my son is the hot head!?"

Layal answers, *"Farkh el-bat a'wwam."* — Like father, like son. — "Calm down, he'll be back while supper is still warm."

Ameer looks into his wife's eyes. He is furious. "You approve of this?"

"I'm just trying to calm you down. Besides, this was your idea, to come back here." Layal takes his hand. "You can't ask your boy to sit at home while his friends are out in the streets. What would you have done?"

Ameer lashes at her in anger. "Why didn't you tell me? I can at least direct them. Don't you care?"

Layal's eyes moisten. "How dare you! I was just over at the house of that fourteen-year-old who died today. It was like being in our house in 'Seventy-Three. My heart stops beating the instant Laith leaves the house, and doesn't start beating again until he's back." A tear rolls down her cheek.

Ameer sees that Layal is about to collapse. She's been keeping a lot to herself lately, and taking on a great emotional burden. She is trying to support mothers who lost their sons and had just participated in a sit-in protest at the Red Cross headquarters in solidarity with Palestinian detainees. He pulls her to him. "You're right, that wasn't fair."

Layal lets her feelings out. "We live here, with *our* people, in *our* land. Everybody looks up to us. We were strangers when we first came. If it weren't for you, your strength, your exploits, everyone would have rejected us. Instead, everybody admires us, and especially you. You're one of the leaders in this new war, as you call it. You just said everyone is fighting. Those who aren't throwing stones are starving, or dying of sickness and wounds. But no one would change a thing. *Not a thing!* The feeling that we're doing something important, for ourselves, by ourselves, is the only thing that matters. You, of all people, can't expect to keep your family out of it."

Ameer is baffled. "What's so special about me?"

"We all try to live up to your standards, your reputation. I have to be an ideal mother, the children have to be model children, and that means Laith has to be a model street fighter." Layal shakes her head. "He told me he wanted to be a leader, just like you, and make you proud."

Ameer is astonished. "*Ya Allah* . . . This is worse than I thought."

The door bursts open and Nidal rushes in, her face desperate. "Karim is gone, too. I'll take you. I think I know where they went."

"Just tell me where they are."

Nidal grabs her father's hand and drags him outside. "I don't know how to explain. It is right next to the cemetery. We'll be fine, don't worry."

Ameer nods. He grabs Nidal by the hand and steps out. He shouts to Khalil, who is outside of his own house, just across the way, patching up fissures in his house walls.

"Khalil! Laith is in trouble. Gear up!" Ameer makes a gesture of hiding a gun in a jacket. He wanted Khalil to bring their compact, folding stock AK's.

Khalil drops his tools. "Right behind you." He runs into his house, grabs two rifles from behind the door and comes out as quickly as he went in.

Ameer says to Nidal, "Go!" She leads the way, dragging her father behind her.

Ameer feels a rush as he races behind his daughter, and somehow feels the pride that these boys and girls must feel. He remembers his first missions, with his father, Tarek, and how thrilled he'd been, how much he admired him. Life has come full circle. Father and daughter going hand in hand to the 'front line.' Ameer's heart is beating in anticipation, in fear for his son, and . . . *for that familiar sensation again, slowly but surely seeping in. The sensory perception is back. Still confused and unfocused, but it clogs his mind. It does not clog his body, as Ameer feels an irresistible surge to forge ahead.*

# CHAPTER 27

Amir speeds into the Israeli Army military compound in Ramallah city and stops his Jeep next to his waiting captain. His trusted officer stands in the middle of the assembly area, supervising the company as it gets ready to move out. Amir scans his troops and their vehicles as he hops out of his car. "*Shalom*, Ron. Are the men ready?"

"Yes Sir. Anti-riot and battle gear."

"The armored cars?"

"Yes, sir. Engines warm. Full line-up."

Amir is satisfied. He knows he can rely on his men. "Good. Saddle up." Amir's thoughts are with Areih. Will he find him in time? Will he find him at all? Where can he be now, and what can he be doing? Is he *already* in trouble? And . . . Why on earth does that *sensation* have to happen *now*?

Ron interrupts his thoughts. "What are the orders, sir? What's our mission?"

Amir leads him to their armored car and waves two soldiers to hop in the back seat. "You drive; I'll brief you on the way. We're going in."

Ron starts the car, turns and signals the men to follow, and drives. "Where to?"

"We have no orders from HQ. Consider it an emergency. A personal one. A group of fanatical settlers have gone out on their own."

"Again!? We're to bring them back? By force if we have to?"

"We're going to bring them back before they start World War Three."

"But do we use our weapons if there's resistance?"

Amir snaps, "No! Areih is with them."

Ron cannot hide a smile. "Areih! He is so like . . . you. What happened?"

"I got splattered with a bucket of shit. He saw me and got all fired up."

"Oh, that explains it."

"You think that's a good excuse?"

Ron says, "No, sir, I meant the smell, sir."

Amir glances at his captain. Ron is struggling to hold in a laugh. He wasn't with him when it happened, but must have heard from the men. Amir has a stern look. "It's dead serious Ron. They don't know what they're doing. They could trigger something that will get out of control." Amir looks ahead as they lead the convoy from the compound.

Ron asks, "Shall I tell HQ we're on a search and rescue mission to retrieve overzealous friendlies?"

"Sure, that will do. But how are we going to find the boys?"

Ron smiles. "It won't be too hard. I have a friend in the Ariel settlement. His name is Isaac. He'll know what's going on."

Amir frowns. "I really dislike those people. How did you meet him?"

"He spends a lot of time with our guys at the roadblock, monitoring traffic and guarding the settlement. He's Mr. Know-It-All in their community."

Amir opens his duffel bag and takes out his *Keffieh* and Palestinian outfit, in order to blend in. "I'll need another two men in Arab dress. How do we get to this Isaac?"

"He will probably be at the roadblock on our way in. Take the sergeant and corporal from the first platoon with you. You've gone undercover with them before."

Amir nods. He knows the two men well, and has in fact worked with them in similar situations. "Let's hope Isaac is there. We'll separate, and you take the lead when I leave you. Keep Isaac on board and brief him on the situation. You'll need good visibility and tactical awareness. Use the usual covering-fire formations, but keep your distances to avoid contact. I don't want any casualties. It's a delicate situation."

"What do we do when we find them sir?"

Amir squeezes the kalash he'd taken from his duffel bag. "They're in for the lesson of their lives. One they'll never forget."

Ron lowers his voice. "Sir, don't make a big deal out of it. Your son is going to be fine, sir. This kind of thing happens all the time, and we always contain it."

Amir looks at the two men in the backseat. They couldn't hear him with their helmets on. "I don't know what's wrong with me, Ron. I'm all sweaty."

Ron tries to calm him down. "We're going in and out. Just tighten up in front of the men."

"I'll be fine. I've had this feeling before, but not so strongly, and it has nothing to do with my son. It usually goes away after a while."

Ron raises his eyebrows in surprise. "You've felt like this before? Like what, exactly?"

"I just feel like I'm already where we're going. It's a sensation. Some sort of a double vision . . . there's a difference, though, this time."

"And what's that, sir?"

"This time the feeling is pushing me ahead. Usually this feeling makes me hesitate and I can't move. I feel frozen."

Ron is puzzled. "And it's been happening for a long time?"

Amir sighs. He's never fully confessed to his experiences before, except to his wife, but this time it is overwhelming. "It's happened to me before, yes. Three or four times." I used to think it was combat stress. Now I think there's something else. I *know* it's something else."

Ron nods ahead. "You'll be fine; I'm not worried about you. The checkpoint, straight ahead." He scrutinizes the area and adds, pointing toward a civilian carrying a rifle and assault vest. "And there's Isaac. We're good to go. He'll take us to your son in no time. All you have to do is blend in and move ahead of our convoy." Ron stops the Jeep near Isaac.

Amir grabs his undercover gear and steps out. "Let's go get my son."

———

Running behind his daughter, Ameer is already sweating, but his main concern is finding his son. There are makeshift road-blocking obstacles here and there, and burning tires and screaming kids everywhere. He shouts to Nidal, "Is it far?"

She turns back with an excited smile, her long black hair flowing in the wind, "We're almost there, Father. Hear the shouting?" She adds, "Are you lost?"

"Almost. How come you know these streets?"

"This is where we play, Father!"

"Play!? *Allah Akbar!* This is a battlefield."

Nidal laughs and slows to a brisk walk. "That's what we play. We throw stones. *Intifada hata a-nasr.*" — Intifada until victory.

Ameer's mind lapses back to when he was rushing the enemy. It was *thawra hatta a-nasr* — Revolution until victory — back in those days. Nidal goes on, "We're fighting, like you did. For our freedom, for our country. Look over there, the boys are gathering stones!"

Ameer is shocked. "You sound like you're part of this!"

"Don't worry about me. I only help in organizing."

Several teenagers, heads and faces hidden beneath black and white *Keffieh* spot her. They toss quick salutes and shout *Intifada sha'biyeh*, their slogan, before returning to their tasks with even more fervor.

"They're saluting you? It looks like you're running the show. I can't believe it, a teenage girl leading young men."

"*Your* girl, Father. All of the *shabab* dream of fighting like you used to. You are their role model. Once we're done with stone-throwing."

Ameer says, "The whole point in throwing stones is *not* to use guns. Stone-throwing is our *last* battle. It represents the image of our people. You children need more guidance." He grabs his daughter by the arm, "Now where's your brother?"

She points to a group of young men at the end of the street. "That's his group. I hope he won't be mad at me."

Ameer and Nidal run up to a bunch of boys gathered outside a two-story house. They have surrounded it, and are throwing stones into the house through its windows, and hurling concrete blocks at the main door. A couple of them are arguing with an old man, who is trying to stop them. It looks like he is the Palestinian owner of the house, in which some adventurous Israelis have taken refuge. Nidal points at a boy covering his head with a *Keffieh*, a Palestinian flag thrown around his neck and on his back, like a cape. "There!"

Ameer reaches his son just as he prepares to throw a Molotov cocktail. Ameer grabs the bottle and tosses it onto the opposite sidewalk, where it harmlessly explodes, the heat from the expanding gases and flying glass forcing him to cover his face with his hands as he bends over Laith to protect him.

As he turns away from the blast, Ameer sees a boy aiming an assault rifle from inside the house, about to shoot Laith. Ameer waves to the boy, who looks up. He drops his rifle. He looks awestruck. Ameer looks back at him for a frozen second, then squeezes Laith's arm, pointing toward his would-be killer. "You see that guy? He was just about to shoot you!"

Laith lifts his chin defiantly. "Not while he burned."

Ameer grasps his son to control him. He can feel his heart pounding as he pulls him near. He waves the other Palestinian boys back from the house as he drags Laith away. "Everybody get back! Back! That's an order! Away from the house! It is I, Ameer, ordering you back! *Lawara!*" — Get back!

Laith's voice is tight with excitement, his eyes are spitting venom. "We cornered a group of Israeli boys, father, and forced them to hide inside this house. The owner tried to stop them, but then he came running out and tried to stop us. We have two wounded."

Ameer is alarmed. "How bad?"

"They were shot. Just leg wounds. The Israelis are scared." Laith mocks. "We heard one of them crying. We'll get them, guns or no guns."

Ameer turns to his daughter. "Nidal, stay here and wait for Khalil. Use your authority to hold everybody back. Don't move from here." He looks back at Laith and takes his arm. *The sensation seeps into Ameer. It controls him. It makes him act, talk, and . . . push ahead. It drives him forward. Forward and toward . . . the very source of it. He feels it's waiting for him. Words are spoken from his mouth,* "Laith, let's go meet the enemy. You might be surprised how much he looks like you." Ameer waves to his son's friends. "Come with me. Karim, Imad, Ahmed, come along. *Now!*"

Laith opens his mouth to protest, but feels his father's squeeze on his arm grow much tighter. He fumbles. "I'm not sure that's such a good idea . . ."

"This is not an *idea*. It's an order. Follow me, and not a word. I do the talking."

Laith's friends follow in amazed silence. Ahmed mutters, "We're with you sir."

*The sensation seems to double in intensity. It clouds his mind with parallel perceptions. Ameer doesn't fight it. For the first time, it comforts him and fills him with energy.* Ameer knows that inside, there would be more than one gun ready to go, and that the Israeli boys are scared. Ameer shouts to them in perfect Hebrew, trying to sound as calm as possible. "*Shalom aleichem!* We're coming in peace. I want to talk to you!"

A voice comes from inside the house. "Come in, if you're a friend." The tone is confident, calm. It even sounds . . . familiar. Is it a trap? Is it that sensation again?

Dragging his son and his son's friends, Ameer enters the house through the garden. He finds eight teenagers, armed to the teeth with Glocks, Uzis and M-4's. They look primed for a fight. He's stepped in just in time. He nods to the boy who'd almost shot his son. He has to make an effort to look away from his face. Ameer has no time for this dreaded sensation now, but it refuses to go away . . . It keeps pushing him towards that same boy, who seems to find the attention natural.

Another well-armed young man seems to be their leader. Ameer addresses him with a military tone and salutes again. "*Shalom.* We come in peace. You lads have no business being here, and should certainly not be carrying that arsenal. I'll escort you to safety. But you have to follow my instructions."

The young man seems to relax. He asks, "What are your instructions, sir?"

"Unload your weapons." Ameer watches the Israeli teens put their safeties on. "No, no. I mean completely empty your guns. Remove the clips, clear your actions and put the rifles on your backs. We'll walk out of here, and my boys will escort us. No one will cause you harm, and no harm will be caused by you. *Understood?*"

The leader smiles and gives the okay to his friends. "We'll do as you say, sir." The young men nod in turn, and obey the order, with surprising swiftness.

Their discipline and, mostly, their compliance amazes Ameer. The Israeli squad of eight teenagers acts as one, and their dexterity with their weapons reminds him of his own when he was their age. Like him, these youngsters probably sleep with their guns. He notices them exchanging looks of consent, before complying with Ameer's orders.

Ameer has a bold thought. Would it work? He says to the Israeli leader, pointing to the wall behind them, "I want you people to stand in line over here."

The leader hesitates, but the boy with the familiar face takes a step toward the wall, soon followed by the rest. The eight boys line up, backs to the wall. Ameer lets out the breath he's been holding. He looks back toward Laith and his friends, and orders in Arabic, "Go, shake their hands one by one — and say your name." His son's expression turns into mixed horror and disgust, and Ameer orders, "*Yalla!*" — Let's go!

Seeing the resistance in Laith's eyes, Ameer starts the process himself. He goes to the first Israeli and puts his hand out. It is the "special" boy who had chosen not to shoot Laith. Ameer's voice is cordial as he says, "Ameer. I'm pleased to meet you."

The young man shakes his hand as his eyes widen, and he mutters in return, "Areih, Shalom."

Ameer feels the sensation grow stronger as he touches the young man's hand. That young boy . . . Even his name . . . *Areih*, lion cub, just like his Laith, except in Hebrew. His handshake with the second boy doesn't produce the same feeling, and Ameer looks back at the first. He opens his mouth, but cannot think of anything to say. Laith, *his* lion cub pushes him forward, eager to finish from this "order".

The tension in the room is easing. Ameer watches the young men's mixed emotions as they greet each other, their defiant looks slowly subsiding. He exclaims, "There, you see. *Al- a'aduw bachar methlak.*" The enemy is human, like you. And then says it again in Hebrew. *"Atem roim, ha oyev enoshi bediuk kamochem."*

The unmistakable sound of an inbound armored motorcade interrupts his satisfaction. It is near. Khalil bursts in, throwing a compact, folding stock AK into Ameer's hands, oblivious to their 'no guns' rules of engagement, and immediately posts two men he's brought with him at the windows overlooking the street.

Khalil says, "They're all around. What do we do, Ameer?" He comes closer to Ameer and whispers, nodding at the Israelis, "We could use them as hostages."

The Israeli boys seem shaken by the sudden intrusion, but remain calm, not even going for their guns when Khalil burst in. Ameer wonders why. The sensation swells again. Every glance at the young Israeli named Areih makes it stronger.

Ameer says to Khalil, "Calm down. We sit tight, and we talk. I want to walk these boys out." He adds, to everyone, "We stay cool and we'll have a peaceful solution."

Ameer peers out the window and watches the armored convoy circle the house and establish a security perimeter. The young Palestinians outside, restrained and controlled by Nidal, withdraw slightly but keep a tight circle around the Israeli soldiers, Molotovs at the ready. A single stone thrown can lead to chaos. The house is surrounded twice, first by the Israelis, and then by the Palestinians. The Israeli convoy encircling them is now trapped as well, by tens of angry teens. Their number is swelling fast. The situation is as tense as it can be.

Ameer needs all his courage and wisdom to sort it out peacefully. He remembers the days when he'd look forward to enemy soldiers so close . . . yet this is different. That sensation is here, guiding his decisions. The incident suddenly seems far more important than just kids stoning soldiers. Ameer finds himself in a deadlock and yet he feels far more comfortable than he should. It makes no sense. He feels like he could just walk out to the enemy and talk to him. *The sensation seems to kick out his last remnants of control, and the blurred perceptions start to flash in his mind . . .*

A cracking sound yanks him out of his inner turmoil. It comes from the stairs to the floor above. Are there more Israeli boys? Are they trying to surprise him? Is that why those below are so obedient? No. It is something else. It is "It." It is the sensation itself. Ameer shivers as he looks up the stairs, hypnotized. The sensation is a thousand, a million times stronger. It is infinite. Ameer yields to it. It overtakes his senses, his emotions, his actions. *The sensation* is coming down the stairs straight toward him. In Peace. It *is* Peace. It is the *spirit* of peace. It fills his body. Invades it.

---

Amir had left his convoy just past the roadblock, ahead of the "hot" area. He and two of his men swapped their Israeli uniforms for Palestinian clothing and exchanged their M-4 rifles for folding-stock AK's. They raced toward the tumult. The source of the uproar was obvious. A snitch had briefed them on the way, and pointed them to an old house surrounded by Palestinian kids, where his boy's group was cornered.

Everyone was delighted to point the way for them when they asked for the trapped Israelis in perfect Arabic. They looked and acted as if they were there to "get" them before Israeli reinforcements arrive. Them being armed seemed to be a morale booster for the Palestinian on-lookers, who pointed with wild cheers. Amir posted his men outside and climbed to the second floor from the back of the house, and into a bedroom.

Now, through the bedroom door, he can see the open space of the large living room below where all are gathered. A flight of stairs leads down, and Amir slowly goes out the door, into the open landing, and onto the first step down. He can see his son and his friends, all holding weapons. Empty, and slung behind their backs. To his surprise, there are Palestinian men, also armed, and Palestinian boys. The scene looks non-threatening. They are ... shaking hands!

*The sensation flows through his every vein, every muscle, and every bone, flooding his senses, controlling his movements. His every nerve twitches with it. It is pushing him forward ... toward ... to that, to 'him', the very source of the feeling. The man with his son, that familiar stranger.* If only he would turn around! Amir hears the man's words about a peaceful solution. *The words resonate in his head. He even feels he is muttering the same words in unison. Amir is driven down the stairs, one step at a time.* Cautious not to startle anyone, he pushes his rifle behind his back, out of direct view. Amir *knows that 'he' is friendly. The sensation 'says' so. Amir even feels 'he' is waiting. The sensation is waiting. The man 'is' the sensation.* The sensation fills him. Warms him.

Like the others, 'he' starts to turn around and look up towards Amir. In the darkened space, Amir squints as he looks into the man's face. The face. His *own* face. He is awestruck. Amir touches his own face as he gazes into the man's eyes. The man, equally mesmerized, returns his gaze, and replicates his movement. *The sensation flows to the man, in a mental and emotional bridge. It is the same sensation he's had over the years, yet this time, he knows its origin: the man. He feels its power:*

*irresistible. His senses, his perceptions, his feelings . . . his entire world swirls around, collapsing into 'his' mind, 'his' world.*

Amir is drawn out of his hypnosis by his son's shout. *"Aba*! Amir!" A Palestinian boy cries out, *"Yaba*! Ameer!" The boy's faces are as flabbergasted as his, as they keep looking at him and then back at 'him'.

———

Amir slowly proceeds down the stairs. For a moment, he looks at the man by the door, whose gun is pointed at him. The man shouts at him, "Put your gun down. Now!"

Amir looks at Ameer, who puts his hand on the pointed rifle's muzzle, motioning it down. Amir nods and slowly slides his own rifle to the floor, as he reaches the last step. Ameer does the same. They are now only a few feet apart. Some of the Israeli boys were slowly retrieving their weapons. Ameer orders, in Hebrew and then in Arabic,

*"Lehorid et ha neshek ou miyad! Selah bel ard, fawran!"* — Weapons down, now!

Amir looks stunned. As the Israeli boys hesitate, he orders, "You heard him. Rifles down."

He proceeds toward Ameer, in the middle of the room. Under the ceiling light. Everyone gasps in the still air. All eyes swing between the two faces. The *same* faces, each staring into the other, locked in fascination.

Ameer tilts his head to the right, and Amir imitates him, to the left. Like someone seeing a mirror for the first time, they observe each other at near contact distance. Amir frowns, and Ameer imitates him. Ameer raises his hand, and touches Amir's cheek. The sensation takes its full meaning; it is embodied by the man opposite. Amir does the same, and shares the same relief in knowledge. This is the sensation. He mutters, "You're real. This sensation, all these years . . . You're not a hallucination. How can this be?"

Ameer speaks in Hebrew, then in Arabic, *"Ata amiti! Inta hakeeki!"* You're real!" He wears a serene face, feels a serene feeling, one he has not known for forty years. "I have seen you before, I have *felt* you before."

The two are interrupted by one of Areih's friends, as he shouts, "Help! My brother has an open grenade!"

All eyes turn to the boy, and follow his look to the quivering young man, holding a grenade. His face is sweaty. His hands are shaking. Ameer and Amir leap to him in concert. They both grasp his hand in theirs, to prevent the grenade lever from flying off, initiating the fuse. Amir has his hand directly on the boy's. He looks at Ameer who understands and relaxes his grasp. Ameer looks at the ground, and finds the missing pin. He holds Amir's hand, to stabilize the grenade, and deftly reinserts the pin, securing it. With their hands still together, Amir asks, *"Mee ata?"* Who are you? Are you Palestinian or Israeli?"

Ameer answers with the same question, *"Inta meen?"* — Who are *you?* — "Are you Israeli or Palestinian?"

Amir says, "You are *exactly* like me!"

Ameer shakes his head. "No. *You* are exactly like *me.*"

Amir stares again at Ameer, then looks at everyone around. What he gets back is nods of approval and inquisitive looks. All are silent.

Ameer observes Amir from his *Keffieh* down to his shoes. "Mirror image." He takes a deep breath. "So, which side are you on?"

Amir smiles. "I asked first."

Ameer looks at Khalil, and hands him the grenade. "Keep it with you, Khalil."

Amir exclaims, "Khalil? *Ata Aravi!*" You're an Arab!

*"Inta yahoudi* — you're a Jew. And yes, I am Palestinian, *ya akhee.*" — My brother.

The two pause at the word, then speak in concert, *"Akhee?"* They hold each other by the arms. The question hangs in the air, stilling all motion, filling the room with the silence of unfathomable yet inexplicable evidence.

A loud, tinny voice comes through from outside. It speaks in Arabic, with a broken accent. "You inside, come out with your hands in the air!" The same command is repeated in Hebrew.

Amir nods towards the window. "My men. They've surrounded us. Must be getting nervous."

Ameer takes one step towards the window, peers outside. "And they're surrounded as well. Boys and girls with Molotov's. We don't want this to end in a bloodbath."

"That's exactly what I came for. Avoiding bloodshed. I came to retrieve my son, Areih, and his friends. What they're doing is wrong."

Ameer walks to his son, puts a hand on his shoulder. "And I came to fetch *my* son, Laith." Ameer pauses for a second, shaking his head as he wonders. "We even share that. Areih *means* Laith." He looks at Areih, puts his other hand on his shoulder. "Areih, Laith . . ." Looking back up at Amir, he asks, pointing to the deadlock outside. "How do we sort this? Do you command your men?"

"I do. I suggest you and I walk out, with the rest of them following, weapons down."

Ameer agrees. "I'll accompany your convoy out of the area, to avoid any friction."

"Good. Let's go." Amir hesitates. "And after that?"

Ameer is spontaneous. "We'll meet again, as soon as possible. We have to sort this out."

"Of course. You even look my age."

"I was born in 'Forty-Eight. Don't say anything. I know." Ameer points his finger to Amir's chest. "You too."

Amir lowers his voice. "We've met. In battle. Jerusalem, 'Sixty-Seven —"

Ameer interrupts, "Beirut, in 'Eighty-Two, and before that, in the Golan, in 'Seventy-Three."

"You attacked our outposts, and an early warning station. Killed everyone inside."

Khalil grumbles. "Must be the one where Anouchka mislead us."

Amir jolts. "You knew her?"

Ameer nods his head. "Yes." He gives Khalil a furtive look, then looks at Amir. "So did you."

"She taught us counter-terror and special operations."

Ameer leans over, whispers in Amir's ear, "She taught you more than that. She thought I was you. Now I understand . . ." Ameer adds a friendly wink.

Amir can't avoid an embarrassed smile.

The Israelis interrupt them once again, as they reiterate the order to come out, through their loudspeakers. Khalil is getting nervous. "Are we talking *girls*, or are we getting out?" He points to Amir. "Your friends are getting nervous, mister. I suggest you give them some sign of life, to calm them down."

Amir goes to the window and bellows to his men. *"Be seder.* We're coming out."

Ameer and Amir exit the house, arms over shoulders, holding their son's hands. The sight of them coming out, followed by both the Palestinian and Israeli boys, in total harmony, brings stunned expressions onto every face. Rifles swing down, and stones fall to the ground. What kind of miracle happened inside that house?

# CHAPTER 28

Three days have passed since that momentous face-off. Three days that turned lives upside down, and raised more questions than could be answered. Ely and Sara, as well as Tarek and Rima, have given a detailed account of the events on that fateful day, in May '48, when the abandoned twins were saved from certain death through two successive chance encounters. Tarek spoke of a God-sent wonder that kept him alive and gave him reason to live, while Ely spoke of that battlefield miracle, the joy of life amidst the fury of death. Discovering that they were adopted, although shocking news in itself, was of little effect compared to their other finding. Their lifelong quest for an answer was now over. The mystery of the unexplained sensation was finally resolved. They had a twin. A twin brother whose path had paralleled yet collided with theirs, causing inner anxiety and emotional stress that they could never understand . . . until now. It was all clear, now.

Moshe and Khalil have organized a meeting between the two families. They chose a motel, on *Jabal-el-Zaytoun* — Mount Olive — overlooking Jerusalem, with the Old City in the background. The nice and calm area is easy to control, with a single access point, along a narrow road. Moshe booked the place, and established a low pro-file, highly professional security perimeter around it. The gathering is kept away from the press, and prying eyes. Moshe is keen to show that the Arab parents are adoptive as well, to negate any speculative claims that Amir is Palestinian, and so he has arranged with the Defense Ministry to give Tarek and Rima permits to be flown in from Tunis to Tel Aviv.

Besides Khalil, Moshe, and a discrete security detail, only the twin brothers, their parents, and their families are allowed. The only excep-tion is a key witness from the past, whom Moshe remembered and located without telling anyone. He sent for him.

The two families gather in a large lounge area of the motel. On the Palestinian side, Ameer and Layal sit on a large sofa, with Roula and Nidal on either side of them. Laith stays on his feet, staring at his cous-ins with a rebellious look. Every now and then, his father asks him to relax and sit down, and Laith complies, but it isn't long before he gets up again and starts pacing back and forth near the window.

Amir and Debbie are on their own couch, trying to stimulate a conversation. Sitting next to them, David and Areih are a little bit more relaxed than Laith, although the psychological barrier with the Palestinian 'family' is there.

The twin brothers are past the barrier, however, and realize, in ret-rospect, what their subconscious has been trying to tell them for years. Their attitude and their feelings are transferring slowly to both their parents and their children. Gradually, conversation starts to flow, as the wives, and eventually the children, throw a question here and an answer there.

Ameer eyes his twin as he pulls Layal closer to him. "*Shu, akhee,* what are our parents doing?"

*Akhee.* Amir wonders whether he will ever get used to that, as he points his thumb towards the main entrance. "They're in the entrance hall, talking. I think Ely is waiting for someone Moshe's bringing. One more secret of his."

Ameer is skeptical. "I am not sure anyone could add to what our parents already know. It looks like a locked case."

Amir shrugs. "I know. Ely says there was neither a living soul, nor a clue, at the burned coach where we were found. But I hope somebody has some records or something . . . We *have* to find out who we really are."

Ameer nods, and throws the question everyone wanted to hear the answer to: "What about you, what do you think? What do you *feel?*"

"I don't think anything. I feel as Israeli as I can be. I don't know otherwise."

"I guess it won't make much difference what the truth is."

Amir raises an eyebrow. "You think so? No matter how bloody things got in all those years of war, I always felt there was something missing, something strange, in what I was doing. Something wrong that had to be corrected and made right."

Ameer laughs. "You just felt bad fighting your own people. We're Palestinians!"

Amir is the only one to smile. "No really. I did not feel bad. I am sure you felt the same. I had that . . . *sensation* at times, that's all. We were in close contact more than once. We've fought each other so many times. Brothers . . . All these years!"

Ameer nods. "I had that sensation too. You know this. Twins sometimes have this sort of spatial communication. I felt like I could see through your eyes, I could hear through your ears. *I felt what you felt.*

We both had the chance to kill each other, and we didn't. That is fate, not luck." He points upward. "Allah is behind this."

Amir hesitates. "We have to learn the truth." He pauses for a second. "I think."

"You mean you'd rather not?"

"If I told you now you're Jew how would you take it? Go home and sleep on it?"

"I'd kill myself." Ameer laughs. "One less Israeli."

His brother shakes his head. "Exactly. For one of us, the truth will not be fun."

Ameer turns serious. "Maybe we should come to some sort of an agreement, no matter who we are?"

"I agree," Amir says.

Layal slips her arm through Ameer's, and looks straight into his brother's eyes. "I think you should make peace. A personal peace between you two, regardless of the world outside. If you two are at peace with each other, and with yourselves, then the rest will follow. This *peace* tried to impose itself upon you, many times before. You denied it, because you didn't know. Now you do."

Debbie smiles wildly for the first time. "You don't talk much, but when you say something, you say the right thing. I totally agree with you, Layal."

Layal says, "You're brothers, regardless of your origin. Just think about that. Twin brothers. I can hardly tell one from the other. Even your voices are the same. You've been through hell and back, both of you, many times. You even 'met' there. Your lives have been the same, yet on opposite sides. What a tragedy!" She points from one to the other. "But it can still be repaired. Either of you could have been carried away by the other parent, and your lives would have been swapped — everything you did, everything that happened to you. Think about it. And this is true also about our two people; Isaac and Ishmael were brothers, both the sons of Abraham. For how long will brothers go on killing each other's families?"

The brothers stare at each other, and respond together, "No more. Never again."

---

Ely stands in the entrance hall, peering out the window. Tarek, Rima, and Sara are there as well, sitting on comfortable couches. Moshe is pacing. Finally, they hear a car pull in. Moshe checks through the window, as one of his men talks with the driver, then turns towards him, and signals 'OK.' Moshe turns towards Ely, to the sound of footsteps outside. "He's here." Moshe opens the door and steps out to greet the visitor.

He is delighted to see Samuel from Dar Moussa, and he recognizes him at once, even after all those years. The very man who helped Ely with one of the infant twins.

"Welcome, my friend, welcome! Please come in, there are some people I want you to meet. You're in for a surprise." Moshe looks inside, nods towards Ely. "I think you remember Ely, only he's about forty years older . . . well, so are you!"

Ely stands and walks out to meet the visitor. Samuel extends his hand, but Ely proceeds to hug him. "You're here! It's been a long time, but you look well. I do read about you in the papers. You're into diplomacy, traveling all around the planet."

Samuel steps back and looks at Ely. "Just trying what I can to help our nation find a peaceful way out of permanent war. It's a pleasure to see you again, sir."

Moshe, as usual, has little time for human emotions. He invites

Samuel to enter. "Come inside, I'll give you more details. Maybe you can shed some light on this matter."

Tarek and Rima stand as Samuel steps through the doorway. Samuel stops and freezes, staring into Tarek's eyes. Tarek is equally struck. For a few frozen seconds, the two men gaze at each other.

Samuel exclaims, "Tarek! Is that you? Rima? Can this be real?"

Tarek says, his voice choking, "Samuel? You're alive. *Al hamdu lillah!*" — Allah be praised! Tarek rushes to hug his old friend.

Samuel looks deeply moved. He hugs Tarek, and barely manages to mutter, "Tarek ... my good friend. My true friend ... What happened to you?" Samuel's wet eyes light upon Rima. "Rima ... How are you? All this time ..."

Tarek's eyes tear up and he says somberly, "It's a very long story, my friend. We'll recount it later." Tarek steps back and looks at his friend. "Time has treated you well." He pauses before going on, as he hugs Samuel yet again. "There are no words to describe the joy of seeing you again."

Samuel is deeply moved. "You're a brother to me. You always were. You always will be ... I feel like I'm back with my family."

Rima cuts in as she hugs Samuel. She too is in tears. "What about your family? Your parents? What happened to your sisters?"

Samuel nods his head. "My sisters are fine, married and all. My parent's trail stopped at a train terminal somewhere in Poland. Like so many others."

"I'm truly sorry. We had real hopes back then." Tarek is quiet for a moment, and then asks, "What about *my* parents? ... You took care of them?"

Samuel has a solemn tone. "I took proper care of them, as I promised." He looks toward Rima, empathetically. "Your parents, too. I brought in a sheikh from another village, the next day."

Rima's voice trembles. "So early? They died that soon? How did it happen? Was it from the battle for my mother's village?"

Samuel nods. "It was even worse than ours. There were reinforcements on both sides. The Legion took positions inside every house—"

"Let's save that for another day, okay?" Moshe interrupts as he was at Ely's side in that battle, too. He goes on, "Samuel, what can you tell us about the twin boys?"

Tarek pulls Rima in a tight clutch, and Samuel puts his hand on Tarek's shoulders, as if to have his permission to bypass the details on their parents. Tarek nods.

Samuel gives Moshe a look of sad irony. "Forty years on, and you haven't learned a thing about humanity." He looks at Ely and Tarek and goes on, "I will tell you now what I never had the chance to tell you, before fate forced us to part." He takes a deep breath. "Rima's family had left for her mother's house, in the next village. Tarek's family had been killed, and he was nowhere to be found. I went to look for him where I had last seen him, just outside the village where we met the Legion soldiers. Along the way, I came across a burnt-up horse-driven coach. A young couple lay dead. The two horses were dead. Someone must have preceded me, as there were no valuables or personal items left on the bodies. I heard a muffled cry. It was Ameer, entangled in bloodied linen, lying next to his mother, on the ground. I picked him up and dashed away, hoping to find Tarek. Sure enough, I found him lying on the ground, a huge purple lump oozing blood on his forehead. The Legion soldiers must have knocked him down when he tried to stop them."

Ely cuts in. "Back at the coach, no sign of anything?"

Samuel shakes his head. "No. Let me go on." Samuel looks at the anxious eyes around him. "I explained the tragedy to Tarek, and convinced him to take Ameer and follow Rima. I remember saying it will only be a day or two. *Forty years* ago." Samuel pauses, as if marking forty years with a few seconds of silence. Then he goes on saying, "As I rode back to the village, I saw Ely's unit at the convoy. I hid behind a bush, just behind them. Ely heard Amir's cry. The other Amir, of course. Sergeant Aaron found him, and handed him to Ely, who held him. That's when Amir started giggling and laughing. I think Ely was mesmerized. I was stunned. Amir had been lying in his dead mother's arms. I had not seen him." Samuel points to Ely and Moshe. "You two argued at first, and Moshe—"

Moshe waves him to stop. "We know all that! Tell us what we *don't* know!"

Samuel reaches for his wallet, and pulls out a piece of paper. "Here. After you left, I went back to the burned carriage, and looked again for clues. I brought a picture I found in a burned frame. It's scratched up, but you can see the twins. There was nothing else."

Moshe snatches the faded picture from Samuel's hand, looking at both sides of it, searching for clues. There were none.

Samuel frowns at Moshe's hasty actions. "Make sure you take care of it. I did, for forty years." Samuel continues. "I remember Ely sending Amir with one of his men, telling him to look for a nursing mother, to feed the child, and tie his horse in front of the house, so he could follow. I knew a family with a newborn, near my house, and I managed to sneak into the village faster than Ely's man. When he trotted into our street, I came out to meet him. And . . . that's it. Later on, you two came back, with all your men. Early evening, you drove off with Amir. I went back the second day, and still found nothing." Samuel turns to Tarek. "Is your son here? Can I see him?" He looks at Ely. "Yours too . . ."

Tarek points to the room inside. "My Ameer is right here with his family. And so is Ely's Amir, with his family."

Samuel starts toward the lounge area where the twins are waiting. "I want to meet them."

Moshe steps into his path. "Wait. We have to know. That's why you're here. We'll tell them the truth, but we have to know first."

"Know what? What truth are you talking about?"

"The boys. Are they Jews or Arabs?"

"Ah! *That* truth. There's no 'Jews' or 'Arabs' for the boys. They're twin brothers. Period." Samuel looks around at everyone in turn, as they still hold their breath, waiting for more. He stares at Moshe. "Don't you remember? That's the one question we could never answer. You were there with Ely when he took the child. You wanted to 'finish him off!'"

Moshe waves it away, avoiding the hostile glares around him. "Never mind that . . . But can't you remember anything else? Any other clues?"

Tarek sighs. "We hoped there might be something more."

Ely adds, "Yes. The boys are looking back at their entire life, and they don't know what to make of it."

Moshe pleads, "Imagine the pressure on them, now that they know that one of them belongs to the other side. One has lived his whole life on the wrong side of the fence, doing serious harm to his own." Moshe glances at Ely and Tarek. "For one of the twins, their world is about to collapse."

Samuel looks at the three men. "If you're hoping for proof that the boy is Jewish, Moshe, then you're going to be disappointed, I'm sorry to say."

Tarek's face lights up with hope. "Are you saying he's Palestinian?"

"No, Tarek, I'm not. I went through the whole convoy, looking for a clue, and couldn't find anything. I remember finding a lot of books and thinking that they were educated people. There was a Koran and a Torah. The evidence could lead to either possibility. You didn't care about that back then, why should you care now? What are your sons thinking?"

Tarek says, "Ameer is perturbed and anxious."

"My Amir, too." Ely says. "I've never seen him so anxious before. I've seen him in pain, I've seen him in anger. But not confused, not this way. They really have to know. Please try to remember. Anything."

Samuel says, "There is *nothing* to remember. Both of you were there, and neither one of you could find anything."

Tarek is surprised. "No one came asking after the smoke had settled?"

Samuel shakes his head. "No one asked, no one cared. I stayed in the village for years, and no one even mentioned the incident. Actually, no one even knew about it. I buried the bodies myself."

Tarek bursts out, "That's it! Ameer's an Arab then. If no one asked about him, and no inquiries were made, then certainly he must have belonged to an Arab family."

Samuel puts his hand on Tarek's shoulder. "I'm sorry, Tarek, but I don't think you can assume that. Believe me, I made some inquiries, and couldn't find anything. There were many people unaccounted for, on both sides. They might have been Jews, in the country without proper papers, like so many were. There was a flood of Jews from the neighboring Arab nations." He looks at the questioning faces around him. "We can't rule out either possibility, and that's the *only* fact. As I said, they're brothers, and that's it."

Moshe's spirit sinks. "What do we tell the boys?"

Samuel doesn't hesitate. "I think it's a sign from *Elohim* for us to not know. I think it's the best possible resolution, for everyone. Twin brothers, who have to learn how to live together, accept each other, share with each other. Just like our two people."

Ely nods. "He's right, Moshe. This might be the best thing we could possibly have for the beginning and promotion of the peace process."

Moshe feels disappointed. "What peace process? We're being stoned to death! They're sending us children so we can't respond. You're speaking of a peace process?"

Tarek glares at him. "That isn't what we came for, Moshe, and it's unworthy of a response. Besides, I think our sons would agree with Samuel."

Ely says, "I agree with Tarek. If we really want peace, what better way to expose the stupidity and waste of war than by the example of our two boys?"

Moshe says, "You can live with the thought that Amir might be an Arab?"

Ely says, "I've done so for forty years. Amir is my son, and I love him as such, that's all I know." Ely has a thin smile. "He's your son in-law. Get used to the idea."

Tarek says, "I'm more worried about the boys. We all dealt with this matter a long time ago. We love them as our own, and will keep on loving them. But how would either one of them feel if he found out that he was wrong all his life?" He looks up at Ely and the other men around them. "Except that, for them, there's no wrong and no right, now. There's no enemy anymore. They're identical twins, and you can't hurt one without hurting the other. Our boys started life together, let them continue it together. It doesn't matter if they're Israelis or Palestinians. What matters is that they are brothers, from this land. They're from both Israel *and* Palestine."

Ely agrees, "Well said, Tarek. I see you're a man of peace. Our sons have given great sacrifice for their nations, and I think they will now have to find ways, together with us, to solve, or rather live with, this conflict."

Tarek adds, "I hope they can handle it. What matters is not only how they've lived their lives, but how they'll live them from here on.

Speculation on the past is just that: speculation. But a peaceful future with two Homelands, Israel and Palestine, living brothers — now that's something to dream of, like Dar Moussa before the war."

Ely says, "What do you say, Moshe? Peace for the brothers, and peace for the land?"

Moshe gazes out a window. For so many years he'd thought only of war. "Peace? I'm for peace, I think . . . But I also wish I knew the truth. My daughter could be married to a Palestinian, for all I know."

Ely laughs and claps him on the back. "Don't you see, Moshe? That doesn't matter, that shouldn't matter! Amir is still Amir . . . It would not change him one bit."

———

A week later, Amir and his brother have taken their families on a picnic to a place near Jerusalem, well inside Israeli territory. Amir hasn't told his brother yet, but the hilltop where they stand overlooks Dar Moussa, which has grown into a small town with tall buildings, wide streets with traffic lights. They even had to *add* green spaces. It is here that their lives began, and then took separate paths. Amir breathes in, as does his brother. The fresh country air, the chirping birds, the white blossoms on the almond trees . . .

Amir gazes at their children playing in the field below them, with Dar Moussa in the background. "What do you think of this view?"

Ameer stands in admiration. "Beautiful."

"Everything is different, yet nothing has changed," Amir says.

"Would you change anything in your life, if you could?" Ameer asks cautiously.

Amir looks around and finds a good-sized boulder to sit on. His brother joins him. Amir asks, "If I could go back in time?"

"I mean, if we'd known, right from the start, that we were adopted, and that we didn't really know where we came from. Would you have done the same things? Fought the same way?"

Amir gazes at the town below. "When I was a boy I'd watch my father get ready to go fight." Amir looks at his brother. "Fight the 'bad ones.' That was you, my brother. You could have been the one with him, instead of me." He shakes his head as he remembers. "Then I started growing up, and war games turned into real war. It wasn't a big change, because we lived with war and death at our door our whole lives, so . . . what else was I supposed to do? But eventually, it all came to seem so pointless. All the killing . . ."

Ameer agrees. "Had you asked me that question, the answer would have been the same. Of course, camp life isn't a nice childhood, especially when you keep moving from one place to the other . . . still, I wonder."

Amir's words come naturally, his thoughts taking up where his brother's stop. Even their thinking runs in parallel. "My enthusiasm, my fanaticism, came in two waves. The first one was as I grew up. All fathers were soldiers; war was in almost every house, death in many. Even at school, the main question was if it would be infantry or armor, navy or air force."

Ameer puts his hand on his brother's knee. With sad eyes, he says, "I know the second wave."

"When I lost Liz, my dedication turned into fanatic extremism. I guess that's where we both lost it."

His brother shakes his head, and Amir knows that the hardened veteran in him is having trouble controlling his human side. His brother says, "I would have given the rest of my life, any time, just for one more game with my little Tarek. He shouldn't have died, before he even started living. I just wanted to say everything I wanted to tell him, one more time. All the time. How much I love him. And hug him, hug him forever."

Amir is just as emotional. "Just one more evening, one more day to do everything she loved to do. A day of nothing but cuddling . . ."

Ameer points to the sky. "As much as I wanted to follow him there, I chose to live. I chose to live, so I could kill." He turns an anguished gaze upon Amir. "For exacting revenge on the other side — on your people. Or is it *my* people? What a tragedy, what a waste of lives, for nothing. Nothing at all. Now we're brothers . . ."

Amir puts a hand on his brother's shoulder. "I remember my mother telling me things I couldn't understand back then. She told me that even killing all the Palestinians wouldn't bring her back." Amir pauses, remembering. "I said, 'it will bring *me* back.'"

His brother raises an eyebrow. "Did it? Did it bring you back?"

Amir shakes his head with a sorry smile. "It took me a while to understand it. Nothing can bring you back; you're as dead as your dead child."

Ameer grins. "Good."

"What do you mean, 'good'?"

He muses, "You got me thinking that it did bring you back and I wondered if I just hadn't done enough killing and fighting."

Amir says with a sad smile, shaking his head, "All this is wrong."

Ameer looks back at him. "Horribly wrong. And we still haven't answered our question—what if we'd known who we were?"

Amir shrugs. "Now that I've met you . . . now that we're here, together . . ."

Ameer peers into his eyes. "What?"

"We could have had this conversation, this relationship, without even being brothers, we're fellow humans, and we should not be killing each other."

"I know. We both have a loaded military history, so there's no doubt about our past attitudes or behavior, but now is the time to make peace."

Amir nods. "You're right. Our story is that of the entire nation."

"Everyone should question their every action."

Amir stirs with enthusiasm. "We have to apply this narrative to the entire nation."

"Convince people to reassess. Show them what war and terror lead to."

"Exactly. Nothing can be done about the past, but what about the future? Where do we go from here?"

Ameer says with an affirmed tone, "Peace. Neighbors. Brothers."

"Right. Most people think there must be another way — even among Israelis, those who are for peace far outnumber the extremists. I know that Palestinians want peace as well."

"We do. It has to be a just and fair peace, a decent life. We need to apply the UN resolutions."

Amir concurs. "Most Israelis would agree to a peaceful Palestinian State by the side of Israel . . . that takes into account the situation on the ground."

His brother pokes him with an elbow. "You're hinting at the settlements. You know they're illegal. Remember, you could be Palestinian!"

Amir doesn't want to get into this argument. "We have to be realistic. Put yourself in my shoes. Do you think removing all those people is feasible? Besides," Amir goes on, "Many of them aren't the crazies you think they are. Some of them are just deeply religious. They truly believe God gave them this land, and they just want to work the fields!" Amir sighs. "Many Israelis hate their guts because they're the main reason we haven't found a way for peace with the Palestinian people."

"You want to compromise on UN resolutions."

"Both sides have to realize that they won't get the full cake, that's all. I agree that we should tell the settlers they can either relocate, or to re-build their settlements in the Negev Desert or in the Galilee. Otherwise, they can stay put, and become Palestinian citizens. Twenty percent of the population in Israel is Palestinians, so why can't you have some Palestinian Jews in the future Palestinian State?

Ameer likes the idea. "*Yahoud Falastinieh*. Mmm . . . I could be the first one amongst them, for all I know."

Amir follows up on his thoughts.

Ameer says, "Our situation, the media coverage . . . we should use it to promote peace."

Amir is pleased. "We're thinking the same way. We have to come up with a plan."

"All we have to do is tell the truth. Show that violence will not solve the deeper issue."

Amir doesn't think it will be that simple. "We will be facing an entire political class of hardcore fanatics. On both sides. They will lie and twist the truth."

Ameer throws in, "We have to do constructive things, jointly. We have to create a synergy that will expand and reach everyone. We build on our situation and go from there."

"You are right," Amir says thoughtfully. "I could have been you and you could have been me. We could swap places right now and no one would know." He laughs. "A highly decorated officer of the IDF and a veteran of the PLO are twin brothers! One of us spent his whole life on the wrong side. Suffering, sacrificing, killing, and dying for the enemy." He looks at his brother. "The good thing is, we'll never know which."

"The good thing is, there's no *wrong* side anymore. No enemy."

Ameer grips his brother's arm. "From now on, we only look ahead. We only use the past as a lesson."

Amir agrees. "These days, people want to listen to those who have been there. I'm still in the military, and I still obey orders. I'll resign if I have to. Nothing is stopping me."

"Same goes for me. I won't hesitate to resign if I feel my position will keep me from my God-given duty of peacemaking between our two nations." Ameer looks at his brother. "Do you realize that this is what's missing? We are the missing link." He has a sparkle in his eyes. "We're the missing link to peace."

Amir is beaming. "And now we have to project that onto every-one else." He stands and stretches. "There's something divine in this. When I think that we've come across each other so many times, almost killed each other, and yet we're now here, face to face, working for peace." He stands and faces Dar Moussa. He gazes at the town and says, "I am questioning my whole life. Yet if I were you, I'd have done what you've done."

Ameer agrees. "Me too. What counts, is what we do from now on. That's the whole point. We have to show how painful and unfruitful the path of war is, and point out the true way. The way of peace." His face lights up. "We should write a book, make a movie. We'll tell both our stories, from the day we were separated. Twin brothers, fighting each other all their lives, killing their own, and losing their way . . . then finding it again."

Amir understands the hurt that has stilled his brother's voice. "Can you talk about it? Little Tarek?"

"I will if I have to." Ameer has a sad smile. "I have to show how my reaction to his death was wrong and pointless. Courage is not in exacting revenge and causing more death, but in forgiveness. And you? Liz?"

"It will help to think that her death can prevent that of others." Amir sighs. "It will somehow resurrect her spirit."

His brother says, "I still think of Little Tarek, and I miss him, even after all these years. I still have the toy AK I carved for him in wood. I *know* he would want other children to live."

Amir takes a deep breath, and exhales loudly, as if trying to flush out the morbid thoughts. He drifts for a second, then pokes his brother in the belly. "You could have killed me!"

His brother returns the punch. "You too."

Amir thinks back to the soldiers he's known who weren't so lucky. He thinks of Anouchka.

His brother frowns. "What's that look?"

Amir hesitates, then says, "In the Golan, in 'Seventy-Three, when you took out that bunker . . ."

"The mission Anouchka planned?"

Amir nods. "I wanted to ask you about her. She used to train us. She was in charge of our special programs, anti-terrorist and undercover work. She trained me."

Ameer winks to his brother. "She trained you after hours too . . . intensely."

Amir answers with a question, "Why do you say that?"

"In our training camp in Russia, she thought I was you, and I got a . . . well, some bonus material." Ameer smiles at the recollection, then sobers up. "It would destroy Layal to know. Even after the years. I'm not a womanizer . . . never was."

"Me neither. When I think about it, I must have been crazy." Amir pictures Anouchka. "She was strong, and beautiful. We were both highly strung."

"If what she did to me was anything like what you two used to do, whew! She did notice something different, but she couldn't say what."

"She called me yesterday. She said she wanted to see me. To see us actually. We'll do that and this chapter of our lives, we keep for us. Except for Ethan, nobody knew. Now it's history. She's teaching and consulting now. Off the military."

"Same with me. My friend Faris knew. He was my best friend; we grew up together. He was killed in our face-off in 'Eighty-Two . . .'"

Amir feels his brother's sorrow. "I'm sorry about that . . . How pointless."

His brother shakes his head. "No apologies. We did what we thought was right. But now it's time to change our aims, and our ways."

"I lost a close friend in that fight, too. We won't let their deaths go to waste." Amir glances at his brother, and watches as his eyes roam over the beauty of the land below. Now was the time to tell him. "I didn't choose this picnic spot by accident."

"No? Is it a special place for you?"

Amir points to their boys, playing on a grassy slope. An old dirt road snakes through the bushes. "You see where David and Laith are standing? That's supposed to be the exact place where it all started."

Ameer shades his eyes and peers. "No kidding?" He points to the town. "That's the village Tarek came from? It's a town now!" He pauses. "Tarek would be amazed."

"If peace ever happens in this land, he could come every day. Samuel told me Tarek's father was sort of a village wise man, and they did everything they could to prevent the bloodshed. Tarek and Samuel were best friends."

"He told me about those days. He is quite stirred to see Samuel again. They will be spending a lot of time together now."

"Like us, they're making up for forty years of forced separation. Just as much as us, they want a peaceful solution to the war. They always have. I think they have their own agenda, which probably includes us." Amir laughs. "Yesterday Ely was with them. They were busy talking."

Ameer gets excited. "We should bring them into our plan. They'll go for it. That's how it all started, with them standing vigil for Dar Moussa . . ."

"And now they can continue. Forty years on."

His brother looks at their children. "Look how our boys get along. I thought they'd be the toughest ones to get together. They're real cousins."

Amir laughs. "You should see my friend Ethan. He looks at me and laughs. The idea that I could be Palestinian caused an earthquake in my circles."

"Me too. Not everyone reacts positively."

"We'll have to deal with those, that's all," Amir says.

"We have a new purpose in life, now. We have to make it happen."

"It *will* happen." Amir thinks about it for a second, then goes on. "We'll deal with it as if it is a mission. Consider every aspect, and make a plan. A plan for peace."

Ameer snaps his fingers. "A plan for peace. Maybe we'll have our own political party. Or a movement for peace. An NGO, make it international."

Amir says, "A movement will be better accepted. We shouldn't get involved in politics other than our quest for peace. We should rally as many people as we can, from both sides, in a simple quest for peace. Our agenda should be limited to the peace process."

Ameer stands and extends his arms as if to embrace the valley below. "It'll be the start of our future, of our peaceful country." He grabs Amir by the shoulder. "Look at our kids. They could have been friends all their lives. All kids should play like that. No more lessons of war and combat drills."

Amir sighs and nods toward the occupied territories. "I wish I could order our troops out."

"And I would stop the young thugs." Ameer says. "We will overcome. Peace will prevail."

Shoulder to shoulder, the brothers stand and gaze at the land.

*One look from both sides*, at their land. They are now ready to share it in peace. A Brotherland. Their Brotherland.

www.ingramcontent.com/pod-product-compliance
Lightning Source LLC
Chambersburg PA
CBHW031030030726
47497CB00004B/1075